TELL ME SOMETHING

AUBREY BONDURANT

Photograph and Cover Design by Sara Eirew

CHAPTER ONE

I looked at my watch and sighed, stealing a glance at my boss. The guy was going to have an aneurysm if the model didn't show up soon, so I stood to the side and out of his way. With Warren Carlyle's pacing and the extra fifty pounds or so he was carrying on his frame, he would be sweating through his expensive suit at any moment. This had to be his worst nightmare as the senior vice president on a million-dollar advertising campaign, to be waiting on Katrina Tross, a hot, upcoming model who was the It Girl of this year.

The location of the hotel rooftop and bar, used for photo shoots such as this, had been confirmed with her agent yesterday, along with the time. But Katrina's agent wasn't answering the phone now. I didn't know Warren very well as I hadn't worked for him that long, but I had witnessed his displeasure and was not looking forward to the fallout if the model's absence jeopardized the Cassius Rum ad campaign.

It probably wasn't a coincidence that Katrina Tross' asking price had quadrupled since our company had booked her eight months ago and now she was a no-show, but I kept my thoughts to myself. No one wanted to hear from an administrative assistant who'd only been part of the advertising world a mere four months. If I was lucky, it would only be for nine more. By then I'd have enough saved up for law school.

I glanced over at the waiting professionals who'd earlier converted a small supply closet into a dressing room: the costly hair stylist flown in from New York, the fashion designer, and one of the best photographers in the business, Bart Chesley, whose asking price was most likely a large chunk of the budget for the day. He was an older man who looked a bit eccentric with his ponytail and a pair of hipster jeans that no one with gray hair should probably be wearing. He was practically steaming over his time being wasted and seemed to have had no issue telling Warren as much a few minutes earlier. Unlike most people, he wasn't intimidated by my boss.

When I thought matters couldn't get any worse, a tall man in a well-tailored suit strode in. My boss's entire demeanor changed instantly as he rushed to greet the stranger, a man who made it obvious he was in charge.

As I watched the newcomer walk closer with Warren, I sucked in my breath. He was, for lack of a better word, gorgeous. Tall, with broad shoulders and sporting short, dark black hair, he had features that were classically chiseled and definitively masculine.

I knew I was staring, but thankfully I wasn't the only one. Trisha, the makeup girl, sidled up next me.

"Wow, he's even hotter in person. All that money and a nice package —he is something," she acknowledged.

I nodded and then realized she spoke as though she knew him. "Who is he?"

She laughed. "Sorry, I forgot you're new. That's Josh Singer, as in owner and CEO of Gamble Enterprises. That includes Gamble Advertising, Gamble Properties, and Gamble Productions. He's the only man I know who can make Warren sweat it."

I knew the name but had never seen the man. "He seems really young to have all that."

Trisha shrugged. "I think the advertising and hotels came from his father. The movie production thing is newer."

"He looks pissed." I watched him speak to Warren in a terse tone that I couldn't quite hear.

"Yeah, well, he's known for his temper. His messy divorce from that Brazilian supermodel a few years ago was quite the tabloid fodder."

We both observed him make a quick phone call and then go over to speak with Bart the photographer, who obviously felt comfortable enough with Josh that he made his frustrations known.

"We only have the space until four. Where the hell is she?" Bart grumbled.

"You know he's kind of intense-looking, but maybe that's what makes him hotter, you know?" Trisha sighed.

All I could do was nod. I snapped out of it when Warren barked at me.

"Haylee."

Walking quickly over to the three men, I met the dark green eyes of Josh Singer and then tried to focus on my boss. "Yes, Mr. Carlyle?"

"You said that you confirmed with her agent yesterday?"

"Yes, sir, I did. I've been trying his phone as well as her assistant's over the last hour, but I've only gotten voicemail."

"And did you leave a message?"

His voice was so condescending that it took all of my effort not to say something smart. Instead, I took a deep breath while trying to ignore Josh's eyes on me. Warren was trying to appear like he was in control, especially in front of his boss.

"Yes, sir, I left several."

We all turned at the same time toward a commotion in the

doorway and watched as Katrina Tross herself came strutting into the bar.

"About damned time," Bart muttered under his breath.

Warren was all smiles for the model, shifting completely into what I called his schmoozing role. I assumed it went with the territory at his level in the advertising world. "Hello, my dear, good to see you. We're running behind, so if we can get you into hair and makeup, we can get started."

Quirking a brow, she gave Josh an assessing look with a sexy smile. "Fine, but I only have one hour."

Warren sputtered and took her assistant to the side. "But we booked one hour prep and two hours for the shoot. We need at least that amount of time as we have three scenes."

The warm sensation of breath in my ear took me off guard, as I had been completely absorbed in their conversation.

"Can you pull out your phone and record this exchange?" Josh whispered.

Flushing, I realized he was inches from my face. "Uh, yes, of course." I hesitated, waiting for my fingers to catch up with my brain, and then fumbled for my cell phone.

After I pressed record, he walked into the frame while Katrina shrugged. "Not my problem."

"Ms. Tross, are you saying that you don't care that the contract specified four hours and you are a half hour late and now demanding that the entire shoot take one?" Josh asked in a low tone.

Her assistant appeared to struggle for words before speaking up. "Mr. Singer, it's just that Ms. Tross has other obligations—"

"Last I checked, a contract was an obligation," he stated dryly. Although I didn't know the man, it was clear his anger was restrained.

Katrina wasn't catching the tone when she gave him a pouting smile. "You can have this face for an hour of pictures and sell your rum with whatever I give you. Considering the peanuts I'm getting paid for it, I think it's only fair."

Josh held up a hand to Warren, who was about to interject. "So if I understand you correctly, because we signed this contract before your asking price skyrocketed, it's no longer worth honoring when you have other higher-paid jobs to attend to?" He looked toward me, and I gave him a slight nod.

"Yes, good. You understand. Wonderful. Shall we proceed then and quit this nonsense talk about contracts?" Katrina gave her purse to her assistant to hold, evidently ready to get to work.

"No, Ms. Tross, we won't. You're in breach of your contract, and since you cannot fulfill it, you can leave." He spoke the words in a tone that forbade any further discussion.

Warren appeared beside himself judging by the color his face was turning, but he was wise enough to keep his mouth shut. He was no longer in charge of this situation; that much was obvious.

"You can't be serious?" For a woman so very beautiful, Katrina was quickly becoming ugly.

"I assure you I'm very serious. You'll be hearing from our attorneys. Good day to you."

Josh turned on heel as she sputtered, "But I'm the hottest thing there is. Even your assistant can't help herself but take my picture over there. You're making a huge mistake."

He quirked a brow at me, and I flushed as he turned back to Katrina.

"She's not taking your picture. She's putting on record your refusal to honor the contract."

Katrina's next move happened quickly. One second I was looking at Josh and the next she lunged toward me. I stepped out of the way just in time as she tried unsuccessfully to grab my phone. Thankfully, her assistant restrained her before she could mount a second attempt.

"I guess we can add attempted assault to the tally," I quipped, earning me a wry look from Josh and a glare from Warren.

Katrina wisely kept her mouth shut and fled out the door with her assistant following.

Pressing stop on the record feature, I viewed it quickly to ensure I had it all. It seemed everyone was waiting on orders from Josh, who, curiously, was still looking at me.

Uncomfortable silence wasn't something I was good with. "I'll, um, email you this video and call Legal." I was happy to do something to break both the tension and the eye contact with the man in charge.

After sending the video and leaving a message for our in-house attorney to call Warren, I overheard Josh talking with the photographer.

"All right, Bart, what do you want to do now?"

The older man gave a little smile and pointed toward me. "We use her."

They all looked at me, and I couldn't help glancing behind me for some other girl. "I'm sorry, what did you say?"

Bart started barking orders with authority. "Get her into hair and makeup. Have the seamstress hem the dress; she's about four inches shorter."

Warren appeared less enthusiastic than the others regarding what was about to happen.

I realized quickly they weren't joking around when Trisha took my hand and led into the small room where she had me sit in the chair.

"But—but I'm not a model," I squeaked. The hair stylist was behind me, letting my locks down from my clip.

"No kidding, chica. Bart, what am I to do with this one? She's shorter and about twenty pounds overweight." Ramone, the clothing designer, was about to have a fit of his own.

Sucking in my breath, I let my temper get the best of me. "She has a name, and you can talk to me directly instead of pretending I'm not in the room. And I don't appreciate having my size six called fat."

I swore I saw a ghost of a smile from Josh as he witnessed the exchange from the doorway. Thankfully, Warren was now on the phone out of earshot.

"Honey, by industry standards anything above a two is fat." Ramone was tsking over my frame as Josh stepped in and met my eyes in the mirror.

"What's your name?"

"Haylee Holloway."

Nodding, he looked toward the designer. "We use Haylee here, or the whole shoot is a wash. You're a genius, Ramone. Make it work."

That seemed to pacify my moody fashion designer as he went over to the clothing rack and started taking inventory.

Over the next ten minutes, my hair was blown out within an inch of its life. As the stylist was flat-ironing it, I watched Warren cross over and talk to both Josh and Bart in front of the doorway.

"Look gentlemen, she's a real pretty girl. I'll give you that, but she isn't a model. She has no training and isn't the image we were hoping to go with. I'm on the phone trying to get a model agency to send another girl. I'm sure we can get someone here in the next hour or so."

I tried not to take offense at Warren's words. It wasn't like he was wrong. I could confidently say I was attractive, based on some male attention I'd received in my twenty-two years. But I'd never been considered exceptionally beautiful and would never have been labeled model material.

Bart shrugged. "Your call, Josh, but I think she's more photogenic than the stick."

I felt Josh give me a once-over from head to toe, and I blushed at the scrutiny. He'd once been married to a Brazilian supermodel, and here I was a girl right out of college from Northern California who'd led a sheltered life thus far and who definitely wasn't a stick figure.

"All right, I trust you know what you're doing, Bart. If anyone can turn nothing into something, it's you."

Well, that was quite the confidence builder. If I'd needed a reminder as to why Josh Singer was out of my league, that sealed it.

I STARED at my image in the mirror when Trisha turned me around. Somehow they had transformed my wavy, shoulder-length brown locks into silky straight perfection that I didn't dare run a hand through—though I was sorely tempted. My ordinary blue eyes stood out like big pools, with the long lashes and coal-black liner they'd used. I never would've thought I could look like a model, not even for a day, and had to appreciate the effort as I smiled at Trisha and the hair stylist.

"You guys are amazing. I look so different."

Cringing as Ramone loudly requested a better padded bra, I then proceeded to get dressed with the help of Trisha and another woman.

I never imagined how much touching models endured. It was a little overwhelming, to say the least, when one of the women reached up no-nonsense to arrange my thong in order to avoid panty lines. Finally, they slid my feet into platform heels, and I looked down at the little black cocktail dress and took a deep breath. Well, no turning back now.

"Let's go," Bart yelled.

Stepping into the bar, I glanced at the bottles of rum strategically placed behind the counter. I felt like a fish out of water as I nervously adjusted my dress, standing there waiting for them to tell me where to sit.

Bart put down his camera, took both of my hands, and looked into my eyes. He obviously realized I was shaking like a leaf. "Relax and take a deep breath, Haylee. Have a seat on the bar stool and turn your body toward me." After this direction, he stepped back to gauge my angle.

I did what was asked simply because I wasn't sure if I was going to pass out or start crying. Neither was a respectable option at the moment.

I must've appeared as awkward as I felt, because as he was about to grab my leg, he paused suddenly. "This is something you'll have to get used to; I'm going to be moving you. Are you okay with that?"

Surprised he would caution me, I was also thankful. Obviously, he knew I was completely new to this entire process. I could only nod again, after which he adjusted my leg, flipped my hair off my shoulder, and turned my body, draping my dress to flatter the shot.

"There. Now I want you to go to whatever place you need to in order to conjure up the emotions I call out." He backed off and went behind the camera to click and wind things.

I was sure I appeared like a deer caught in headlights and could only blink at the noise and flash as Bart snapped a picture.

He spoke in low, concise tones. "I want aloof, dear. You're waiting on someone and can't be bothered to make eye contact with any other man in the bar. You know you look good, and there isn't a thing you want to do to attract their attention."

I stayed frozen, trying to register what he was saying, and then closed my eyes. Opening them at the sound of footsteps coming toward me, I was stunned to see it was Josh Singer instead of Bart this time.

"Haylee, correct?" His voice was low and kind.

Piercing green eyes once again completely transfixed me and I could only nod.

"Well, Haylee, I'm Josh. I don't think we formally met."

I tried to smile as he took my hand. "It's nice to meet you." Swallowing hard at his touch, I was a little unnerved that he was speaking to me as if we were the only two in the room.

"You, too." There was that ghost of a smile again.

I admitted, "I'm nervous, and I really don't want to blow this for you, but I'm not sure I'm equipped to pull this off." I was being brutally honest even if it would cost me my job, this shoot, and whatever self-esteem I had left.

"Some girls would think this would be a fantasy come true: hair, makeup, playing dress up."

"I'm so not that girl, Mr. Singer."

He chuckled, seeming a lot less intimidating than I had originally thought. "You can do this. If you can work for Warren, I think you must have it in you." He whispered the last part, causing me to smile wider.

"All right, I'll try." I took a deep breath and concentrated on the aloof, confident, sexy woman they wanted me to portray. It was satisfying to see Josh's surprised look and his smile toward Warren.

Bart started snapping off some shots as he took me through the motions. A short time later, he called it a wrap on the first scene.

I WAS in curlers and wanted to kill someone. I'd never been more humiliated in my life as when I overheard Ramone speak to Josh and Bart outside the dressing room.

"We cannot do swimsuit; she's not waxed."

I didn't dare look in their direction but could tell by their silence that neither man knew quite what to say about that information. It wasn't every day that a woman's bikini line was an open topic.

Finally, Josh spoke. "Um, well, don't we have a suit that ah, well, that doesn't show, you know?"

I'd been a pretty good sport thus far, but this was too much. "You make it sound as though it's a jungle. I simply said I'm not bare and can't believe we're discussing this," I mumbled. As Josh walked in behind me, I noticed he was trying to hide his laugh.

"Haylee, you will look great in the swimsuit," Bart declared, coming in and taking my hand. "I'm the best in the business, and you have my promise."

I sighed, losing some of my initial embarrassment.

"As for the other, can we get, uh, well, a wax job?" he asked Trisha, who evidently was the lucky one to be saddled with the task.

"Of course, but she'll be red," she responded, shrugging.

Josh hesitated. "That's fine, we'll deal with it. That is if you're okay with it, Haylee?"

For a moment I was shocked that he was leaving it up to me. "Yes, I think so." The decision made, I resigned myself to face my fate via hot wax.

After the impromptu waxing, I came out of the dressing room in a two-piece suit that was white, of all colors, and fought my anxiety. I worked out when I could and actually loved running, but I was highly aware of my shortcomings in that moment. I wasn't fat, contrary to Ramone's comment, nor did I feel like a size six was heavy by any stretch, but I also wasn't completely toned. Hell, I would've at least skipped the damn bagel this morning had I a clue I'd be in a bikini later in front of a camera.

Dreading the fact that I was about to be in front of everyone and looking at the fake tan they had just applied, I wanted to run and hide, but instead I continued down the one flight of stairs from the bar to the hotel pool. I stole a glance at Josh, wishing he would find something else to do. Wasn't he the owner? Did he have to be here the whole time, watching me with those intense green eyes?

Luckily, the pool scene was the shortest one. Bart moved me around, and I concentrated on doing exactly as I was told. I could only hope he would be true to his word and make me look good.

"Okay, that's a wrap on this one," Bart called out.

The stylists moved in quickly to scoop me up and get me back into the small dressing room. I visibly relaxed the moment the robe came on and was grateful that I was more than halfway done.

The last scene entailed smoke and a jazz performance up on stage—they'd made the bar look like a typical lounge.

They put me in a glamorous, dark burgundy dress that was red-carpet-worthy. My hair was in a messy up-do with my lips painted crimson. I was positioned at the lounge table and watched as they placed my drink and the bottle within view, reminding me this was an ad for the rum. One of the staging staff placed a cigarette in front of me in an ash tray. My nose wrinkled in response. "What's this?"

The props coordinator explained. "In this scene you're a smoker."

"I don't smoke," I said directly, looking at Josh. I didn't care who he was or how appealing he looked. I wanted to make it clear that this was not an option.

"Fine, leave it burning for a couple shots then," he relented.

I was mollified and Bart took the first few pictures.

"Good, now put your legs up on the other chair there, relax back as if you've come here a million times and hold the cigarette up in your right hand. You're not smoking it, but if you could appear like you are for a shot or two?"

I picked up the offending cigarette and heard Josh laugh as he started toward me.

"No, hold it like this."

As much as the idea of holding a cigarette was offensive to me, his nearness was making it worth it.

"Good," he commented, going back as Bart snapped a couple more.

Standing above his camera, Bart paused. "That's great, Haylee. Take a break and go on over to the bar. I need a moment to think of what I want to do there."

Sighing, I went over to the bar and lay down fully, flat on the polished surface. Looking up at the ceiling, I enjoyed the small rest. But then I smoothed down the dress and propped myself up on my elbows to steal a glance over at Josh, who was simply staring at me. The intensity of his gaze robbed the air from my lungs until his voice broke the trance.

"Stay there, Haylee. Look toward me. Now raise your legs up and cross them," he encouraged. Obviously happy with my accidental pose, he directed Bart to take some pictures.

"Excellent." After a few more shots, they called a wrap.

All of the tension left my body as I hopped down and returned with Trisha to get back to myself.

MY FACE WAS FRESHLY SCRUBBED with minimal makeup when I came out from the dressing room back to the rooftop, where the hotel staff was busy rearranging everything back to normal. It was a relief to be rid of the false eyelashes and heavy cosmetics and back in my business attire. While everyone was busy, I found Bart packing up his equipment.

"So, did it go all right?" I asked.

The older man smiled kindly and took my hands. "It went beautifully, bella. Here's my card. If ever you want to model again, you call me, okay?" He beamed, kissing both my cheeks while I blushed at the unexpected compliment.

Bracing myself, I watched Warren stalk over. He was all business.

"Okay, Haylee, dress up is over. Go get Legal on the phone to see if they have the necessary documents drawn up so I can get this Katrina mess behind us."

Giving him a curt nod and Bart a small wave, I acknowledged it was time for me to get back to reality.

While I was finishing up the call with the general counsel's assistant, I saw Warren give Bart an annoyed look. I knew instantly that they were in some sort of discussion that was not going my boss's way. Not a good sign when they walked towards me.

"The general counsel said he can meet with you at ten o'clock on Monday, Mr. Carlyle. He has the contract in hand—" I started after hanging up the phone.

"To use your photos, we need your signature," Warren interrupted. "It's just a formality since you were posing instead of Katrina. Call Legal back, get the release drawn up, and get it signed before you leave the office tonight."

It had been a long day, and I'd been hoping to catch a cab home from here, but it was evident that I'd have to make my way back Downtown to the office after all. "Certainly, I'll call them right back."

Josh walked up, once again with those eyes on me. "I want to thank you for stepping in today, Haylee. Did Warren talk about your fee?"

Shifting uncomfortably, I looked at my boss, who was obviously caught off guard.

He attempted to answer, only to have Josh hold up his hand to stop him. Josh glanced back at me with an intense expression.

"Uh, we hadn't discussed it yet, but he did mention the release. I'll make sure I have that signed by the end of the day, Mr. Singer." I looked between them, unaware of what was causing the tension.

Josh gave me a smile that didn't reach his eyes. "I think forty thousand is fair, don't you, Warren?"

My jaw almost dropped open.

Warren lips pursed. "Yes, yes, of course I was about to bring that up. Please make sure Tom includes that fee in your release package. That is all." He effectively dismissed me.

Thankful to escape the friction, I grabbed my phone to call Legal again. By this time they were probably tired of hearing from me. Meanwhile, I stole a peek at Josh and found his gaze meeting mine. Fumbling over my words to the receptionist, I had to turn away. Jesus, it wasn't enough that he casually gave me almost a full year's salary in one afternoon, but the way that man looked and then looked at me—way too hot for comfort.

I needed to get a grip. Josh Singer was not the kind of guy a girl like me flirted with or even entertained a fantasy about. I had one goal in mind, which was to save up for law school and I needed to remember that.

CHAPTER TWO

The first thing I did after arriving back in the office was down a Diet Coke from the break room to get some caffeine in my body. I hadn't eaten all day and had a new respect for models now that my fatigue was threatening to take over from the shoot.

The Legal department was two floors up in the building, and I headed there to sign the release necessary for Cassius Rum to use my pictures.

One look from the legal assistant was enough to convey her irritation at having to stay late on a Friday evening. "Tom is waiting for you." She gestured toward our general counsel's office door.

I'd never met the man, but Tom Goldstein gave me a nod to come in as he finished up his phone call. He appeared to be in his late forties and was pleasant looking. "Hi, Haylee, I'm Tom Goldstein. I have the paperwork here for you to sign: the release and authorization of your payment." He handed over some official looking documents.

"Nice to meet you, and thanks for doing this on short notice. It was all sort of last minute," I admitted as he watched me sign.

"Between the breach of contract with Katrina Tross and Mr. Singer being there, well it sounds like quite an interesting day," he empathized. "You'll get your payment next Friday when payroll processes it. I hope that's all right?"

I could hardly believe it. "Yes, of course. Thank you. Do you mind me asking what law school you went to, Mr. Goldstein?" I was always interested in anyone in legal, considering that studying law was what I wanted to do next year.

"Not at all, and call me Tom. I went to Harvard Law School. I love it up there, especially in the fall. Why? Are you interested in law school?"

Warming to his smile, I shared my plans. "Yes, I'm saving up and hoping to go next year."

He nodded, seeming pleased. "Did you already take the LSAT? Wait one second. Let me get these papers to Maureen so she can go home, then I'll be back." He gestured for me to take a seat as he went out to give her the documents.

I heard another man's voice and then Tom returned with Josh, explaining to him what I guessed was my release.

"Yes, this next Friday's payroll, sir," he said.

Seeing Josh again so soon was messing with my senses. Jesus, I needed to eat some food and then go home and take a cold shower or something.

"So, did you need anything else from Haylee this evening?" Josh asked.

"No, sir. We were just discussing law schools and if she'd taken the LSAT yet," Tom supplied.

Both men looked at me expectantly. "And did you?" Josh questioned.

I swallowed at his sudden interest. "I, uh, yes. I took it in June." My hands were knotted in my lap, and I realized I should probably be standing. I shot to my feet and almost groaned as that put me within inches of my problem.

"What was your score?" Tom inquired.

Josh seemed equally interested.

"It was a 172."

My face heated when Tom whistled.

"That's a great score. You could get into any of the top ten schools with that, most likely."

I nodded but felt unprepared for this part of my personal life to become the business of the owner of the company. "Thank you. I hope so. If you don't need me for anything else, Mr. Goldstein, I'll leave you two gentlemen now."

I was about to make my escape toward an In-N-Out burger, fries, and, hell, maybe even a chocolate milkshake, when Josh threw me for a loop.

"Actually, Haylee, I came back to speak with you. Tom, thanks for taking care of the paperwork. Nice to see you again." He shook the older man's hand.

Josh walked me to the elevator while I fought my nerves.

"You're blushing. What are you thinking about?" he inquired in a tone that I hadn't heard him use before. It was intimate and soft.

His observation made my face burn even further. I was sure that I was going to faint from sheer hunger or the madness of the day. "Well, if I'm being perfectly honest, Mr. Singer, I was blushing at the fact that you've seen me pretty much at my most insecure today. Not exactly the impression I wanted to make with my boss's boss."

Watching his eyes, I could tell he was surprised at my admission.

"I hope that you can always be honest with me, and please call me Josh."

"Okay. What was it that you wanted to speak with me about?"

After the doors of the elevator opened, he walked beside me toward my desk, which was in front of Warren's corner office.

Looking around, I was surprised that I didn't see my boss. Shouldn't he have returned to the office if Josh was here?

"Not here. Have you eaten?"

The question was innocent, and yet I felt completely flustered. "Uh, no, I haven't."

"I'm being presumptuous. You probably have plans on a Friday night?" He went around my desk and picked up the small photograph of my parents. For a moment, he studied it and I found his prying eyes unnerving.

"I was going to hit In-N-Out Burger, but no plans after."

His brow arched, and I knew that I'd probably come across like a teenager to him. "Are these your parents?" His voice was low and intimate again.

"Yes."

"Do you have a car parked in the garage?"

"No, I take the bus in."

"Good, we can take my rental car. Lead the way to In-N-Out Burger."

The way he said it made me giggle. He was like an Ivy Leaguer trying out another language, enunciating every syllable.

His brows shot up.

And because I didn't want him to think I was laughing at him, I confessed. "Sorry, it was just the way you said In-N-Out Burger. It made it sound fancy. We can go somewhere else if you'd prefer. I mean, it's fast food." I couldn't picture this gorgeous man in his impeccable suit hitting up a fast food restaurant.

After we made our way to the garage, I was even more convinced of this when I took in the Mercedes waiting for him. Feeling his hand on the small of my back, I tried not to let my nerves get the best of me.

"I think a burger and fries sound really good about now." He opened my door.

Once seated, I felt the cool leather on my bare legs and

inhaled the scent of the car. It was hard not to do so when in a vehicle this rich.

"Are you, uh, smelling the car?"

Embarrassed for a moment, I shrugged. "The leather of a new car smells amazing. I can't help it."

He looked amused as he navigated out onto the streets of Los Angeles right smack into rush hour. "Do you like LA?"

Wondering what it was he wanted to speak with me about, I remained patient. He was a man who seemed to be in control at all times, and at this moment he wanted small talk. "It's okay. The weather is nice, but traffic not so much." It had taken five minutes to go a half mile, and we had four more to go to the nearest In-N-Out Burger.

"Where are you from originally?"

It would have been nice if there'd been less traffic so he'd have to keep his eyes on the road. Every time he glanced over I got flustered. "I grew up north of San Francisco and did my undergrad at Stanford." I was trying not to babble. This wasn't a date and a get-to-know-you. He was my boss's boss and the owner of the company.

"Do your parents still live there?"

"No. They're both deceased."

He murmured, "I'm sorry."

The awkward silence weighed on me while he appeared to absorb my answers. "Where are you from?" I asked, curious to learn something about him.

He seemed startled by my reciprocating question, and his gaze met mine again.

Was this type of inquiry considered bad form in the business world? I wasn't sure. Then again, we were on our way to eat fast food after a day of discussing my bikini line. How much weirder was this day going to get?

"I grew up in Virginia, outside of DC, in a town called

McLean. Now I'm based primarily out of New York City, although I travel quite a bit."

I wanted to ask him where his favorite place in the entire world was or how he liked New York City, but I felt like it would highlight my lack of worldliness. Besides, Josh Singer didn't seem the type to talk for no reason. I didn't even realize I'd sighed until he did the same.

"I guess I'm not very good company."

His vulnerability was surprising. Turning toward him, I admitted, "Honestly, I was sighing because I want to ask you more but then felt like it might be inappropriate, or you might think I'm the one who isn't good company."

He turned toward me at the next red light. "I wish you would just ask me your questions. Too many people worry about what I might or might not think."

Based on his comment, I wondered if it was lonely in his world. "Okay. Among the places you've traveled, where's your favorite spot in the world?"

Smiling, he appeared to think about it. "If you're talking about a beach, then I would say Moorea, which is in the French Polynesian Islands. For culture, I would say Prague or Istanbul."

"Nice. Um, do you want to grab a table or do drive-thru?" We were turning into the parking lot.

"I'm good with drive-thru if you are."

We got in line, and I continued my questioning. "Where's the most charming place you've ever been?"

He seemed thrown by the question at first. "Ah, the most charming place would probably be Ireland. What are we ordering?" It was now our turn at the speaker.

"You want me to choose?" I was surprised when he nodded, after which I leaned across him without thinking. "We'd like two cheeseburgers, two fries, and two chocolate milkshakes, please."

He stiffened at the contact, and I quickly moved back, trying not to notice that he smelled amazing. Even better than the leather seats.

"Sorry, I didn't mean to invade your space." I retrieved cash out of my purse and felt his eyes on me. His expression told me he was amused that I was planning to pay. "You're driving me home and just gave me forty thousand dollars. The least I can do is treat you to a junk food dinner."

I expected him to be stubborn, but instead he accepted my twenty and gave it to the teenage girl who could only stare dumbly.

Yeah, I know how it feels, honey. He's way out of both of our leagues.

As he handed me my change, I felt his hand on mine, thinking it was unfair that I be so affected while he simply went through the normal motions.

"So, do you want to eat in the parking lot, go to your place, or continue on to my hotel room?" He must have noticed my stunned look as he hastily added, "I didn't mean that the way it sounded. I meant—You know what? Why don't we just pull over here?" He parked the car on the far side of the lot. "I didn't mean to make you feel uncomfortable, Haylee." His voice was quiet.

I was torn between the longing to rip into my cheeseburger and the desire to unbuckle his pants and devour him. I doubted either of those scenarios was in the business etiquette handbook.

"You aren't. I knew what you were asking, and considering traffic, I think eating here is the best idea. I'm starving."

He seemed to relax as we both dug into our burgers.

Meanwhile, I tried to remember my manners. "Well, what do you think?"

"It's good. Is this your go-to place for dinner?"

"Ah, no. Can't keep my size six, still-too-fat-for-modeling figure by eating here every night."

He chuckled with an appreciation for my sarcasm.

"It's more comfort food to follow a long hard day with no workout planned after. Slug food."

He quirked a brow.

"You know, slugging on the couch after a junk-induced food coma?"

He seemed to find that humorous. "When are you going to law school?"

Well, that was quite a change in subject. "I'm hoping next year in the fall." I was feeling better by the minute as I started on my fries.

"Why are you waiting?"

He seemed sincerely interested, but I didn't want to make it about money. This was a man who wouldn't understand having to save up for something. "I had a lot happening directly after graduation and wanted to work for a year first."

He frowned at my vague answer. "Do you like working for Warren?"

I stopped chewing and swallowed hard. Warren was a bully around the office, and I wasn't particularly fond of him. But Josh was his boss and since one of the traits I held dear was loyalty, I answered carefully. "He works hard at his job and is well respected in the industry."

He appeared disappointed by my response. "You do know that he didn't plan to pay you for today, right?"

I'd suspected that Josh was responsible for the payday, but hearing the confirmation made me a little sick to my stomach. Warren hadn't seemed appreciative of me stepping in at all. Given his personality, he probably thought of it as an extension of my job duties to fill in when requested.

"Mr. Singer, I'm not sure what you expect me to say. I'm not surprised, if that's what you're after. However, I don't think it's appropriate for me to discuss my feelings on the matter with his boss and the owner of the company."

"I admire your loyalty. Warren has been through five assistants in the last three years, so I'm well aware of his reputation. But you're right. He works hard for me and works harder for his clients, so I can excuse his lack of soft skills most of the time. You started calling me Mr. Singer again, by the way."

My head was spinning. "Okay, *Josh*." I put emphasis on his first name. "Why did you ask me if I like working for Warren?"

"Well, that leads me to what I wanted to discuss with you."

My palms started to sweat. Isn't this where in a romance novel he'd propose an arrangement whereby I went back to his hotel room to see exactly what was under that suit?

"I want you to work for me."

In my mind, that sentence ended with *as my personal sex slave,* but in reality I grasped that he was proposing an authentic job. "Uh, what?" was my eloquent response.

"I want you to come to New York and work as my second assistant. Nigel has been with me for a number of years and is the best in the business; however, he has a personal situation which currently precludes him from traveling with me. Plus, he'll need to take time out of the office from time to time to address these personal issues. I would need you in New York most of the time, but you would also travel with me."

I was stunned. "I would move to New York?"

"Yes. I think you will find the salary quite a bit higher than what you're earning here."

"But the cost of living is higher, too. I would need to find a place to live, and I have two more months on my roommate agreement here." I stopped, realizing I was rambling to someone who wouldn't appreciate why.

"I recognize this is catching you off guard. Ask me your questions while I drive you home. I'll give you my cell phone number so that you can text me anything you may think of later this evening. I'm leaving Sunday morning and would want you to come to New York with me then."

"I, um, wow. But you don't even know if I'm a good

assistant. Not to mention, I would leave Warren without any notice."

"The fact that you're worried about leaving without notice tells me what kind of assistant you are. I need someone who's loyal and who I can trust."

"I have a million questions," I murmured, after giving him directions to my apartment building.

"Well, let me break it down to make your decision easier. You want to save money for law school, right?"

I nodded.

"I will pay you a hundred thousand in salary and provide free housing. That ought to allow you the ability to do that."

Housing alone was a fortune. "I've only been to New York City once. Where would I live?"

"In Manhattan, only a few blocks from the office. I need you close by so you can come into work or travel at the last minute. Matter of fact, we'd leave for Cancun next week if you take the job. So, fair warning: you won't have much time for a personal life. This position is very demanding."

We had pulled up to the curb, but I still wasn't sure how to respond to any of this.

"I'll take care of the last two months' rent to satisfy your agreement here. For your convenience, the apartment in New York is already furnished. As for your belongings, I'll pay to have them moved out there. Or if you prefer, you can put things in storage."

I already had my parents' belongings in storage. I only had my clothes and some other odds and ends to worry about.

"Give me your phone," he requested.

I pulled it out, handed it over, and then watched him deftly type his number into my contacts.

"Text or call me with any more questions. I'm at the Four Seasons and will expect you either way on Sunday morning for breakfast at nine o'clock."

I was surprised that he wanted to meet, no matter what my decision, and had to test him. "What if I say no?"

His answer was thoughtful. "I'll be disappointed, but you would continue your current position with Warren if that's what you want. I like to think I'm giving you a choice as I'm not a man who usually has to resort to ultimatums."

My mouth went dry as I thought there weren't many women who'd tell Josh Singer no. Ugh, I needed to get my mind out of the gutter. I also needed some space away from this magnetic man if I was to make a clear, professional decision. "All right, I'll think about it. Here, let me take the trash. Don't want to ruin the new car smell." I gathered up the fast food bags and got out.

"Thanks for dinner, Haylee. And I mean it: text or call with any questions. I don't care what time it is." He had rolled down the window.

"Okay, and you're welcome." I stepped away from the car and felt his eyes on me as I turned and walked toward my three-story, Spanish style apartment building and up the two flights to my door.

CHAPTER THREE

My roommate's name was Angela, and I'd been lucky to find her on Craigslist for a six-month sublet while her usual roommate was in Spain on a temporary work assignment. Angela was a CPA and worked for a prestigious accounting firm. At the moment, however, she was getting completely decked out to hit the town. As I glanced at her short skirt and sparkly top, I found it hard to imagine her a tax genius by day.

"Hey, lady, long day for you. Whoa, love the hair. Very sexy," she pointed out, greeting me at the door. I put my purse down and followed her into the hall bathroom where she started putting on her makeup.

"Yeah, it was a crazy day for sure. Where you off to?"

"*We,* meaning the both of us, are going out. It's been a long, boring, number-crunching kind of week, and there's a hot new club where one of my clients put our names on the VIP list."

The last thing I wanted to do was go out. I had a ton to think about, but the thought of spending the night fretting and overanalyzing it all seemed depressing. Plus this could potentially be my last night out in LA with Angela.

"Okay, you know what? I'm in, but I need to change and do something with this." I gestured toward my face, wishing I'd left on my makeup from the shoot.

"Please, you're gorgeous. I'd kill for your curves, and the hair is seriously hot. Just put on some makeup and throw on something skimpy."

Laughing, I hurried into my room, slipping on a short mini and an off-the-shoulder club-worthy shirt. I doubted very much this ensemble would cut it in New York. Then again, it didn't sound like I'd have a lot of time for a social life there. In fact, the way Josh had presented it made me think about all of the time I'd be spending with him instead.

How did one travel all over the world with a hot boss and not completely make a fool of oneself?

And why me? No matter what else he had explained, he hadn't clarified why he would ask me when he could easily hire someone local. A secret hope he might have felt the same spark I had sent a shiver through me. But then what? He was the owner of the company.

Damn. What I needed was to drink and dance and then come home and slug it tomorrow with a hangover. It wasn't my most mature idea, but it was the plan of the moment.

I met my roommate in the hall after doing up my eyes the way Trisha had, grabbed my ID and some cash.

Angela whistled. "Wow, the smoky eye looks amazing on you."

I smiled and returned the compliment by remarking how great she looked in her outfit.

As we called a cab and headed out, I brought her up to speed with all the events of the day.

"Holy shit. You filled in for Katrina Tross? What did the pictures look like? Have you seen them?"

I realized I had no idea how they'd turned out. I thought it had gone well, but what the hell did I know? Shrugging the question off, I supplied the subsequent details of Josh coming to the office and his job offer instead, but I left out the fast-food dinner as it seemed too bizarre to explain.

"Wait. You were offered a free move to New York, a furnished apartment, and the opportunity to travel the world for a year? Plus he's paying off your sublet here. Uh, yeah, tough decision, my friend. I'm sorry we won't be able to get that three bedroom we talked about once Susan is back from Spain, but clearly this is a much better opportunity."

I sighed, thinking she was right. It was a terrific opportunity.

"So what's the problem? Is the guy creepy, or what?"

"Well, that's one of the issues. He's gorgeous, like seriously hot, like I-get-tongue-tied attractive."

Before I knew it, she was on her phone and then flashing a picture of Josh Singer my way. "Is this him?"

Nodding, I took her phone and sighed. "Oh, yeah, that's him."

"Holy shit, he's smoking hot. What kind of offer is it?" She narrowed her eyes, and I rolled mine.

"A professional one. Sheesh."

She laughed and took my hand as we got out of the cab in front of the club. We then proceeded to the front of the line and toward the VIP entrance. "Sorry, honey. You know I didn't mean any disrespect. Although if I'm being honest, a nonprofessional offer from a guy who looks like that could be interesting, too. He's like tie-me-up-and-use-a-flogger-on-me gorgeous."

I shook my head, knowing Angela had an affinity for those types of books. But yeah, he was kind of tie-me-up hot. And I'd have to google what the hell a flogger was.

"So, do you want my opinion? DO IT," she shouted as we entered the loud club.

I could only smile. Then we made our way into the vibrating center.

A FEW DRINKS LATER, I watched Angela meet up with one of her coworkers while I thought about the one question I couldn't shake.

I was sure I'd regret texting him later, but at one o'clock in the morning, four drinks in, it seemed like a great idea. ***"Why me?"***

I was surprised at how quickly he texted back.

"Where are you?"

Smiling, I thought about Josh in a place like this. An image of Mr. Conservative bumping and grinding made me giggle. ***"Out at a club."***

"How much have you had to drink?"

It was tempting to ask what he was wearing, but even in my drunken mindset I knew that was over the top. ***"A few. You didn't answer my question."***

As I waited for his text back, I felt my phone vibrate with an incoming call instead. Oh, shit, it had to be Josh. The music was deafening, but I answered anyhow.

"Hello," I shouted and could barely hear his response. "Hold on."

I found Angela, who was happily lip-locked with a guy from her office, and told her I was making my way home. She smiled, telling me not to wait up. Good for Angela, I thought, walking outside.

The cooler air hit me, and I realized I was still holding my phone with Josh on the other end. "Um, are you still there?" I wondered for a moment if he'd actually called.

"Yes, I'm here. Where are you?" At least he didn't sound annoyed.

"It's a club called Fancy. Downtown. I'm about to catch a cab home." My feet were killing me.

"Stay there. I'll be by in a few minutes and drive you."

Did I hear him correctly? "No, no, it's late. I'm fine to take a cab." It began to sink in that I was talking to the owner of the company I worked for, and I started to freak out a bit.

"I'll give you a ride, so wait for me out front. I mean it."

He didn't leave room for me to argue, and when he pulled up ten minutes later, I had to fight my anxiety. After opening the passenger door, I slid in.

"Jesus, you call that a skirt?" That was the first thing out of his mouth.

I should have been offended, but instead I started giggling. "It's a club skirt, and mine is long compared to some."

As if on cue, two women came out in skimpier attire.

He only raised a brow and muttered something about being too old.

He was silent most of the trip, and I was surprised when he cut the engine after pulling into my apartment parking lot. "I'll walk you up." His voice was back to intimate.

When my face hit the night air, I started to realize what I must look like through his eyes. "I'm fine, really. Look, I'm sorry. I drank too much, and I had just thought to text you a question, and then you called, and now you're walking me up, and shit—" I missed a step on the stairs, and he steadied me up against his body.

He'd changed his clothes and was now in jeans and a soft black T-shirt. My hand found his chest, and I was able to feel the hardness of his muscles beneath the soft material. Jumping back, I realized what a silly girl I must appear to be to him. At the top of the stairs, I unlocked my door and was about to bid him good night when he invited himself inside.

"Where's your roommate?"

"She's going home with someone from the club. I mean, she's not slutty. It's her coworker, and they've been seeing each other. Crap, Haylee. Just. Stop. Talking." I clamped a hand over my mouth, completely embarrassed.

"Why did you ask me that question?" He had crossed the room and was looking intently at me.

My lips went dry, and I cursed mentally at the fact that most of the moisture from my mouth was now pooling between my legs. Merely from his intensity. "I just— I don't know. It doesn't make sense, that's all." My eyes shifted down.

His fingers lifted my chin. "You make me want to get to know and trust you for some inexplicable reason. Does that answer your question?"

It really didn't and instead led to many more. But my brain was fuzzy and I was exhausted, so I merely nodded, wondering if and secretly hoping that he would kiss me.

"So, is that a yes, then?" His voice did this honey thing that made my stomach flip-flop. "Or are there any other concerns?"

"I, uh, no. Are you sure you haven't changed your mind?"

Smiling, he gave me an entertained look. "No, but tell me, what's holding you back from taking this opportunity?"

Before I could filter my response through the tiny sober part of my mind, I blurted out, "That I'm way too attracted to you for you to be my boss."

He stepped back, and my brain registered what had just come out.

"Oh, shit, I didn't mean to say that out loud." I felt the tears of embarrassment well up.

He cupped my face and wiped them away before they made tracks. "Text me yes. Right now, so that in the morning you see that you've agreed."

Since when was a text message a binding agreement? But my heart and fuzzy head weren't computing, so I nodded dumbly and fumbled with my phone.

"There, I just sent it," I proclaimed.

He checked his phone and seemed pleased. "Get some sleep and get your things in order. Tomorrow I'll email you the nondisclosure agreement that you'll need to sign before working for me. I'll see you Sunday morning. And, Haylee?" He was at my front door and looked back. "The feeling is quite mutual." With that, he left.

It took me a full minute to realize what he was referring to, but once I did I was dumbfounded. Josh Singer was attracted to me, too. And I'd just agreed to move to New York to work for him.

CHAPTER FOUR

My new life started with me staring out at a bustling Times Square from the window of the town car that had picked us up at the airport. I felt like a tourist and couldn't help it. Looking over at Josh, I found that he was smiling at me while I took in the sensory overload that was New York City. So this would be home for the next nine months.

We'd taken his private plane and were now pulling up outside of a tall, modern-looking apartment building. The doorman greeted Josh and came out with a cart to help with the luggage.

"Hello, Miss. I'm Rafael. I'm on the door most nights, and Jim is your day man. I'll meet you upstairs with your things shortly." He seemed friendly and appeared to know Josh.

"Um, what floor am I on?" I asked as we both stepped into the elevator together.

"You're on twenty-four." Josh pressed the button.

The butterflies in my stomach increased with each passing number. It would be the first place I'd ever have all to myself.

Following his steps to the end of the hall, I noticed how quiet it was and wondered what my neighbors would be like. Seeing only two other doors at the end of the hall, I wondered who else lived on the floor. Nice building in Manhattan with a secure entrance, mere blocks from Times Square— Yeah, I had a feeling I'd have nothing in common with either of them.

"Don't use your address on anything, including your HR forms. Instead, you can set up a PO Box tomorrow at lunch for a mailing address. There's a post office a block from the office."

"Do I get to ask why?"

He unlocked the door for me, apparently choosing to avoid the question.

Turning on the light, I went in and glanced around. It looked a lot like one of those extended-stay hotel rooms, with a small kitchen off to my right and a queen-sized bed over to my left. I opened the door next to the bed to find a good-sized closet and then walked to the door on the far side of the space. This revealed a bathroom which boasted a pretty glass shower. The flat-screen TV on the wall was a nice touch as I'd be able to watch television in bed.

"It's not really made for entertaining, but the view isn't bad."

After making my way over to the window, I sucked in my breath at the lights of the city spread out before me. "It's amazing. I've never before had a place that I didn't have to share. Any company will just have to watch the TV from the bed."

I hadn't realized how it sounded until it was out of my mouth.

His eyes darkened as he turned toward me.

Swallowing hard, I pictured him in my bed, but something told me we wouldn't be watching much television.

"We'll need to discuss any company before you bring people here. Matter of fact, I'd appreciate it if you tell anyone who asks where you're living that you're staying with friends."

That seemed a little strange, but I didn't have a chance to think about it because Rafael knocked on the door and then brought in my suitcases.

"I'll leave you to get settled and see you in the morning," Josh said, turning to go.

I was anxious to get unpacked, but in looking over at Rafael, I was even more worried about offending my new doorman.

"Wait, quick question." I dragged Josh over to the side, out of earshot of the other man. "I'm not really sure. Do I, um, tip Rafael?"

The question seemed to completely throw him.

Noticing my hand was still on his arm, I suddenly dropped it, incredulous that I'd touched him with such familiarity.

But instead of looking annoyed, he reached his hand up and tucked my hair behind my ear.

I could only stare and hope that after his touch I'd still be able to comprehend his answer.

"No. At a hotel it would be appropriate but not the doorman of your residence. Holidays are a time to do that."

He spoke to me in a voice that didn't make me feel stupid. "Thanks. I guess I'll see you tomorrow morning, then." I was sorry to see him go, but he suddenly seemed in a hurry as he stepped back and toward the door.

"Yes, tomorrow morning. Good night, Haylee."

With that, he and Rafael were both on their way out.

I grabbed my key from the counter and did a twirl around the room. My new life was looking pretty damn sweet thus far.

I SPENT the next couple of hours unpacking and getting my work clothes steamed out, ready for the week. The sound of my stomach growling reminded me that I hadn't eaten. Since I didn't have any food, I would need to go out. Already dressed casually in yoga pants and a tank top, I threw on a sweatshirt and tennis shoes. It was much cooler here at night than in LA, being that it was fall in the Big Apple.

Once I made my way downstairs, I asked Rafael where to find good local places for food. I settled on Thai a couple blocks away and also found a small convenience store along the way. With bags in hand, I headed back into the lobby.

"Ah, Ms. Haylee. Here, Mr. Singer wanted me to give you these menus for places that deliver. In New York City, you name it, and you can have anything delivered. They will bring it to the front desk, and then I can call you or send it straight up."

I smiled, thankful, and then realized how strange his instruction had sounded. "Rafael, when did Mr. Singer tell you to give these to me?"

"Uh, about an hour ago. He wanted to ensure I kept an eye out for you and requested that I inform him if you stepped out of the building. It's a good city, miss, but if you don't know it—Well, it can be dangerous. Mr. Singer is simply a cautious man. I hope you're not upset."

"No. Not at all, but can I ask you something?"

"Of course. Anything."

"Does Mr. Singer live in this building, too?"

His expression was one of confusion and then he laughed. "You didn't know? You're in his guest apartment. He occupies the entire twenty-fourth floor, the penthouse, miss."

"Thanks."

Oh, boy. On my way up, I tried to figure out what this meant. But at least I didn't have to wonder any longer why he wouldn't want my address given out.

SLEEP ELUDED me most of the night. It could've been nerves regarding my first day at the office or the fact that I was on a West Coast internal clock. But I was pretty sure it was the green eyes that I knew were sleeping next door to me that occupied my thoughts.

Grateful for my Diet Coke in the morning, I googled where my new office was located and then left early, hoping someone would be there to let me in. It was a beautiful morning, and the air smelled of autumn. The sidewalks were packed, and the bustle made me smile as I stopped for a bagel and walked the five blocks to work.

I found my building by eight o'clock and was thankful the security desk was expecting me. After giving me a temporary badge, they told me to go up to the top floor. Once there, I was pleasantly greeted by a well-dressed, forty-something-year-old man who introduced himself as Nigel.

"Hello, my dear. You must be Haylee," he acknowledged kindly.

His British accent was charming, and the sincerity in his eyes made me hopeful that we would become friends. "Yes, you must be Nigel. It's nice to meet you."

"This is your desk. We both sit directly outside of the executive elevator with Josh's office through that door. I'll show you that in a moment. How was the trip?"

"It was good. It's been a whirlwind, but I'm really happy to be here. I hope you don't mind me being early. Jo— I mean, Mr. Singer said nine o'clock, but I wanted to arrive before he did."

"No, I certainly understand. I typically get here early on Mondays to get his schedule sorted, and I'm in by eight-thirty on most other days. We might as well jump in before he gets here."

I smiled, eager to get started.

First, Nigel brought me around Josh's office for a tour. I was impressed with the space and thought the dark wood and rich leather represented him well.

"We have two floors of this building which make up the executive headquarters. That includes Human Resources, Accounting, IT, and a small legal department. The Gamble Advertising office is six blocks away. We have two floors in that building as well, but it's much more of a client-facing office."

In other words, Josh separated his Gamble Enterprise operations from Gamble Advertising. That was good to know.

"I'm glad you're here, my dear. I've needed to take more personal time lately with an illness in the family, and, well, the travel has just been impossible. Josh is very particular about whom he trusts."

It was a relief that he didn't feel threatened by me. This was going to be short-term, and I was happy to help in any way I could.

"Mr. Singer should be here any minute. He has a ten o'clock call, so how about at that time you go on down to HR? They're one floor down. They'll give you all of your paperwork. Then IT can give you your hardware along with your building badge. Your badge will allow you direct access to Josh's elevator and this office."

It sounded good to me. "Okay. Thank you."

Josh came off the elevator.

I followed Nigel's lead and stood at my desk. I thought I had a handle on my nerves until Josh turned toward me in his pinstriped suit.

"Good morning," he greeted.

My mouth went dry. "Good morning, Mr. Singer." I didn't sound like myself.

He must have sensed it as he paused and raised that damn brow of his.

NIGEL CAME out of Josh's office after fifteen minutes. "He would like to see you briefly, Haylee."

Walking in with a notepad and pen, I smoothed my Chanel suit and thought about how the pink twill had been my mother's absolute favorite.

"How was your evening?" he asked, taking me off guard. I had thought we would start off all business.

"Um, it was good. I'm unpacked, and Rafael was kind enough to offer me a ton of takeout options."

"Ah, yes. Well, I'm sure that's preferable to going out late at night in a strange city."

My face broke out in a smile at his veiled suggestion to stay in.

"Nigel, I trust, is getting you settled in?" He steepled his fingers and leaned back in his chair.

I nodded and observed Josh behind his desk with the city stretched out behind him. This was the man of power whom others must see. Instead of being intimidated, though, I was completely aroused. It was an unfortunate feeling, considering I was at work and wasn't sure what in the hell my boss was thinking. He seemed to reflect a myriad of conflicting emotions.

"Our trip to Cancun has been postponed from Wednesday to Sunday. From there, we'll go over to Hong Kong for a few days. It's sometimes easier to string these international trips together."

Feeling slightly let down that I wasn't getting the opportunity to travel with him sooner, I could only nod.

"You look disappointed." He seemed to have my number, which was unnerving and pleasing at the same time.

"Oh, I just was looking forward to the travel."

He glanced at his watch; his call would be starting soon. "Everyone thinks traveling for business is sexy until you do it often enough you realize it's a lot of work and can be quite tiring in reality."

I didn't think before I responded. Lowering my voice to a whisper, I leaned over the desk. "It isn't the travel that I find sexy, Mr. Singer."

I got the desired response with the darkening of his eyes and the quick intake of his breath.

Nigel's voice cut through over the intercom. "Sir, your conference call is ready for you."

Smiling, I crossed to the door. With a glance back, I saw that Josh was tracking me and had yet to pick up the call.

SHIT, what had I been thinking? I was starting to have serious regrets over my little flirtation after my hour with Human Resources, who informed me that as part of the orientation they would be emailing me shortly the links to the sexual harassment training. Although I'd already gone through it in LA, it hadn't resonated like it did right now.

Trying not to think about the fact that I'd probably already violated the office policy with this morning's comment alone, I went over to IT. While there, I received my laptop and building badge. I was thankful they managed to sync up my smartphone with the work server so that I wouldn't have to carry around two separate phones.

When I went back upstairs, I found Nigel on the phone, so I booted up my new laptop and worked for the next hour setting up my email and then arranging my office desk. As noon approached, I suggested that Nigel go to lunch while I man the phones.

Hesitant at first, he then seemed relieved. "Mr. Singer is out at a lunch meeting, but I should be back before he returns. Do you want me to grab you something?"

"Actually, when you get back, I need to step out and set up a PO box for my mail." I was glad that he didn't ask where I was staying, but realized he might already know.

"Not a problem, my dear. I won't be long."

With the time to myself in the office, I figured I might as well get the sexual harassment training over and done. Accordingly, I clicked on the provided link and brought up a cheesy interactive video. Rolling my eyes and putting my chin in my hand, I started watching. I was ten minutes in when Josh came off the elevator.

"Streaming movies already? I wouldn't have thought you'd be that bored your first day. Where's Nigel?"

Good to know he had a sense of humor in the office. "He stepped out. I'm just watching this sexual harassment video since I thought you were still at a lunch engagement." As soon as I mentioned sexual harassment, I knew that my face heated.

Smiling, he leaned over my shoulder to watch. His closeness was unsettling as was the delicious smell of him: a mix of soap, cologne and, well, just pure virile man.

"It cancelled. Are you learning anything, Haylee?"

That buttery voice of his did things to me. Damn. "Well, it's kind of cheesy and, frankly, a little annoying at what they think constitutes harassment."

I was pretty sure that we were crossing a line currently with his proximity to my ear but was hard pressed to move a muscle.

"Show me."

When I clicked on the next slide, we saw the character of Jose asking Carmen, a coworker, out on a date. She told him that she had other plans. He then asked her out a second time the next week. She proceeded to tell him that she had to wash her hair, after which she complained to another coworker that he wasn't getting the hint. The question presented was whether or not the coworker should report it.

"And the correct answer is?" he baited me.

Turning toward him, I realized our faces were inches from one another. "That Carmen should've just told him she's just not interested instead of making up some lame excuse. As far as Jose knows, she actually did have other plans the first time. And the second time, maybe she was just in dire need of a hair wash. He's clueless and maybe didn't mean to harass her in the least, but now it's escalating to HR, and that's crap."

His gaze slid to mine, and he gave me an amused smile. “Maybe Carmen doesn’t want to hurt his feelings by telling him that she’s not interested. What then?”

My stomach dropped, and I swallowed hard. He’d leaned back on my desk so that I had to swivel my chair to look up at his face. Now I wondered if I was misreading the situation entirely. I didn’t exactly have a lot of experience with men, especially with older, powerful men-who-could-have-any-woman-in-the-world kind of men. All of a sudden, every ounce of my self-confidence was on the brink.

“She could just tell him that she has a boyfriend. That would keep him from asking again, and it makes him feel like it was nothing personal.”

“So she should lie?” The question was posed innocently enough, but I could feel an edge to it.

“I guess it depends on how close she is to him. If she sees him often and is a friend, I guess you’re right. She shouldn’t lie. But if he’s some random guy she’s met on a work trip or only sees sometimes, then…”

“It’s not a lie if she doesn’t know him?”

Uh-oh. I was failing whatever test he was giving me. “I didn’t say that. What I’m saying is sometimes a white lie is better than hurting someone’s feelings.”

He seemed to acknowledge the difference but pressed on. “And if he’s someone she sees every day? What then?”

“Well, I guess maybe Carmen first needs to figure out if she’s been giving Jose mixed signals.”

His brow arched, and I felt like a foolish teenage girl. Perhaps I had misunderstood him when I’d been drunk.

“Or maybe Jose figures out that Carmen was just being nice, and he was misinterpreting the situation. In that case, Jose simply needed a reality check.” I couldn’t maintain eye contact as I laid out that depressing scenario.

“I didn’t mean—”

Thankfully, he was unable to finish his thought because Nigel came in.

God, I was humiliated. "Mr. Singer, can I pick you up anything for lunch since you're back early?" I was on my feet, gathering my purse and trying to act nonchalant.

Josh gave little indication that he heard me, and Nigel just looked between us.

"A sandwich would be fine, Haylee, thank you. Nigel, if you would call Alan from accounting up here, I'd like a few minutes with him."

"Yes, of course," Nigel said while our boss went back behind closed doors.

"I guess I should ask what kind of sandwich he likes." I turned toward Nigel, hoping he wouldn't read anything into the awkwardness he'd walked in on.

He only smiled and handed me a three-page, typed-up document. "Everything personal is in here, but do me a favor and don't let our boss see it, all right?"

Nodding, I tucked it into my purse.

A BLOCK down the street at the post office, I had to wait in line. By the time I was done setting up my PO box, half my lunch hour was gone. At least I had some interesting reading. I skimmed over the basics of the personal document Nigel had handed me and honed in on the surprises.

Thirty-two years old. Doesn't drink soda. Cigarette brand was Marlboro Red Box. Holy crap, he was a smoker. I hadn't noticed, so he must take care with the smell on his clothing. I was disappointed but moved on and read that he worked out three times per week with a trainer doing mixed martial arts. His various charities were listed as well as his personal properties, which included the condo in New York and a house in Charlotte, North Carolina.

The second page listed his pet peeves. Laziness, gossip, insincerity, rudeness, pettiness, and dishonesty. I could talk with the man for ten minutes and figure that out. Musical tastes included country music. Huh, didn't see that one coming. Wasn't a fan of dance clubs or loud music and DOES NOT DANCE. Okay that was in all shouty-capital letters, so it must be nonnegotiable.

The final page was a number of topics not to bring up.

Marriage, dating, and relationships in general. Well, I'd only flirted and not actually brought up any of that.

Money and finances. Well, at least I hadn't done that.

His smoking. Ah, so it was a don't-ask-don't-tell policy, then.

Quickly scanning the rest of it, I found food preferences and accordingly ordered him a club sandwich with an iced tea. I got myself a soup and Diet Coke.

After I arrived back at the office, Nigel motioned that I could just go into Josh's office with the food since our boss was busy on the phone.

I walked in quietly.

His back was turned, and he was looking out the window, but when I set his lunch down, he turned around.

His eyes met mine. "Chelsea, I'll call you back."

And just like that, I was front and center, wishing I wasn't.

"Did you get your PO box established?" As always, he asked a question that wasn't on my mind.

"Yes, it's set up."

"Good. Look, there's a lot—"

"Sir, Mr. Hines on the line for you. He said it's quite urgent." Nigel's voice cut through.

Josh's eyes reflected his frustration. "Dammit, I have to take this."

His tone was apologetic, and I felt bad about adding drama to his already busy day. "Yes, certainly."

I walked out feeling relieved.

THE REMAINDER of the week was spent establishing a routine and learning how to plan travel and all of the other details of Josh's schedule. I was comforted that he had a private travel person named Maria who took care of the actual flight and hotel itineraries.

On Friday I was invited out by Zach, the IT guy who was around my age. He asked if I'd come over to Jersey City for a drink or two and indicated there would be a group, including his sister and roommates.

Considering I didn't have any friends in the city and it was in fact a Friday night—without any indication from Josh that he wanted to spend a minute in my company outside of the office—I accepted. After the subway took me across the river to Jersey City, it was a short walk from the third stop.

I was pleased to see Zach's friendly face toward the back of the bar. He was sitting at a table with some other twenty-something-year-olds.

"Hey, you made it. Fantastic. Everyone, this is Haylee. She works in my office. Haylee, this is Jason and Kyle, my roommates. Debbie is Kyle's girlfriend, and that's her friend, Natasha."

Smiling, I took a seat, happy to get off my feet. Meanwhile, Jason ordered a round of shots.

Oh, shit, I wasn't a lightweight, but shots were definitely going to set me over the edge if I didn't get some food in me. After throwing back the first one, I requested a menu and ordered some chicken strips and fries. At least those would help soak up the liquor.

I was having a good time talking with everyone, but by midnight I was drunk. Not fall-down-stupid intoxicated but silly-fun drunk. So were all of my companions for the evening. I reached into my purse to check the time on my phone and noticed the three missed calls and two text messages asking where I was. They were all from *Carmen,* which I'd thought a clever way to input Josh's cell phone information.

I considered calling but realized it would only break the good mood I was in. Instead, I sent a text. ***"I'm fine, just out with friends, see u Sunday."***

The response back was immediate. ***"Where are you?"***

Why did he make me feel like I was breaking curfew? ***"Jersey City."***

No response back.

He was probably either seething or tracking my phone about now. Crap, he would have the resources to do it, too. How ironic would it be if he called Zach to take care of that? Smiling at the thought, I told everyone I needed to go. It would take an hour, at least, to get back to my place, and I wanted to ensure I didn't miss the last train.

"I'll walk with you to the subway," Zach offered.

It was tempting to say no, but I wasn't sure I could find it again from this direction, particularly given all the alcohol in my system.

"So, it seems like you had a good time," he tested along the way.

"It was really nice of you to invite me. Thank you." We stood in front of the subway entrance, and I noticed him getting nervous. "It's good to have a friend in the office, Zach. I'll talk to you when I get back from my trip. Thanks again." I wasn't taking any chances and was down the stairs before he could try to kiss me or say something that would make the situation weird.

He was a super nice guy, but I didn't want to date someone I worked with.

Yeah, right. Evidently, the exception would be my boss and the owner of the whole damn company. I wanted to kick my own ass for being so naïve.

My phone buzzed, and I realized I had another text.

"How are you getting back?"

"I'm about to hop on the subway," I responded.

IT TOOK AN HOUR, but I was finally in familiar territory again and waved hello to Rafael upon entering the building. As I came off the elevator onto my floor, I was rummaging for my key. When I glanced up, I saw one of the doors at the end of the hall open and Josh appear in the doorway.

The vision he made in bare feet, lounge pants, and a white T-shirt made me swallow hard. His jet-black hair was unkempt enough that he might have just woken up.

"Do you have any idea how worried I was?" His voice was quiet.

I took a deep breath before commenting. "I'm a grown woman and was safe."

He ran a hand through his hair, and we just stood there staring at one another. "Who were you with?"

"Zach from IT and his roommates and their friends. It was a large group of people." I'm not sure why I didn't take the opportunity to make him jealous, but he didn't seem in the mood for it.

"I see. And you had to go all the way to Jersey to get drunk with Zach?"

"I'm not drunk, and it was a group. I wasn't there with him; he just happened to issue the invite."

"So he didn't try to kiss you?"

Before I could second-guess what I was doing, I marched up and grasped both sides of his face, bringing it down to mine and putting my lips on his.

His initial surprise shifted to desire in about two seconds. He tangled his hands in my hair and met my insistent mouth with his own.

"Jesus, Haylee," he managed a minute later, pulling back.

How could a simple kiss cause so much heat? "No, Zach didn't kiss me."

"You need to get some sleep. Make sure you drink some water before you go to bed." His voice sounded regretful.

I didn't trust myself to say anything as I'd already gone far enough with my brazen action, so I only nodded and walked on shaky legs to my door. I hadn't been prepared for how that one kiss would leave me hungry for more.

CHAPTER FIVE

On Sunday, we left for Cancun via commercial jet in first class, which meant no alone-time with Josh on the flight. There had been absolutely no mention of what had happened in the hall on Friday night. It was as if we were both pretending it hadn't occurred, yet I couldn't stop thinking about that kiss and wondered if he was similarly afflicted.

It was my first official business trip, and I looked forward to it. Upon arrival, we made our way to his current resort, which was midway down what was known as the Strip. This resort, I would learn, was a little over five years old and offered an all-inclusive vacation. So far in the afternoon daylight, the city didn't look like a spring break mecca. But considering it was off season and the middle of the day, perhaps I wasn't seeing the place at its prime.

Getting checked into the hotel definitely had its benefits when you were the owner. We were each shown to a spacious room when we arrived on the same floor. I went about setting up Josh's computer in the office of his suite and then ordered up a fruit and cheese plate and got things ready for his first appointment. On the agenda today were meetings regarding a new resort being built further down the Strip. Evidently, construction would start next month.

"This is Hector, the hotel manager. Hector, this is Haylee, my assistant." Josh introduced the man who'd knocked on the door.

"*Encantado de conocerte*. Nice to meet you," Hector greeted in both Spanish and then English.

My response took them both aback. "*Estoy encantada de conocerte también*. Nice to meet you, too."

"*Ah, usted habla español*?"

"*Si*."

"*Ah, muy bien*. I'll see you later, Haylee, and if you need anything during your stay, please do not hesitate to contact me," Hector offered before going into the office with Josh.

After their meeting, Josh came out and found me staring at the view off the balcony. "I didn't know that you spoke Spanish," he said, regarding me.

"I like to keep you on your toes, Mr. Singer," I teased. I was tempted to reveal that it was one of four languages that I knew, but I figured some things were better left demonstrated than said.

"What do you think of the view?"

"Beautiful. The water is so blue that it makes me wish I could ditch the job and lie by the pool all day long with a margarita in hand."

A smile tugged at his lips before he exhaled. "Look, I need to warn you about Roberto, my head contractor. He's a little over the top and very into your personal space. He thinks he's being suave with the ladies, but with too much cologne, a bad hair piece, and being in his fifties— Well, he can be a bit much."

"Here's hoping he isn't handsy."

My joke clearly missed its mark. Josh gave me a dark look. "If he touches you inappropriately, I'll break his hand."

A shiver moved through me because I didn't doubt it. "Uh, okay, tiger. Look, I'm pretty sure if he's handsy, I can take care of it myself without any broken bones. But I appreciate the offer of assistance."

Roberto arrived right on time, and when the door opened, I immediately smelled his cologne. Gold chains, chest hair, a bad comb-over, and a very large midsection made up the rest of Roberto.

"Oh, my, Josh, she's lovely. How do you keep your hands off her?" He kissed my hand and then both cheeks.

I felt myself blush, and Josh quirked a brow as if to say I told you so.

"It's nice to meet you, Mr. Velas."

"Oh, no, the pleasure is all mine, and you must call me Roberto. And you are?"

Josh answered for me, clearly done with the fawning. "This is Haylee, and she has a boyfriend."

Meeting his eyes, I had to bite my lip to keep from laughing out loud. He was using my sexual harassment lie.

"Undoubtedly, you would, a woman as lovely as you. Now then, you must join us for dinner tonight. Josh is an amazing man, but I can only talk so much business."

I was a little stunned that he took such a familiar tone with my boss and looked to Josh for guidance.

"Maybe you could add one to the reservation. I believe we're going to the Argentinian steakhouse that you love so much, Roberto."

AFTER THE MEETINGS FINISHED, I joined the two gentlemen at the steakhouse. Dinner soon shaped up to be very entertaining. Roberto was the complete polar opposite of Josh, and I became the buffer between them. Roberto was very animated in his storytelling and recalled how his housekeeper had become his latest love.

"Sometimes I think a woman has to put it out there for a man. I mean, men, we don't do subtlety. So I come home from work, and there she is vacuuming my house, completely naked. I mean, that sends a message, don't you think, Haylee?"

I about choked on my drink. "Uh, yeah, I'd say so." I stole a quick look at Josh, who didn't seem as amused as I was.

Roberto went on, changing the subject with talk of his daughter who was now in the States attending college.

I was happy to call it a night directly after dinner, but not as much as Josh appeared to be. He looked like he'd gone four rounds.

"The man is exhausting but also happens to be the best general contractor in Cancun," he commented.

We got into the car, which was better than a cab at this hour, and drove in silence back to the hotel. Where our legs touched slightly, I could feel the heat between us. Once we arrived and made our way up to our floor wordlessly, I waited for an invitation to his suite.

"You should get some sleep, and I'll see you in the morning. We'll tour the construction site for the new resort and then be off for Hong Kong tomorrow afternoon."

I tried to hide my hurt feelings at the rejection and decided to go for it. "I'm not tired."

As I moved closer, he stood his ground, looking at me apprehensively. His breath caught when I put my hand on his chest. He closed his eyes, and I could almost feel his inner turmoil. "There are some things you don't understand."

"Tell me, then."

He was on the verge, I could feel it. But then he backtracked, putting his hands in his pockets as if to keep himself from touching me and turning away. "Good night."

Watching him go to his door, I felt tears threaten. Rather than take a chance that he would see them, I turned on my heel and walked back to the elevator instead of my room.

Hearing him call after me, I purposefully ignored it. I wasn't stupid enough to go traipsing around Mexico by myself, but I needed to clear my head.

Once I got to the lobby bar, I ordered a margarita and took it onto the nearby balcony. There I sat down, thankful that I was alone with the night. The sound of the ocean was peaceful, and I kept thinking about what Roberto had said. There was no way I was being too subtle as I'd practically thrown myself at Josh. Which only meant one thing: he wasn't interested.

"Haylee, what are you doing?" Josh's voice came from behind me. I heard the distinct sound of a lighter and saw the puff of smoke as he walked toward the railing.

"Please don't smoke around me." My voice was flat, and I didn't bother to meet his eyes.

"You don't need anything more to drink."

Looking up, I met his agitated eyes. "Maybe you don't remember, but I'm a grown woman. You quite obviously are only my boss, and I'm off the clock." I was being petty but didn't care at the moment.

"That's right, I am your boss, and I'm ordering you to go back to your room."

Downing my drink in one last gulp, I stood up a little unsteadily.

"Jesus," he muttered.

Defiant, I responded, "As you wish, Mr. Singer."

I was about to walk away when he tugged my arm back, and suddenly his mouth was crushing down on mine. The taste of smoke was strong, but my desire was stronger as his tongue expertly explored my mouth. My tongue shyly met his while his hands grasped either side of my face, holding me in place. I was completely at his mercy and lost in the moment until he pulled away suddenly.

"I know you don't understand, but you need to go back to your room. We can't do this."

My emotions were heightened, which made the rejection sting all that much more. To make matters worse, he spoke to me like I was a child. "Obviously, it's *my* inability to understand. What an incredibly condescending asshole thing to say."

"You've been drinking."

"Yes, I have, and maybe that's what's giving me the courage to put it out there." I fished through my purse and held out my hotel key card. "Here's my extra room key. I'm going to bed and wish you'd join me. If you don't, then we go back to merely professional in the morning. If you do, well, we'll figure it out. Just do me a favor and brush your teeth first because the cigarette thing is a real turn-off for me."

I turned on my heel, my heart beating double time in my chest the entire way up to my room. I'd never done anything remotely like this in my life.

When I got to my room, I wasn't sure what to do. I started with brushing my teeth and then my hair, leaving the latter soft and down. I gulped down a bottle of water and, after pacing fifteen minutes, took a quick shower. All the while I listened for the door. I turned off the lights, turned them on, turned them back off, and took a deep breath.

An hour had passed, and reality was hitting me smack in the face. He wasn't coming.

After donning my luxurious hotel robe, I lay down on the bed, willing myself not to cry. Rejection cut deep, and knowing I'd have to return to normal with him as my boss tomorrow wasn't making it any easier.

I heard the sound of a key slide in before the door opened. My breath held. When I rolled over on the bed, I saw Josh in my doorway. He was still dressed as I had left him, but now had his laptop and cell phone in his hands.

This wasn't exactly what I'd envisioned. Sitting up, I raised a brow. Was he coming in because he wanted me—or was he looking for his assistant?

"If we do this, we do it my way, which I'll warn you is complicated. First thing's first, you talk to my attorney."

I was too stunned for words.

"A nondisclosure agreement protects me in the business world. But in my private one, having a sexual relationship, especially with someone I employ and who essentially lives in my apartment, is not the smartest idea. It gets complicated and requires an even stricter version of a privacy agreement. My attorney is the only one who knows the, uh, circumstances, by the way, and that I'm here right now. Here's the document, and here's my laptop ready to dial Mark Hines in a video conference. If we're going to do this, then you'll need to follow without reservation everything he asks of you."

"Okay, I'm going to get dressed first." I got up and grabbed a T-shirt and shorts out of my suitcase. If I was doing a video conference with his attorney at—shit, twelve-thirty—I needed to be clothed properly.

When I came out of the bathroom, I saw that Josh had taken a seat next to the window in one of the hotel chairs. His eyes and expression were unreadable.

The laptop was on the desk with the document laid out in front of it. Had this been what he was doing over the last hour, composing this with his lawyer?

I sat down and pressed the button. A man's face, presumably that of the attorney, immediately came up on the screen. He must have been wakened from sleep and appeared to be in his home office. He was younger than I'd supposed, maybe the same age as Josh.

He greeted me with a sincere smile. "Ms. Holloway, my name is Mark Hines. I'm Mr. Singer's personal attorney. I take it that Mr. Singer has informed you of the nature of this call."

Glancing over at Josh, who still was revealing nothing, I found that I was suddenly nervous. Unfortunately, I was also not entirely sober. "Um, yes, Mr. Hines, and please call me Haylee."

I sensed his hesitation and then blurted out, "It's all very personal, so calling me Ms. Holloway sounds really formal."

His eyes sympathized. "Okay, Haylee, call me Mark. The document is in front of you, correct?"

I nodded.

Josh seemed to be fixated on me, still not giving anything away with his silence.

Then it dawned on me. This was a test. His world meant potential lawsuits and risk when it came to everything. Gold diggers were probably the norm. Given my position working for him, not to mention his past, it was no wonder he was cautious. Right now he was throwing down a challenge to see if I was willing to go through with it.

What should have been a turn-off instantly became a turn-on when I realized how desperately he must want me that, after midnight in Mexico, he'd dragged his attorney out of bed and come up with this agreement.

"So I'm going to read the document, sign, and then verbally agree?" I questioned.

Mark appeared hesitant. "Actually, I'll read each paragraph to you, and then you'll verbally agree."

Annoyance fueled my next words. "I don't need to be read to like a three-year-old. I can read it myself, sign it, and then verbally agree while recorded."

Josh came up behind me. He and Mark shared a look.

"Haylee, I have no doubt that you're smart," Mark started and then paused.

Josh tried to explain. "This is to ensure you understand—"

I could only be condescended to so much. "I have a 172 on the LSAT and graduated with a 4.0 from Stanford. I think that I'll understand it fine without having it recited to me. We can go paragraph by paragraph with me reading it, but I'm not going to be treated like I don't know what a legal document is or what it means."

Mark looked surprised, his mouth twitching with amusement as he waited for Josh's response.

"Fine." Following this concession, Josh took his seat back by the window.

In the end, it took twenty minutes. Then I signed and watched while Josh took the papers and headed out, presumably to fax or scan them from his hotel room office.

"Once I receive the document, I'll acknowledge receipt," Mark explained looking as awkward as I felt.

"Sorry you were woken up for this."

Blushing, he dismissed the burden. "I can assure you that I'm accustomed to a lot of middle-of-the-night calls from Mr. Singer." He must've seen my expression, for he turned an even brighter shade of red and apologized. "I'm sorry. I didn't mean for this particular thing, never for this before. I only meant that we've worked together many years, and with international business as it is, I keep different hours."

I put him out of his misery. "It's all right. This is uncomfortable for me, too, to say the least, but I appreciate your discretion. Thank you."

He seemed genuine when he nodded. Probably to pass the time, he asked, "So, what law school are you looking at?"

Smiling, I appreciated the change in subject. "My father went to Stanford, and I liked it there for undergrad. But I may be leaning more toward Yale or Harvard."

"I'm a Yale alum and still live in New Haven. I love it here. But with your scores and undergrad GPA, you should have no trouble getting in wherever you want. Matter of fact, do me a favor?"

"Uh, what's that?"

"Send me your application essay once you've finished it. I sat on the board of admissions a couple years back and can tell you what works and what doesn't."

That was huge, bigger than huge, and my smile must've showed it. "Mark, I don't know what to say, except thank you."

"It's not a problem. We lawyers have to stick together. But I have a feeling you'll do great."

Neither of us had noticed Josh reenter the room. "I certainly hope that wasn't a pep talk for entering into a sexual relationship with me."

I was mortified, but Mark seemed to take it in stride.

"We were talking law schools. As for the other, I can offer no comment. I've received the email, so let me print and verify all the pages were received." He stood up and went to his printer.

One look at Josh, and I felt like he'd pounce the moment Mark was done.

Mark confirmed receipt and gave a brief good night, obviously anxious to get back to bed and end the awkward call.

"So, are you properly turned off yet?" Josh asked once the laptop was closed.

Laughing, I joked, "Uh, well, Mark was a nice fluffer, so I'm good." I could thank Angela for the knowledge of that word and many others like it.

He seemed to appreciate my humor, throwing back his head and laughing. "You do know that you can change your mind." His voice was now the honey tone that turned me much the same.

"Having you wake up your attorney in the middle of the night because you couldn't stand to wait any longer to touch me is honestly a huge turn-on."

His eyes heated with desire. Then he crossed to me and fisted his hand in my hair.

"We do this my way. You sure you're up for that?"

I quirked a brow. At this point, he could suggest I stand on my head, and I'd gladly do it.

"Go put this on."

Taking the silk robe from his hand, I hurried to the bathroom to do as he requested.

WHEN I CAME BACK OUT into the room, the lights were off, with the exception of the small desk light.

Josh was still wearing his slacks and collared shirt. He reached for my hand and led me over to the bed.

My eyes flickered down to see he had unwound my robe belt and now had it in his hands.

"My way," he reiterated as he gently pushed me onto the bed and slipped the robe off completely.

I swallowed at being laid out naked for him on the bed. At least the low light helped with the uncertainty of it all.

Moving both my hands above my head, he tied them together with the silken robe tie. "Are you okay with this, Haylee?"

I could only nod. I didn't have a lot of sexual experience, let alone familiarity with being tied up, but in this moment, I felt a yearning like I'd never felt before. The binding only heightened the anticipation.

"You're beautiful," he murmured, nuzzling my neck and then working his way down.

I was completely at his mercy, but hearing that he thought I was beautiful gave me confidence I could trust him. I realized that for him, control was important. He didn't want me to do the touching this time around, and I was happy to oblige. When I felt his breath on my breast, I arched up.

He chuckled. "You're impatient, aren't you?"

A small moan was my only reply when his tongue teased one of my nipples. My back bowed in response; my breaths came out short and stuttered from the pleasure.

His mouth rained kisses over my stomach, and when I felt one of his fingers enter me, I took a deep shuddering breath.

"Jesus, you're so wet, so incredibly tight for me, aren't you?"

"Yes," I whispered, knowing I was shamelessly ready for him.

And yet, he still took his time. His mouth caressed over my hips and then down, down.

"Oh—" I gasped, feeling his breath again right at my pubic bone and then another finger inside me. He licked and nipped, causing my body to become taut with anticipation as I breathed in the scent of him.

"That's it; just feel it." His words were against my cleft, and then his mouth descended, triggering my hips to buck in response. "Relax, baby."

Easy for him to say, I thought, as I couldn't even grip the sheets. I was tightly wound with an electric current running through me. "I can't; it's too much," I pleaded.

He chuckled and then started the real assault with both his fingers working inside me and his mouth greedily and fully claiming me. His tongue fluttered over my clit.

My back arched, involuntarily pressing me against the friction. I felt nothing but pure, raw sensation.

"God, you taste good," he marveled.

His tongue flicked with both patience and insistence, giving me sensuous torture along with pleasure. He groaned as my body tightened and then exploded.

Crying out, I rode waves of passion until there was nothing left.

"You're so damn responsive," he murmured, working his way back up my body, kissing each of my breasts and then up to my neck.

I lay there completely spent, trying to steady both my breathing and heartbeat.

He lifted the comforter up over me as he snuggled me close, fitting my naked backside against the side of him.

Despite the uncomfortable position of still being bound, I tried to wiggle back into him, feeling his laugh.

"Insatiable."

"I thought we'd have sex now?"

"My way means that I say when and how I want you. Get some sleep. We have a long day tomorrow."

I was disappointed and tried not to pout. My first-ever orgasm, and yet I already craved more. I wasn't sure if his denial was a control issue or if there was something he wasn't telling me. "I'm still tied up."

He reached around and settled my hands in front of me. He then loosened the silken tie but didn't unknot it altogether. "I don't trust that you won't try something if I untie you right now."

"But I want to touch you," I whispered.

I felt him sigh. "Another time, or weren't you satisfied?"

I sensed a touch of agitation in his voice and did my best to flip over to face him. Not so easy with my hands tied, but I managed and searched his eyes.

"I've never felt that before," I admitted.

His gaze narrowed. "You've never had someone go down on you?"

"Well, that, and I've never had, well, you know, an orgasm."

He looked stunned, and then skepticism crept into his eyes. "As sexual as you are, you're telling me that you've never come before?"

What in the hell did he mean by that? "As sexual as I am?"

Exhaling, he raised a brow. "You know what I mean."

"Actually, I don't. Why don't you spell it out?"

"Haylee, obviously you've been with other partners—" he started.

"What does *obviously* mean exactly? Do I have some sort of stamp on me that I'm unaware of announcing my experience?"

Rolling his eyes, he put his hands behind his head. "Go to

sleep. This isn't a conversation that I'm going to win."

I didn't like that we were leaving it on this note. "I've been with two guys: one in high school and one in college."

That seemed to get his attention. He rolled toward me.

"The boy in high school—it was the first time for both of us. So in his defense, neither of us knew what to do, let alone have the opportunity to do it. Back seats of cars and before parents come home isn't exactly conducive toward good sex, evidently." I wasn't sure if Josh wanted to hear any of this, so I stopped talking.

"And the guy from college?" he prompted.

"We met at a frat party. Both of us drinking, went upstairs. Such a cliché, but I was in a place where I felt a need to do that type of thing. Anyhow, we tried dating a couple times after that, but turns out when I wasn't drunk he was obnoxious, and the sex still wasn't good. I guess I wanted to ensure he wasn't a one-night stand. So there you have my sexual history in a nutshell, and none of it included an orgasm or oral sex, at least not for me."

"I didn't mean to make it seem that I thought poorly of you. I simply had a different read on your experience."

I sighed. "Considering I kissed you first and gave you my room key, I guess I can't blame you for having that impression. Please know that I've never done anything like that in my life, ever, okay?"

"What made you do it this time?"

"Because life is short, and I've never wanted anyone the way I wanted you."

I went to kiss his mouth, but he shook his head.

"It's okay, you don't have to."

I didn't understand what he was talking about until he made his way south. "Josh, what are you—?" Oh, his fingers were back inside me.

"Someone who has been deprived this long deserves two."

CHAPTER SIX

I woke slowly and stretched. The first thing that dawned on me was that both my hands were untied; the second was that my bed was empty. Looking at the time, I saw it was past eight o'clock in the morning. We had a construction tour scheduled in an hour.

My robe was draped over the back of the chair, and I slipped it on when the knock came at the door. I looked through the peephole before opening it and then smiled at the man with a tray.

"Room service, Ms. Holloway." His nametag said he was Jose.

After signing for the meal and thanking Jose, I opened the covers to reveal fresh fruit, pancakes, and bacon. There was also an envelope with *Haylee* written in the unmistakable penmanship of Josh.

Smiling, I opened it, already moved by the romantic gesture. But I cursed when I read the words.

Decided to go to Hong Kong solo and early. Please enjoy the resort for the day and fly back to New York whenever you'd like. I'll see you back in the city in a few days and

don't read anything into this. It's business, not personal. –Josh

"Not personal?" I seethed, pacing the room. He conveniently left me at the resort after our first sexual encounter and flew off to Hong Kong without his *travel assistant*? Not personal? How did it get any more personal?

I called the travel line and spoke with Maria to confirm that, indeed, Josh had taken off about an hour earlier.

So now I was supposed to make my way back to New York. It was like a walk of shame the morning after, only I got to do it for three thousand miles all the way back East.

After a shower and some time to think, I decided that I would follow my father's words of wisdom. He'd once told me that saying nothing spoke volumes. Considering he'd been a successful divorce attorney and had seen many reactions in his day, I figured he probably knew what he was talking about.

On the bright side, this was an opportunity for me to get my mother's winter clothes from storage in San Francisco. With that in mind, I made some travel plans of my own and set off for the airport.

When I landed in San Francisco, I cruised through customs quickly and then drove twenty minutes north in my compact rental car. The large storage unit was expensive to maintain each month as it was in a mega-secure facility, but it was worth it. Many of the items inside were heirlooms and irreplaceable, passed down for generations. They were also well organized. My mother had been meticulous about how she stored the furniture after selling our house the summer following the death of my father.

Once in my storage bay, I smiled sadly at the familiar furniture and ran my hands lovingly over the wardrobe rack. Now that

I was living in New York, I'd have the opportunity to wear the vintage winter clothes that had belonged to my mother and grandmother.

I'd had a privileged upbringing in San Francisco suburbia, but I would've traded it all to have my parents back. Being an only child meant I'd been the sole recipient of my parents' undivided attention. Even so, I'd have given anything to have a sibling with whom to share this grief. It had been a while since I'd had myself a good cry, but surrounded by my parents' things, my childhood memories, and my emotions from this morning, I allowed the tears to flow.

When I heard my phone ring, I frowned at the unknown number but answered because, technically, it was a workday. "Hello."

"Where are you?"

Josh's voice took me off guard. "Um, where are you?"

"Which unit are you in?"

Was he actually here?

"One fourteen," I replied, wiping my eyes the best I could before walking over to open the door.

Nothing should have shocked me any longer with Josh and his unpredictability, but I was still stunned to see him standing there.

"What are you doing here?" I asked.

He stepped inside and took a look around before focusing back on my face. "Your parents' things?"

"Yes. I was collecting some of my winter stuff. I didn't have any of it with me in LA, well, for obvious reasons."

"Are you all right?" His hand came under my chin.

His voice had the tears dropping again. "I haven't been here in a while. It's emotional, in a good and bad way, to be surrounded by so many things from my past."

"Why's it all still out here? I told you I'd pay for your move. We can transport these belongings back East."

"I know and thank you, but I don't know where I'm attending school and then where I'll live after that. This storage facility is better than most. It's known for its security, and my mom was adamant about that with so many valuables. Plus, I'm scared to death of something breaking in a move."

He nodded his understanding and then took a seat on the sofa and patted the cushion beside him. "Will you tell me about your parents?"

"Don't you need to fly to Hong Kong?"

He took my hand, pulling me gently into his lap. "I never pretend to be interested for the sake of doing so. If I ask you something, it's because I truly want to know."

This was a fundamental part of him. He never cared if the moment got awkward or needed some conversation filler. Instead, he was measured in what he asked and decided to talk about. He reclined slightly on the cushions and settled me between his legs, waiting for me to speak.

"My mom was born and raised Southern, daughter of a governor. My dad grew up in Northern California, but he worked in the South on my grandfather's second-term campaign as an intern one summer. They met, fell in love, got married, and she moved out to California. He was a divorce attorney. My mother was a homemaker who involved herself in local charities and with my school. I had a good childhood: private schools, nice vacations, all of their attention, love, and support." I paused and thought back to the night that had forever changed my life.

"Then one evening, out of the blue, my parents called me into the living room. My mother had been crying; my father was more serious than I'd ever seen him. I instantly thought I was busted for having had sex in the back seat of my boyfriend's car. We'd done that for the first time a week earlier. I was so naïve and self-centered."

Josh hugged me. "You were a teenager. You're supposed to

be self-centered at that age. So I take it they told you news about your father's health?"

Sighing, I recalled the memory. "Yes. My father was a smoker in my younger years but had quit when I was in middle school. So we were all shocked when he was diagnosed with lung cancer. When he quit, we ignorantly figured all the risks disappeared." I waited, appreciating that Josh was still intently listening.

"How long did he have?"

"Less than a year. He tried one round of chemo, but that seemed worse than the cancer. He'd hoped to watch me graduate, but unfortunately he fell a few months shy." Josh's arms came around me, and I swallowed past the lump in my throat. "At least he knew that I'd been accepted to Stanford. That made him proud."

"I bet it did. And your mom?"

"After my father died, we packed up and sold the house. My mother's father passed away that same year, and my mom went into a deep depression. I never knew my mom to smoke cigarettes, but evidently her dad had been a heavy smoker while she grew up, and it turned out she'd smoked for quite a few years in her youth. I didn't realize then that she already knew she had the early stages of emphysema. Combination of her smoking and the secondhand smoke exposure.

"She insisted on moving down with me during college. I wasn't thrilled with the idea, but the thought of leaving her alone was worse, so we moved down to Palo Alto and got an apartment there. At the end of my freshman year of college, my mom told me she was sick. By my junior year, she was on oxygen. A month after my graduation, she passed."

"She attended your graduation?"

"Yes, from a wheel chair and on oxygen, but she got to see it. The last couple months while I studied for the LSAT, we composed her bucket list. We went through places she'd always wanted me to see, things that were important to her for me to know about, such as traditions, et cetera. I guess it gave her peace to know that we made plans together for the future. I don't know, I guess it doesn't really matter."

"Of course it matters. I think it's a gift to have had that time. Is her death the reason you didn't go directly into law school?"

"Yeah, that, finances, and my little mental breakdown." I was trying to make a joke but realized it fell flat when he stiffened. "I was only kidding."

He kissed the back of my neck and swept my hair to the side. "Tell me about it."

"I'd planned on attending law school, but the medical debt was high, and there were a lot of things to take care of. I wasn't focused."

"They didn't have medical or life insurance?"

"My father did, but there were still sizable medical bills. It's astounding how much cancer costs even with insurance. Selling the house helped, and although I didn't have a lot of insight into the finances at that point, my father's law partner told me that my mom was debt-free. With my dad's death, our medical coverage stopped and since my mom wasn't yet sixty-five years old and didn't qualify for Medicare, she had no insurance. I had to sell their cars, and my mom sold a lot of her jewelry. So no law school fund. Rather than go into student loan debt, I chose to save up some money. I took the experience I had working for my father during the summers—filing, preparing documents, and helping schedule—put it on a resume, and got the job with Warren in LA."

"Tell me about the breakdown."

I winced, having hoped I'd steered successfully away from that bit. "It's not something that's easy for me to talk about. Tell me something personal that no one else knows about you, and then I will."

Exhaling, he massaged my shoulders gently. "I had a vasectomy in the third year of my marriage."

I hadn't figured on him reciprocating with something so deeply personal. Yet when he didn't elaborate, I had to ask. "Why?"

"Aside from the obvious reason that I don't want to have children?"

"Something must have convinced you to make that decision when you did."

He paused before changing the subject. "Were you hospitalized and treated?"

I recognized we were trading vulnerabilities and took a deep breath. "Yes, briefly on the hospitalization, and I was on antidepressants for a few weeks, but they made me fuzzy." My voice was small. I wished I could simply erase that part of my life.

"Did you try to harm yourself?" His voice was quiet and nonjudgmental, but I still felt deeply exposed.

"No, but I stopped taking care of myself. I couldn't get out of bed. I didn't talk to anyone. Or shower. I just cried and wanted to give up. Not the same as slitting my wrists, but not exactly healthy, either." I could feel his hands rubbing my arms, warming me up from the chill. "What prompted the vasectomy?"

"Betrayal."

Letting out a harsh breath, I took his hand and brought it to my lips assuming she must've cheated on him. I gave it a kiss and turned towards him. "I'm sorry."

"Who found you, got you help?"

Having needed help both embarrassed and stung. "My father's partner and best friend, Charlie Hastings." I hoped not to have to elaborate, but Josh wasn't having it.

"What happened?"

"He and his wife, Beth, had been checking up on me, but I hadn't returned their calls. He found me crumpled on the bathroom floor, dehydrated and out of it. He called an ambulance and they, uh, put me in a place for a few weeks. He even paid for everything and then moved me down to LA. I owe him a great deal, and yet he refuses to see it that way." I got up and paced, trying to mentally shrug off the memory. "The thing is that I'm not that girl anymore. She wasn't strong enough to pull it together. So talking about her and what happened isn't easy."

"That was just a few months ago. I think you should cut yourself some slack."

With a forced smile, I took a seat again, feeling more myself by the minute. "I'm not going back there. I don't need the meds, and I don't need the counseling. It was just a reaction to a tough situation. I'm stronger now and realize only I can change my fate and the way I choose to look at life. I may not believe that life has a big happy ending, but being depressed is a choice. I'm choosing not to be."

"Depression isn't something you can just flick on or off like a switch. I think it's commendable that you have adopted a can-do attitude, but it isn't always so simple. You lost both your parents at a very pivotal time in your life—"

It was easier to keep a handle on my emotions when I wasn't receiving sympathy. "I appreciate what you're trying to say, but I don't need you to psychoanalyze me. You surely wouldn't want me returning the favor. Now, I'm not pretending I won't have moments where I'm sad about things because I know I will. But this is something I need to do for myself. No one else can help me with it."

"All right. I won't say anymore. Everyone has their own way of dealing with things, and if this works for you, then I'll respect that."

"Thank you." I breathed a sigh of relief that the conversation was over.

"I don't want to get married again, ever, nor have children. I walked away in Mexico because I don't want to hurt you. I should've been strong enough to have let you go to your room and not used the key, but instead I called Mark and—"

I put my finger to his lips. "I'm really happy that you called Mark. And I'm glad we're clear on what it is you want and don't want. In the interest of full disclosure, I want to get married someday and have kids, and I mean plural because being an only child when you lose your parents sucks. But before doing any of that, I want to go to law school, get a job, and settle somewhere. That means I don't want a long-term relationship now that might derail that plan." Just the thought of anything long term at this point in my life petrified me as I wasn't ready to deal with that kind of complication.

"So we figure this out until you leave for school next fall?"

"Considering we both want different things and are heading in separate directions, I think it would be good to have an expiration date up front." It would be nice to know when something was set to end as opposed to having the rug dragged out from under me. Losing both parents had taught me that nothing was for certain, and time went by in the snap of a finger.

Drawing back, he stroked his thumbs under my eyes and wiped away the residual tears. "I need to catch a plane to Hong Kong."

Frowning, I got up from the couch only to be pulled back down.

"I needed some time by myself to process," he maintained, searching my eyes.

I knew I wasn't doing a good job of hiding that I was upset. "How's that working out for you?" Considering he'd essentially followed me here, he was clearly a walking contradiction.

"Look, it wasn't personal."

Rolling my eyes, I felt all of the anger and embarrassment from the morning return. "It sure as hell felt personal. After a night of your face in my hooha, the next thing I have is a note saying you're leaving me in Mexico."

The corners of his mouth twitched. "Hooha?"

My gaze narrowed. "That would be what you take from that sentence. Bottom line is you hired me to be your travel assistant. Then you leave me to do the walk of shame back into the office. What was I supposed to think? And what was I supposed to tell Nigel when I came back without you?"

"What's a walk of shame?"

I got up, and took a deep breath. "Google it. I'm not taking the time to explain it as you have a flight to catch. I'll see you once you return to New York."

"Okay, and maybe I'll lookup *hooha,* too, while I'm at it." Smirking, he pulled out his phone.

I busied myself gathering two of the hard-sided suitcases I'd seen in the back and packing them with several coats and a couple more of my mother's gowns, including her wedding dress. I don't know why I wanted it with me, but it made me feel better to have it in my possession. I finished up and found him still engrossed in his phone.

"All right, according to the urban dictionary, a *hooha* is also known as female genitalia, aka vagina, aka punani. Well, that's a new one. Also considered a happy place. I guess I won't be clicking on images."

Shaking my head, I tried not to smile.

He gave me a devilish grin. "Now, then, the walk of shame. Let's see. It's known as the walk across campus in the same clothes as yesterday after you slept with someone and spent the night in his or her room."

He glanced up at me after reading a bit more. "First of all, you are showered and changed. And secondly, I would never put it that way." He looked mildly offended.

"It was a figure of speech. Even if I am flying back across the country to New York, it feels like I might as well be skulking across campus in last night's clothes. You never did tell me, by the way, why you're here. And how did you know where to find me?"

He appeared uncomfortable but answered the question. "I had a layover and called Maria to see what your travel plans were. She told me about you renting the car. So I waited in the Hertz lot and followed you. I was curious."

"You could've called me."

He shrugged. "I didn't want to send mixed messages." The twinkle in his eye showed he got the irony.

I blew out a breath. "Yeah, cuz showing up here didn't. Look, you wanted time alone. It's fine. I get it, but next time, please tell me to my face so that I don't feel like—I don't know—how I felt this morning when I got the note."

"How did you feel?" He genuinely seemed to want to know.

Considering I was still raw from the sting of it, I decided to be frank. "The tray showed up, and I thought what a romantic gesture. Then I saw the note, and I thought maybe it was something cute, but it wasn't. It made me think that somehow I'd done something wrong or—I don't know."

He moved closer and cupped my chin. "Tell me."

"I thought maybe my reaction was weird, or my thighs were too big, or I said something wrong last night during."

His eyes widened.

"Look, I know that sounds ridiculous to you, but for a woman, these are the stupid things that go through our head when a man just up and leaves after something intimate like that. Obviously, I got over it by the time I took a shower. You said not to take it personally, but, well, after what happened, I thought it particularly unthoughtful to tell me to think of you leaving me as 'business.' That's all."

"I don't know what to say." He seemed contrite, but I noted that the first words out of his mouth weren't an apology.

"Well, you asked. I'm simply being honest even if it's more than you want to hear. Anyhow, I'm ready to go."

He looked down at the two suitcases and took them out to my car to load while I locked up.

WE TOOK our separate cars to the airport and met up at the rental counter after turning over the keys.

"I'm going to get checked in. I think you need to make your way to the international terminal that way." I pointed and turned toward the domestic terminal.

He frowned. "Let's call Maria and get you on my flight to Hong Kong."

Hesitating, I glanced down at my suitcases. "You want time alone, and I get it. I feel better now that you've told me that to my face. Meanwhile, I filled two large suitcases that are meant to get back to New York and not by way of Hong Kong. It's fine. Really."

But suddenly he didn't seem to think so. "We can have the suitcases shipped. Come on, I'll take care of that while you call Maria."

After Maria worked her magic and we got checked in, I looked over at Josh while we were in the lounge. "Why did you change your mind?"

His stunning green eyes were serious. "I figured if we're doing this, it might be better to work out the awkwardness overseas, where no one knows what the norm is, rather than back in New York."

His answer was pretty black and white. I guessed I wasn't getting a *because I thought I'd miss you* from him anytime soon.

"So the hotel situation: am I going to have to drink enough each night to get up the nerve to give you my key? Or will you—I don't know—inform me ahead of time if you plan on coming by?"

If he noticed my sarcasm, he chose to ignore it. "This is new territory for me, and I'm a little paranoid about how to maintain professional boundaries what with the new personal ones."

I was a little offended. "I would like to think I'll be professional. You don't have to worry about me embarrassing you; I promise not to hop on you in a conference room in front of your staff."

He glanced at me, evidently amused. "You're not the only one I'm worried about."

Holy crap. Was Josh as turned on by my presence as I was by his? It was hard for me to believe. He always seemed in such control.

"Do you have one of these?" He showed me his iPad.

I shook my head. "No, but they seem pretty cool. Plus, you can play Angry Birds on a larger screen than your phone."

He quirked a brow.

After I motioned for him to hand it over, I swiped over it with my fingers, clicked on the app section, and downloaded one of the Angry Birds versions for a demonstration.

"What kind of game is that?" He looked a cross between appalled and intrigued.

"Stress release. You shoot birds at pigs or monkeys. It gets addictive. Try it, at least."

He seemed apprehensive, but a few minutes later he was shooting birds with expert precision.

"See, and now you are properly educated in mindless stress relief. You could even put it on your phone if you like."

He gave me a look that conveyed his irritation at having been sucked in.

I couldn't help laughing.

"I have enough work without that distraction," he told me. "But if you need to kill some monkeys or pigs on a larger screen, feel free to borrow the iPad anytime."

Smiling, we checked the clock and made our way to the boarding gate.

First class on a 747 was spectacular. We went upstairs where I marveled at the individual pods with flat screens and leather chairs that reclined into full beds. I was immediately greeted by a flight attendant and asked what I'd like to drink.

Josh negotiated with the man beside me, and he had seemed inclined to trade, so I got to be seated next to Josh. It wasn't as though we could snuggle and watch television, as the pods were designed for individual privacy, but we would be able to talk. That would be nice.

"So, what's the business in Hong Kong?" I was watching him study some charts and grids on his laptop.

"You really want to know?"

"I don't ever ask a question for the sake of asking it. If I ask, it means I really want to know."

Having his words used back on him garnered a smile. "All right, I'm looking at the prospect of purchasing a small advertising business there. Currently I don't have anything in the Asia Pacific region, so I'm thinking of expansion by acquisition. I'll go over their financials and strategy most of the day. The cocktail party they plan to throw in the evening is an attempt to wine and dine me."

He probably got a lot of that with people courting his money. "So they want to be bought, I take it?"

"Very much. They lost their competitive edge when their chief rival went global two years ago while they stayed local. They need new leadership and the owner seems to be agreeable to it."

The fact that he shared these details with me meant a lot. "How do they feel about American ownership specifically, though? Any ill will?"

"Culturally, there may be. I guess we'll see. But unless you can understand Chinese, I doubt very much we'll know either way."

It was on the tip of my tongue to reveal I'd taken eight years of Cantonese, but I figured it might be better to surprise him with that information later.

After finishing a movie and dinner, I glanced over to see Josh was still in business mode. He'd barely touched his meal. Anyone who ever thought he lived off of his inheritance obviously had never seen the man work.

Once the flight attendant took my tray, I stood up and went to the lavatory where I brushed my teeth, washed my face, and put my hair up in a ponytail. Happy that I'd brought comfy clothes, I quickly dressed into yoga pants and a sweatshirt. Now ready for sleep, I walked back to my seat.

Josh glanced over and then did a double take, groaning.

I smiled innocently. "What?"

"You look about fifteen years old with your pony tail and outfit."

Quirking an indignant brow, I leaned over and whispered, "I can assure you I'm all grown up."

His eyes darkened.

I was satisfied I'd gotten my point across. So while gathering my blankets, I was unprepared for the honey voice.

"Haylee…"

God, what that voice did to me.

It was clear he suspected as much when he met my gaze and then motioned me closer. "You do know that when you whisper things like that to me I imagine doing some very naughty things to you," he murmured.

It was my turn to suck in my breath. Then I smiled and returned the sexy sentiment. "I can assure you that I'm imagining all of those things right now."

I got the desired effect when his breath came out strained. "Sweet dreams."

As I woke up, I stretched and then glanced at my watch. Three more hours to go. That meant I'd slept a good seven hours. Looking over, I noticed Josh still looked immaculate, without a hair out of place, and was reading his paper. I wondered if he'd slept at all.

After making myself presentable in the lavatory, I returned to my seat and requested a Diet Coke and some hot tea with my breakfast. This earned me a dubious look from Josh.

"Yes, double caffeine, and once I finish, why don't we go over anything you need me to do as far as logistics are concerned for this trip and for the London trip in a couple of weeks?"

When he nodded, I realized he'd been chomping at the bit to get me back into admin role so he could get some things off his plate.

We spent the remaining flight time going over details, including his trip to London in a couple weeks and a charity golf tournament scheduled for Miami in a month. I took careful notes until they announced the plane was descending. Then we both put away our laptops.

"We'll be expedited through customs as they'll give us passes to the first class line. Then we'll grab our bags and head to the arrivals lounge."

I wasn't used to international travel and appreciated him letting me know what to expect. "So, business dress to the hotel, then we'll go to the office for a full day. About six o'clock back to the hotel followed by a scheduled pickup at seven in order to go to the cocktail reception. When we arrive, I'll have the concierge get your tux pressed out."

Agreeing, he then took me off guard. "Does it bother you to do these things for me?"

I had no idea where this was coming from and matched his

low tone so that no one could overhear us. "It's my job, so of course it doesn't."

He weighed this but didn't let it go. "Yes, but it doesn't feel strange given the other part? You don't resent it?"

Turning to face him, I was frank. "It never crossed my mind. I'd feel worse if you felt I was incapable but kept me around because of the other. If anything, I want to make sure I'm doing the job that you're paying me for and doing it well. It might sound cheesy, but I value your respect above the other."

He held my gaze for the longest time. "Sometimes I think you hold me in higher regard than I probably deserve."

"I think we all need someone who does."

I left him to process that and turned my attention to gathering my things for landing.

CHAPTER SEVEN

Upon arrival, we cruised through the express customs line. I felt scruffy and ready for a shower. But I noted the arrivals lounge was impressive. We both walked in and made our way to our private suites.

"Take your time; we aren't in a hurry," Josh told me.

Taking advantage of his offer, I washed my hair and lingered over blow-drying it straight. I turned on some tunes from my phone, rubbed in my lotion, and was bopping to Ed Sheeran when the knock came at the door.

Considering I was merely in my towel, I hoped it wasn't someone wanting to use the room. I was surprised to see Josh outside the door, completely dressed in suit and tie.

"Oh, shit, did I lose track of time?"

Smiling, he moved me further into the room. "No, we have plenty."

"Ohhh…" was all that I managed.

Backing me into the chair, he captured my mouth. His kiss was sensual with soft lips. Meanwhile, he made short work of ridding me of my towel. Next, he moved down to my breasts, paying special attention to my nipples.

Moaning with pleasure, I murmured, "Once again, you're fully dressed, and I'm not."

He nipped at my waist. "This is how I like you. Remember, my way," he murmured, and made his way back up to my face. He worked my aroused flesh with his fingers while devouring my mouth. "That's it, Haylee. I want you to come while I watch."

Hearing my name again was about to send me over the edge. His lips glided down my neck, sending shivers down my spine.

"I can feel it building. Let it go." His thumb found a rhythm, circling my clit. I felt my body start to convulse. His voice was low and demanding. "Look at me."

My eyes flashed open. I felt the intensity of his watching while the orgasm ripped through me.

He kissed me deeply, stroking my tongue with his and then his mouth trailed down over my breasts and stomach, finally diving for my wet center.

I hadn't even caught my breath. "Jesus, Josh, I can't, oh…"

His tongue lapped at the wetness running down my thighs while his fingers spread it over my tender lips.

"You taste like peaches," he groaned and then focused in on my swollen nub, teasing it back to engorgement. He sucked and tongued my clit with such precision and perfect pressure that I was sure I would go insane.

"It's the lotion. Oh, God." I surrendered fully to his erotic assault and let myself ride yet another explosion.

I was putty, completely and totally unable to speak or move.

Then he got up and went to stand in front of my mirror, pulling out his toothbrush and acting like it was an everyday habit to devour a woman and then simply brush his teeth.

"You all right?" he questioned, giving me a smug look.

"I'm sorry, Haylee can't come to the phone at the moment as she's passed out from unbelievable orgasms and unable to walk for at least the next hour or so. Please leave a message, and I'll return your call after the sexual euphoria has passed."

He chuckled, looking quite pleased with himself as he watched me fumble with the towel. "Hmm, only an hour. I may need to work on that, then."

I shot him an incredulous look. "Oh, no, you don't. As much as I loved that, I swear if I don't get to see you naked this next time I'm going to die from curiosity, not to mention sexual selfishness."

He cocked a brow. "I get pleasure from giving you pleasure."

I felt that he was holding something back, but now wasn't the time to push. I smiled instead. "I'm a lucky girl, then."

That seemed to satisfy him. "Don't you need to get dressed?"

I moved toward him and leaned into his relaxed frame. "Are you going to watch?"

His eyes danced with mischief and then turned serious. "Perhaps when we have more time. I'll meet you out in the lounge."

I couldn't resist one more kiss and cupped his face, bringing his lips down to meet mine.

"What was that for?" he asked, a bit taken back.

"Because I won't get to do it again for the rest of the day."

He brushed my cheek with his hand and gave me one more before leaving.

I CHOSE to wear my Tahari black dress, something that dipped below the knee with a little flair, and the matching jacket with white piping. Classic and professional, I thought, looking at my reflection.

When I met Josh in the lounge, he was back in business mode. It was hard to believe that mere minutes ago his face had been between my thighs. I received a quick glance, and we made our way out to the waiting car.

The Four Seasons checked us in quickly. I gave Josh's tuxedo to the concierge to press before we went upstairs to our individual rooms. Mine was on the fourth floor, and his was on the tenth in a suite. We agreed to meet in the lobby in ten minutes to make our way into the office.

The office building of the company Josh was looking to acquire was tall, like most of the buildings in Hong Kong. We were immediately greeted and shown to the thirty-second floor. The CEO of Windom Advertising came out to greet Josh, who introduced me to him.

"Ken, this is Haylee, my assistant."

"So nice to meet you. First time to Hong Kong?"

"Yes, it is. Nice to meet you too," I said, smiling.

He turned to introduce me to his assistant, Ana, who seemed very friendly and overly helpful towards Josh.

"Mr. Singer, if you need anything, anything at all, please let me know."

She was a small woman, probably in her late twenties. When she briefly lapsed into her native language to make a comment toward Ken, I tried to keep my features neutral.

"Ana will get you set up down the hall, Haylee. We have a space for you to make calls or set up your computer. Maybe you can join us on a tour of the office later this afternoon following lunch," Ken offered.

I gave my thanks and, with one last look at my boss, followed Ana through the office.

"Have you worked for Mr. Singer long?" she inquired sweetly as she took me down the hall.

"Only a couple weeks."

"Well, if you need anything, my extension is 5004. Dial 9 to get out for external calls."

"Great. Thanks. What time is lunch? Do you need help with setup?"

She waved me off. "No, my dear, we have it under control.

Matter of fact, you'll be on your own, I'm afraid. You might try the sandwich shop downstairs."

In the US it was customary to order extra for the assistants even if they weren't eating with the executives, but perhaps it was different here. "All right, thanks. Uh, where's the ladies' room and the kitchen?"

She looked put out to have to extend our time together, but her manners must have kicked in. "Of course, let me show you." She led me down the corridor and to the left, where I could see a number of desks, and finally into a large kitchen. "Water, coffee, sodas are here. And the ladies' room is located two doors down."

Another woman came in and was introduced to me as Patty. She smiled and then spoke with Ana in Cantonese, in which conversation Ana explained who I was.

It took everything in me not to react to Ana's next words. She told Patty that I didn't seem too bright, but it was obvious in looking at me that intelligence wasn't why I'd been hired.

Patty shook her head a little and then smiled at me. "It was nice to meet you." Well, at least Patty hadn't wanted to join in.

"Anything else, or can I get back to work now?" Ana almost inserted enough false sweetness in the question to disguise the passive-aggressive comment.

"No, thank you, Ana. You've been most helpful." Grabbing a Diet Coke from the refrigerator she'd shown me, I tried not to let my thoughts wander toward a fantasy of pitching it down the hallway at her head.

The rest of the morning was spent catching up on email and calling Nigel to coordinate Josh's schedule for the next couple of weeks. I hesitated but then thought, what the hell. So I asked Nigel, "How are things on the personal front?"

He sighed heavily. "Did Josh tell you the details?"

"No, not at all, and I would never ask him. But from what you've alluded to, it's health-related and obviously not yours. As someone who has been through it—both my parents had cancer—I want you to know that I'm here for you, Nigel."

That seemed to break down his last defense. I heard his unsteady breath. "It's stage three colon cancer. My partner, David, has been going through radiation and chemo, but we had to take a break because of the radiation burns. He started back up this week. Surgery to remove the tumor is set tentatively after Christmas, assuming we stay on course, followed by more chemo."

Sighing, I thought of all the things well-meaning people had said to me that hadn't helped. I decided to give support rather than mere sympathy. "Stage three and operable are the most positive things you said in that sentence even if it might not seem that way. Those words mean it's beatable. I'll definitely be thinking of you both."

"Thank you. It means a lot, and I know you're right. I need to keep thinking positive. How is Hong Kong?"

"It's okay. I think that Josh will be held up in meetings all day, and then we have a cocktail party tonight."

"Traveling overnight and then hitting the ground running is no fun," he sympathized. "I don't know how Josh does it so well."

"I don't know, either. At least I got some sleep on the plane, but I don't think he even closed his eyes once." It was a little unnerving now that I thought about it. I hadn't once had a glimpse of the man sleeping.

"He's an insomniac, but one who seems to function fine with it. Merely a couple hours a night, and he seems as fresh as anyone else who requires eight."

Filing this information away, I finished up Josh's schedule and then let Nigel get on with his evening as it was late his time. Next I focused on travel itineraries and my emails for the next few hours. I was so engrossed in my tasks that it took my stomach growling to remind me it was well past lunch time. I passed Ana's desk as I made my way down the hall, managing to restrain my temper when I realized she and the receptionist had obviously taken lunch for themselves from the executives' order.

"I'm stepping out to get a sandwich if Mr. Singer looks for me."

"I'm sure he'll get what he needs from me, but I'll pass on the message if he asks." Then in Cantonese, she spoke to the receptionist. "What a stupid twit. Clearly he's only keeping her around for one purpose."

The girl laughed and spoke back to her in their language. "She's not even that skinny. Big butt."

Smiling tightly, I took some satisfaction from the fact they didn't know I'd understood what they were saying. "Well, then. Be back shortly."

Big butt? I didn't have a big butt. I just wasn't so tiny that I had barely any butt at all—like each of them.

JOSH POKED his head in to my office space and gave me a small smile later that afternoon. "You look tired."

It was nearing four o'clock Hong Kong time, and I was feeling the effects of jet lag. "You don't look tired in the least, which makes me kind of jealous."

"Are you ready to take off for the hotel? We finished up early, and I have a call with the Sydney office in an hour."

His schedule didn't have any mention of a call. "Is this something I should have on your calendar?"

He shrugged. "I just added it. I figured I'd use it to get us out of here early."

Smiling, I shut down my computer. I was happy to go back to my hotel room as it would give me more time to get ready for this evening.

When we arrived in the hotel lobby, Josh turned to study me. “You’re welcome to skip tonight if you’d like to crash.”

“I wouldn’t miss it.”

“Really? I would if I could. All of the schmoozing gets tiresome.”

Rolling my eyes, I decided it was time to fess up about being able to understand Cantonese. “I have something I need to tell you before the party if you have a few minutes.”

He cocked his brow. “Why don’t you get dressed and meet me up at my room about five-thirty? We can discuss it then.”

As I got off the elevator on my floor, I turned and suddenly had to ask. “Do you think my ass is big?”

He seemed to lose the ability to form words. “I, uh—Why on earth are you asking me this?”

Winking, I gave him a saucy smile and walked away, very sure that my assets were on display. “It came up, that’s all.” Glancing back, I had the satisfaction of seeing his eyes fixated on the very topic.

A HOT SHOWER did the trick, not only to rejuvenate me, but also to de-wrinkle the dress that was hanging on the bathroom door. After twisting my hair up, I reapplied my makeup, thankful for the extra time. Fastening my black stockings with garters, I found myself excited about Josh seeing them. The dress was a simple black cocktail dress circa 1950: Christian Dior with a floaty bottom, off-the-shoulder straps, and a belted waist that flattered my figure. Grabbing my clutch and finishing off with a beautiful red lipstick, I made my way up to the executive suite that Josh occupied.

When he opened the door, his eyes widened in response to me.

I gave him a flirtatious smile, keeping quiet when I realized he had a phone pressed to one ear.

He motioned me in, and I remembered he was finishing up his Sydney call. Still talking, he poured two glasses of whiskey and handed me mine. He gave a little clink to the glass and, with a small smile, sipped it slowly.

I took the opportunity to survey his spacious suite. It had an entire living room the size of my apartment, with a full-sized sofa and loveseat. A dining table and a small bar were one step up, next to the picture window overlooking the city. I walked over and admired the view.

"All right, gentlemen, I trust this is in good hands. Thank you." He hung up the phone and turned his attention to me.

"What was the toast for?" I turned toward him.

He simply grinned and walked up the step to join me by the window. "To you looking lovely."

Flushing at the compliment, I drank slowly. Whiskey wasn't really my thing, but the warmth that spread through my belly felt good.

"Turn around for a moment," he requested.

I put my glass down and thought that he meant for me to do a complete turn-around, but he stopped me halfway.

"Now, on the subject of your ass, who in the world told you it was big?"

Looking over my shoulder, I smiled at him.

He cupped it through my dress. "It's perfect, really. Not too big, not too bony, very spankable." Just like that, his hand smacked my backside.

Turning around, I feigned an indignant look. "Ouch. Not nice."

He chuckled and threw back the rest of his drink.

"Turns out Ana and the receptionist had a very colorful chat about how there's only one reason I work for you, and then it was mentioned that I had a big ass."

Confusion furrowed his brow. "They actually said this to you?"

Smiling, I shook my head slowly. "Oh, they had no idea I could understand what they were saying."

It was finally sinking in. "You understand Chinese?"

"I know Cantonese and some Mandarin. In Hong Kong, or at least in that office, most speak Cantonese, which is good because it's easier for me to understand that dialect."

"You can read and write Chinese?" He was completely taken aback.

Taking Josh off guard probably didn't happen often. "I can speak and understand Cantonese and Mandarin, although understanding the latter is harder. You do realize there's more than one Chinese dialect, right?"

He only shook his head.

Finally, something I knew that he didn't. "Cantonese is the official language of Hong Kong—well, along with English. Meanwhile, Mandarin is prevalent throughout most of mainland China, Beijing, Singapore, et cetera. I never really got the hang of the whole Chinese character thing, so it's sort of like being illiterate. I can speak it and understand it, but writing and reading is another story."

"And you learned these languages when?"

"I took it in high school. One of my friends was a foreign exchange student from Hong Kong, and I had the opportunity to practice with her a lot. Then I studied both languages in college, too. I didn't know how I'd do here, but I understand the dialect pretty well. You really didn't read my resume that I had on file with Warren, did you?"

He went over and poured himself another drink, having the grace to look chagrined. "Evidently not. What other languages do you know?"

"Spanish, as you know, and I can speak French, although not as well as Mandarin or Cantonese."

"So you can understand the conversations in the office, what they've been saying?" Now he was getting the usefulness of my skill set.

"Yes."

He took another drink. "They aren't aware that you understand them? You didn't let on?"

"It took all of my willpower not to throw my Diet Coke in her face, but no, they haven't had a clue. I'm merely playing the ditzy secretary they all think I am."

His expression conveyed annoyance. "You are anything but, and I didn't mean to insult you by interrogating you about it. I..." He laughed at himself. "You surprise me. Just when I think I know you, I'm completely thrown for a loop. I find myself utterly intrigued."

I felt a flush of pleasure. "The feeling is mutual." Pulling out a dining room chair, I put my leg up, sliding my hem to show my stocking and garter. "Sometimes I don't fasten these correctly and may need some help. Matter of fact, we could maybe be a little late for the party?"

Instead of the amusement I'd expected, a dark storm of emotions was reflected in his eyes, making me feel as though I might be consumed from the heat of them.

"We should go before we're late," he indicated quietly.

His mood shift caught me completely off guard. "What just happened?"

He wouldn't meet my eyes. "Nothing. We need to go."

"You aren't telling me something," I murmured softly.

His eyes snapped to mine. "Don't try to change me. I'm a private man and like it that way."

It was said without anger, but I could tell that I'd inadvertently hit a nerve. "I'll meet you downstairs." I set my glass down, grabbed my clutch, and walked out his door.

His footsteps came behind me on the way to the elevator. "Haylee..."

Damn his honey voice. "Don't. One minute you're telling me about being intrigued, and the next you're telling me not to change you. What in the hell just happened? Did I do something wrong? I feel like you're holding something back, Josh."

He exhaled as we got into an empty elevator heading for the lobby. I felt his hand tugging on my pinky. "You didn't do anything wrong. I am who I am. Besides, I thought I made it clear that we do this my way, which means I decide when and how."

When I looked at him, I saw a little bit of sadness in his eyes, but tugged my pinky away once the elevator doors opened. I didn't know what to do.

After getting in the car waiting outside, we sat in the back seat, silent for a few minutes until he turned towards me.

"Haylee, look at me."

Meeting his eyes, I saw passion and fear reflected. I wanted so badly to tell him that I wasn't his ex-wife, that whatever had happened with her I wouldn't do the same thing to him, and that he could— Shit, what? Change? I blew out the breath I'd been holding and closed my eyes for a second before taking his hand.

"I'm sorry," I murmured and witnessed confusion cloud his eyes.

"You have nothing to apologize for."

"I wanted you to confide in me when you confide in no one. So even if I didn't think that was asking you to change, it was."

He gazed at me for the longest time and then relaxed. "If anyone should apologize, it should be me. You're right, I'm hot and cold, and you're only asking questions. I'm just not equipped to answer them at this point. Okay?"

Nodding, I squeezed his hand, willing myself to be patient. Meanwhile, I vowed that once I got some time to myself, I would evaluate whether or not I wanted to put myself through this for the next few months. His emotional roller coaster had such a profound effect on me and my mood that I questioned whether this thing between us would be healthy.

I didn't want to rely on anyone for validation. The only person I had to depend on in this world was myself. I needed to remember that, especially now.

After getting out of the car, we went inside toward the club-level suite where the party was being held. Josh took me over to the side before entering the room. "Do you think you can withstand another night of listening to conversations among those who decide to talk badly about us?"

I batted my eyelashes dramatically. "No problem."

"We'll plan on recapping after the party. They really won't know what hit them come tomorrow morning." He looked amused with the notion.

I wasn't sure what he had in mind, but something told me that Josh Singer would ensure that anyone who crossed him would regret it.

Ana was one of the first to greet us, with eyes only for my boss. "Ah, Mr. Singer, let me get you a drink. What's your pleasure?"

He came ready to play. "Haylee knows how I like it; I'll let her take care of the drink."

Biting my lip, I tried not to laugh at the expression on Ana's face. I snagged a couple of appetizers on my way to the bar, intending to enjoy at least the food while I was here. A few minutes later, I sidled up to Josh and handed him his drink.

Ken, now standing with Josh, introduced a couple of the top guys to me.

They both rubbed me the wrong way immediately. Each lingered a little too long over my hand, and one of them even caressed his thumb over my fingers. Hearing what they said to each other in Cantonese sealed the deal.

Giving Josh my best fake smile, I was happy to hear the

music start. It provided some background noise as we moved out of earshot.

"What were they discussing?"

"Well, after Stan and Charlie creeped me out with the hand thing, they discussed how I might give head. Apparently, they'd seen me eat a cocktail shrimp earlier."

His eyes darkened.

"It's fine. The fact that they can compare a small cocktail shrimp to giving head kind of tells you everything you need to know about their penis size."

He chuckled. "If it makes you feel better, I didn't like either of them, either. I figured they wouldn't have anything good to say. How about Ken?"

"I don't mind him, but I think that he tends to turn a blind eye toward bad behavior. This is kind of like being a spy."

That garnered a smile. "You make a sexy spy."

THE NEXT FORTY minutes were spent listening to conversations, some good and some bad. I was relieved when Josh came over because I was ready to leave.

"Are there any redeeming people who work for this company?"

"George told Ana to shut up when she called me a whore."

His eyes flashed with fury. "Explain to me exactly how you aren't losing your temper."

"I know I'm not a whore, so why would I let it bother me?"

He held my gaze. "Nice try. You want to pummel her."

Nodding, I cracked a smile. "I really do, and I think I can take her. My size six gives me a good weight advantage."

He chuckled, scanning the room. "Oh, my money is definitely on you. Do you mind giving it another ten minutes? I'm waiting on the owner, and then we're out of here. I can think of better things to do with my time."

I wasn't sure if the innuendo was intentional, but it suddenly had me hot and bothered. So much for worrying about an emotional roller coaster. At the first hint of being alone with him later, my mind flew down only one track.

"No, I don't mind."

Matter of fact, it gave me an opportunity to use the ladies' room. Once I opened the door, I tried not to let the presence of the women at the sink, Ana and Helen, the HR director, make me turn around and leave.

"Haylee, you look lovely tonight," Ana commented, too sweet to be sincere.

I smiled, replied with a thank you, and headed into a stall.

They chattered on in Cantonese, oblivious to the fact that I could understand them. But while they were laughing and carrying on, the topic of their conversation made the color drain from my face.

After taking a few minutes to compose myself, I waited until they left before returning to the party. I caught Josh's eye at the same time an older gentleman came up to greet me.

"You must be Haylee. I'm Tom Wang, Windom's owner." He kissed my hand.

I tried to conjure up a genuine smile when all I wanted to do was leave. "Hello, Mr. Wang. It's very nice to meet you." We made small talk about the company and Hong Kong. Then he took me off guard.

"You've met my daughter, I take it?"

I was confused. "Uh, I'm not sure if I have, Mr. Wang."

He waved Ana over.

Dread seeped through me.

"Ana is my daughter. She manages the office and maintains the everyday tasks now that my wife has retired."

Surprising me, Ana told her father in Cantonese, "Haylee has been very sweet and very helpful."

So Daddy didn't know how nasty she could be?

"You know how I feel about speaking our language around people who don't know it. It's rude." Tom smiled apologetically. "Ana was saying how helpful and sweet you were. I believe Josh said you were making your way back to your hotel soon. I'm sure it's been a long day with flying in overnight. But I look forward to a breakfast meeting tomorrow with the both of you."

Thankfully, he'd already spoken with Josh, so we said our goodbyes and headed out to the car.

JOSH WAS quiet on the ride back to the hotel, but in the elevator he turned to me. "What happened in the ladies' room that had you pale as a ghost when you walked out?"

I was surprised he'd noticed. "It's nothing."

His eyes narrowed with annoyance. "Don't tell me it's nothing. Ana came out ahead of you, along with that other woman. What were they saying?"

I was tired from the day, and my feet hurt. Reaching down, I took off my shoes one at a time, choosing to ignore his question because I simply didn't have the energy for it at the moment.

As soon as the doors opened, he blocked my way and then hit for the doors to close. "Why don't we recap in my suite?"

Part of me wanted to be by myself, but a deal was a deal. I'd promised I'd go over the conversations of the evening. I felt my heart beating double time as I crossed the threshold of his suite at this late hour. His mood was tough to gauge.

Once seated in Josh's living room, I related all of the dialogue throughout the evening and then the tidbit about Ana being Tom's daughter.

He didn't look surprised.

"You knew?"

He shrugged. "I wondered why an office manager had so much confidence and that untouchable flair to her, so I asked Ken."

Sighing, I shared my thought that Tom wasn't aware of Ana's true nature.

"Agreed. So now tell me what happened in the ladies' room?"

Swallowing hard, I got up from the sofa where I'd been sitting. "I really don't want to discuss it. It was more petty stuff, and I'm tired."

I could tell I was pissing him off, but I didn't know how to go about sharing what I'd overheard.

The knock at the door surprised me, but it seemed as if Josh had been expecting it. At the door, he spoke in low tones and walked back into the living room while pouring himself a drink. In his hand was a small package that had evidently just been delivered. He slid out what appeared to be a prescription bottle. After uncapping it, he took out one of the pills, and washed it down with his whiskey.

It was tempting to ask what he was taking, but it wasn't my business. Maybe he'd forgotten his medication at home or something.

"I need you to call Henry in Mergers and Acquisitions. It's about eight o'clock in the morning his time. He's expecting my call about whether or not I'm purchasing the company."

"Okay. Do I have time to change?" I already knew the answer but needed confirmation that he wasn't in the mood to do me any favors.

"No."

Over the next thirty minutes, I conferenced in Henry and printed out legal documents. From what I could gather from their conversation, Josh was going through with the purchase. After he signed the paperwork, I excused myself to go into the office to fax them to Henry.

I wanted to slip down to my room to change into comfortable clothes but knew that Josh would be furious. When I walked back into the living room, he was off the phone and watching me.

"Did he email confirmation he received the documents?" I asked.

"Yes. Now, come here." His voice had an edge to it. No honey this time.

After standing there a moment, I tentatively walked over to stand two feet in front of him.

"Do you want me to fuck you?"

My mouth went bone dry. Although I wanted to be offended by his words, I became undeniably turned on by them. "What?" This was so unlike the Josh I knew thus far that I wasn't sure what to say.

"It's a fairly easy question to answer. Yes or no, Haylee?" He seemed to know what hearing my name on his lips did to me and was clearly using it to his advantage.

"You seem angry with me," I worried in a soft voice.

He stood up and moved around behind me. "Yes, well, I don't like playing games, and yet here we are."

I'd been drinking some at the party and was dead on my feet. Even so, I was pretty sure I was missing something here. I felt his hands glide down my back and come around my waist to undo my belt. "I don't know what you're talking about," I managed to say on a whisper.

"I'm talking about the fact that you seemed to be an open book of information all day. But then I didn't explain why I wouldn't fuck you earlier. After that, you started to hold information hostage."

"I would never consider the two the same thing. I hadn't even thought about earlier." I felt my zipper run down my back and cool air hit my skin.

"You didn't think about me fucking you when you showed me your garters earlier?"

My dress pooled at my feet. "I was trying to be playful. You smacked my ass, and I thought I'd tease a little back."

He stepped in front of me again, looking down the length of me and giving me a hand so that I could step completely out of my dress.

I stood there wearing only my bra, panties, garters, and stockings. Thank God I'd chosen my one set of sexy lingerie this evening.

"So, you didn't want to be fucked and didn't want to talk about why I wasn't fucking you."

His temper appeared to be rising. "Please stop talking like that."

He laughed bitterly. "Are you going to tell me that the word *fucking* is turning you off?" He moved behind me again. I felt his fingers reach between my legs where they found me drenched through my panties. "I think not."

"I don't want to talk about it. I want to go to my room."

The last part was unconvincing, but his hand pulled back. "If you wish to leave, then go," he snapped harshly.

Turning, I searched his eyes. "Josh, I'm not trying to hold anything hostage."

He gave me a cruel smile and scoffed. "Aren't you? Aren't all women?"

"Please don't make it like this between us." I put my hand on his chest.

"Did you see me take that pill earlier?" His eyes looked haunted.

"Yes, why?" I had no idea where this was heading. Was he sick? Did he have a drug problem?

I didn't see it coming until it was out of his mouth. "Yes, well, in order to get it up and keep it up after the vasectomy, I've had to resort to taking those little blue, damned pills. And the cruelest part is that I still don't come. So there you have it. My big dark secret that I wasn't ready to share with you. But you backed me into a corner. Now, what was said in the bathroom?"

"But I don't understand." My head was spinning.

Then, just like that, I was being carried over to the large picture window overlooking the city. He placed my hands on the glass and spread my legs apart as if ready to do a pat down on me. But instead, he stepped behind me and lowered his zipper. "I want to know what you heard earlier." His fingers reached around me into my thong and found me pathetically ready for him.

"I don't…" I felt my panties rip.

"You don't—what? Want to be fucked?"

God help me, I could feel my whole body trembling with desire. He was hard against my backside with his other hand teasing my nipples. I was lost and would do or say anything at this point.

"Tell me, Haylee. Tell me you want to be fucked."

I felt him tease the back of me and stroke my swollen folds. "Yes, I want you to fuck me," I admitted finally.

He came around to my front. I saw not only passion but also anger in his eyes. "Then tell me what you heard." His fingers were now teasing my throbbing clit. When I'd start to feel it build, he'd stop.

Somewhere in the sexual fog, I was remotely aware that he was using sex as a weapon, but I was too inexperienced to know what to do about it and too turned on to want to stop. "I heard, um, Ana. She was talking to the HR girl about you and your ex-wife. They were discussing a rumor about you pushing her and a miscarriage as a result."

He moved behind me, but not before I saw the flash of hurt register on his face. I cursed the fact that he'd bullied me into telling him.

"This won't be gentle, so tell me now if you want to leave.

Otherwise, I'm going to have you hard right now."

I swallowed, bracing myself as I wanted it too much at this point. "I'm staying."

He shoved inside of me. He was so large that I could feel myself stretching to accommodate his size. Gasping, I felt him thrust into me fully, vaguely sensing his fingers digging into my hips, holding me in place as he pumped hard and fast.

The first wave of pleasure ripped through me quickly as my body had been primed for it. I rode thrust after thrust. He gripped my ass and pushed deeper inside me before reaching around and working my clit with his deft fingers until I came again.

Mercifully, he braced me while he pulled out, as I wasn't sure I could stand a minute longer.

"Haylee, I—"

I wasn't sure what he'd say next or why it was so important to me, but I dropped to my knees and dove for him with my hands and mouth, ignoring his protests.

"Jesus, Haylee, no. You don't—"

Looking up through my eyelashes, I watched him wage the war between raw lust and whatever he'd been about to say. Working his length thoroughly with my mouth and tongue, I used my hand to pump him hard.

He tensed, and I realized standing probably wasn't the most relaxed position. I broke contact, took his hand, and led him down the step to the couch. There I none too gently pushed him down and followed with my mouth again.

"Christ—"

I wasn't listening; instead, I was frenzied with only one goal in mind. I wanted him to come. And maybe I wanted payback for his taking such control over me earlier. My fist worked his shaft while my mouth was greedy for his taste. I felt his thighs tremble and wondered if he was getting close. Sucking harder, I demanded it with my tongue working his length.

He started to come in my mouth, but abruptly pulled me up

and thrust back inside of me. He completed his orgasm deep inside my pulsating core.

We were both left exhausted, situated half on the sofa and half on the floor.

He carefully slid out and sat up fully on the living room couch, watching me with hooded eyes while I stood up.

Walking over to where my dress lay, I dragged it up, situating the belt half-ass and zipping myself as best I could with shaking fingers.

"Listen, I—"

Holding up my hand, I fought the tears, knowing that I was overly emotional but not able to help it. "No, you don't get to talk anymore tonight; instead, you can listen for a change. I didn't tell you what was said in the restroom at first because I knew it would upset you and because I didn't believe it. But you used sex as a weapon to bully me into telling you. I knew you were holding something back from me, but I was willing to let you take your time and tell me when you were ready."

He swallowed hard.

"I need to go." Grabbing my purse, I made a quick exit, rushing back into the elevator and down to my room. I fought my tears the entire way, but let them flow as I washed the makeup off my face and ran a hot bath. I knew I'd handled that poorly. I'd more than wanted the sex, but I hadn't been prepared to deal with the overwhelming emotions afterwards.

Hearing the knock at the door, I chose to ignore it until it became pounding. Meanwhile, my phone was ringing. I turned off the water, threw on my robe, and opened the door, ready to give him a piece of my mind. Then I glanced at his face.

He looked devastated.

We stood there staring at each other for the longest time.

"You were in the bath?"

I could only nod, not trusting my voice.

"Come on." He took my hand and led me back into my bathroom. Cupping my chin, he kissed me softly on the lips and then the forehead. Gently, he peeled off my robe.

After stepping into the tub, I eased down in the water and watched as he undressed from his tuxedo shirt and pants. He slid into the bath behind me, situating me between his legs and cradling my back against his strong, hard chest. I could feel him breathing in the scent of my hair.

"I know you probably want to be alone, but I had to know if you were okay."

"You didn't hurt me if that's what you're asking. Physically," I clarified.

He rubbed my arms and seemed to struggle for words. "I was so convinced that you were backing me into a corner and have no excuse for the way I acted or how I lashed out at you. I behaved terribly."

"You could start with actually saying I'm sorry."

"I'm not very good with apologies."

My temper completely snapped. "What's so hard about two little words? It's pretty easy. Here, I'll even go first. I'm sorry that I didn't want to tell you what Ana and Helen were gossiping about in the bathroom this evening. It took me off guard, and I knew that it would upset you. I simply didn't think that I was doing anyone favors by spreading malicious rumors."

He hugged my waist and buried his face in my neck. "I'm sorry."

Breathing deep, I forced myself to relax back in his arms. "I hate that you told me about the pills like that. Something so personal and painful for you shouldn't have been thrown out in anger."

He took my hands and held them. "No, it probably shouldn't have, but to be honest, I'm not sure there'd been another way to tell you. I didn't want you to feel sorry for me. Why do you think the second NDA was so important for you to sign—it was in case you found out. I didn't have the pills with me in Mexico or earlier this evening but called my physician to have the prescription delivered. You're the only person who knows—with the exception of my doctor, who prescribes me the pills while telling me that it's all in my head."

"So tonight is the first time you've—?" I asked quietly, kind of liking that fact.

"The best orgasm of my life," he revealed, sighing. "Look, what those women were discussing, the rumors? I didn't touch her. She fell, and I wasn't even in the same damn room when she did. But she was going down the stairs and not watching because she was angry with me because I'd figured out she was cheating, so I guess inadvertently..."

I turned around, straddling his legs, and put my finger to his lips. "You don't need to explain anything to me. It was upsetting to hear, but I didn't believe it for a second. But promise me you won't ever use sex as a weapon again."

"I promise," he vowed, kissing me senseless. He soaped up my arms and then my breasts, slowly working his way down.

Closing my eyes, I couldn't believe that my body was ready to respond again so quickly.

"Haylee..."

My eyes fluttered open, and I feasted on his lips again, feeling his fingers working me. Deepening the kiss, I could feel him grow hard against me. Before he could protest or overthink it, I rose up and impaled myself on his impressive erection. I relished the sound of his groan as I rocked into his hips.

He gripped my backside, helping set the rhythm. "No, don't close your eyes. Look at me," he commanded softly.

The intimacy was overwhelming being face to face like this. I could tell this territory was as new for him as it was for me. My hands plowed through his hair while his hand made its way between our bodies and rubbed my most sensitive spot. Gasping, I increased the cadence and rode him harder.

"That's it. You feel so good."

I tipped over the edge of reason and realized I was taking him with me when he groaned. I enjoyed the look of surprise and satisfaction in his eyes.

We sat like that in the tub awhile before I noticed the patch on his arm. "What's this?" I ran my fingers over it.

"Nicorette patch."

My face split into a grin. "You quit smoking?"

"I'd been meaning to for a while, even had the patches with me. I guess I had the proper incentive this time."

I kissed him again deeply, enjoying the touch of his mouth on mine and toying with his lips. God, he was a really great kisser.

"I know I should have asked this before we had sex, but I'm not on the pill. The couple times I had sex, my partners wore condoms, but with your ex being unfaithful—" God I'd already failed Safe Sex 101.

"I had a checkup and got tested after I found out she cheated. I'm clean, and I had the vasectomy, which is more effective than the pill anyhow."

Breathing a sigh of relief, I murmured against his neck, "Water is getting cold."

He lifted me up and kissed my forehead. "Let's rinse." Leading me into the shower, he turned on the water. We quickly washed, and then he spent an inordinate amount of time drying me thoroughly with little kisses along the way.

His strong arms came around me and picked me up, carrying me to the bed and laying me down gently. "Time for sleep. You have to be exhausted."

It was nice when he climbed into the bed behind me. I was almost asleep when I heard him murmur, "Haylee?"

"Hmm?"

"I don't think your ass is fat at all."

I fell asleep smiling.

CHAPTER EIGHT

I woke up a little disoriented by the weight across my body until I realized it was Josh's arm. He was half on his back and half facing me, looking vulnerable while sound asleep.

Taking the opportunity to study him, I noticed he appeared much younger than his thirty-two years. I hadn't noticed how long his lashes were until now, when his eyes were closed. I had no doubt he was the most attractive man I'd ever seen. Even close up, he seemed flawless and simply gazing at him caused butterflies. Of all of the women in the world, why did he want me?

Well, that was a nice insecure thought. Rolling my eyes, I slipped out of bed quietly. The last thing I needed was to start feeling doubt and then question my self-worth.

Hopping in the shower, I convinced myself that even if he was gorgeous, I was attractive, too, and we all had faults.

When he stepped into the shower in front of me, however, I forgot all about faults. The man was breathtaking.

"Good morning." He cupped my face and kissed me soundly.

"Hey, you brushed your teeth. That's hardly fair," I protested.

A smile spread across his face. "It's quite all right. I'll simply pick alternative places to kiss."

And just like that, he was kneeling in front me with his mouth on my center. My climax was hard and fast.

As he rose, I realized he was hard for me.

"I can't guarantee how long it will last or if it's still from the pill yesterday, but it seems like a shame to waste it."

I didn't even have time to comment before he lifted me up. I wrapped my legs around his waist, sheathing every hard inch of him inside of me. I loved hearing his intake of breath from the pleasure.

"Jesus, Haylee, what you do to me."

Squeezing my legs, I pulled him in even deeper. As I met his thrusts, the burn started working its way down to my toes. Was there any limit to the number of orgasms one person could have in a week? I was pretty sure I was about to find out as I exploded and then felt him do the same moments after.

The warm water was no longer reaching me in the corner. Now that I was coming down from the height of passion, I started to shiver.

"You're cold." He pulled out and inched me down the length of him, taking me back into the warm stream of water.

"Much better." I took the soap and leisurely explored his impressively chiseled chest before smoothing my hands down to his abs and trim waistline. I had never studied a man's body and found myself mesmerized. Massaging his biceps, I marveled at the strength he had before exploring down each forearm and then into his wrists and large hands. Looking up through my lashes, I saw his eyes watching me, curious, when I then kneeled down. I soaped each leg, taking my time with his shapely calves and moving on up to his powerful thighs.

Pausing, I soaped up my hands and took his length in both hands, caressing the soft skin and then underneath his length. I smiled, moving around to his back where I soaped up his broad shoulders. I admired the muscles in his back and traced my fingertips further down. Damn if his ass wasn't made like a sculpture, I thought. I rubbed my hands over the taut muscles and dared to slide one down between his cheeks. I heard his small groan and loved the power that came with turning him on. Finally working my way down the back of his thighs, I finished the job by hugging his back tightly to me and enjoying the moment.

"You're all clean, Mr. Singer," I declared in my best seductive secretary voice.

His body shook with a chuckle. I squealed when he turned and wrapped his hands around my waist, grinning at me. "I probably shouldn't be so turned on by that. You do know that I'm sorely tempted to keep you in your room all day naked, don't you?"

I could see the seriousness in his eyes, and it was enticing, but he had important work to do. "Places to go, people to see, flights to catch."

He gave me a fake pouty face.

This teasing side of him was so rare that I stood a few seconds stunned, not realizing he was exiting the shower and speaking to me again.

"Unfortunately, you're right. I need to get back up to my room and get dressed."

Washing quickly, I climbed out of the shower, donned my hotel robe, and stepped into the bedroom in time to see him putting on last night's clothes.

"So, going up to my room right now, that's the *walk of shame* you referred to, isn't it?"

I couldn't help bursting out laughing, "Sorry." I didn't mean it in the slightest.

"I have nothing to be ashamed about. Mind-blowing sex, sleeping a full night, and then the best shower I've ever had. I've earned this walk."

Giggling, it hit me that I was seeing Josh smile more now. Knowing I might be the reason for that was humbling, but it made me a bit fearful of what this softer side of him might come to mean to me.

"All right, time to get back to reality. I'll meet you in an hour. We can take our luggage with us to the office and leave from there," he suggested.

"Sounds good."

He came back, giving me a resounding kiss. "Ready for the big reveal today in the office?"

That made me smile. "I'll follow your lead."

I THOUGHT the deep plum Dianne Von Furstenberg wrap dress was appropriate and added a chunky necklace with matching suede pumps. DVF said sexy, feminine, and sassy all in one. I zipped up my suitcase and proceeded down to the lobby.

Josh was freshly dressed in a black pinstriped suit and stood off to the side, talking on the phone.

I could see his profile and felt a flutter in my belly that I'd been in the shower with this stunning man only an hour ago. He exuded authority and, with it, a sexual electricity that was beginning to occupy my every thought. Even with our newfound sexual, uh, accomplishment, if you will, I wondered what the status of our relationship would be going forward. It felt a little too soon to wonder if we'd start spending nights together. I supposed I needed to adopt a wait and see approach.

Walking toward him, I was rewarded with a double take and then a slow assessment as his eyes raked over my body. He ended the appraisal with a small smile when he finished up his call.

"Is that your *fuck-you-I-knew-Chinese-all-along* dress?" he teased.

I laughed in response. "I like that. Yes, it is."

We walked out to the car. In the backseat, I felt his fingers find mine. "So what's the game plan?"

He raised a brow. "I figured I'd leave you in the driver's seat. I bought the company as of midnight last night. Perhaps you want to do the honors of the firing."

I instantly felt sick to my stomach.

"Are you all right?"

I knew he would be disappointed, but the truth was that although I was angry at Ana and some of the others, actually ending their employment left me feeling guilty. I knew in my gut that people like Ana didn't belong in a company influencing people. She was like a poison. But firing her still wasn't something with which I was comfortable. And of course there was the fact that she was the owner's daughter. "Yes, I'm fine, but I'm a little overwhelmed at that prospect, I guess."

He seemed to buy that and went back to checking his email.

Looking out the window, I sat back and tried to get myself psyched up for this morning. "What time did you want to try to leave today? The flight is at three o'clock." I was anxious to fly home.

"As soon as possible. I'd rather spend time in the lounge than one more minute in that office."

I had to ask the obvious question. "Then why buy the company?"

"Because I know business, and at the end of the day, this one will be profitable. I have plans to grow it and the perfect man to put in charge. He's looking to make a move from London to Hong Kong. Once I make sure he has an assistant who secretly knows Chinese, he'll be good."

I managed a forced smile. "Who, exactly, is being fired?"

"You tell me. Remember, driver's seat."

Biting my lip, I tried to remain objective. "Well, who are you letting go because of performance unrelated to what I overheard?"

"There are a few people, but I want for you to make your decision based on what you witnessed."

"But what if they are a big asset to the company, and I—"

He cut me off. "I don't care. I want them out."

"Okay. I guess I would say Ana, Stan, and Charlie."

He nodded, clearly not surprised.

We made our way up the elevator, and I felt jittery, wishing I'd had breakfast before going in. Obviously, sex had muddled my priorities this morning.

As soon as we were off the elevator, Ana greeted us. "Mr. Singer, Haylee, everyone is gathering in the conference room for the news." Clearly, she was aware of the logistics of the sale.

Josh gave her a curt nod. "Lead the way."

Just like that, we were thrust in front of fifty people. Standing to the side, I admired the way that Josh could command a room by simply entering it.

He offered a small smile that didn't meet his eyes. "As I'm sure some of you are already aware, Gamble Advertising has purchased your company as of yesterday evening. My HR director and my regional vice president will be traveling over in the next couple of weeks with details regarding what this will mean to you each individually. Obviously, you can expect some changes, but I'm excited to work together to expand your Asia Pacific reach and to grow your foothold in this region.

"I want to thank Tom for his many years of leadership and hard work in founding this company and taking it to the point it is today. I also want to thank Ken for his guidance and hospitality in bringing me here. I welcome you to the Gamble Advertising family. Haylee, how do you say that in Cantonese?"

All eyes turned toward me.

With measured calculation, I made sure I glanced around the room toward all of the faces when I translated for Josh.

Helen's eyes hit the floor, Stan and Charlie squirmed in their seats, and the poor receptionist, Cindy, looked like she was about to cry. Only Ana had the nerve to look pissed off at the discovery. Well, at least that cemented any second thoughts I had about her losing her job.

"My assistant has educated me on the differences between Cantonese and Mandarin, having studied both. Hopefully, by the next time I come here, I will be well versed myself." His words were light, but his tone wasn't. He made a point of looking at Ana before giving a smile to both Ken and Tom.

"I know you probably want to take some time with your people, gentlemen, but, afterwards, if I could have a few moments before Haylee and I depart for the airport, I'd appreciate it."

They both nodded, offering breakfast in one of the conference rooms. Josh declined politely. Obviously he was anxious to get this over and done with.

We went out the door and into the lobby, intending to wait on them, but I wasn't surprised to see Ana approaching quickly behind us.

"Can I borrow Haylee for a moment?" she asked sweetly.

Josh turned toward her and gave her his full attention. "I don't think so. I need her with me, actually, while we talk with your father."

Her face faltered. Then she made the mistake of challenging him. "That's right, he is my father which means he won't make a deal without protecting me, so I would suggest—"

He didn't let her finish, taking a step forward. "I'd proceed very carefully, Ana, before you start making threats." He must have seen her eyes dart toward me because he continued. "And I think your time with taking shots at Haylee is done, too." He spoke in a low, menacing voice.

She swallowed hard.

Ken and Tom came out of the meeting. They glanced from her toward Josh and then toward me.

"I need a minute with you, Mr. Singer," I whispered.

He hesitated but then took my arm and led me to a vacant conference room.

"I can't do this. I'm sorry. I mean, I appreciate you giving me this opportunity, but to take away someone's livelihood just like that? I find no satisfaction in it." I could tell he was going to argue and mitigated. "I do know they need to be gone because to have any of these people here would be toxic for this company. I suppose you're disappointed, but I feel like I'm about to throw up." I forced myself to hold his gaze and breathed a sigh of relief when his eyes softened.

"I'm not disappointed and would be more upset if you found delight in firing someone, to be honest. Although I've definitely had more experience with this and in doing what's necessary, I don't take any joy from it, either."

I sighed, embarrassed that I couldn't go through with it.

"Why don't you wait for me downstairs in the lobby? This won't take long and I'm not going into the details of why. They are all getting generously compensated to allow them time to look for alternative employment. And remember that Tom is getting a good chunk of change with the sale of his company. So you could say that, indirectly, Ana will benefit from that as well."

I nodded and was thankful to make my way out. It was times like this that I missed my father the most. He would've offered great advice, as he'd been both practical and realistic in his views. My mother loved me, but my father respected my opinion and would guide me into making my own decision, which would result in the least amount of regret. Josh had been more than understanding, but it didn't make the weight of chickening out any easier.

"Ready?" Josh asked, meeting me in the lobby. He didn't give away anything he might have been feeling.

Nodding, I proceeded with him from the office building out to the car. The drive to the airport seemed extraordinarily long as I stared out the window, taking in the enormous Hong Kong Harbor and thinking of all of the ships making their way across the world.

We were early for our flight and settled into a nearly empty lounge. I took the opportunity to finalize some details for our upcoming Charlotte and London trips. After we caught up on logistics, we lapsed into a comfortable silence.

"Haylee…"

I looked up at the sound of my name and saw his green eyes watching me intently.

"Today was stressful. You handled it well."

I didn't think I deserved the compliment. "I wish I'd been stronger. I'm sorry."

Leaning in close, he said, "You have nothing to apologize for. I have something for you that will hopefully put a smile on your face." Reaching into his bag, he pulled out a box with a bow.

"When did you possibly have time to do this?"

He gave me a look that pretty much conveyed *that is what I pay people for*.

After undoing the bow and paper, I saw the brand new iPad. "This is very nice, but—"

"Not at all unselfish. Open it up. I had them charge it, and then this morning I added some apps for you."

Taking it out of the box, I found five different types of Angry Birds. My face broke out in a smile. "It's very thoughtful of you. Thank you."

He looked pleased with my acceptance of the gift. "Here's

where you connect to wireless in settings. When we get on the plane, you can hook up to the Wi-Fi network. And here is the instant messenger feature. You can put in your email address and set it up for personal use."

"I can't wait to get the Kindle app. My mom had one in the hospital. Reading helped to pass the time when she was there for her treatments."

"What happened to the Kindle?" He surprised me with the details he picked up on.

"I gave it to an older gentleman who was there the same days as my mom. He didn't have visitors, and he was really grateful for it."

Something flashed in his eyes, but it was gone by the time he got up.

"Let's get boarded and get home. You have lots of Angry Birds to play."

I WAS SEATED one row in front of Josh. With happy couples or business associates in the other pods, there was no trading this time around so that we could sit next to one another.

Once I settled in, I waited until we were in the air to take my backpack to the lavatory and change into my yoga pants and sweatshirt. Opting for pigtails in order to get a reaction out of Josh, I came out and went down my aisle. After putting my bag away, I looked over and gave him a little smile, then sat back down, enjoying the way his eyes had tracked me.

After lunch, I wondered if I should try to sleep or watch a movie and was unprepared for Josh's face suddenly next to mine.

"Hi," he greeted, grinning.

Turning, I grinned back. "Hi." He was so unbelievably adorable. It was all I could do not to act giddy like a teenager with him kneeling down next to me.

"Could you do me a favor? Turn on your wireless and hook up your instant messaging on your iPad."

"Uh, okay, sure." I watched him return to his seat, feeling curious as I logged onto the Wi-Fi and then set up my instant messenger with my personal email account.

It wasn't long before I received my first message from *The Gambler.*

How appropriate, I thought, smiling.

"Hi."

I changed my nickname to something other than my email address and settled on *Peaches*, hopeful he would remember the reference to the way he'd said I tasted.

"***Hi back.***"

"Nice nickname. Your yoga pants are torture again, by the way."

"Oh yeah?"

"You had every man in first class watching you stretch up to put your backpack away, so yeah."

Hmm. Was he a little bit jealous?

"***You up for playing a game?***"

"Angry birds?" I quipped.

"Eyes Rolling. No, something a bit more personal…"

"I'm intrigued…"

"This game starts with yes or no answers. Do you want to play?"

"Yes."

"***Good, now I want you to have the flight attendant make up your bed, ok?***"

"Ok."

Standing up, I waited for the flight attendant to come and make up my bed. While thanking her, I glimpsed Josh sipping his whiskey and seemingly engrossed in his tablet. He didn't spare me a glance.

After lying down, I closed the pod around me and was propping myself up on my pillows when the next message came in.

"Are you comfortable?"

"Yes."

"Good. I want you to take your blankets and put them over you. Cover yourself up, all right?"

"Yes."

"Now I want you to take your left hand and reach down and touch yourself."

I groaned because, unfortunately, this wasn't a department in which I'd ever been particularly successful.

"You still there?" came the next message.

"Yes."

"Is this making you uncomfortable?"

"Yes and no."

"Talk to me."

"I've never done this before."

"The talking or the touching?"

"Both."

"Never?"

"I've tried but never successful at it. I used to think something was wrong with me, but obviously now I know different, thanks to you."

"I wish I could touch you right now."

"Me too!!!"

"What if you imagine that it's me, my fingers feeling if you are wet for me?"

Reaching down with my left hand, I felt the pool of dampness. ***"Yes, I am."*** I typed with my other hand.

"I want you to put one finger inside yourself. Do you feel that liquid honey, Haylee?"

Even when he typed my name, it made me hot. I did his bidding and felt myself slick with desire. ***"Yes."***

"Good girl. Now take two fingers and rub your clit for me. Start with small circles. We're only getting you warmed up."

Moving my fingers as directed, I felt my body start to respond.

"That's it, baby. How does it feel?"

"Good."

"Now I want you to imagine my tongue where your fingers are. It's licking, sucking, and tasting you. Close your eyes and imagine your hand running through my hair as you push my mouth deeper into you."

I had to stifle a moan, feeling my body respond to my fingers and his words.

"Type a Y if you're feeling it."

"Y."

"Good girl. Now I want you to rub faster. That's it. Now take those fingers and dip them down into your wet pussy and bring them back up. You're drenched for me. I know you are."

"Y," I typed, slightly out of breath. My body was begging for release.

"Rub around and feel the ache. Can you imagine it's my fingers and my mouth?"

"Y."

"Do you know how much I want you? How many things I want to do to you?"

"Tell me." I needed to hear it.

"I want to possess all of you. Do you know what that means?"

"N."

"Reach down, way down, and feel how slick you are. Are you dripping?"

"Y."

"Take your fingers and suck on one. Taste yourself, and know that I would possess your mouth. You would take me in deeply and suck me dry."

With that mental picture, my body writhed with anticipation.

"Now move your fingers down again and feel that delicious slit of yours. Put two fingers inside that drenched entrance and squeeze that sweet pussy around them. I would have you there, deep and wet. Do you like that?"

"Y."

"Now take those fingers and dip them down lower, taking that honey with you and feel that gorgeous pucker and know that I will someday possess you there, too, baby. Does that scare you?"

"Y."

"Don't be afraid. We'll work you into it, my sexy girl. Now rub harder."

"Y."

"Now come for me, my sweet, beautiful, Haylee."

And just like that, I did. After stuffing a pillow in my face to keep myself from crying out, I lay there stupefied, a little in awe and a little self-conscious of the fact that I'd had an orgasm in an airplane via sexting with my boss. I yawned, feeling tired now, and realized I was ignoring the blinking iPad.

"Talk to me."

"Sorry, I was a little busy."

"So does that mean??????"

"YYYYYYYYY."

"You don't know how much that turns me on."

I smiled and then typed my saucy response. ***"Does that count for mile-high club?"*** I could hear his chuckle through my pod and giggled.

"I'm not sure on the particulars of that one."

I googled it for fun. ***"According to Google, the mile-high club does not have any provisions for self-indulgence."***

"Pity."

"Do you want to play?"

"Some other time, perhaps. You should probably get some sleep."

I figured it was probably for the best since I wasn't sure how I would go about sexting him back. ***"A different game, then?"***

"??"

"It's called Tell Me Something. So tell me something I don't know about you."

"I don't think I like this game."

"It doesn't have to be some deep secret, simply something I don't know about you. It can be personal or something curious. I think it would be a nice way to get to know each other better. I'll even go first. I can't stand food-scented candles. I don't understand why you would want your house to smell like cookies or chocolate or fruit. It gives me a headache."

"I'll file that away for future reference. All right, one thing, and then you sleep."

Smiling, I typed a ***"Y."***

"Careful, I'll start again with the first game."

"One thing, and then I'll leave you alone."

"I can't stand soggy cereal. So I pour the milk, take 3, maybe 4, bites and toss the rest."

"Funny, thank you for humoring me. Night."

CHAPTER NINE

We arrived back in New York after the long plane ride from Hong Kong. After getting into the back of his town car, I could feel Josh's eyes on me.

"You're blushing," he noted quietly.

I'd been thinking about our little game a mile high.

He hooked my pinky between us on the seat on the ride home from the airport while I felt heat already spreading from the anticipation of being alone with him.

It was late by the time we got back to the building. As we walked in through the lobby, I waved hello to Rafael.

"Why don't you go on up? I'll grab the Thai food from the front desk and meet you at your place in a few minutes," Josh suggested.

Grateful to be home, I dragged my suitcase inside my apartment and thought it sure would be nice to sleep in tomorrow morning with absolutely nothing on the agenda.

Though I left my door open, I expected to go over to Josh's place for food. But ten minutes later, he came into my apartment instead, holding the takeout bag and shutting the door behind him.

"Hungry?" he asked suggestively.

I smiled, watching as he set the bag down on my counter and then crossed the room. He pulled me to him before crushing me with his kiss.

"This is all I thought about the entire plane ride, these damn pants," he muttered.

I giggled as he dragged them down while frantically moving me toward the bed. The back of my knees hit the mattress, and I took him down with me. We wasted no time in finishing up what we'd started on the plane.

Lying there beside him after, I realized that my underwear and pants were still around my knees and his were in much the same shape.

"So I take it that you don't need the pills any longer?" I asked lightly, hoping he wouldn't take offense.

Chuckling, he pushed up and searched my face. "It would appear not. If only I'd known the cure was a twenty-two-year-old, I wouldn't have wasted the last few years. It kind of irks me that Dr. Winters was right about it not being a physical condition caused by his surgery."

"Hmm, well if you had known four years ago that a twenty-two-year-old was the answer, it wouldn't have been me, and I don't like that scenario. Unless maybe, in that case, an eighteen-year-old would've been the solution."

"Twenty-two is bad enough. When do you turn twenty-three?"

"Hoping for a smaller age gap?" I teased.

"I'll take anything I can get."

"My birthday is in March and yours?"

"It's in July. So I get four whole months when there's only a nine-year difference instead of ten." He rolled off and pulled his pants up. "I'm going to run home and change, maybe take a quick shower. Then if you're up for it, I can come back and we can eat?"

It didn't make sense that he wasn't inviting me to his place, but I was too happy to be back in my own space to argue. "Sounds good."

I dashed into the shower after watching the door close.

A short time later, I was taking down two plates when Josh came back in, not bothering with a knock. His hair was slightly damp, and he smelled wonderful.

"I ordered the drunken noodle, some pad thai, peanut butter chicken stuff, and some pork dumpling things. Is there anything you don't want?" He opened the bag and took out the boxes to set them on the counter.

"Nope, it all sounds great. Thanks for thinking of dinner."

Dishing up a little out of each box, I watched as he did the same. I walked over to the bed and sat on it cross legged with my plate. Considering I didn't have any place to sit aside from this, I wondered why we weren't at a table in his place.

He joined me and gave me a curious look. "Do you wear that to bed?"

I glanced down at my oversized Stanford T-shirt and blue running shorts. "Yeah, why?"

His eyes twinkled with laughter.

"What? Why did you ask that?" I was totally lost on what was so funny.

Shrugging, he put his fork down. "Okay, don't take this the wrong way, but you dress impeccably at work. That gave me a different impression of what you might wear at night."

I guess I'd never thought about what to wear to bed as none of the guys I'd previously been with had ever spent the night. My eyes shifted from my attire to his. I was fairly certain his lounge pants and T-shirt cost more than what I made in a day. "Well, I have my mom to thank for—"

Josh's phone interrupted the rest of my admission about inheriting my work wardrobe.

As he looked at the number on his screen, he frowned. "I

have to take this." He then stepped out of my apartment, closing the door behind him.

By the time I finished eating, he hadn't returned. After clearing my plate, I packed up the boxes and then left his plate on the counter. I was about ready to call it a night when he finally did come back, looking annoyed.

"I, uh, have a lot of work to do this evening. I'll probably be pretty busy tomorrow, too."

He was evading something, and my eyes rolled of their own volition. In fact, since tomorrow was Saturday, I'd been looking forward to doing anything I wanted. "I have plans tomorrow, too. Let me know if you need anything workwise. Otherwise, I'll see you Sunday afternoon when we leave for Charlotte. The car will be here at two o'clock."

"Wait. What plans do you have?"

Glad my back was to him, I turned slowly and smiled. "You first." I said it sweetly enough that he knew the point I was making.

"Touché. I'll see you Sunday. Sweet dreams." He kissed me long and slow before sighing with regret and leaving.

I puttered across the room and plugged in my phone to charge. As an afterthought, I plugged in the iPad and logged into messenger. I was pathetic, already missing him.

Looking through some of the apps, I realized I had FaceTime and emailed my Aunt Jeanine, or Aunt J, as I called her. Now that we both had iPads, we'd be able to use FaceTime instead of doing our traditional Saturday phone chat tomorrow. It would be nice to see my only living family member face to face for a change.

It was tempting to go straight to bed, but I glanced at the suitcases I'd had shipped from San Francisco. They wouldn't unpack themselves. At the very least, I needed to take out my mom's coats and dresses which had trekked across the country.

THE NEXT MORNING I felt quite accomplished, having gotten a run, laundry, and a manicure out of the way, all before ten o'clock. Later that evening as I was finishing up my FaceTime call with my aunt and uncle, Josh knocked.

His brow arched at my fancy black-and-white ball gown and flute of champagne. "Uh, what's the occasion?"

I was momentarily confused until he pointed to my dress, and then giggled. "Right. Sorry, I've had a few glasses of champagne. It's my mom's birthday today, and since she loved fancy ball gowns, and I was FaceTiming my aunt—"

His phone rang, and he winced. "Shit, hold on." Taking it, he said tersely, "Yes." He stepped back out to the hall to have the conversation, shutting my door and the ability to hear anything he was saying.

Once I'd undressed carefully, I hung my dress back up in the closet. Slipping on a large T-shirt and nothing else, I puttered around. I was about to give up on him when a soft knock came at the door.

He didn't wait for me to answer this time but simply stepped inside. "I came by to tell you we need to leave earlier than planned tomorrow for Charlotte. I'd like to have the car pick us up by noon instead of two o'clock."

I wanted to point out that he could've sent me an email, but calling him out for his excuse to see me seemed counterproductive.

"Okay, I'll call Maria and the car service."

"Another oversized T-shirt for bed?" he teased.

Already on hold with the phone to my ear, I lifted my shirt up slightly, revealing there was nothing on underneath. I got the satisfaction I was after with his intake of breath. "Not so unsexy now, is it?"

Giving me a wicked smile, he lifted me onto the countertop

and inched my shirt up to my waist. “Sexiest shirt ever,” he muttered, diving toward my center.

Maria came back on the line while I tried unsuccessfully to keep him from attaining his goal. “Uh-huh, no. That’s great, Maria. You’re the best. I— Oh, sorry, I stubbed my toe.”

His lips trailed kisses down the insides of my thighs.

“Got it. Let me call the car service for the airport pickup.” I hung up, and he grinned. “You’re naughty. I’m trying to get something done for my boss and—” My breath hissed when his finger dipped into my entrance.

“You were the one with no panties. Matter of fact, I think that you should go without them every night from now on.” He suckled my hypersensitive nub with his mouth.

I was about combust on the countertop. “Hmm, I’ll take that under advisement. Now, I have another call to make. Are you going to behave?”

He looked up at me with a wicked gleam in his eyes.

I couldn’t help laughing. “Give me five minutes.” I dialed the car company and gritted my teeth as he slipped his finger back inside of me. “Yes, we have a pickup that I need to change to noon tomorrow. For Joshua Singer.” Oh, Lord, he was moving his finger, and now there were two. “Yes, yes, sounds good. Thank you.” The last word was on a squeak as I disconnected and let him take me over the edge, shamelessly right there on my countertop.

“Come here.” He lifted me, and I wrapped my legs around him. Once we were settled like that, he moved me toward the bed and set me down on the edge of it. There, he slipped my shirt over my head and ran his hands down my entire length.

After stripping him of his polo shirt, I made quick work of his belt and zipper and pulled his erection free. “Ahhh…” I closed both hands around him and enjoyed it when he threw his head back in pleasure.

He stepped away from my reach and kicked off his pants and

boxers. He grinned at himself in his white socks. "Sorry, but there's no way I can do this with just these on."

Laughing at the picture he made, I helped him lose the socks before he followed me down onto the bed.

He kissed me deeply while my hands reached between us and found his arousal again. "I can't seem to get enough of you, Haylee."

His honey voice saying my name had me shivering. I gasped when his fingers parted me and he spread my wetness lower. "Easy now, not tonight. We need to break you in slowly." He slipped a finger in a place I never dreamed I'd find pleasure. In and out, spreading my liquid desire back further as his eyes locked on mine. "Tell me you want it here."

"I—"

He must've sensed my embarrassment. "It's only us, and you just have to ask yourself if it feels good. It's okay to tell me. I want to have you everywhere, but only if you like it."

Nodding, I swallowed hard. "I like it."

He flipped me so that I was now on top of him and lowered me onto his burgeoning erection. "You feel so tight, so unbelievably wet. Ride me, gorgeous."

I started to move and felt his fingers dance over my backside again and massage me there.

"That's it, I'm going to fill you completely." He tormented me by inserting his finger.

I felt myself in a frenzy of absolute overstimulation and came harder and faster than ever before while he thrust up and found release of his own.

After tucking me in beside him, he turned off the side lamp and then brought the comforter up to cover us.

I reached over to set my alarm before I forgot and then burrowed back into his arms.

"You undo me," he confided.

Playing with his strong hands, I traced the lines. "How so?"

"You're so trusting of me with your body and then honor me with such pure and unfiltered pleasure. It's a potent thing."

"You make me feel safe enough to trust you that way."

His kisses floated down my neck, and then his hands skimmed down the length of my legs as if he couldn't touch me enough. "I interrupted you when you were telling me that today was your mom's birthday."

The bubble of mindless post-sex bliss popped. I exhaled heavily. "Yeah, it's a silly thing, but my mother liked to dress up and have champagne on her birthdays. So my aunt and I did that today via FaceTime, which is thanks to the new iPad."

"Where does your aunt live?"

"She and my Uncle Paul live in Perth, Australia. They own a fabulous restaurant there, or at least so I hear as my uncle is the chef."

"You should go someday to visit."

"I was thinking of taking a few weeks before starting law school, actually. It's tough for them to get away in that kind of business and I don't know when I'd get another opportunity once I'm back in student mode."

"I think it's nice that you do these things for your mom."

Sighing, I figured I'd keep quiet. Voicing my thoughts made me feel guilty.

"What?" he asked.

"Nothing. It's what she would've wanted." I hoped he'd leave it alone.

"And what about what you want?"

I fought my irritation. "I want to honor her. Besides, it was nice talking with my Aunt J. It made my mother happy to know that we'd do this every year."

He seemed to absorb this. "So dressing up and drinking champagne today was at your mother's request?"

"She had this thing about birthdays and special events she was going to miss, so she planned out a lot of things. I think I told you about the bucket list. I also have a card for every one of my next forty birthdays."

"Wait. She wrote you out forty birthday cards?"

"Yeah, she detailed out all of the major holidays and events. I have a letter for my wedding, for my firstborn, and so forth. She wanted to make sure she was a part of it, I guess."

"I see," he murmured.

I turned toward him, knowing he wanted to say more. "What?"

He looked thoughtful and then spoke with measured words. "I think it's wonderful that you have something to remember your mom by, but I wonder if, for instance, on your birthday, knowing you'll open that card and be sad as a result might make it tough."

In one sentence he had managed to sum up everything I'd been feeling. "I'd feel so guilty not to. I promised her, and sometimes I love that I will be able to read what she wrote and recognize that she was thinking of me. But then other times I get overwhelmed because I know it's coming."

He stroked my face. "Can I offer some advice?"

I nodded while fighting my tears.

"Nothing says it has to be done on that day. If you're dreading the happy occasion on which she wanted you to think of her, then what's the point? Instead, maybe read it when you're ready. If it's close to Christmas, maybe you open the card for it on the twenty-third instead, for example. Then you can spend Christmas knowing how she felt but not anticipating the pain of reading the letter. Or open it after the holiday. The point is I think you should pick when you want to have those moments instead of letting the calendar dictate them."

I really liked his idea. "Maybe. I realize she never intended these letters to make me sad. She wanted me to know that she was thinking of me, it made her feel at peace that I would have a part of her this way."

"I think you're right. But, Haylee, it's only been a matter of months. The pain is fresh. Until it dulls, you need to do what you can for you. She would want that."

"Thank you," I whispered, drying my eyes.

He kissed my nose. "When my dad died ten years ago, I felt so cheated that it was sudden. I kept thinking, if only I'd had more time or known it was coming. If only he'd imparted more wisdom to me, it would hurt less. But turns out, it doesn't. I see you honoring your mom, and her death still hurts you. It still robbed you of time with her."

"How did your father die?"

"Massive heart attack on his second day of vacation. Go figure."

"I'm sorry. It's never easy. How's your mom?"

"I'd say she's resilient. Even if she wasn't, she would still make me think she was. So where in this plan of your mother's did you go to law school and become a prominent lawyer?"

"Ha, you're very perceptive."

He smiled, and I enjoyed being able to share this with him.

"My mom had a lot of amazing qualities, but believing in equality for women and wanting me to be independent and successful weren't on the list. In her mind, I should instead be looking for a man to take care of me. Luckily, she didn't fight me on Stanford. Where better to meet a successful man than a top-rated college? But law school? Oh, man, did she not want me to go. In her old-fashioned world view, the man was supposed to be the lawyer. My role would be as a dutiful, supportive wife."

"Ah, so law school is from your father?"

"Absolutely. He used to say it was our little secret, but his little girl would never be some man's arm candy."

"Good thing I admire your brain," he quipped, running his hand over my ass. "So your mom wanted you to be a housewife, cooking and cleaning and taking care of your husband?"

"Oh, my God, no. I was to be a proper Southern wife, which

meant no cooking or cleaning but coordinating the people who did. My talents would be concentrated on throwing beautiful parties, catered of course, looking poised and perfect in designer clothing, and exercising social responsibility. A proper Southern woman knows how to smile her way out of the rudest of situations and say 'bless her heart' to anyone, the perfect passive-aggressive comment." I ended in a Southern accent.

"Well, you'll probably love North Carolina then. There's definitely that Southern thing there," he chuckled.

I sighed, enjoying this conversation but feeling slightly remorseful. "I didn't mean to paint my mom in such a terrible light. All that said, she was a wonderful mother. I never had a nanny, my parents seldom went away without me, and I went to bed every night knowing that I was loved. My mom was the yang to my dad's yin, and I got the best of both of them." My eyes were starting to get heavy.

"I think you may be the yang to my yin," Josh said on a whisper.

CHAPTER TEN

Once a year Gamble Advertising held a meeting for the vice presidents at the headquarters office in Charlotte, North Carolina. For a week, all of the VPs around the country came in for strategy sessions regarding ad campaigns and networking. We took the short trip down on Sunday afternoon in preparation for the Monday start.

Everyone was staying at the Marriott hotel close to the office with the exception of Josh, who owned a house fifteen minutes south of the city. I was disappointed to drop him at his front door without receiving an invitation inside, but why should this house be any different from his home in New York? Clearly both were off limits. At least the time saved would give me an opportunity to get checked in and go for a run in the hotel gym. I hadn't run in weeks and knew the longer I went without, the harder it would be to get back into it.

I was three miles in on the hotel treadmill with my iPod's workout play list blaring in my ears when a good-looking executive type walked into the gym and gave me an assessing glance. Since I was at a full sprint in nothing but a sports bra and running shorts, he was getting quite the view. With my luck, he was one of the Gamble VPs.

I took a headphone out of the ear closest to him when I realized he was trying to talk to me from the next treadmill over.

"Uh, sorry, I just said you're kind of putting me to shame. Maybe you should slow down," he joked.

"Five more minutes, and your ego will be safe again." I smiled and put my headphones back in.

After completing my remaining time, I slowed the machine down and wiped my face before taking out my earbuds.

"My ego thanks you," he quipped with an easy grin. He was tall and handsome in a classic, boy-next-door way. On top of that, he had a great smile.

I laughed in good humor.

"I'm Brian, by the way."

There were two men on the VP list with that name. One was Brian, the regional vice president from Charlotte, and the other was Bryan, the new VP out of the Dallas office. "Nice to meet you. I'm Haylee."

His eyes widened in recognition. "Haylee Holloway, as in the assistant to Josh Singer?"

Frowning internally at the way he asked, I managed a smile. "Yeah, not exactly the way I wanted to meet any of the VPs this week." I slowed the treadmill way down and threw on my shirt.

His smile widened. "Come on. If you had been down here with full makeup on, barely walking, I might have a low opinion. But the way you're running and, no offense, but like, really sweating, I have nothing but respect."

I had to grin at that. "So are you Brian with an I from Charlotte or Bryan with a Y from Dallas?"

"I'm Brian with an I from Charlotte."

"Ah, nice to meet you, then, Brian with an I." I stopped the treadmill.

Surprisingly, he stopped his and took my hand warmly. "Nice to meet you, Haylee with double Es, right?"

Laughing, I nodded. It was curious that he knew that I spelled my name that way, but maybe he'd seen it on an agenda or something.

"So I have a dinner tonight, but tell me you'll be at the bar when I get back?"

This was dangerous territory. Even if I wasn't involved with Josh, I didn't want to start something with someone I worked with. Yeah, I was a big ol' hypocrite.

"For what?" I'm sure I would be in the lobby, but didn't want him to think it would be because of him.

He gave me a smile. "I'm traveling to Hong Kong directly after this meeting to take stock of the new company, so I'd love to pick your brain. Maybe you can teach me Cantonese."

The surprise that he knew about that lowered my guard a little as did his business reasoning. "Sure, we can talk Hong Kong if you're back early enough from dinner because I'm not someone who stays up late."

"I'll eat fast and skip dessert."

"See ya, Brian with an I."

"Bye, Haylee with two Es."

THE HOTEL LOUNGE was made up of several tables and with a large bar area. My eyes surveyed the room. Among a few faces I didn't know, I spotted Warren.

"Haylee, how nice to see you." He gave me an awkward half hug and then introduced me to the other two men at his table. "This is Bryan Foster from the Dallas office and John Warner from Chicago. Gentlemen, this is Haylee Holloway, my former assistant and now Josh's."

Both men were attractive and well-groomed, and we exchanged pleasantries.

"Where's Josh?" Warren queried, looking around.

"He had a dinner engagement. I'm not sure if he's coming back here afterwards or not."

"We finished our dinner early, but I'm sure everyone will be congregating soon. The hotel bar becomes the most happening place all week. Why don't you pull up a chair?"

I was about to make my excuses when I heard the voice of Brian with an I behind me.

"Oh, good, Haylee, you're still here. Warren, nice to see you. Hey, John," he greeted, shaking hands all around. "Sasha was just around here. Oh, there she is with Josh."

I watched Josh and a fashionable woman in her thirties walk into the bar and approach us. Though I'd never met her, I knew Sasha was from the New York office. She was simply stunning. Black, shiny hair cut into a chic bob, artfully done makeup, and designer clothing—she was as put together as it got, New York uptown style. I appreciated her nicely tailored black pant suit and gorgeous, four-inch killer heels. Her lips would give Angelina a run for her money.

Everything about her looked professional. She exuded a combination of sex appeal, confidence, and professionalism that, on my best day, I would never have been able to pull off.

One glance told me she hardly gave me a thought at all.

Brian did the honors of introducing us. "I don't think you've met Sasha Brooks. She's the vice president of our New York advertising branch. Sasha, this is Haylee Holloway, Josh's new assistant and the kind of girl who puts a man to shame on a treadmill."

Blushing, I noticed that both she and Josh narrowed their eyes at Brian's remark, probably wondering where it had come from.

Sasha's smile didn't meet her eyes when I shook her hand. I

imagined there were very few who got the privilege of a true smile from her, and Brian's comment hadn't helped. *Thanks a lot, Brian with an I.* Just what I needed.

Sighing, I made small talk with everyone and finally excused myself. I was eager to head back to my hotel room and get some sleep for the next day.

Josh had barely looked in my direction. Considering he hadn't tried to contact me, it was safe to assume he was annoyed. Shrugging it off since I hadn't done a thing wrong, I fell asleep wondering what tomorrow would hold.

THE NEXT MORNING WAS HECTIC, getting the breakfast caterers in and setting everything up for the meetings.

Juliette, the office manager in Charlotte, was a few years older than me and full of energy. She knew absolutely everything about everyone in the company, as she had worked here for the last eight years. When she showed me pictures of her adorable infant son, it was hard to believe she'd just had a baby as her figure was so petite.

She and I decided we would switch off taking notes in the meetings. Thankfully, she volunteered to go first. That way I could use her format and get a sense of what would be expected when it was my turn in the afternoon.

After Josh went into the first meeting with barely a glance at me, I made myself comfortable in his spacious office. I finished up a conversation with Nigel and then called Maria to finalize our London plans.

That's when Josh walked in, looking surprised to see me.

Finishing my call, I hung up the phone. "Sorry to take over your space. I thought you were in meetings until lunch, so I was making some calls."

He stopped and stood there, staring at me.

"I'll leave." I started gathering my stuff.

He moved toward me. "No, you don't need to. I'm only here now because what's the point of being the boss if you can't walk out of a meeting every now and again?"

"Good point."

He wrestled with what to say. "I was caught off guard last night at dinner when Brian asked to take you to Hong Kong. I got the distinct impression his request involved more than your administrative skills."

I instantly bristled. "Well, how about the fact that I can speak fluent Cantonese? Maybe he could want me for that skill set."

He crossed over to the window and closed the blinds, all the while never taking his eyes off me.

I swallowed hard. This one act of his was turning me on. It was like he was setting the stage.

"Considering his comment about your running, I highly doubt that was the only reason."

I could only sigh in frustration. "First of all, I was only working out. He was funny. I laughed. He mentioned Hong Kong and that he knew I could speak the language. That was it."

"I've known Brian for a lot of years. At dinner he was pumping me for information about you." He crossed back to his door and locked it.

"So, what did you say about me traveling to Hong Kong with him?" I honestly didn't care to go, but it pissed me off that I was being judged for merely running on a treadmill.

He crossed toward me. Once again, his dark green eyes never left my face. "I told him that I needed you with me."

"Oh," I managed.

He touched my cheek. "Did you want me to tell him that he could take you to Hong Kong, Haylee?" He got me right in my sweet spot with the way he said my name.

I shook my head.

"Not even a little bit?" he teased. "Brian is a good-looking, successful guy: never married, no kids, decent, fun. So what's the problem?"

I chose to leave him unsatisfied with my answer. "Geography, for one." I lifted my chin in defiance.

His eyes darkened. "Cute. Now tell me why you don't want Brian."

I wasn't budging. "Why don't you tell me why you don't want me to go to Hong Kong with him first?"

His eyes, now the color of jade, searched my face. "Because I'm not interested in sharing you."

This is what I'd needed to hear from him. But I forgot all about words when he crushed his mouth to mine. His tongue swept out, tasted mine, and his arousal pressed up against my center. I wanted him right here and now in the office.

"I have to get back in there," he murmured, regretfully pulling away.

I kissed his sensuous lips again, enjoying the moment. "Okay, so no more jealousy?"

He stiffened at my question and then looked resigned. "I don't like to think I'm the jealous type, but evidently I'm exhibiting the symptoms with you."

I stroked his face and kissed him again.

"Tell me something before I have to go," he entreated softly.

I smiled at his remembrance of my game. "I would never make you jealous on purpose. It's not a game I like to play or enjoy being on the other side of. I do recognize that I'm really friendly and somewhat flirtatious. But understand that's simply a natural ease I have with most people. It's nothing I'm trying to do for a reaction or attention. Now, your turn."

"I'm naturally an introvert. However, in my position I constantly have to be an extrovert. Sometimes I come across as intense or difficult to read. In fact, I'm simply uncomfortable in social situations."

I'd guessed that might be the case a couple of times, but it was something to hear his admission.

With one more kiss, he reluctantly left me.

I wished we'd had time for more.

"HAYLEE, they want you in the large conference room pronto. Sorry," Juliette said, coming into the small conference room where I was setting up lunch.

I walked in to the large room and found all eyes on me.

Warren was up front with three big easels. "Haylee, come on in," he said with a smile.

A brief look toward Josh revealed nothing. I glanced around the room, but apparently everyone was waiting on Warren to speak.

"So, you may have all heard about what happened four weeks ago. We had a major almost-catastrophe with the Cassius Rum campaign when Katrina Tross decided not to honor her contract. Like a champ, Haylee stepped in at the last minute and was lucky enough to play model for a day."

I resented the tone in which he was portraying how fortunate I'd been but then was completely floored when he turned each of the boards on the easels around.

They all showed me. Me in the bar, me at the pool, and me in the lounge. Only it wasn't me. At least, it didn't look like the me I knew. Instead, it looked like a real, honest-to-goodness, sexy, glossy magazine model.

I could only stand there, blushing.

"I think I speak for Warren and for Cassius Rum when I say you saved the day quite literally. The client couldn't be happier with these shots. They chose these three to go into this month's Glamour, Maxim, Cosmo Life, and Vogue magazines," Josh interjected, far more complimentary than my former boss had been.

I swallowed hard and then moved closer to the pictures. "I, um, I was happy to help. Thank you for this."

Everyone clapped and then congratulated me in the surreal moment.

"Cassius Rum is asking if you'd be available to do another shoot this spring for their summer campaign. They're also talking about some possible appearances in Vegas," Warren informed me.

"Uh, yes, of course. I mean, I'll have to work it out with my job schedule, but I'd be honored." I sincerely meant it. It was flattering that the client hadn't pitched a fit, having been promised a supermodel and ending up with a size six administrative assistant still red from a bikini wax.

"I don't think Josh will have a problem with your work schedule when it comes to making a client happy. In fact, we could do a backstory about your being an assistant and then stepping in last minute. The girl next door becomes an overnight model," Warren proposed.

I wasn't sure I could form words and looked toward Josh, who was no help. I swallowed hard. "Do you think I could speak with you for a moment alone, Warren?"

"Yes, certainly."

We made our way outside the conference room into the hall. Relieved that Josh came out, too, I faced my former boss.

"Um, I really appreciate the opportunity, but I don't want that kind of publicity."

He looked completely taken aback. "But this could launch you into a full-blown modeling career."

I didn't want to offend him. "And I appreciate that you would do that for me. I truly do, but I'm attending law school next year. Although I'm thankful for any opportunity to do modeling on the side in order to help fund that dream, I don't desire an actual career of it."

He glanced toward Josh and then back at me. "All right. My client will be happy that you're willing to do their summer campaign. The pictures are yours, by the way. Take them home, frame them."

I smiled, happy that he understood. "Thanks, for everything, Warren. I can't tell you how much it means that you would give me this opportunity. Truly."

He seemed appeased and gave me an awkward pat on the arm. "Of course, kiddo."

I watched him walk back into the large conference room. Rooted to the spot, I was still trying to take it all in.

"Are you okay?" Josh inquired.

Nodding, I sighed. "I think so."

"I can have those pictures framed for your apartment."

I looked at him, focusing back on reality. "I really don't want them. Maybe smaller ones, but those—Those are just too much. I mean, to have pictures that big of myself on my wall is kind of weird."

Throwing his head back, he laughed. "You never cease to surprise me."

Was that a compliment? I didn't have a chance to figure it out as Brian interrupted.

Making my escape, I gathered my poster-sized photos and put them in Josh's office. The last thing I needed was to be on display in the meeting room for the rest of the afternoon.

LATER THAT DAY, after only taking notes for an hour, a few things became apparent to me during the meeting of Gamble VPs. Warren was the senior man who made his opinion known whether it was asked for or not. Josh tended to sit back and take it all in, only commenting when necessary—which ensured that everyone listened to what he had to say. And lastly, everyone talked over or dismissed the one woman in the room, Sasha.

"All right, moving to Sasha and Delayne Diamonds," Brian started out with the next agenda item. "They were very unhappy with the last campaign they ran with our competitor. Obviously, they're looking for something different from us. What do you have, Sasha?"

Giving Brian a smile, she started out, "I was thinking we might focus on their vintage line, a black-and-white throwback."

She definitely had my attention with the word vintage.

Warren spoke over her. "How would you do black and white when diamonds are white?"

"Well, I was thinking of muted colors, but—"

"I think it goes without saying that we need a big splash on this one. Show Delayne they made the correct move coming to us," Warren interrupted.

I watched her swallow and could feel the tangible tension when she tried to continue. "We could do an engagement or wedding focus with the vintage spin…"

Everyone shook their heads and looked unimpressed. I watched her confidence strip away with one comment after another.

"Isn't their vintage line the least profitable part of their business? I don't think they'd want to put their ad campaign dollars towards something with such a small niche," John from Chicago pitched in.

"Plus engagement and wedding would need to be done in time for the holidays which would prove impossible at this point. For some odd reason, Christmas and New Years are big engagement holidays," Warren remarked.

Brian then spoke, clearly taking control of the situation and, in my mind, protecting Sasha from any more of Warren's comments. "I think that we should do a smaller breakout session tomorrow and discuss some possible new options for diamonds."

Sasha appeared to be biting her tongue, and I felt some sympathy for her. She continued on, however, discussing her other clients as though she hadn't been grilled. Her ability to shake it off was impressive.

LATER, while Juliette briefed everyone else on the plans for the evening, I excused myself to go to the ladies' room and walked in on Sasha dabbing her eyes.

She immediately tried to recover when she realized I was there, but I knew without a doubt she'd been crying. She gave me a brief nod and then went about washing her hands.

I contemplated what to say. "For what it's worth, I absolutely loved the vintage idea."

She turned to look at me and sighed.

Just in case, I prepared myself for a tell off.

"Thanks, Haylee. Now back to the wolves." Resignedly, she turned and made her way out.

No matter how tough she might appear, I recognized she wasn't above being affected by the criticism.

CHAPTER ELEVEN

After returning from Charlotte on Thursday, I spent Saturday evening packing for our trip to London. Josh had been right about travel getting old quickly. It had been nice to be back in New York, though, at least for the weekend. After hitting the Statue of Liberty as well as the Empire State building, I'd finished this afternoon with a half-price Broadway show. I wanted to make sure I took advantage of my time in the city.

I was becoming more efficient with my packing as I had the list down pat. There was an exception to the usual items this time, however. I was bringing one of my formal gowns for an art gala on Monday evening. It would be nice finally to have an occasion to wear one.

The six-hour flight to London felt a whole lot easier than the much longer flight to Asia. Josh worked for the first couple of hours and then shut it down and glanced over at me. "What are you doing?"

I was typing away on my laptop. "Finishing my personal statement for law school. I need to have everything submitted next week."

"That's good. Obviously, you're prepared."

I smiled. "Being prepared is the only way I know how to relax. I know that sounds strange."

"It doesn't. Actually, it speaks to me as I'm much the same way."

I saved my document and turned toward him. "Did you read ahead in school?"

He nodded. "I did. My friends used to make fun of me, but I was always worried about being behind—which was really about not being ahead."

I couldn't help laughing. "I was the same. Tell me something, something about you in college. What were you like?"

"Undergrad or MBA?"

"Let's start with undergrad. I want to know about eighteen-year-old Josh."

He gave me a wry smile. "I was entitled, like a lot of freshmen at Harvard, I guess. My dad was an alumnus, we had money, and I was known. I went there with my best friend from childhood. He was much more extroverted than I was, had charisma in spades. I was the one who made sure he studied. I suppose that's what made us a good team."

"Are you still friends?"

"Yes, you know him. Brian Carpenter, your biggest treadmill fan, is my childhood friend. We grew up next door to one another, went to Harvard together, and met Mark there freshman year."

I was shocked. "Mark-the-attorney Mark?"

"One and the same."

"Wow. Well, that's wonderful you have such good friends." And a little strange that he would be jealous of Brian, considering their long history.

"I told you, I have a hard time with trust. I keep the people that I can confide in closest to me, and it's served me well. Mark and Brian are two of the best people I know."

"I can see that. So no big-time parties, fraternities, girls?" I teased.

He shook his head. "Not really. My father was adamant about no fraternity, so we spent the first year in the dorms. But the three of us rented an apartment by sophomore year. Mark met someone junior year who he was serious about, so it was mainly Brian and I. We all finished up Harvard together. Brian and I stayed there for our MBA while Mark went on to law school at Yale. So now it's your turn. What was Haylee like in college?" He wriggled his brows as if to suggest I had some seedy secrets.

Laughing, I marveled at this rare side of him. "Sorry, there isn't much to tell. My mom was there with me, and we shared an apartment. Studying was my escape when I sat through her chemo appointments. I had a notion junior year that I'd go out and try the party scene because I was tired of missing out. So I went to a fraternity party and drank too much. That's where I met the douchebag I told you about. The episode didn't exactly inspire me to go out anymore."

"Any good friends?"

"I wish I could say yes, but my priority over the last few years hasn't been forming or maintaining friendships." Matter of fact, I'd yet to call my former roommate, Angela, to let her know how the move and new job were turning out.

"But you're so outgoing."

I smiled. "I am, but I didn't click with fellow students. They were all so carefree, talking about what they were going to do on Friday night, while there I was without a dad and about to lose my mom. I spent a lot of time in hospitals, though, and got to know a lot of the staff and many other patients. I guess the whole thing gave me a sense that there's no permanence in relationships. People in high school went off to their separate colleges. Individuals in college went on to their careers or more school. People in the hospital went back home or, unfortunately, they died. I've learned it's easier not to get attached. But then I hear about how you and Brian and Mark have been best friends for years. I'm envious of that type of long-term relationship."

He reached over and took my hand. In that moment he didn't seem to care who saw it. "I'm impressed that you could keep your focus on school. A lot of people wouldn't have been able to. A 4.0 at Stanford is commendable, especially given what you were going through."

"Thank you. Now enough of the sad talk. I wish I had better stories to tell you, but maybe I can make up for it in law school. I have a feeling you have plenty that you aren't telling me. Perhaps I can get them from Mark or Brian?"

He smiled, and we went on talking about a lot of things, ranging from where we grew up to our favorite movies and things to do. It made the flight go by quickly, but more important, it made me appreciate how much I enjoyed talking with Josh and getting to know him. Even if I didn't believe in any relationship actually lasting, it was still important to feel a connection in the moment.

I COULD HARDLY CONTAIN my enthusiasm when we traveled into London from the airport, and I got my first glimpse of Big Ben. When I found Josh's eyes on me, I gave him a smile. "All this history in a modern city is amazing."

He returned my smile and hooked my pinky. It seemed to be our car ritual. The simple gesture made me flush with pleasure.

We traveled to the hotel, which was in the financial district of London. My breath stuttered when I caught sight of the classical architecture. "Even the hotel is amazing."

The driver opened up my door, and we walked into the lobby of the Chancery Court Hotel. The entrance smelled like Japanese cherry trees and looked like a London postcard, with high ceilings and large flower arrangements. It was classy and elegant, and I instantly loved everything about it. I checked us in and smiled at the British woman behind the counter with her sophisticated accent.

As we made our way to the elevators, I glanced down at the room numbers and realized we were next to each other. "There must be a mistake. They have me booked next to you in another suite." I was about to step off the elevator and go back to the front desk.

Josh's hand took my arm, pulling me back in. "It's not a mistake. I asked Maria to ensure we had adjoining rooms, explaining that I needed you close by."

I was speechless for a moment. Then on the top floor, we got off the elevator and walked down the hall to our respective rooms.

After stepping into my lovely suite, I smiled at the spacious room, complete with a sitting area and a large bathroom. I unpacked my evening dress and hung it up, then did the same with my suits for the week. Exhaustion had started to set in with all of the travel and once again, I wondered how Josh managed it.

A soft knock camenot from the main door but from the one on the side. Ah, right, the adjoining rooms. Opening the door, I smiled at Josh standing there.

When he saw my face, he frowned. "You're tired. You should get some sleep."

I imagined I had dark circles under my eyes, and I didn't bother to stifle my yawn. "It's not even nine o'clock, but I feel like I could probably crash."

He gave me a quick kiss and stroked my cheek. "I'll see you in the morning." He closed the door halfway, allowing me some privacy.

I WOKE UP AFTER MIDNIGHT, London time, and saw light coming under the shared door to Josh's room. After quickly brushing my teeth and ensuring my hair wasn't sticking up all over, I padded quietly over to the adjoining door and opened it slightly.

He was propped up in bed with reading glasses on, working on his laptop. He was the absolute epitome of sexy, I thought, smiling.

He looked up and met my eyes. "Hey, you. Feeling better?"

I nodded and climbed up onto the end of the bed, enjoying the way his brows raised in surprise. The surprise turned into a smile when I crawled up and straddled his hips. After removing his reading glasses and putting the laptop aside, my hands skimmed over his chest. "Hi," I breathed.

"Hi, yourself. I guess someone got a power nap." He rubbed my back.

I bit my lip and put my hands on his bare chest. "You are so sexy like this."

Doubt was reflected in his gaze. "With my reading glasses and a laptop?"

"Mm hmm." I dipped my lips to his neck where I worked little kisses and nibbles back up toward his delectable mouth. I could feel his hands moving down my hips and then cupping my backside. I shimmied down the length of his body so that I could move the sheet to expose him in nothing but boxers.

I felt him harden when I slipped my hands down to stroke his flesh. He felt like silk and grew larger as I moved my hands down the length of him.

His eyes focused on me. "Haylee," he whispered.

Simply saying my name had me completely undone. I ran my fingers over his taut abs and traced the vee down to his hips.

"Tell me something," he requested.

I gave him a sexy smile. "When you say my name like that it makes me instantly wet."

He smiled roguishly. "Haylee, Haylee, Haylee."

I couldn't help giggling. "Now tell me something," I returned, feeling his hands pull down my panties.

"I was thinking about you and selfishly wanting to crawl into that bed behind you and wake you up. Then you were here, so maybe I'm really asleep and dreaming."

That admission from him warmed me completely. I shifted so that he could get my thong off fully and then repaid the favor, sliding his boxers down his legs.

He helped me out of my shirt, and his hands were instantly on my breasts.

Hovering over his arousal, I positioned myself so that I could sheath him fully.

"Jesus, are sure you're ready?"

"Considering you've said my name now for a fifth time, yeah, I really am." I got the satisfaction of his groan when I placed his wide tip between the lips of my swollen sex, coating him in my slickness. His breaths turned shallow and fast when I lowered myself down. I enjoyed every inch as he filled me to the hilt.

"Ah, fuck, you're so sweet."

I loved the fact that I got to control the tempo and rode him up and down, relishing the pleasure that was so evident in his eyes. When his skilled fingers found my slick sex, I completely lost my ability to control things. I moved faster and faster, now frenzied with my climax about to hit and the fact that I could feel Josh getting close. As I exploded, I leaned down to whisper in his ear. "Come in me."

That turned out to be his undoing. A powerful shudder ran through him, and his climax rushed deep inside of me.

After collapsing onto his chest, I felt his lips on my neck. He withdrew slowly and rolled me onto my back, then gathered me close.

We lay like that for minutes or hours. I wasn't sure. But when

I realized I was about to fall asleep, I made myself get up, kissing his cheek before slipping out the side of the bed.

"Where are you going?" He pulled me back to him.

"To bed. I know you like your space—"

He snuggled me tight. "Stay. I like this."

My head was in the crook of his arm and our legs were entwined. I sighed at the delicious skin on skin contact. "How could I say no?"

I tried not to read too much into it, but it felt good to be held in his arms.

THE DAY in the London office was uneventful. Josh was pretty much in meeting after meeting all day. Unlike Hong Kong, however, every single person was nice to me. They were professional, and I enjoyed listening to their accents.

Josh had plans for a working lunch, so I was excited when two of the assistants took me down the street to a local pub for a meal. I ordered the bangers and mash and tried my best to pretend the food was good. In fact, it had sounded better than it actually was. The highlight was ordering a round of pints. It seemed socially acceptable to have one with lunch.

I was smiling on my way back into the office. Then I came face to face with Josh as I came off the elevator.

"Do you have a moment?" He looked at me strangely.

I bit my lip. Busted. "Yes, certainly."

We went into a vacant conference room, and I started to apologize. "I'm sorry. We only had the one beer, and it was nice. Everyone is just so kind, but the bangers and mash, not so great. I mean, I thought I'd like British food, but so far—" I was rambling and saw his lips twitch as he obviously tried not to smile.

"That's all very interesting, and I'm glad this trip is going much better for you than Hong Kong. But what I needed to see you about is the golf charity event in Miami. I found out there's a conflict with someone attending and need you to cancel my appearance. I'll keep the donation, however."

I wondered briefly if the conflict had anything to do with his ex-wife. "Oh, sorry. I thought maybe I was busted for the beer."

That amused him even further, and he shook his head. "No, the British are different from us about drinking during the day. I'm glad you got out. Plus, I have to say you're kind of adorable once you've had a drink."

"Because I ramble?"

He nodded and gave me one of his small smiles. "I should be done at the office about five o'clock, then we can head back to the hotel. The gala starts at six. I don't plan on staying long, only an hour or so."

For the gala I dressed in my mother's vintage Jean Desses dress. Aside from her wedding gown, it was my favorite piece. The layers were flattering, and the look was soft in a beautiful, bubblegum pink color. Because it was strapless and had a stunning bust line, it didn't require a necklace.

I let my hair down and spent some time with a curling iron, putting in nice chunky curls. Then I did up my eyes. Satisfied with the look, I was about to grab my clutch and head next door when Josh framed the connecting door in his tuxedo.

I felt a burn of desire flare up simply from watching him devour me with his eyes. His slow smile caused a flutter in my belly.

"What's that smile for?"

He offered his arm. "You said your father never wanted you to be arm candy, and yet here I am thinking you look like a delectable confection."

"Hmm, too bad I don't get to be *your* arm candy tonight." I knew that as soon as we got to the gala, we would need to separate and put back up the professional barrier.

"True, but I get to unwrap you later. Right, Haylee?" His voice went an octave lower.

I stepped closer and straightened his tie. "You said my name on purpose, didn't you?"

He gave me a contagious grin. "Maybe I like knowing how that affects you, Haylee."

Damn. I probably should've kept that tidbit to myself. Closing my eyes, I breathed in the scent of him. When I opened them again, I could see his clouded with desire.

"I guess since you know how it affects me, you now have to think about that all night."

Bingo. I saw a shudder go through him. "Fair point. Let's go so we can get back here as quickly as possible."

I definitely liked that idea. I kept it in mind as he led me out to the car and we drove to the art gala a few blocks away.

UPON ENTERING THE ART MUSEUM, I was glad I'd decided on such a formal gown as there were diamonds and furs all around me. A waiter came by with a glass of champagne which I gladly accepted.

I gave a small smile to Josh, who appeared hesitant to leave my side. "It's okay. Just text me when you're ready to go."

He looked relieved that I wasn't feeling abandoned and sauntered off toward a group of gentlemen, all of whom seemed to recognize him.

After an hour of smiling my way through the crowd and scanning the art around the room, I made my way to the ladies' room. Cursing my luck, I saw I'd started my period. Worse yet, at a party in London and wearing a formal dress, I was without a freaking tampon.

"Terrific," I muttered. Wadding up some tissue, I came out of the stall and searched around the ornate bathroom for a dispenser. Beautiful paper adorned the walls and a chandelier hung in the middle of the posh sitting room, but I couldn't locate a dispenser. There was nothing near the door or on the far wall. What was it with the British?

Sighing, I didn't grasp I had an audience until I turned and saw a beautiful woman watching me with one eyebrow arched and her expression amused.

"Please tell me the party isn't so bad that you're looking for an escape window?"

I couldn't help laughing. Her accent told me that she was American, too. "No, no. I was looking for a dispenser."

She was gorgeous, with her blond hair in a sleek chignon and a beautiful red dress which accentuated a small waist and an impressive tall, willowy figure.

"Condoms or tampons? Which I guess is kind of personal, considering I'll know how you'll be spending your evening." She laughed.

I chuckled, too. "Tampons, unfortunately."

"Well, that I can help you with. Here." She opened her clutch and offered me one.

"You're a lifesaver. I really can't thank you enough. Um, I'm Haylee. I figure the least I can do is introduce myself after this personal conversation."

"I'm Catherine, and it's a pleasure. Another American at a stuffy party across the pond is always a good sign."

I excused myself to go back into the stall and was pleased that she hadn't left when I came out to wash my hands.

"I'm not trying to be fresh as I check out your dress, but it looks a lot like a Jean Desses design."

I instantly beamed. Not many people knew vintage fashion. “It is a Jean Desses. I’m impressed you know that.”

“It’s gorgeous, and I should know that as I’m in fashion. I especially love vintage designers.”

It was as if we were destined to become friends. “Well, in that case I should tell you that I have a green one at home and a whole wardrobe of vintage 1950-1960s clothes.”

She looked genuinely interested. “I think we should take this out to one of the tables as I’m intrigued. Which designers do you have?”

We walked out of the ladies’ room and over to a nearby table. On the way she snagged a glass of champagne.

“I don’t want to keep you from any mingling if you need to…” I hesitated, suddenly self-conscious because Catherine was put together and poised. And if she was in the fashion industry, time was probably valuable to her at functions like this.

But she waved a hand. “Please. I only came because I was in town for business. It was this or spending the night alone in my hotel room. And, well, I love dressing up.”

I studied her dress and its lines and the fact that she wore it impeccably. “Calvin Klein?”

She smiled. “Nice eye. It is Calvin Klein. God, I should hire you away from whoever you work for now. So tell me more about your collection.” She was sincere, down to earth, and a fresh breath of air compared to the kind of people I had expected to meet at a party like this.

“Well, I have several Chanel, Oleg Cassini, and Givenchy pieces. And then I have a few YSL, Pucci, Halston, DVF, and Ralph Lauren. Let’s see, what else... Oh, Balenciaga, Valentino, and Tahari.”

She looked impressed. “You seem so young. How did you amass such a wardrobe?”

“They were my mother and grandmother’s dresses. My mother was obsessed with Jackie Kennedy and Audrey Hepburn.

She was the daughter of a governor in the South in the late 60s. She would love that I'm wearing the dresses and suits now for work and for parties like this."

Catherine's eyes suddenly looked sympathetic. "When did she pass?"

I sighed. She was very perceptive and easy to talk to. "Last year. Now that I'm working in New York, I finally have an occasion to wear a suit every day and use her purses and coats."

"I'm in New York, too. So tell me, what's your very favorite piece?"

That was an easy question. "The Valentino wedding dress. It's simply exquisite, the type of dress that makes you sigh."

"I'd love to see the collection—maybe what you think are the top ten pieces. For both personal and professional reasons, I'm truly interested. Maybe I could come by sometime? Not to invite myself, but I feel like I've found a kindred spirit. Plus, now that I'm divorced and out there dating again, I find that I need younger friends. The women in my age group are either married, divorced, busy with kids—or they're so embittered they don't want to go out at all. Jeez, I'm not coming off as too depressing and desperate, am I?"

I laughed and shook my head. "Not at all. As for coming by, well, I'm kind of crashing with friends currently. But I'd love to bring my dresses by your place. Anytime. As for the other, I don't know anyone in New York aside from my boss and a couple of my coworkers. They're all men, so it would be nice to have a female friend in the city."

"Here's my card."

I glanced at the title and was momentarily stunned. "Fashion Editor for Cosmo Life?"

She smiled. "I'm still thinking of stealing you away from your current job. Any interest in fashion?"

It was tempting. "I like what I'm doing, especially with the travel, and my boss has been great about helping me relocate to

New York. If I didn't have plans for law school next year, I would definitely be interested. I love fashion."

"Law school, wow. Well, then it works out better this way to be friends, don't you think?"

I'd completely lost track of Josh and the fact that he was probably looking for me by now. As if on cue, my eyes caught his across the room. I watched his approach and was ready to introduce him, only to see his surprised expression when he noticed Catherine.

She wore the same look of recognition. "Hi, Josh. I knew you were traveling but had no idea you were in London." Her eyes were wide and her face flushed. It was obvious she was interested in him. But then, how could a woman look at him and not be affected?

"Catherine, it's good to see you. I didn't know you were here, either." He kissed her cheek in a familiar way.

"I had a fashion show to attend. Then of course I came here because it was the hot ticket of the evening. We need to do dinner again soon and catch up. It's been a couple of weeks."

My stomach knotted at the thought that they had a personal relationship, but the truth was I liked Catherine too much to be jealous.

"Oh, my, where are my manners? Josh, this is Haylee. Haylee, this is Josh Singer, a friend from New York."

We both looked at her with surprise, and then Josh chuckled.

"Haylee is my assistant, Catherine. She's helping Nigel out as he's had to take some time off." He scratched his chin. "Uh, how's it that you two know each other?"

Now it was my turn to smile. "Ladies' room, actually."

Catherine laughed. "I'm trying to steal her away from you to come work for me. Obviously, I didn't know it was you she worked for. But anyone who knows fashion like she does should work in the industry."

He gave a slight smile. I couldn't tell if he was more uncomfortable with my job offer or with the fact that Catherine and I had become fast friends. "Well, she sort of does work in fashion, at least on the side. Haylee did the Cassius Rum shoot."

Her eyes widened, and she glanced back at me. "Oh, my goodness. I knew you looked familiar. Josh told me all about you stepping in for Katrina Tross. What a mess that could've been, but the spread turned out amazing. Matter of fact, it's in my magazine this month."

Another reminder that Catherine and Josh must speak with each other often. "Thank you. Bart Chesley was wonderful, and Mr. Singer was more than patient with my jitters."

She contemplated a moment, and then her face lit up. "Josh, I need her for an idea that's forming in my head. Haylee, I just had this vision of a vintage spread, and since they're your clothes and you're a model, it's fate. You have my card. I fully insist you call me next week. We'll put something together."

As evidenced by his expression, Josh was in the dark.

Catherine smiled. "You will let me borrow her, right?"

"Uh, yes. I guess I'm confused, though. What vintage spread?"

Catherine winked at me. "See, you work with a man who doesn't know fashion at all. I struck up a conversation with her because she's wearing a Jean Desses original gown. Then we got to talking about all of the designers she has in her collection, and I asked if she minded showing it to me. But now that I know she models too, we could talk about an actual spread."

I was unprepared for the disapproval I heard in Josh's tone. "I had no idea you had such an extensive designer wardrobe. Maybe you'd save more money for law school if so much didn't go toward your clothes."

My face burned with embarrassment. I was momentarily stunned to have him speak to me like that, especially in front of Catherine.

Luckily, she came to my defense. "Your collection is from your mother and grandmother, right?"

I could only nod, fighting the hurt that he could say something so rude and think so little of me. One look at my face, and he had to know how upset I was.

Catherine glanced between the both of us and sought to ease the strain. "Uh, I'm sure he didn't mean to assume…"

My temper ignited and I finally found my voice. "No need to apologize for him, Catherine. I'm quite used to not getting an apology from Mr. Singer. Perhaps if he'd ever seen my Old Navy jeans or my three-pack underwear from Sears he might not have made the same assumption."

I got the desired effect when Josh flushed.

I faced Catherine. "The highlight of my evening has definitely been meeting you. I'd be delighted to call you next week and look forward to showing you my favorite pieces, especially the beautiful wedding dress." For some reason, it gave me satisfaction to mention this particular garment in front of Josh.

She gave me a sincere smile. "It was my highlight, as well. Are you leaving?"

Josh found his voice. "I'll escort you back to the hotel."

I shook my head. "No, no, you two catch up. Like I told Mr. Singer earlier, I'm on my way from this event to visit with some friends I have here in London. I'll meet you in the lobby tomorrow morning, Mr. Singer."

I could see in his eyes that he knew I was lying, but there was no way I was giving him a chance to accompany me back to the hotel.

"Oh, good, sweetie. Go and have some fun. I forget that the night is probably young for you." She leaned in and gave me a hug. "I look forward to talking next week. It's been a pleasure."

I could tell she meant it, and I was grateful for the solidarity. I didn't bother to glance at Josh again. Instead, I quickly made a beeline for the exit.

I hurried back to the hotel and went straight up to my room. There I changed out of my gown and put on my Old Navy jeans, cursing Josh all over again for humiliating me with such a rude assumption. After pulling on a sweater and shoving on my boots, I went back down to the lobby, thankful that the front desk clerk could give me directions to the nearest late-night pharmacy.

RELIEF FLOODED me once I was on the busy sidewalk, mingling with the crowd and luckily not running into Josh. I'd feared he would take off after me, and I wasn't ready to speak with him. Of course, the fact that he was with Catherine didn't thrill me, either, but considering she had a lot more in common with him and lived in New York—Well, perhaps it was for the best. I wasn't typically insecure, but my emotions were heightened at the moment.

I stopped in the pharmacy and made short work of buying the essentials, which included chocolate. Tucking my purchases into my purse, I walked back toward the hotel. But since I wasn't yet ready to go back inside, I decided to stop in at the pub across the street. Happy that it wasn't insanely busy on a weeknight, I took a seat. Smiling at the bartender, I asked for a cider and had started to relax when I felt my phone vibrate.

"Hello."

"Where the hell are you?" Josh's voice was angry.

"Are you kidding me? That's the first thing you're going to say to me?"

"Haylee, you're trying my patience."

I looked at the phone as if I wanted to strangle it and promptly hung up. Asshole. Not my most mature moment, however, considering he was technically my boss and this was, in fact, a business trip.

The phone rang back, and I sighed. Maybe we could start this over. "Hello."

"If you hang up on me again—"

I cut him off. "Unless your next words are *I'm sorry,* I have nothing more to say to you."

"What in the hell was I supposed to think with your high-end clothes and a new outfit every damn day and then to hear that they were all designer—"

I hung up on him again. It felt good to switch off my phone entirely. I gulped down my cider, and the bartender poured me another one.

"On the house, love. That sounded brutal. My name is Greg."

"Nice to meet you, Greg." I smiled, and we spent the next hour laughing about some of the differences between American and English customs. I was in an exceptional fit of giggles over the word fanny, which meant something entirely different in London and was quite offensive—it described female genitalia—when I saw Josh walk in.

He was still dressed in his tux, but his tie was undone. He looked both pissed and sexy as hell.

"Uh, Greg, it was nice meeting you. Thank you for saving my night," I muttered, pulling out some bills to pay my tab.

He glanced toward Josh. "Boyfriend?"

"No. Worse, I'm afraid. He's my pissed-off boss." I smiled at Greg one last time and stepped around Josh and out the door.

He followed me, walking in silence next to me into the lobby of hotel.

The front desk clerk smiled. "Oh, good, you found her."

I gave her a tight smile, and we went up in the elevator in more silence.

He still hadn't spoken to me by the time we got up to our rooms, but the tension was palpable. I went through my door, closing it behind me, and then directly into my bathroom. I planned to take a quick shower and go to bed. If he wanted to ignore me the rest of the night, that suited me fine.

Unfortunately, it didn't appear I was getting such a reprieve. He strode into my room through the connecting door without even a knock.

"I am so pissed off, it's probably for the best if we don't speak tonight."

Then why was he coming into my room? "You're pissed off at me? You've got to be kidding. How hard is it to say you're fucking sorry, Josh?"

"I'm not the one who took off in a foreign city and then hung up on me twice. And what was with the bartender?"

I threw my hands up, not believing his audacity. "And what's with Catherine and you?"

That got my point across. I saw his jaw clench.

"I'm not playing tit for tat. You're at the bar picking up on men, and I'm out searching for you, having to ask the front desk where you went. By the way, why did you need a pharmacy?"

The change of subject took me completely off guard. "What?"

"The pharmacy. The clerk said you asked for directions. What did you need there?"

His gall knew no bounds. "You know what? I'm not sure what hurts most: the fact that you would honestly believe I'm squandering my money on designer clothes even after I told you I'm saving for law school, or that you would say something like that in front of someone I'd just met and respect, even if you for a moment thought it was true. You humiliated me, and then you add insult to injury by being pissed off at me because I needed a moment. I wasn't hitting on anyone tonight. I was only being friendly with the bartender. And now you're demanding to know what I purchased at a pharmacy. I can't even—"

"I'm sorry," he cut me off, saying it softly. "Oh, shit, Haylee. Please don't cry."

I wiped my eyes, knowing I was being overly emotional but unable to help it. I let him engulf me in a hug and sighed. "Why couldn't you have said that at the party? I don't understand it. You knew you were wrong, and yet you merely stood there."

"I know. The only defense I have is that Catherine would have seen through it. You were standing there hurt, and I wasn't sure how to apologize as a boss would to his employee. Hell, I don't know if I've ever had to apologize to someone I work with before, especially in front of an audience. I froze, knowing I was completely over the line. Then on the phone I was worried and pissed off, so I didn't say it. I told you I'm not good at them."

I sighed, realizing this was new territory for him. Josh Singer, multi-millionaire and my boss, probably wouldn't have commented to begin with, let alone have to say he was sorry. But it still smarted.

"Thank you for apologizing," I accepted quietly.

"Now, will you tell me what you needed at the pharmacy?" The man was like a dog with a bone.

"Tampons. Happy now?" I flushed three shades.

He made it worse with his next question. "You started your period tonight?"

"Ugh, yes, and I really don't want to discuss this at all."

He only chuckled. "I was married, so it's not like I'm unfamiliar with a woman's menstrual cycle. It doesn't embarrass me at all."

"Well, that makes one of us." My eyes focused on my feet.

He lifted my chin. "Haylee, it's natural."

I groaned, thinking this conversation was anything but natural and wanted to pull away, but he wouldn't let me.

"I want you to feel comfortable with me, even about this. How are you feeling? Are you cramping?"

"God, this is way too personal."

He dipped his head and kissed me. "I want to be personal with you."

I felt my stomach flutter at that statement.

"Come on, I'll draw you a bath."

I hesitated. "Josh, I don't—I mean I can't, you know, right now…"

"It's not all about the sex. Come on, let's get a bath started. My room has a huge soaking tub."

He took my hand and led me through his room and into his large bathroom. He started the water and put one of the towels on the warming rack. "Not sure how safe these things are, but I like the idea of one."

I liked the idea of a toasty towel as well and sighed at the sight of the large jetted tub. A warm bath would feel like heaven.

"Did you take anything: ibuprofen, Tylenol?"

"Uh, no. I didn't think to buy any, but I managed to grab chocolate."

He smiled and made short work of rounding up two pills and a glass of water for me. "Here, they will help you sleep better."

After undressing, I tossed them back and settled into the tub. My eyes opened when I heard the water splash.

He was getting in with me. "Scoot up so that I can get behind you."

I did as requested and then lay back on his chest.

"Catherine adored you. Must have been some ladies' room conversation." He soaped up my shoulders and massaged them.

"I genuinely liked her, too. She has an enthusiasm and sincerity that's refreshing."

He paused and then rubbed down my arms. "Funny, she said essentially the same thing about you. She's excited about having a twenty-something-year-old friend in the city."

I laughed. "Yeah, well I'm pretty boring, so if she's looking to party it up, she might be disappointed."

"Probably for the best. Her divorce has done a number on her self-esteem and the last thing she needs is to go wild and crazy.

She's a professional woman who needs to remember she could easily become Page Six news."

"So you guys are friends?"

He reached around and started washing my breasts. "Yes, we're friends."

I sensed that wasn't the whole story. "But she would like to be more?"

He sighed. "Yes, and I'm trying to be a good friend to her post-divorce. But she's panicked about being thirty-three-years old and now unmarried without kids."

"Did you know her ex-husband?"

His hands felt amazing as they made their way to my legs. "Yes, I knew him, not that we were friends. He's an executive with Morgan Stanley."

"What happened?"

"Her story to tell."

I should've expected that from him. "I just meant that she's beautiful, successful, fun, and—well, she's nice. It doesn't add up unless he was a complete asshole. Actually, it doesn't make sense why you're not interested in her."

"I would think it would be obvious. Marriage, kids—Plus, as much as I like Catherine, I've only ever thought of her as a friend."

"Looking at the two of you, it would be easy to imagine you together. You look like you'd fit as a couple."

His arms went around me. "I felt the same way when I saw you laughing tonight at the pub with that twenty-something-year-old English bartender. Same thing on your night out with Zach. But I'd like to think the perception of what fits and the reality can be very different."

"Can I ask you something?"

"You can ask anything, but whether or not I'll answer depends on the question."

In other words, his marriage was off-limits. "Are we exclusive?"

He tensed. I assumed it was because I was pushing the boundaries of what he was willing to offer. This relationship might be temporary, but the thought of him with another woman didn't sit well at all.

"I haven't been with anyone else, if that's what you're asking. I guess I had assumed we were exclusive," he confided.

I sighed in relief. "I like that assumption."

He shifted and started to rise out of the water. "Water is getting cold. Come here. Let's get you dried off." He helped me out of the tub and wrapped me up in a warm towel.

"I'm a fan of the toasty towel. Might be worth the fire risk."

He took one for himself and smiled. "I think you're right about that. Did you, um, need some time in the bathroom before bed?"

My face heated. "Uh, yeah. I'll go back to my room and then get dressed."

"You're cute when you blush."

My face flushed even further. "Good night." I smiled, giving him a kiss.

"You're sleeping with me tonight, aren't you?"

Okay, this threw me. "Um, you want me to?"

He kissed my forehead. "Get dressed in your pajamas and come back to my bed. I'll massage your back."

Damn if he wasn't the best boyfriend ever, I thought, after crawling into the bed a short time later. He massaged my lower back precisely where it was always sore this time of month.

CHAPTER TWELVE

The next day involved a lot of shuffling of meetings with an unforeseen crisis concerning the purchase of the Hong Kong business. Something about the government and taxes, but I wasn't brought up to speed on the details.

From the grim look on Josh's face, it was evident he wasn't happy. Now at ten o'clock at night, we were still in the London office, conferencing with both Brian, who was on site in Hong Kong, and a bunch of attorneys. I didn't know how he did it, but Josh still looked impeccable in his suit after a fourteen-hour day.

Hours earlier, he'd offered me a chance to go back to the hotel, but I wouldn't hear of it. I think he was relieved since, in my opinion, he couldn't have handled all the logistics of the many calls. Not that he wasn't brilliant, but men like him didn't bother with the details of how to videoconference. Hell, they didn't need to.

"Gentlemen, I trust this is now in good hands." He wrapped up the call and glanced at me after finally hanging up. "Let's go." Annoyance from the day was evident in his tone.

We walked back to the hotel in silence and then took the

elevator up to the hotel suites. "Do you want me to order room service?" I inquired as we went through his hotel room door.

"Sure, that's fine." Terse, he didn't offer any further guidance.

Most girls might have taken his abrupt mood personally. But having witnessed a portion of how his day had gone, I didn't blame him for being irritable. Plus, we were still in business mode. Compared to Warren's moods, Josh's were pretty easy to anticipate.

Calling down for a couple of burgers with fries, I threw some chocolate chip cookies into the order, too, because why the hell not?

In my room, I quickly changed into my jeans and sweatshirt, happy to take my hair down and remove my makeup.

A short time later, Josh walked in from his adjoining room with the tray full of food. I was on the phone with Nigel, catching up on the coming week's schedule. I hadn't even heard room service knock with the delivery.

"Right, Nigel, I'll ask him. Talk to you tomorrow." I hung up and looked toward Josh.

"Ask me what?" He lifted the lids from the burgers and glanced over at me with an expression that let me know what he thought of my meal choice.

I shrugged. "What? You had a long, bad day, and you probably shouldn't leave the ordering up to a woman who's hormonal if you want a salad."

Well, that got him. He laughed out loud. "Fair enough."

He set the tray on the small table, and we both dug in. "What were you going to ask me?"

"Nigel asked if you wanted him to make your travel arrangements for Thanksgiving. It's next Thursday." Nigel had also mentioned that last year Josh's mom and brother had come into New York, the year prior Vegas. Josh clearly spent the time with his family; it was just a matter of where that time would be this year.

Judging by the annoyed look on his face, however, deciding this wasn't high on his priorities. Or he didn't want to discuss holiday plans with me particularly.

"I don't know. It's a week away."

"I know. I mean, imagine two assistants trying to plan a whole week ahead of time—it's crazy."

He paused in chewing his food, arching a brow. "Are you being sassy, Ms. Holloway?"

Holy hell, the way he said that spiked my libido instantly. I not-so-innocently dipped my fry in ketchup and sucked it off while watching his eyes darken. "I wouldn't dream of it, Mr. Singer," I retorted, batting my eyelashes.

He reached across the small table and wiped the ketchup from the side of my mouth.

I took the opportunity to take his finger and suck it gently, getting satisfaction out of his breath catching.

"You need to get some sleep," he suggested regretfully.

He was always concerned about me getting enough rest. It occurred to me there must be a reason behind it. "Why are you always so worried about my sleep? It comes from somewhere."

He sighed and then was surprisingly open. "I'm an insomniac most nights. At one point in my twenties, I wasn't aware of how that made me push people. I had Mark up all night on a deal, and he fell asleep driving home. He was fine, luckily; the car wasn't. It was an important lesson for me to pay attention and ensure that no one else I cared about got put in jeopardy because I didn't allow them to get enough rest."

I was speechless and caressed his face to show my gratitude for this confidence. "Thank you for sharing that."

"So, you should probably get to bed."

"I can always sleep on the plane." Then, before he could

protest, I was down on my knees, undoing his belt and freeing him.

"I don't know what in this lifetime I did to deserve this, but I'll take it," he mumbled.

Smiling, I licked the pre-cum from his tip, enjoying his sounds of pleasure.

"Ahh, Christ… how long do your periods last?"

I paused and tried not to be embarrassed by his frankness. "About four to five days, I guess. Why?" I went back to licking his shaft from base to tip.

He groaned. "Because I want to be inside you. I want to make you come."

"Hmm, can't you enjoy being on the receiving end for a few days?" I moved lower and paid attention to his balls.

He gripped the table. "Dammit. I'm not going to last long with you doing that."

His cock hardened further with my fist stroking his length. I took him all the way into my mouth, using my tongue and lips to suck him harder.

After a few minutes of my delicious torture, he let go and spilled into my mouth, hot and thick.

Swallowing all of it, I then kissed his tip lightly before climbing back into my chair.

After slugging back my soda, I went back to eating my burger and watched as he zipped himself up. "So you moved most of your meetings from tomorrow to today. Does that mean you want to leave early tomorrow?"

His brows raised. "And just like that, we're back to business?"

"The lines are so blurred that I honestly have to kind of go with it. Otherwise, I'd be insecure as either your girlfriend or your assistant, and I don't think you'd appreciate either type of unease. I figure when we're alone, they will need to blur. When we're in public, well, it's only business."

He contemplated this while eating his fries. "Girlfriend, huh?"

Crap, I hadn't realized I'd said that. My face heated. "You know what I mean, and that wasn't my point." I refused to be embarrassed and lifted my chin. "Plus, since no one knows but the two of us—well, except for Mark, technically—I figure I can call you whatever I want."

Smiling, he seemed to enjoy my response. "You are sassy tonight."

Hmm, yes, I was. "Does it freak you out to be called a boyfriend?"

Gathering up his dishes, he took a minute to answer. "It's strange at my age, after having been married, to be a boyfriend again. But I guess I like that you would consider yourself my girlfriend."

Okay, so in other words I was taken, and he wasn't? I tried not to read into it.

"I worried about how you—or me for that matter—would be able to balance both the work and the personal. For what it's worth, so far I'm liking the way we weave in and out. Although I know it isn't always easy, you've been nothing but professional. You're unlike any other woman I've met. Maybe it's your age that makes you so refreshing. I don't know."

"You could spend time with other girls my age and let me know," I quipped, mildly insulted.

Chuckling, he shook his head. "Point taken and no, thank you. I'd meant it as a compliment."

"So you're saying you're happy to be banging your secretary?" I'd thought I was being funny, but his eyes narrowed.

Clearly pissed off at the dig, he crossed to me and framed my face. "Don't ever insult yourself or me by referring to us that way again. You wonder why I want to keep things a secret? It's to avoid people saying or even thinking something like that.

People don't need to put a disrespectful label on it, and neither do we, okay?"

I could only nod.

He took my mouth greedily as if to prove the point. Then, pulling back, he nipped my bottom lip. "I'm going to run the bath. Meet me in there when you're ready."

It was incredibly sexy how he not only took charge but also was adamant about making me feel like what we had wasn't cheap. Swallowing hard, I checked my feelings and took a deep breath. I needed to remind myself that this was only temporary. It didn't matter if he thought of me as his girlfriend or put a label on it. If I let myself believe for a moment that we had a future together past me leaving for school, I risked a broken heart.

Josh was in his robe when I padded into the bathroom. I wasn't sure where his thoughts were, and he didn't reveal them as he peeled off my robe.

After sliding into the tub, I was pleased when Josh stepped in behind me. He soaped my back like he had the night before. "Tell me something?" I whispered.

Behind me, he let out a breath. "I'm an asshole who doesn't like to say he's sorry."

I giggled. "You're supposed to tell me something I don't already know."

Chuckling, he admitted, "All right. I have a fear of needles. My mom tells me I would hyperventilate when I was a child when I knew I had to get shots."

I smiled since it was easy to assume Josh was fearless.

"Now tell me something," he returned, soaping my breasts.

His touch made my breath catch. "I was only teasing when I made the comment about banging your secretary. But I think subconsciously I needed your response to reassure me that I mean more than that to you. I don't know why, because your actions have never made me feel cheap, but hearing you get angry over it cemented the reassurance in my mind. I'm sorry. It wasn't my intention to push you into setting me at ease, but I do feel better now that you have."

He was quiet. I wasn't sure what he was thinking, so I twisted to get a read on his face, but he kept me in position with his hands.

"Stay where you are," he whispered. His hand traveled down my stomach and then lower.

"I'm still on my—"

"Shhh, I promise I won't go any lower than this," he assured me, putting the pad of his thumb on my clit. "Okay?"

Groaning in pleasure, I could only nod.

I felt his breath at my ear. "Do you know what you do to me with your honesty, Haylee?" he asked in his honey voice.

I shook my head as he rubbed me softly, teasing.

"You completely beguile me. Does that feel good?"

I squirmed under the tutelage from his hand. "Yes." It sounded like it was someone else's passion-filled voice answering.

He increased the pressure and tempo. "Relax, and let your body feel it."

I did, exploding in record time as I felt his lips on my neck.

"That's it. Now again."

I started to protest, but his hand had already started. "Josh, I can't—" I practically begged.

"Yes, you can. Let it go."

I did, completely coming undone under his hand as his hot breath caressed my ear.

"Good girl."

I felt like jelly and barely registered when he lifted me out of the tub and dried me off.

He left me for a moment and returned with the panties and T-shirt I had laid out on my bed.

"Here, get dressed, and then let's get you into bed. You're exhausted."

That was an understatement, I thought, barely able to keep my eyes open. By the time he enveloped me in his arms, I was completely asleep.

I WAS STILL GETTING DRESSED the next morning when Josh entered my set of rooms, hot and sweaty, apparently having visited the gym first thing.

My mouth watered at the sight of his body on display in shorts and a T-shirt.

"You and I have plans for today before we fly home. As soon as I get back from a breakfast meeting, we're going."

"What plans?"

"A surprise. So pack your things and be ready when I get back in about an hour or so."

I was intrigued and started packing.

After I'd ordered room service and Josh returned from breakfast, he changed quickly and we headed out. Although it was sunny, the air was crisp. I was glad I'd dressed warmly. Meanwhile, instead of stepping into a car at the curb, Josh turned right.

I walked alongside him for two blocks until we came to a stop in front of a sign that read *Big Red Bus Stop.* Sure enough, a double-decker bus pulled up a short while later, and we boarded.

"I was told this was the fastest way to see the sights around London," he noted as we wound our way upstairs.

We found ourselves alone in the open-air top since everyone else had opted for the warmth downstairs. After guiding me toward a seat on the side, he slid in beside me and put his arm around me.

"This is awesome." I beamed, hardly able to keep the grin off my face.

Chuckling, he shook his head. Taking a tourist bus in London was probably never anything Josh Singer had thought he'd be doing, but the fact that he was doing it for me filled me with enormous pleasure.

I pulled out my phone, prepared to take some pictures, and held it up in front of us. "Do you mind just one?" I wasn't sure how he felt about a couple selfie, but was about to find out.

"So long as you take it off your device when we get home." He took my phone, getting a longer arm-reach, and snapped the photo of our faces together.

"Sure thing. I'll put it as my computer wallpaper," I retorted, looking at the picture. It was the very first one I had of us together.

"Very funny. Okay, milady, your adventure awaits. We can get off at any location you want, but I do have a couple of planned stops as well."

I was ecstatic to see everything as we proceeded into traffic and my tour of London began.

It turned out you could see quite a lot from the top of a double-decker bus. I snapped photos of Parliament, Big Ben, beautiful churches, the London Bridge, the Eye of London, Trafalgar Square, and Buckingham Palace. We got off at the Tower of London and were ushered to the front of the line and given a private tour of the royal jewels. It was the same story when we got to Big Ben and the Parliament building. Early in the afternoon, Josh had a car meet us, and we were whisked across town to Harrods Department Store.

"Oh, my gosh," I remarked, stepping inside while he grinned at my enthusiasm. My hand squeezed his.

Happily, he didn't let go as he led me downstairs.

The store was magical. After lunch and perusing all of the shops, I looked over and smiled. "Well, Mr. Singer, you get the prize for the best surprise ever. You've thought of everything today."

"I do enjoy the details. Now back to reality, unfortunately."

Once we picked up our luggage from the hotel, we set out for the airport.

It had been a day that made it hard to remember he was my boss. Considering those moments were so few, it was difficult to want to return to the real world.

He must have felt the same because he put his coat in between us and held my hand underneath it, stroking my thumb for the duration of the ride.

I lay back in the seat, enjoying the simple intimacy.

CHAPTER THIRTEEN

I felt pretty good about Josh and myself during the next few days in New York after we arrived back from London. This confident view lasted until Thursday afternoon, when I went down to the office lobby, intending to grab some lunch. As though in slow motion, I watched Josh greet a tall blond woman with a kiss on the cheek, a gesture she returned by capturing his lips completely.

I couldn't look away, not even after his eyes met mine and he set her away from him slowly.

My face heated, and I turned on my heel, moving quickly outside into the safety of numbers in the café next door. I changed my mind about getting my soup to go and instead took a solo seat in the corner. It was tempting to text Nigel and pretend I was sick, but this was my bed, and I had to lie in it. So much for not getting jealous. Sucking it up, I returned to the office when my lunch hour was up.

"Hey, Nigel, I'm back. You go ahead," I offered, knowing he had a late lunch appointment with a friend of his.

"All right. This arrived for you via messenger."

The box made me curious, and I opened it to reveal a very expensive designer pair of jeans and a beautiful lacy thong with matching bra, both made of the most luxurious silk.

"Do I even want to know?" Nigel asked, raising a brow.

"I don't even know." It dawned on me, though, when I opened the card.

Because every girl should have a designer pair of jeans and something underneath that makes her feel like a million bucks. I expect a call this week. —Catherine

I tucked the card into my pocket, not wanting Nigel or Josh to see what was written. "It's from Catherine Davenport. I met her in London, and she may want to feature my mom's vintage dresses in her magazine." I filled him on the rest of the details, omitting Josh's comments and our subsequent fight.

Nigel smiled, looking impressed. "That's amazing. She's a force in the fashion industry. Based on today's gift, I definitely think you should ring her."

"I will. Enjoy your lunch." Putting the gift under my desk, I intended to call her straightaway. I'd never really had a good girl friend and was moved by such an extravagant gesture.

"Oh, Mr. Singer requested to see you when you returned. Be back in an hour."

Shit, he was here.

I knocked lightly and opened the door when I heard Josh's voice telling me to come in. "Nigel said you'd like to see me, Mr. Singer." I was glad that I was looking exceptionally put together today in my red Ralph Lauren dress with matching shoes.

He took his time looking me up and down. "Who was the gift from?" He leaned back in his chair, looking every bit the powerful business man.

My pulse leapt at the sound of his voice. "Catherine."

His look of surprise gave me a small feeling of satisfaction.

"I see. Are you going to tell me what she sent?" There was quiet tension in his voice.

"Designer jeans and a lacy thong." I watched his jaw tick.

"Did Nigel leave for lunch?"

I felt my mouth go dry. "Yes."

"Are you off your period?"

Oh, shit. We were crossing a line not previously crossed here in the office. "Yes," I admitted in a whisper.

"Good. Come here." He wheeled his chair back. "I want your ass right here on my desk."

Swallowing hard, I watched as he crossed the room and locked the door, but I stayed rooted to the spot. "What if someone comes upstairs?" We were the top floor of the building, but there were several individuals who had direct access via the elevators to the space outside his office.

He gave me an annoyed look and went to the control panel on the side of the wall, locking the elevators as well. "Your ass, Haylee, on that desk." His tone had an edge to it.

I moved to where he had instructed, edging up onto his desk and twisting at the waist in order to watch his graceful movements.

He shrugged out of his suit jacket and walked toward me almost like he was stalking prey.

It was so unbelievably hot.

"Take off your panties," he ordered.

I shook my head.

He cocked an eyebrow, coming to stand in front of me. "Defiant today?"

I nudged my chin up. "Considering I just saw you lip-locked with a blonde downstairs, you'll have to excuse me if my panties don't exactly want to jump right off."

That at least earned me another tick in his jaw. "Okay, evidently we're hashing this out now."

My body rebelled against the idea of talking. As he was about to step away, I locked my legs around his waist and hauled him toward me. "Hash later."

And just like that, his mouth was crashing down on mine. He wasn't gentle, and I didn't want him to be as our mutual frustration spilled out into the kiss. Suddenly I was frantic to have him inside of me.

"Dammit, I'm breaking the rules with you all over the place." His teeth grazed my neck while his hands worked up under my dress. He sucked in his breath when he found my garters. "I'll buy you more underwear," he promised.

A moment later I discovered what he meant when I felt the crotch rip. Swiftly, he was inside of me, holding my hips and driving like a man possessed. I gripped his waist and held on, feeling the pressure build when his thumb found my most sensitive spot between our bodies. It wasn't long before I came completely undone.

He followed with one last thrust and a groan, emptying fully deep inside of me. "Christ, Haylee." He pulled out slowly and grabbed some tissues from the box he kept on his desk, wiping himself before doing up his pants again. "My bathroom has washcloths."

I slid down and found myself off balance in more than one way. After walking into a surprisingly spacious bathroom, I made quick work out of cleaning up. The underwear was a lost cause. It was tempting to leave them in his trash, but I couldn't take the chance they might be found, so I took them with me.

Josh was on the phone when I walked out. Well, this was awkward. I guess I should go?

As if reading my mind, he held up a finger, indicating I should wait. After finishing his conversation, he studied me.

My eyes drifted to where we had just been on his desk, and I flushed.

"Well, now, that could be a challenge." He chuckled.

My face split in a grin. "I'll need to ensure I don't look at that spot when I come in. I should probably get some Clorox wipes or something."

He shook his head. "I can still smell you right here, and I'd like to keep it that way, at least until they clean tonight."

He made me want to hop up there and go at him all over again. "Oh," was all I could manage.

"Come here," he commanded softly.

I walked slowly around to him and was not prepared when he dragged me down into his lap and inhaled the scent of my hair.

"Do you trust me?"

"I want to, and so far I haven't had a reason not to. Are you going to tell me who the blonde was?"

He leaned back so that we could see eye to eye. "She's a colleague's daughter and in town for a week. I took her out last night, and today she came to meet me for lunch."

"I guess she decided to make you the meal," I offered sarcastically.

"She kissed me, and I broke it off. She isn't used to taking no for an answer."

"I bet." He hadn't ended the kiss fast enough for my taste, but now wasn't the time to be petty. "And does our exclusivity include kissing?"

Nodding, he claimed my lips, kissing me slowly. "When I told you that we'd be sexually exclusive, I meant it, Haylee."

"So you didn't want to sleep with her?"

I realized he was trying to figure out whether to be truthful or not.

"You can be honest," I coaxed, meaning it.

"You know my history when it comes to sex."

I did, and it made me hot and bothered when I thought about the first time he had tied my hands up. "Yes, but now that you can, I didn't know if you maybe want to make up for lost time."

He chuckled. "I'm having more sex now than I've had in the

last five years. And, yes, if you're doing the math, that does include the last year of my marriage. So between work and keeping up with you, I think it's fair to say that I wouldn't have the time or energy to sleep with anyone else."

He hadn't really answered the question.

"But…" I hedged.

"But obviously part of me is curious if I'm, you know, able to. The thought of losing you isn't worth the curiosity, though, and that's all it is. Curiosity. I have social obligations that dictate I have a date, and I don't want to hash out the details each and every time. If I was interested in taking another woman to bed, I wouldn't have bothered telling you that we were exclusive."

It troubled me that he seemed to have all of the decision-making power in this process. And I'd given it to him on a silver platter. If I was being honest with myself, it wasn't the kiss that was upsetting me the most, considering he had stopped it. It was the fact that he'd chosen to spend his time with her over me when I'd sat at home last night waiting for a phone call or knock. Sighing, I recognized it was time to change that scenario. "So to clarify, you're going to date other women, so I can date others, as well?"

He frowned. "I'm going out with other women from time to time, but we wouldn't be dating, just—"

"Going on dates?" I supplied cynically and heard his teeth grind.

"Do you want to date other guys?" he snapped.

I snapped back. "I want to go out to dinner and go to a show with someone instead of by myself, so I guess the answer is yes. And if what you're saying is you have to go out from time to time, and it can't be with me, then I'm assuming the same goes for my plans that can't include you."

"Well, I don't want to go out, so that's the difference."

"Are you planning to see her again?"

"Haylee."

"Don't you *Haylee* me. It's a reasonable question, considering she doesn't like to hear no for an answer. Your words, Josh."

"This is exactly why I didn't want to argue about this here and now. I need to get back to work, and Nigel is returning any moment. I don't need the aggravation of this here in the office."

Checking my temper, I went out to my desk, first putting my torn underwear in my purse. I then walked back in and, to his shock, wiped the desk with my Clorox wipe.

"If you didn't want to do this here, then you shouldn't have done me there." And with that, I turned and went back to my desk.

As I shut his door, I heard his chuckle. Asshole. I smiled in spite of my irritation. After I settled in, I called Catherine to set up lunch during the next week and thank her for the amazing gift.

NIGEL INSISTED that I join him and his partner for Thanksgiving. Truth be told, I was excited finally to meet David after hearing so much about him. I was also anxious to wear my new designer jeans, which made my butt look incredible, if I did say so myself. Catherine was certainly right about the silk underwear, too, as I felt like a million bucks.

I kind of wished Josh was in town so that I could show him how sexy I felt, but I think he'd been relieved to hear that I was celebrating Thanksgiving with Nigel. He'd flown to Virginia to spend the long weekend with his mom and brother.

The subway was easy enough to take into Brooklyn, where I was instantly charmed by Nigel and David's brownstone. David was adorable with his bow tie and big brown eyes. For a man who had lost his hair to chemo, he was rocking it like a nerdy Jason Statham. He took me for a tour, showing me all three floors and their latest remodel project in the basement. I learned that gardening was his true passion as he led me out to the back yard, leaning on me for strength, a measure for which I told him to stop apologizing.

Nigel was an incredible cook laying out a feast with a full turkey and all of the traditional side dishes. Listening to them talk over dinner and witnessing the affection between them, I could see how they complemented each other.

While helping Nigel clear the table, I heard my phone ringing. I looked at the unknown number, wondering if Josh was calling me.

"Hello."

"Haylee, it's Bart Chesley. I hope I'm not interrupting your Thanksgiving evening?"

"No. Actually, I'm about to head back to my apartment. Everything okay?" I could hear something in his voice, anxiety maybe.

"Yes, well, unfortunately we have a model who got shingles. The shoot is tomorrow morning, down in the Bahamas. I don't suppose you could come down?"

I jumped on the opportunity since I had nothing else planned for the long weekend. "I'd love to."

He gave me all of the details, and I got booked on the first flight down there the next day.

My morning was hectic once I arrived at the resort in the Bahamas. Bart introduced me to Gina, who was hair and makeup for the day. Soon the two of us were off and running, taking care of all the prep work.

The first shoot was in a bikini, and I was thankful it was a tasteful, black one this time. The idea was to look like the girl next door, down here on vacation. I could definitely do this role much better than filling in for a supermodel.

Then I got a good look at my significant other for the shoot. Uh, yeah, he was not relatable; he was gorgeous. Well over six feet tall, clean-cut with close-cropped dark brown hair, he already had his shirt off, displaying impressive washboard abs.

"Hi ya, you must be Haylee. I'm Will."

Oh, boy, he had an Australian accent.

"Hi, it's nice to meet you, Will."

His eyes were blue, his smile revealed perfect white teeth, and I was suddenly a bit more insecure about this model shoot. Guys like him belonged on billboards. Girls like me were pretty but definitely not exceptional.

"You're from New York, yeah?"

"Yes, well, originally from California, but I'm in New York now. You?"

"I'm in New York, too."

And with that, the staging crew was ready for us to take our places. As we got into the shoot, I realized that it was a lot easier for me to do action-type activities in front of the camera rather than merely posing, which is what I'd had to do in the other shoot. In-the-moment shots were more natural. It also helped to have Will. As it turned out, he wasn't simply easy on the eyes but was funny and easy to feel comfortable around.

"I'm so glad I got you as my partner on this job," he confessed in between scenes.

I checked my phone for the umpteenth time, having not heard from Josh yet. "I'm really glad I got you, too," I said sincerely.

"Boyfriend?" he inquired, watching me with my phone.

Embarrassed for having checked it so often, I shook my head. I couldn't tell him either way, and I wasn't sure I wanted to.

"Good, that means I can call you. Maybe we can get together once I'm back in a week or so."

I waited to feel guilt, but it didn't come. I wasn't going to be the girl sitting at home every night while my secret boyfriend went out with other women and spent the holidays without even texting me.

"I'd like that, Will," I said smiling.

CHAPTER FOURTEEN

The week after Thanksgiving, Catherine and I made plans to meet at her work office for lunch. I was excited to see her again. My self-confidence when it came to modeling had grown after the opportunity in the Bahamas, and I was enthusiastic about showing off my mom's dresses. With my garment bags in hand, I was thankful to be ushered right to her office on the forty-third floor of the building.

"Haylee, how lovely to see you. Here, let me help you." She grabbed half of my bags and hung them onto a rolling wardrobe cart.

Her office walls were quite impressive with framed pictures of celebrities and magazine covers from over the years.

"It's great to see you again, too. Thank you for taking the time." I meant it.

"Are you kidding? This is a treat. I would suggest we sit and chat, but I'm way too anxious to see the dresses. Are you wearing a vintage Chanel suit now?" she questioned, spinning me around.

Happy that I'd chosen the dark tweed for today, I smiled and nodded. "It's like finding someone who speaks the same language. I am indeed wearing Chanel. 1968."

"Gorgeous. So you tell me: where should we start?"

I started with the Jean Desses green dress and then the pink one she had seen previously. From there, I moved on to the Dior trapeze dress, which had her oohing and aahing. Next was an Oleg Cassini classic suit and two Chanel dresses. The black Givenchy was one of my favorites, along with a colorful Pucci dress. They all had her smiling in appreciation.

"And now for the finale, I present the Valentino wedding gown."

Her eyes got big, and she clapped her hands together. "It's exquisite. May I?"

I nodded, liking that she asked before touching the lace.

"I have to have these dresses in my magazine, especially this one. Please tell me you'll do it."

She seemed so worried I might not that I rushed to reassure her. "Of course I'd love to. It would be amazing to show them off."

"I'd want them for my February issue, which means shooting next week. We'll need shoes unless you have them?" She went down a mental checklist.

"I have some, but I don't have any for the wedding dress or something that would go with the Pucci print. But I'm happy to show you what I do have."

"Good. As for a male model, I'll have to set up some interviews."

"If you don't have anyone in mind, I'd love for you to interview a model I know." I gave her a quick rundown on Will, and she looked curious.

"Sounds good. Why don't you give me his number, and I'll set up a meeting."

It would make me happy to work with Will again instead of

taking a chance on a stranger with whom I might not feel as comfortable.

"As for a photographer, I need to make some phone calls." Catherine was jotting notes.

"I could see if Bart is available."

She appeared taken aback. "Bart Chesley?"

"Um, yeah, I mean he gave me his cell number…"

"Haylee, Bart is one of the best in the business. If he would do this, it would be huge. I know he's friendly with Josh. Maybe he could place a call?"

"Well, actually, I saw Bart last weekend. He called me for a last-minute shoot in the Bahamas, and he said to let him know about any modeling that I did. Unless you think he'd be insulted that I would ask him directly. I'm not sure of protocol."

She still appeared a little stunned. It was unnerving because I got the sense that Catherine was never stunned. "So he called you directly to ask you to do the shoot?"

"Uh, yeah, on Thanksgiving."

"Well, screw protocol. If you have his number and have a rapport, go for it. Are you kidding me? This is all coming together like it was meant to be."

"Okay, I'll call him." I pulled out my phone, and she looked astounded again. Evidently she wasn't expecting I'd do it this instant.

I was pleased when Bart answered on the second ring. After a few niceties and compliments about how this weekend's pictures had turned out, I asked the favor and then glanced over at Catherine. I hung up with a smile on my face.

"He said absolutely he'd do it. To have your office call him to work out the dates."

She seemed impressed. "As if I didn't love you enough already, you have Bart Chesley on speed dial."

My face heated. "I hope he didn't feel weird. From the look on your face, I'm wondering if maybe I overstepped. He knows I work for, uh, Mr. Singer, and I don't want that to be the reason." Crap, now I was overthinking it.

She took both my hands and reassured me. "Honey, Bart Chesley wouldn't do a favor for the pope unless he wanted to. He works because he loves the art, or because he likes the people who ask him. His price tag is high, but he's worth every penny. And he has a laundry list of models with whom he has worked only one time, if you get my drift."

I guess I did. I had only thought of Bart as a nice older man who was kind to me and gave me my first break.

"As for your fee, I'll have the legal department draw it up. What's your rate?"

Now it was my turn to be dumbfounded. "I honestly don't know. Both times I've sort of stepped in, so whatever you think makes sense, really."

She mulled this over. "I'll talk to Josh about the other shoot you did. I want to make sure I'm fair to you."

I was uncomfortable with that thought but smiled. "So now I kind of have a favor to ask, but please know that you can absolutely say no." I started to get a little anxious about even asking. I never minded giving favors, but requesting them was tougher.

"Name it. Here, let's eat. I had salads brought up for lunch. I'm sure you could probably put away anything, but I've got to watch what I eat. Especially now, being middle-aged and divorced."

Her self-deprecation threw me. It went to show that someone could look like they had everything from the outside and yet be hurting inside.

"Well, I was thinking about the jewelry. I'm assuming you want vintage, especially the wedding jewelry, and Gamble Advertising represents Delayne Diamonds. They have this vintage line that has everything from wedding rings to everyday-type diamonds. Sasha Brooks is their rep, and, well, since she's new to the account, I was thinking it could be an amazing opportunity for her."

"Done. Sounds perfect, actually."

That was really easy. Too easy, when I thought of a woman like Sasha. "Thank you, but Sasha is—Well, she's proud. She needs to feel like she's earned it."

Catherine took a bite of her salad and contemplated. "Why are you doing this for her? Is she a friend?"

The question threw me. "To be honest, I don't know her very well. But I watched as she got ripped apart by a good old boy's network when she pitched the vintage idea. I think this would be an awesome way of telling them all to shove it."

Catherine appeared to understand this. "Fair enough." She scanned her phone and frowned at her calendar. "After tomorrow, I'm traveling for the next couple weeks."

"Would tomorrow work, by any chance?"

"I'm booked all day, but I could do after work."

"That would be perfect. How about a meeting and then maybe happy hour? Sasha is single, beautiful, successful, and you mentioned wanting to go out."

Her face lit up at the thought. "That sounds great, actually, as long as you think she isn't one of those catty women. I can't handle any more of the type who pretend to be a friend and then stab you in the back."

Considering my first impression of Sasha, I decided to play it safe. "How about we do the presentation, and you can judge for yourself? I think that she can be nice, but she sees women as a natural threat. To be fair, I think it's a defense instead of mean-girl mentality. All the same, I won't mention happy hour to her unless you do."

She seemed satisfied with that answer and then remarked, "There aren't a lot of women in the corporate world who look out for one another. It's nice you're doing this for her. I hope she can appreciate it."

We finished up our lunch with small talk. I looked forward to calling Sasha when I got back and crossed my fingers she would be as excited as I was.

JOSH WAS on a conference call when I arrived back at the office. After Nigel left early for one of David's appointments, I settled in and called Sasha.

"Sasha Brooks here."

"Hi, Sasha. This is Haylee, Josh's assistant."

"Yes, hello. What can I do for you?"

"I have what could be an opportunity for you to feature that vintage diamond line." I filled her in on the details of the shoot and Catherine.

"I don't know what to say," she finally admitted after my explanation.

"I was hoping you'd say yes. The only kicker is that she has to meet you tomorrow, though not until the end of the day. Time is tight because she wants to try to get the spread in the February issue. That means the shoot has to be in the next couple of weeks."

"Oh, shit, that's quick. Do you have the dresses there in the office? I would need to see them in order to get a sense and then I'd need to talk to the client. Actually, maybe I should get the project first before I mention it, not like they'll say no." I could hear her brain running a million miles an hour.

"Mr. Singer is leaving at six o'clock for an appointment, so why don't you come by his office here after that? I do have the dresses, and I'll help you work on whatever you need tonight."

"That's great, yeah, I'll come by. Thank you, and I'll see you then."

We hung up, and I found myself looking forward to this evening.

I DIDN'T SEE much of Josh until he was ready to leave for his business dinner, and even then he had a phone to his ear. He gave me a smile and a wave on his way out. Although I was used to this routine, sometimes it irritated me that I never knew if we would see each other later. I'd intended to tell him about pitching to Catherine, but the more I thought about it, the more convinced I was to keep it to myself. Given his inability to share his plans, perhaps it was time that I wasn't so forthcoming with mine.

Sasha trekked over from the Gamble Advertising office six blocks away, arriving at my office on time. Not surprisingly, she looked impeccable and appeared genuinely excited for the opportunity.

The first fifteen minutes were spent showing her the dresses. I saved the wedding gown for last.

"Wow, the whole collection is amazing. But this wedding dress is absolutely stunning."

I smiled, knowing she meant it sincerely. You couldn't look at the Valentino and not fall in love.

"Do you think she wants different jewelry for each dress?"

"I think so, although I can't tell you for sure which gowns she'll pick, so I think we should give her options for each."

Taking out her notepad, Sasha was clearly eager to start. "Okay, let's go through the wardrobe. I brought the catalog of everything vintage, so maybe we can make a list of those pieces we think will go with each dress." It was going to be a late night, but her enthusiasm was contagious.

We were finishing up with the preliminary list of items when Josh walked back in, still in his suit. He appeared completely surprised by the image of Sasha and me with our heads together at my desk, both looking at my computer. "I— Hello, Sasha."

She straightened up, looking way too guilty for something so innocent.

"Oh, Josh, sorry. I didn't know you'd be here."

Since this was actually his office, he raised a brow.

I interjected quickly. "Sasha was nice enough to come by and help me pick out dresses for the Cosmo shoot."

"Uh, great. That's nice. I, um, forgot something. If you ladies are planning to be here awhile, you're welcome to use my office."

It was almost eight o'clock, and I wondered if he'd come back here for me. "Thank you. Appreciate it."

As if remembering he supposedly forgot something, he went into his office and came back out with a folder in his hand. "Ladies, have a good evening."

Once we heard the elevator ding, we both took a deep breath and then burst into giggles.

"You know it's bad when my boss's boss is shocked when I'm being nice," Sasha divulged, sitting back in her chair. "Why are doing this for me?"

"First and foremost, I liked your idea. And, well, the vintage opportunity presented itself, so it kind of made sense. Also, I like the notion of you showing Brian, and especially Warren, that your idea was a good one."

She mulled this over. "Thank you. Sincerely."

IT WAS close to eleven o'clock by the time the cab dropped me off, so I was thankful for Rafael's assistance in getting my dresses upstairs.

A short time later there was a knock at my door. I opened it and smiled at Josh, who was dressed in his pajama pants and a soft white T-shirt. I ran my hand down his chest, a gesture that seemed to amuse him.

"Petting me now?"

"You are very soft and I like this look on you, very hot."

To that he simply raised that sexy brow of his. "Soooo…" he prompted, closing the door.

Removing my shoes, I proceeded to undress in front of him, hanging up my suit and walking into the bathroom in my bra and panties to wash my face. He leaned against the doorframe, watching me. I was becoming more comfortable and kind of liked that we could share these personal moments.

"Sooooo what?" I pretended ignorance.

"So, are you going to tell me what tonight was about? You and Sasha together in the office?"

I turned and smiled slyly. "I could, but I'd rather let it play out, let it be a surprise. Do you mind?"

"Does it have something to do with today's meeting with Catherine? I take it she wants to do the shoot."

I crossed over and put my arms around him, enjoying the feel of his warmth. "It does, and yes, she is. In the next couple of weeks, actually. But the part with Sasha, I would prefer for it to come up through the chain at the appropriate time."

He ran his hands down, settling them on my hips, and leaned back so that he could kiss my forehead. "And what if I wanted to know now?"

"I would tell you as I don't want any secrets between us. But this is business, and I'd like for it to come from Sasha to Brian and up to you, the way it would if you weren't standing here stroking my back at the moment."

He gave me a kiss then, and I melted. "I will let it be a surprise, then, my sweet Haylee." He nuzzled my ear.

It made me happy that he trusted me.

"Let's go to bed," I purred, turning out the lights and taking his hand.

If Sasha was nervous the next evening, she didn't show it as we headed up to Catherine's office.

Catherine was warm in greeting her, but I could tell that her guard was up. Toward me, I had never seen these defenses.

After I made the introductions, Catherine gave some background as to what she was looking for.

"I thought about it, and I decided we'll do a chronicle, going from boy-meets-girl to dating to engagement to wedding to honeymoon. We could start with meeting at a party, then perhaps a date scene, then out to a fancy dinner in the Givenchy gown where the boyfriend pops the question. Next would be the bridal shower, and on to the wedding dress, which will be the centerpiece. I was thinking we'd do the wedding night with vintage lingerie. Do you have any, Haylee?"

"Uh, no. I sure don't."

"Well, I have a perfect Dior set that I think would photograph wonderfully on you. Not to worry, it covers more than a bikini. Then for the honeymoon, we feature the Pucci and do a green screen, so that we can have you on the beach or something."

"I think that all sounds amazing." I meant it, and Sasha echoed the sentiment.

"So what do you have for me, Sasha, as far as jewelry?" Catherine asked.

I had to hand it to Sasha. Fifteen minutes later I was sold on all of it, and I could tell that Catherine was impressed. "You put this all together in the last twenty-four hours?" she queried, looking at the pictures.

Sasha nodded. "Yes. With Haylee's help, I did."

"It's impressive. So from here, I take it you need to talk to your client. You can let them know they'll get full credit and pricing, if they want it listed. I might suggest you give them some leeway in choosing the jewelry they wish to push, but tell them that I'm set on the pale pink diamond pendant necklace for the wedding gown. That, girls, was a great choice, and I have the perfect shoes in mind to complete the look."

We both nodded, and she folded up the book.

"If possible, I'd like to speak with your client no later than Tuesday next week when I'm back in town," Catherine said, looking at Sasha.

Considering any client would jump at this opportunity, Sasha assured her that she would be in touch with the details the next day.

"So, Sasha. Haylee and I were planning to make our way downstairs for happy hour. I'm newly divorced, and she's kind enough to reintroduce me to the single scene. Would you like to join us?"

Sasha smiled. "I'd love to. If you could excuse me for a moment, I'd like to call my boss and let him know about this. Then I should call my client."

"Of course. There's a conference room out my door to the right. Please feel free to take as long as you like. Haylee and I can discuss more about the scenes and a few other details."

Sasha smiled, mouthed *thank you* to me, and quickly went into the conference room.

"You're beaming like you won something," Catherine remarked.

"I feel like we did. She worked hard on this. It was important that you saw that instead of merely doing me a favor."

"I can respect that, especially now that I've met her. Are you comfortable doing the lingerie scene?"

"I think so. I mean, I've done bikinis, and Bart is amazing at making me feel relaxed. Is Will going to be the model?"

She smiled. "If he's as great as you say, I think so. We're meeting on Tuesday. Also, Bart did get back to me. How does December twenty-third work for you? Sorry it's so close to the holidays, but he's coming into town to see family, so he'd like to combine the trip."

"That's not a problem. I'll check with Mr. Singer and confirm, but he's always said he'd be flexible when it comes to modeling."

"Honey, I meant for your holiday plans. You have some, right?"

"Uh, yes, I have a couple options. I'm working that week either way, though." Shit, I hadn't even thought of Christmas plans yet.

She sighed. "Well, if you need me to talk to Josh about getting a day off, let me know, and I'll have a chat with him."

I tried not to think of the irony of her thinking she'd have more pull than I would.

IT WAS obvious by the time we made it downstairs that I was not the one who could show Catherine what the single life was like in New York City. Not only was I unfamiliar with the city, but I also had no clue how business professionals did happy hour.

Sasha, thankfully, was more than willing to take the lead. Catherine and I were happy to be her pupils for the evening.

"Okay, first rule when it comes to happy hour, ladies: never go to the bar next to your work. Because guess who you will see there? Work people."

Huh, well that made sense.

"Secondly, go to a bar that's next to a firm with a lot of successful men because they will simply go downstairs to grab a drink."

If anyone seemed to have self-assurance when it came to men, it was Sasha with her flawless olive skin and the pencil skirt and white blouse accenting her curves. Her killer stilettos appeared to be the icing on the cake. I had a feeling I could learn a lot from her when it came to how to act cool and collected around the opposite sex.

When we entered the bar, I noticed right away the ratio of men to women was indeed in our favor. The décor was modern, with funky light fixtures, chrome tables, and a huge bar with colorful liquor bottles behind it. Mirrors were everywhere. Although we stayed downstairs, it looked like there was an upper level. It was happy hour central, with suits and ties everywhere.

Sasha smiled at the bartender and held up three fingers.

He obviously knew exactly what she wanted since he nodded and then pointed over to a high-top table with two stools. Within a minute, another stool was brought around and three martinis delivered.

"Wow, that's some service. You come here a lot?" I was impressed.

Sasha smiled and shrugged. "Enough, although I haven't been out in a while. I like to bring my single female clients here since there's a big law firm upstairs. Lots of men."

Sasha nudged me under the table when I tried looking around. "Third rule of Operation Trolling for Hot Guys: we don't look around. We're here for these amazing blackberry martinis and to talk to one another. We don't give a shit about who's around us or how cute the men are. Let them come to you, ladies."

The rules made me giggle. We made small talk, and I appreciated that Sasha was actually quite funny once she was comfortable around people. By the end of the evening, I'd had a great time in the company of two dynamic, successful women, and Sasha had given her phone number to a hot attorney.

IT WAS LATE by the time I got home and sank into bed. I lay there waiting for Josh, hoping he'd come by. Finally frustrated that I'd wait on him, I picked up my phone and texted him.

"Had three drinks and miss you. I'm home now in my lonely bed."

Fifteen minutes later my door opened, and I watched as he crawled in beside me.

"Lonely bed, huh?"

I stroked his bare chest. "Very lonely."

Reaching down, I cupped his thick erection in my hand and marveled at how soft his skin was while he could be so hard at the same time. He shifted and lifted me up so that I was on top of him, and I scooted down and took his hard length in my mouth. I liked it when I could take him by surprise. His deep guttural groan let me know he was enjoying it. Working my way up, I kissed his chest and took some time to tease nipples before finally aligning his erection to my wet center and sinking down onto him one inch at a time.

He took deep breaths with the contact. "I— Jesus, Haylee."

"I definitely like this position," I hummed, now filled with him and gasping with pleasure at how deep he was.

The added bonus was the fact that he had access to my most sensitive spots and took full advantage of it. He rubbed my clit in slow circles and established a rhythm. As I was about to come, he took control, gripping my ass and thrusting up until we both went over the edge together.

I lay on top of his chest, catching my breath and loving the way he smelled and felt under me.

"How was happy hour?"

"It was good. Sasha definitely has it down. I think she'll be good for Catherine."

"Hmm. Well, I heard something today from Brian. Seems that Sasha presented to Catherine today an idea for Delayne Diamonds to do the jewelry for this vintage spread in her magazine. Do you know anything about that?"

"Surprised?" I kissed his neck.

He gently moved me off and tucked me into his side. "I was,

but then I realized I shouldn't have been. You have a very business-oriented mind. But I do have a question."

"Mm?" I was getting sleepy.

"Did Catherine want Sasha to present, or was that exercise merely to make Sasha think Catherine wasn't merely doing a favor for you?"

"I think you know the answer. Sasha is proud, and I wanted Catherine to know that the diamonds would do her shoot justice and that the whole idea wasn't simply a favor to me."

"Why did you do this for her?"

I was a little uncomfortable with the question. "Technically, it was for Gamble Advertising, but the truth is that I liked her idea during the meeting in Charlotte. She got shot down before anyone actually listened to her, and I didn't like seeing Warren bully her. Then this opportunity, well, it presented itself."

He brushed my hair back and kissed me. "You are special, Haylee. Not many women would do that for someone else, let alone for Sasha-B-Fierce."

"Huh, that's her nickname?"

Now it was his turn to look uncomfortable. "Not ever to be repeated, but it's what Brian calls her sometimes. It's a compliment, but I don't think one she'd enjoy hearing."

"I think it's fitting, and they should be a couple."

He sighed. "No matchmaking, especially in the workplace. It could be disastrous. I know that's totally hypocritical, but I don't care. By the way, I hope you and Catherine didn't have me as a subject of your conversation."

That earned him a swat. "Narcissism doesn't suit you. But no, neither one of us would ever gossip. One, it would make me feel disloyal toward you. And two, I'd feel guilty as hell regarding her since she likes you, and I really like her."

"Well, it isn't the ideal for me to have you two become friends for that reason. But at the same time, she's one of the best people I know in the city."

"Don't you have someone you could set her up with?"

That earned me a swat. "No matchmaking, especially by me. I want no part of it."

"All right, no more talk of that. So the shoot is set for the twenty-third of this month. Bart called, and he can do it. I'll check with Nigel about the day, but considering David's surgery is two days after Christmas, the both of them will be staying in town for the holidays, so Nigel should be able to cover for me at the office."

"Shouldn't be a problem. I believe Brian plans on being there at the shoot, so I thought I would be, too, if that's okay."

As if I would say no. "Of course it is." I wanted to warn him not to get weird about the wedding dress, but to hell with it. He'd have to deal.

"Who's the male model?" Although he inquired lightly, I knew there was nothing light about it.

"Catherine's planning to interview a couple of candidates." I didn't want to reveal I had offered up Will until my hot Aussie friend had met her and she'd decided whether to use him or not.

"So I guess now is as good a time as any to ask about your plans for the holidays. Are you traveling?" Josh asked.

"I'm not sure yet. The Hastings, you know, my father's former partner, invited me out to California. Nigel invited me to have dinner with him and David, and I have other friends I can spend it with, too. A lot of options, but I'm not sure what I'm up for at this point."

That appeared to ease his mind a little. "I don't want you spending Christmas alone. I'll be home in Virginia, but I could come back if you needed me to."

I fought the lump in my throat and the slight disappointment that he wasn't inviting me with him.

"Thank you. I appreciate it, but I'll be fine."

CHAPTER FIFTEEN

The next few weeks went by quickly as, in complete awe, I experienced the holidays New York style. I spent an entire Saturday simply marveling at all of the window displays and Rockefeller Center's tree. It truly was magical and was almost enough to take my mind off of the first Christmas I'd spend without any family.

I mailed off a package to my aunt and uncle and was pleased when the gift I'd bought for Josh arrived in the mail. What did you get a guy who had everything? Something silly, I figured, not even knowing if he'd reciprocate or when I'd even have the opportunity to give it to him. I'd hardly seen him over the last few days. He'd been booked with an engagement pertaining to the holidays each evening. Although I didn't ask, I was pretty sure he knew it had been that time of month for me. It was unsettling that he'd know that, but then I realized this was the first mature relationship I'd ever had. That sort of knowledge was probably par for the course.

I woke up early the morning of the shoot on the twenty third and headed out to the location of the studio. There I was greeted by Bart, who was busy setting up his equipment in the small intimate setting. The space was made up of one room with a smaller dressing room off to the side. This setup would mean that Bart would be close—and so would everyone watching. Seeing Gina put me instantly at ease. She'd been wonderful with hair and makeup in the Bahamas.

Will showed up and appeared astounded to see me. "Haylee?"

I smiled big. "Catherine didn't tell you I was your partner, I take it."

He shook his head and hugged me tightly. "No, but she said that someone recommended me. How are you?"

We caught up, and I was delighted to hear he was leaving in the morning to go home to Australia for the holidays to spend them with his family. Gina came over, assessing my face and nails, obviously ready to get to work. When Will asked about my plans, I hesitated slightly but then explained that I was traveling out to California to visit with a friend.

A short while later, I watched Brian and Josh come in with Sasha. All of them had the same expression on their faces once they took a look at Will. Yeah, he was hot. Even though I didn't seek to make Josh jealous, I could tell by his narrowed eyes that he wasn't pleased with my male counterpart.

Will chatted on with me until Bart came over to show us the photos from the Bahamas shoot.

I had mentioned the post-Thanksgiving modeling opportunity to Josh, but I hadn't shared a lot of details, namely Will. Judging by the expression on Josh's face, he was none too happy to see the two of us in the Bahamas.

Suddenly I realized I was being rude by not introducing Will to everyone. "Sorry, Will. This is Sasha Brooks, Brian Carpenter, and Josh Singer. They're all with Gamble Advertising and represent Delayne Diamonds."

Will shook each of their hands. I felt a growing unease at the way Josh was studying him. Will didn't help matters when he put his arm around me.

"So you two know one another?" Brian looked amused.

Will jumped in before I could form an answer. "Yeah, we met on the Atlantis shoot last month. We had a lot of fun that day. Luckily, we get to work together again. Right, Haylee girl?"

Nodding, I mentally cringed at his term of endearment for me and stole a look at Josh. His lips were now in a firm line. Fortunately, I was saved from any more awkwardness when Gina took my hand and led me to my chair to get started on my hair and makeup.

First up was the purple trapeze dress. For this I'd wear my hair half up and half down and black platform shoes.

Sasha approached, introducing Lucy, the rep from Delayne Diamonds. With Lucy was a man who looked like he was a bodybuilder, evidently hired to ensure the safety of the jewelry.

After I had donned the dress and was ready for the shot, Lucy draped me in the first set of diamonds. I was to be the girl standing against the wall at a party with a drink in my hand.

"Great, Haylee. Give me a touch of lonely and insecurity as you scan the room," Bart instructed.

I scanned and swallowed hard when I saw Josh's eyes on me. They didn't give anything away.

A few more pictures and poses with Will coming in to meet me, and then I was swooped off to get ready for the next shot.

The date scene was a simple one with my cute floral print YSL dress. Will and I pretended to be at a small intimate coffee shop table and leaned into one another, emulating the body language of a successful date. He made me laugh with his disaster story of a first date, and before I knew it, Bart called a wrap. Turned out just chatting with Will made it feel natural instead of like work.

Next up was the black Givenchy gown. The scene was a romantic dinner for two at a fancy restaurant. My hair was mostly up, and I was positioned so that the slit in the dress exposed my left leg, where I wore a diamond anklet and black stilettos.

"Now that's hot." The voice had to be Brian's.

My face heated. Nothing like posing with an entire peanut gallery mere feet away lobbing comments.

The props people were still busy fussing with the table setup, so I opened the ring box to take a peek. "It's absolutely gorgeous, isn't it?" I said to no one in particular.

Will glimpsed at it and shrugged.

Admiring rings must be more of a girl thing. Confirming that thought, Sasha and Catherine came over to take a look.

"I have to get a peep, too. God, it's even better in person. Exquisite," Catherine said, and Sasha nodded.

Both Brian and Josh appeared uncomfortable when I glanced over. Then Bart called for the scene to start, and we were back to work.

"Great body language, you two. Haylee, do you think you can give him a kiss? Make sure the ring is visible on the side of his face," Bart requested.

It was no hardship to kiss Will, but it was certainly awkward with Josh looking on. I noticed he stepped away the moment the shot was over.

The final scene before we broke for lunch was the bridal shower. For this I wore the pink Jean Desses dress in which I'd met Catherine. It was perfect for a fancy bridal shower. Lucy came in and changed out the diamonds while Gina put my hair back in a twist. She made the look subtle with nude lips and pastels.

"Okay, my dear, make sure we see the ring. Play with the bow and look like you're excited about what's in the box."

I did a few more shots, some while sipping on a mimosa and others while holding up a lacy garment.

"Good, fantastic. That dress shows up well with that background," Bart remarked. "Okay, that's a wrap on this one."

By lunchtime I was grateful we only had three scenes remaining. The lingerie scene was the first up, so I took my water and my fruit and regretfully stayed away from the sandwich and chips.

"Man, Haylee, is that all you're eating?" Brian asked.

"You'd stick to fruit and water, too, if they were putting you in underwear for the next shot," Sasha quipped.

He took it good-naturedly and gave me a wink.

I kept the robe on as long as possible before the next shot, but I had to remove it partially when the ring of diamonds was placed around my neck, all thirty-two carats of them. This was the most expensive piece and would set off the ice-blue ensemble in the scene for which I hoped Josh would not show up.

I was not in luck, as everyone was standing around mere feet from the bed, including my boss.

When Will took off his shirt and Gina gave him oil to set off his abs, I swear both Sasha and Catherine audibly gasped. I might have appreciated the view myself if my secret boyfriend hadn't been watching me watch Will.

"All right, Will, sit up against the headboard. Haylee, you're going to lie across his lap on your side. Light the candles, and let's do this." Bart instructed everyone to take their places.

I swallowed hard at the intimate shot we were about to do and dropped the robe, refusing to look at anyone in the room aside from Will. The problem was that his appreciative look made me blush two shades anyhow. "Stop," I whispered, embarrassed.

"Sorry, you're absolutely stunning," he reassured me.

"Thanks." I awkwardly tried to position myself. I was sure the pose would photograph well, but looking good in print and looking natural in real life were often two different things.

"Lean up more, Haylee. Good. Someone get her a magazine," Bart called.

I did a scene flipping through it.

"Let me see both the engagement and wedding rings."

They would be hard to miss, I thought, since I was wearing a four-carat solitaire and a band worth another two carats.

"Okay, you two. Will, stretch out on the bed, flex the abs. Yes, across the bed, and Haylee, I want you to be on your stomach facing me and up on your elbows reading the magazine. Good, but too much cleavage. Pull it up a little."

Shit. I sat up and tugged at the corset, managing to catch Josh's dark look before I got back into position.

Bart looked a little frustrated. "I can't see the ensemble very well in either shot, so new plan. Will, I want you to sit on the edge of the bed, feet on the floor. Haylee, stand in front of him, and Will, put your hands on her hips."

He moved over to us and placed us in the intimate position, with me turned slightly more than Will toward the camera. "Good," he encouraged, taking a couple pics and then coming back.

I was stiff, but how could I help it? I was in lingerie in front of everyone who was looking on.

Will's fingers tickled my side.

"Hey." I giggled at his funny face.

"I thought it might relax you. Do you have plans for New Year's Eve?"

"I'm not sure, but I don't think so."

"Well, let me know. I'll be back the day before. We should do something."

"A little less chatty, please. I need more sexy, smoldering looks," Bart interjected.

I couldn't help it; I giggled. Then Will laughed. When I looked at Bart, even he was now smiling.

"Okay, you two, I'm going to get above you. I want you both

across the bed gazing at each other. I want tender and smoldering looks."

Sure enough, there we were giggling at the fact that Bart was standing literally between us looking down. Finally, Will turned serious and caressed my face. He pressed his thumb on my bottom lip, causing me to catch my breath. Even if I was completely involved with Josh, Will was too good-looking and sweet for me to avoid some reaction. Damn.

"Good. I like those shots. Catherine, what do you think?" Bart asked her to come over and look while Will and I sat on the bed waiting.

"Holy intensity, you two. You sure you aren't a couple?" Catherine joked.

Blushing, I glanced over to where Josh was now ignoring me, apparently completely engrossed in his phone.

"You looked amazing," Gina confirmed, taking off all of the heavy eye makeup for the next shot.

Everyone was hanging out while Gina did my hair. She started chatting with Bart about her holiday plans. It was obvious the two of them had worked together a number of times over the years. Turning toward me, she asked, "Are you sure you're set on traveling to California, Haylee? Because you're welcome to come over to my house for dinner. I'm just over the river in Jersey."

Oh, shit. She'd overheard me tell Will my fictitious plans. Now everyone seemed to be focused on me at once, including Josh.

"Uh, yes, I'm going out to LA to meet my old roommate, Angela." I figured she would be the best excuse as no one knew her, and there wouldn't be a lot of questions.

I was grateful for Bart's interruption. "I'm almost ready. You can get her into the dress."

"All set. Let's go," Gina announced, having sleeked my hair back into a fun ponytail.

I loved the Pucci dress. It was vibrant and cool and the perfect vacation dress. It paired great with the vintage pearl and diamond jewelry. My oversized sunglasses and beach bag completed the look. We posed in front of the green screen and clinked champagne glasses for the next few shots. Catherine had mentioned something about inserting a beach scene for the actual finished product.

"Show us the rings, Haylee," Bart ordered.

We managed to go through a couple more poses, one of which had me on Will's lap in a beach chair. Luckily, this shot was the simplest of them all, and we were done quickly.

Now for the crowning jewel. Gina pulled out all the stops for this one, arranging my hair into a bridal up-do, and Lucy came over with the pink diamond pendant necklace and matching earrings.

"God, it's perfection, isn't it?" Sasha proclaimed while she and Catherine looked at me in the jewels. It was the culmination of our three combined efforts, and we savored the moment. Sasha did the honors with champagne while Catherine handed me a box.

"I knew as soon as I saw these they were meant for this dress."

I flipped open the lid and found the most breathtaking shoes I'd ever seen. "Oh, my God, Catherine. They're beautiful."

"Blush-colored Valentino lace pumps with bows," she supplied.

We all sighed while I could hear Brian's voice carry.

"What the hell are they all staring at?"

Josh answered in a mildly amused voice. "Shoes. Women and shoes."

Even Lucy came over to covet them, another box in hand. "All right, ladies, for the final engagement/wedding ring combo, I thought we'd let you pick. Here are the five we have to choose from."

"Huh, well, would you look at that? It's the only time I've ever seen so many women quiet," Brian teased.

Sasha tossed him an amused look over her shoulder.

"Haylee, you do the honors. You're going to be in your mother's wedding dress; pick the ring you would most want," Catherine offered.

I had to keep myself from glancing to see if Josh was within hearing distance. I could have passed on the offer, but what the hell. This was like a trial run for my mother's amazing dress, and there was one exquisite ring which had first caught my interest online. It did so again here in person. "This one," I declared.

Lucy smiled and nodded. "That's my favorite, too. 1950s vintage, four-carat round center stone with intricate side stone baguettes. And the wedding band that goes with it sparkles."

We all just nodded dumbly, and I had to ask. "How much does this retail for?"

"Together, the set is over a hundred thousand."

"Holy shit," again from Brian. Again a reminder of just how close everyone was to us.

"Cheapskate," Sasha admonished. Not for the first time, I saw sparks fly between the two of them.

He only shrugged. "Not cheap, merely practical. Would you wear that much money on your hand, Haylee, for real?"

"No way, but it's fun to pretend for the day," I admitted before making my way into the changing room to put on the dress. I don't know why I was feeling so nervous, but the thought of having Josh see me in the gown I eventually planned to wear at my own wedding left me feeling out of sorts.

I stepped into the dress and turned around for Gina to zip me up. Catherine and Sasha were there smiling, and for a weird moment it felt like it would if I were an actual bride trying on *the* dress in front of my girlfriends.

"Oh, Haylee, your mother would be so proud," Catherine exclaimed.

And just like that I was sobbing, embarrassingly so. Catherine, Sasha, and Gina all sought to soothe me while I felt the weight of the holidays coming up.

I finally took a deep breath and calmed myself. "I need a few minutes. Could you tell Bart and Will?" I watched as they all went out searching for tissues and to talk to Bart.

It wasn't long before Josh came in. "You okay?"

I faced him, watching his eyes widen at the sight of me in my dress and probably at my running mascara. We both were speechless until Gina came back in with tissues.

"I, uh, heard you crying and wanted to make sure you were all right," he explained, breaking the spell.

I had to fight the urge to cross the small room and have him envelop me in a hug. "I, um, I got overwhelmed. I've never put this dress on, and I was thinking of my mom. I'm sorry. I didn't mean to worry anyone, and I didn't mean for you to have to redo my makeup, Gina."

She waved me off, wiping tears of her own. "Honey, I'm a mama, and you don't have to apologize. Hell, it feels more like a real wedding with the tears. So let's get you touched up and out there, okay?"

I gave one last apologetic look toward Josh and then let Gina work her magic. When I finally came out, Will was in his tux, munching on a protein bar and chatting with Bart while Josh and Brian were talking with Catherine and Sasha.

"Ah, bella, you look beautiful," Bart approved, coming toward me.

I bit the inside of my cheek and tried not to cry again. "Thank you, Bart."

Will's reaction was sweet. "Love, aren't I the lucky man today? Now, why don't you think of what you'll pig out on after this shoot? Pizza, pasta, or maybe a hamburger. Take your mind off of the sadness, yeah?"

My hand squeezed his, and I smiled. His joking was what I'd needed to distract me, and I was back in work mode.

"Okay, take a seat on the settee. And Will, you stand behind it, reaching down. I want it with your arms reaching up, Haylee," Bart requested. He positioned my dress so that my beautiful shoes were showing, and I reached up so that my ring would be as visible as Will's. "Beautiful. Okay, now stand up. I want you two to do the *kiss the bride* moment by joining hands. Cock the foot back so we can see that shoe. Great, great."

I swallowed hard as Will dipped his head to kiss me. My heart fluttered for a beat. There was an overriding sweetness that I'd never felt when Josh kissed me. It made me long for something I hadn't known was missing.

"You're gorgeous," he whispered, winking at me afterwards.

I was thankful he was so good at setting me at ease. Posing seemed natural and simple with him. "Thank you."

"Now can you pick her up in front of the green screen? I'm thinking an over-the-threshold shot," Bart requested.

I groaned at the thought of being picked up and panicked as Will took off his jacket and loosened his tie as directed. "I'm heavy."

"Haylee, please. You're what, a buck-o-five?"

"I'm definitely not one hundred and five pounds." Now I was even more flustered.

"So what, one-fifteen?"

"Will, let me give you some advice: stop guessing a woman's weight," Brian supplied from three feet away.

"Finally, he spreads words of wisdom," Sasha laughed.

"Sorry." Will winced, giving me a sheepish smile.

"You're fine, but I'm one hundred and thirty pounds, for the record."

His expression showed his shock. "Wow, you're heavier than you look."

That hadn't exactly been a compliment, and my narrowed

eyes reflected that. "All right, careful with the dress," I warned before getting scooped up.

It felt odd to be picked up by Will. Josh must have felt the same uneasiness, for when I risked a look, I saw him turn and leave.

"God, you're heavy," Will jested, earning a swat and getting me back in the moment as we laughed.

Bart took his last shots with Catherine approving that we had enough. It was a wrap.

I'd never been so exhausted after a shoot, both emotionally and physically. I was confused over my reaction to Will's kiss and not sure how to feel about Josh's jealousy.

I WAS RELIEVED to be back in my jeans and thankful when Catherine had all of my dresses back in their bags, ready to be delivered to Josh's office that night. I'm sure it must've seemed weird to her, but I couldn't very well give her my home address. I'd just have to go back by the office to get them tonight.

When I came out of the changing room, everyone was gathered around chatting. The exception was Josh, who hadn't returned. Sasha was all smiles as she relayed how happy the client had been with the focus on the jewelry.

"Bella, it's a pleasure as always. Merry Christmas to you and safe journey to the West Coast." Bart was all packed up and kissed both my cheeks.

My hands took his. "Merry Christmas, Bart, and thank you. I can't tell you how much it means that you would photograph me again."

"It's always a pleasure. Perhaps I'll do your actual wedding someday."

"Maybe. Take care, Bart," I managed, feeling weird all over

again that the day in question might include Bart and my dress, but would never include Josh.

Catherine gave me a hug. "Merry Christmas, Haylee. I can't wait to see these pictures. Josh said he had a flight to catch and had to leave early."

Will gave me a kiss on the cheek, and I promised to call him when he got back in order to talk about New Year's Eve plans.

I embraced both Sasha and Gina and turned down the offer of a shared cab. I wanted to make the short walk to the office by myself so that I could take a breath. I also wanted to put Josh's gift on his desk since it wasn't like I could leave it at his place. He obviously wouldn't get it until after the holidays, but how was I supposed to have known he'd leave from the photo shoot.

"I'll walk with you," Brian offered, surprising me.

Although I would've preferred to do it alone, it wasn't like I could say no. "Uh, sure, I guess."

Brian and I walked in silence the first block. "So, are you going home to see family for the holidays?" I asked, making small talk.

"Yes, flying out to Virginia tomorrow morning. So what's the deal between you and Josh?"

Stopping after a few steps, I waited until he noticed I wasn't walking beside him any longer.

"I know it's none of my business," he said, stepping back toward me.

"Agreed. It isn't any of your business. I will simply say that he's my boss, and I'm lucky for the opportunity he's given me." I didn't need this shit now, especially with my emotions all over the place.

"So are you and Will an item?"

"Again, none of your business." I could absolutely refute being anything more than friends, but at the moment I didn't feel I owed anyone an explanation.

He contemplated, and I remembered what Josh had said

about Brian asking about me in Charlotte. "And if you're about to ask me out, please don't. I think you're a nice and funny guy, and I'm flattered. But if you want my honest opinion, I'm not the girl for you."

He laughed out loud. "Oh, I think you have enough guys at the moment who would like to date you, Haylee girl, without me adding to the mix."

I narrowed my eyes at his use of Will's endearment.

He laughed some more. "Come on, it's freezing. Let's walk."

We fell into step again.

"I'm curious. So who's the girl for me, then, if you're not? You sounded like you had someone in mind."

"Oh, I think you know."

"Inter-office relationships can be tricky." His innuendo was unmistakable.

"Are they? I wouldn't know."

"Because they aren't tricky, or because there isn't something going on?"

I stopped again. "Why don't you spit it out, Brian? Or better yet, go ask your best friend."

He smirked as if he'd been hoping I would suggest he do just that. "Okay, I've known Josh forever. And I have to say that in the last couple of months since he's met you, he's been happier than I've seen him in a very long time."

Oh, shit, this wasn't what I'd expected to hear. I'd assumed his intention was to make it sleazy. "Oh," was all I managed.

He took my arm and sighed, falling back into step. "And I did ask him, but he's towing the same line you are. So I think one of three things is happening. Either there's nothing going on, and I'm being completely offensive to you right now. Or there's something definitely going on, and neither of you want anyone to know. Or what I think is most likely is there's potential for something, and if I know him, he isn't acting on it because of the position he's in."

There he went with the assumption Josh wouldn't act. "What would you recommend, then, if I were theoretically in the third situation you describe?"

We'd arrived at the office building and went into the lobby. There he turned toward me. "I would recommend that you keep doing what you're doing, but at some point, you'll probably have to make the first move."

My lips twitched. If he only knew that's exactly what I'd done.

"So I'm curious. What made you reach out to Sasha? She wasn't exactly nice to you when you first met."

We stepped on the elevator heading up to the office. "I imagine it'd be exhausting having to fight to take charge and be heard. I saw that in your meeting in Charlotte. She has to work three times as hard, all while getting half the respect. I'd be bitchy too if I had to go through that every single day."

He appeared to consider my words. "I respect her fully, for the record, and can appreciate how hard she has to work in this industry. But I can't seem to figure out a way to make her believe she doesn't always have to fight."

"You're a smart man, Brian with an I. You'll figure it out." We both stepped off the elevator as Josh came out of his office. I hadn't expected to see him tonight.

He looked equally as surprised. "I didn't think you'd be back this evening."

"Catherine sent the dresses over here, and I wanted to bring them home tonight. Plus, I needed to grab some things."

Brian decided to take his leave. "Merry Christmas, Haylee. Amazing job today. The client will be thrilled, and I can't wait to see the photos."

"Thanks, Brian. Merry Christmas to you, too. Good night."

"See you in Virginia, Josh."

Josh gave him a brief nod in return.

Once the elevator doors closed, we simply stood there looking at one another until Josh finally broke the silence.

"Did you request Will on the shoot today?"

Shit. Catherine must have said something. "I suggested that Catherine interview him. He was easy to work with in the Bahamas, and I wanted to feel relaxed with someone on this one."

"Why didn't you mention it to me?"

"I didn't think it was relevant. Today was a job, and Will is a male model who I recommended but Catherine ultimately chose."

He smirked and then turned to go into his office, forcing me to follow if I wanted to continue the conversation. "Yeah, it's not relevant in the least that you recommended the same guy from the Bahamas to do a lingerie and wedding scene today."

"Will and I are just friends, and I'm at ease with him. I'm sorry if today was rough for you to watch. It didn't exactly make me comfortable, either, if I'm being honest."

"You know what? This isn't the type of conversation I want to have in the office." He grabbed his jacket.

My temper flared. "Right. So you can fuck in me in your office, but we can't have this discussion. Why don't we take it back to your apartment, then?"

Well, that earned me a glare. "Where's this coming from?"

"Where's what coming from?"

"The hostility over things that we've already established as boundaries."

That was laughable. "You mean you set them as boundaries, and you started with the hostility. I'm merely returning it."

"I was going to suggest taking this to your place, but since you seem opposed to the idea, let's discuss it here. How many times have you been out with your friend Will?"

I didn't appreciate his tone, but I had nothing to hide, either. "I met him in the Bahamas over Thanksgiving weekend and again today. That's it. How many times have you been out with Catherine?"

"What the fuck does she have to do with anything?"

My hands clenched with frustration. "Because you don't tell me what plans you have or who you have them with. Tell me something. Do you have a New Year's Eve date? Are you going out with anyone?"

He stood quiet, and I knew the answer.

"Catherine?"

"Are you guys discussing me now? I told you early on I value my privacy: in my apartment, in my life. You said you trusted me."

"Trust is a two-way street. You shouldn't care that Will was the model today because, again, we value privacy, and we don't have the type of relationship where we tell each other who we're seeing or when so long as we aren't sleeping with them."

"It was one kiss, Haylee, and I'd had too much to drink. I was caught off guard last night, so it took a moment, okay?"

He must've recognized I had no idea what he was talking about when my faced drained of color.

"I didn't even know you were out with her last night, let alone about any kissing," I said quietly.

He looked frustrated. "Look, last evening was to make sure Catherine understood that we were friends; we will always just be friends."

"Fine. Maybe I should kiss Will and figure out if that's what I want, too."

Well, that did it. His eyes darkened and his mouth thinned. "First of all, you did kiss him today, several times, and secondly, so much for never wanting to make me jealous and play games, right?"

"I'm simply trying to catch up. So far I've seen you kissing one woman in the office lobby, and now I hear that you kissed another one last night. I like Will and wouldn't mind working together again."

"So you want to kiss Will, to go out with him?"

"I don't know," I answered honestly.

"Which one: kiss or go out with?" His temper was building.

Instead of warning me to retreat, it was only pissing me off further.

"I don't want to be made the fool. You're out with all of these beautiful women, and I'm not going to sit at home waiting on your phone call or for you to come by. You didn't even text me once over the Thanksgiving holiday. You call the shots, and I wait pathetically for them. I won't be that girl."

"Dammit, Haylee, you aren't that girl. I thought we agreed to this. Then you become friends with Catherine, and all of a sudden we're fighting."

"I don't want to argue anymore with you." I told myself it didn't matter. Why was I expending energy over something with an expiration date anyhow? Arguing over this was silly and almost pissed me off as much as he did.

He paced and then sighed. "Fine. No more fighting. You know what? I think you should go out with Will."

He moved closer to me and then crushed his mouth down on mine.

All of my frustration and emotions came to the surface as I met his hungry kiss with one of my own.

He nipped my lower lip and then held me with a fist in my hair. Dominance and hunger were coursing through his body, and I wanted all of it.

"See if he turns you on the way that I do," he mumbled, unfastening my jeans and taking them down to my boots before frantically cupping my sex.

I whimpered, wanting more.

He massaged me with unrelenting fingers. "See if he makes

you as drenched as I do, if you want his fingers inside of your tight pussy like this."

Clenching down around his fingers, I heard the hiss of his breath. He turned me around abruptly, set my hands on his desk, and entered me from the back in one stroke. I savored the burn of not quite being all the way ready for him.

"See if you don't wish it was me fucking you instead."

I couldn't talk, couldn't do anything but meet his thrusts and enjoy this sweet torture he was inflicting on me. My body was on sensory overload as I felt him building.

"I want you to remember the feeling of me inside of you." He reached around for my clit, giving me the push I needed to have me coming at the same time he did.

We both stood there for what seemed eternity. Wincing as he withdrew, I heard the sound of him zipping up but didn't bother to turn around while I reached down for my panties and jeans and tugged them up.

His strong hands helped me, and then he embraced me from behind. "I told you I would never use sex as a weapon or punishment again, and I broke that promise," he whispered quietly.

I turned and brushed his face briefly before crossing over to my purse. "It wasn't punishment as much as it was angry sex." I had in fact wanted it as much as he had. But again it highlighted that I was missing something. Sweet and tender wasn't the way that Josh Singer did things. I pulled his gift out and handed it over. "This is for you. It's your Christmas gift. Have a good trip to Virginia tonight, all right?"

He looked at the package and then back at me. "So this is how we leave it?"

I swallowed hard. "I think we both need some time. This feels too complicated for a short-term relationship. I'll see you when you get back and Merry Christmas." I kissed him on the cheek and headed downstairs before he could see my tears.

I was numb while driving in the cab back to my apartment

with my dress bags, half hoping Josh would delay his flight and spend the night with me instead. Stupid girl, I thought, letting myself into my apartment. He'd never promised more, and here I was disappointed that I'd never asked for it.

A gold envelope with a red bow was placed on my kitchen counter. I knew it had to be from him. Opening it, I smiled at the first class ticket to Perth to see my family there. It was incredibly generous and thoughtful. I was tempted to call or text him but thought it better to focus on getting through the holiday and get a rein on my emotions before dealing with *us*.

CHAPTER SIXTEEN

It was Christmas Eve, and I had things to do before I could barricade myself in my room and shut the world off. I made myself get up and shower and put on some makeup even though I didn't want to. Then I went to the grocery store and laundromat before settling in to spend an hour composing Merry Christmas emails and sending out text messages. It would make it easier if I didn't have to respond to holiday messages asking how I was doing but instead preempted them.

I called my aunt and uncle, explaining that I was at a friend's house and had left my iPad at home as an excuse for being unable to FaceTime. I put on background music in order to complete the lie and so I could make it short. My Aunt J sounded relieved that I was spending the holiday with people, and we ended with laughs and a promise I would call her in a few days.

Finally, I thought, almost done. Fixing a bowl of cereal, I took out the bottle of pills I hadn't used since my breakdown. They were prescribed sleeping pills, and I could take up to two. But one was enough to put me out for eight to ten hours, so I'd start with that.

My way of controlling the oncoming depression was to fast forward through the holidays and avoid it. Maybe it was a cop-out, but it sure as hell beat crying my eyes out and feeling sorry for myself.

I had about twenty minutes before the medicine took effect and designated this time toward opening my mom's gift and card. The card was incredibly sad. My mom had known she was dying when she wrote it and that we wouldn't spend this Christmas together. It took three attempts before I finally got through it. God, how I missed my parents. Christmas hadn't been the same for years without my father, but now that both of them were gone, the pain was overwhelming.

After opening the box from my mother, it took a moment for me to recognize what it was. The note with it confirmed that my mom had taken the stone from her diamond engagement ring put into a bezel setting. Earlier, she'd told me she'd had to sell it to pay bills. I figured I'd never see it again. I put the necklace on with trembling hands and buried my face in my pillow before letting the pill work its magic and floating off into a dreamless sleep.

I didn't stir until nine o'clock the next morning. The problem with the sleeping pills was that you didn't wake up rested. Instead you felt groggy and lethargic. I took a few minutes to check my email, to which I had replies from quite a few people.

I also had a text from Josh that simply said, ***"Merry Christmas."***

I texted him back, ***"Merry Christmas, Josh."***

And that was it. He was with his family. What else could I expect?

After taking a quick shower, I ate a bowl of cereal, downed a Diet Coke, and then settled back into bed. This time I'd take two pills. I'd never taken the max before, but I wanted to sleep for as long as possible and not wake up in the middle of the night. I lay back down, hearing the buzz of my phone a short while later but not able to coherently figure out if it was a text or a call. Drifting, my last thought was that it would have to wait.

Was that Josh's voice? I must've been either dreaming or hallucinating. So this is what two pills did to someone? I wondered what time it was, but I couldn't bring myself to lift my eyes open to check. So heavy. Jesus, now I was hearing Rafael the doorman's voice while I felt myself being carried. I mumbled in my sleep to a dreamed-up Josh and was back out.

The next thing I knew, I had a light shining into each of my eyes. What the hell? And then a strange man's voice and back to dreaming of Josh. My sheets felt extraordinarily soft, I thought, snuggling deeper into them and breathing in his scent. Never would I take two pills again; I was now dreaming of smells. And was someone saying my name?

"What?" I asked, not knowing if anyone answered. Then I heard my name again and felt a cool hand on my forehead and soft lips touching mine. Hmm, maybe I would take two pills always. I was kissing Josh, and suddenly I was snuggled up next to his hard body. Yes, definitely two pills from now on.

The third time I awoke, I managed to open my eyes and then promptly closed them again because I must still be dreaming. This wasn't my room. Let's try this again. Right eye open, left eye open, still not it. What the hell? I moved into a seated position and rubbed my eyes. Definitely not my room.

This room was big. I couldn't tell what time of day it was because the large windows on one side had blackout shades drawn. I glanced over to the other side and saw a small, sleek alarm clock and focused: one-thirty. Was it am or pm?

My hands smoothed the sheets and I experienced deja vu from my dream, for they were the most luxuriously soft sheets I'd ever felt. The bed was massive. From what I could see, everything around me was in gray and blue hues. I needed a light and fumbled on the table for one before giving up. Feeling along the wall, I finally found a switch and shielded my eyes as a reading light shown down from over the headboard.

Okay, that was progress. So was the fact that I was still in my oversized T-shirt and workout shorts. I swung my legs over the side and looked down at the hardwood floors that gleamed. I tried to get on my feet but was still too unsteady.

"Hello?" I called out in a croaky voice. I was relieved when Josh opened the door.

"Hey, how are you feeling?" he asked quietly. He came to sit next to me on the bed and searched my face.

"Groggy, but otherwise fine. Where am I?"

"My bedroom."

I thought about the irony of finally being in his place only when passed out. "How did I get here?"

"I called Maria to find out which flight you were on, and she said you didn't book through her. Then I called your old roommate, Angela, and she told me she received an email that you were staying in New York and having dinner with Gina. I called Gina— You get the picture."

Oh, my God. Covering my face in my hands, I felt ashamed beyond belief.

"Don't worry. I smoothed it over by calling them back and letting them know I had misunderstood and you were in Northern California with family friends."

"Thank you," I whispered.

He rubbed my back and sighed. "Haylee, what happened? Were you ever traveling to California?"

Shaking my head, I tried to get a handle on my humiliation. "I just needed to be by myself. I didn't want to go anywhere, but I also didn't want everyone to worry about me. I hated to lie, but I needed to be alone." I finally glanced at his face and realized what a mess I must look. "What time is it? What day?"

"It's the twenty-sixth, and it's one-thirty pm."

"Well, that's good, then. First Christmas down." I was trying to play it cool and saw his temper the moment it ignited.

"Don't you dare make light of it. I thought maybe you were trying to kill yourself. That maybe our argument coupled with the holidays might have pushed you over, and I wasn't there for you when I should've been. Even my doctor who came to check on you said that with your history you should be talking with someone and shouldn't have been left alone. I can't believe I said the things I did to you right before the holidays. Once I found out you weren't where you said you'd be and you didn't answer your phone, I couldn't get up here fast enough. I should've been your rock."

My tears started falling.

Josh took a deep breath and took my hands.

I bit my lip and tried to explain. "I would never take my life, not even when I was in the darkest place. Please don't feel guilty. You didn't sign on for the burden of providing my happiness when you met me, and you can't be my rock; no one can. I have to learn to be my own rock."

"That's crap, Haylee. I can be your rock when you need it."

"Rocks are permanent. Even if you think that your parents or your spouse are your rock, they leave you and you find out that they can't be that any longer. I guess what I'm saying is nothing is permanent. Relying on other people for your happiness or to lift you up ends up disappointing you in the end."

"That's depressing," he sighed.

Yeah, it kind of was. "I'm sorry I lied, but I couldn't stand the thought of you feeling guilty, and here you are feeling it anyhow. I'm sorry you had to come up here and ruin your holiday plans. Plus, this wasn't the way I wanted to see your apartment."

"You didn't ruin anything. I was calling Maria so that I could go out to California to see you. I missed you, and then I started feeling terrible about the way we left things."

I put a finger to his lips. "No more guilt or feeling sorry for me, please. I'm not that fragile. I can stand you being angry or pissed off at me, but I can't stand the thought of you feeling sorry or guilty, okay?"

He smiled and his hand drifted across my cheek. "How do you feel?"

"A little bit sleepy. I could probably crash another couple hours." I yawned as if on cue.

"Well, we have plans, but you can sleep soon. I need you to shower and dress comfortably. Just pack your passport and whatever toiletry stuff you'll need over the next few days."

"What do you mean? Are we flying to California?"

"Not unless you want to. I had another surprise in mind."

"All right, but for the record this isn't a *feel sorry for me* trip, is it?"

He laughed. "Uh, no, it's an *I want some alone time with my girlfriend* type trip, okay?" He kissed my forehead, and it made me smile like a loon. "You're welcome to use my bathroom. There's a steam shower that might feel good."

"Thanks, but I'll get back to my place where my stuff is. I also don't want this to be the circumstance in which I see your place."

He seemed to understand and took my arm, helping me out of bed and to walk unsteadily through his bedroom door.

"What are you doing?" he asked, looking at me as I covered my eyes.

"I don't want to see it yet," I giggled and was unceremoniously tossed over his shoulder.

"Well, if I'm leading the blind, it's easier to simply carry you."

He took me out his front door and into the hallway while I sneaked a peek. His place was spacious and very gray and chrome with the windows floor-to-ceiling on the far wall. Closing my eyes again, I hoped there would be another opportunity to see it.

"Okay, what do I pack?" I questioned, fresh from the shower and in a sweatshirt and the yoga pants he loved.

"Just your bath stuff."

I stood with my hands on my hips. "Am I going to be naked the whole time?"

"Most of the time," he retorted.

I went and put my arms around him and breathed in his scent. "We could start with a little preview." My hands made their way down to his glorious ass which was wonderfully set off in jeans.

But his hands came around, taking both of mine and holding them in front of me. "As much as it pains me to turn that offer down, we have a plane to catch. Now throw some shampoo and a toothbrush in a bag, and let's go."

"I need underwear," I chided, crossing to the drawer.

He moved to block my way. "Nope, you won't need it."

"How about a swimsuit? Or a dress or something?"

"Nope."

"What about workout clothes? I'd like to go running."

This at least got some consideration. "Fine, a pair of workout shorts, shoes, and a T-shirt. That's it."

I threw in my sports bra as well as a couple of pairs of underwear since I wasn't running commando. Some hair stuff, makeup, and my hygiene kit—and I had my small duffle bag set to go. "Okay, I'm packed."

"WAKE UP, beautiful. We're landing soon."

We had boarded Josh's private jet a few hours ago, and I'd fallen asleep within minutes of takeoff. Stretching, I smiled apologetically. "Sorry I wasn't much company."

"You're fine. I had some business stuff to do anyhow, and now we can hopefully enjoy some work-free days."

That sounded wonderful, and then panic set in. "Wait. I took off, and Nigel is out starting tomorrow with David's surgery. I'm scheduled to be in the office."

He only smiled. "I gave everyone the week off. It costs more to heat the place and turn on the lights than it's worth to keep the office open. Plus, the boss is taking a real vacation for the first time in years. Besides all that, if I need something, I know where to find you. I've already let Nigel know that you're on call all week, so he has nothing to worry about."

Well, then, I guess it was good to be the boss. "Sounds like you've thought of everything. It makes me feel kind of good that the boss is taking his first real vacation in years with me. Thank you."

His hand squeezed mine, and a few minutes later we were on the ground. The sun had set, but I could tell from the balmy temperature and the shadows of palm trees we were some place tropical. We descended the steps of the plane onto the tarmac. There Josh shook the hand of an older gentleman who loaded our bags into the back of a Jeep Wrangler.

I still wasn't sure where we were, but gauging from the palm trees and warm, moist air, we were on an island. The two men spoke for a few minutes, and then Josh came back with keys in his hand. "Shall we?"

We drove in the Jeep for about twenty-five minutes. I sensed there was water on one side of the road and looked toward the road signs for any sort of clue.

"Okay, I give up. Where are we?"

"Tortola in the British Virgin Islands. You can't see it now, but the water is beautiful here."

"I can't wait. Are we in a resort?"

"You'll find out soon enough," he hedged with mischief in his eyes.

I enjoyed studying his profile from the passenger side as he navigated the winding road. He was the most relaxed I'd ever seen him, and the thought of having him all to myself was almost too good to be true.

A short time later we pulled into a driveway with a large iron gate into which Josh punched a code.

I had expected someone to come out, but instead it looked as though we were alone as we entered through the front door of an elegant two-story house.

"Wow." I stepped inside the foyer and glanced at the beautiful staircase, marble floors, and the gorgeous open room that led out to what looked like a pool.

"I was hoping you'd like it."

"Is this yours?"

"No, it's a rental, but the pictures seemed nice online."

"And it's only the two of us, no one else?"

He took my hand and led me into the gourmet kitchen. "Just the two of us, not even a chef. Hopefully they stocked some food." He opened the refrigerator, which was completely packed with meats and produce.

"Um, who's cooking?" A chef I was not.

"Don't worry, I'll be the head chef, and you can be my sous-chef. Are you hungry now?" He put his arms around me.

I shook my head. "No, but I would love to see the house."

We started out on the first floor and then proceeded upstairs. The master bedroom was impressive with its large four-poster king-sized bed and the French doors that opened onto a balcony. I stepped outside and could hear, and practically feel, the ocean only steps away. "I can't wait until morning to see everything."

His arms came around me from the back, and I sighed with pure contentment.

"Tell me something you're thinking right now," he queried softly.

"I'm thinking that I can't wait to wake up with you tomorrow morning without having to hurry out of bed for anything. We haven't done that, and it's something I'm looking forward to for the next few days."

"I didn't know it bothered you," he murmured.

I shrugged and turned toward him. "Well, of course you wouldn't as I've never mentioned anything until now. And I wouldn't use the word *bother*, but I like the idea of waking up with you tomorrow. That's all."

"My refreshingly logical Haylee. You don't expect me to be a mind reader. I can't tell you what an amazing gift that is."

I could only laugh and mentally thank my father who once told me, 'Honey, men are pretty black and white creatures. No matter how obvious the hint a woman gives a man, it would be easier if she simply told him what it is that she wants. Men are not good at guessing, believe me.'

"It feels good to be here. Tell me something," I requested.

"I loved my Christmas gift, and I may even start eating cereal again."

It hadn't been much to get him a bowl that separated the cereal from the milk to avoid soggy cereal, but then what did you get a millionaire who had everything? "Well, your gift was beyond generous and very thoughtful. Now I'll definitely get to go see my family before I start school. Thank you."

"I'm pleased to see you happy and not so down."

"I wasn't down; I was merely coping. Yes, it was a weak thing to do, but I needed the easy way out this year. Next year, hopefully, I'll be stronger."

"There isn't a part of you that isn't strong." His arms wrapped around me and lifted me up. "Light as a feather."

"Are you comparing your strength to Will's?"

"Maybe. So who feels like they can lift you easier?"

"You can." Men were so strange in what made them jealous.

His thumb traveled along my bottom lip, and then his mouth found mine. It was a different kiss than I'd ever had from him. Sweet and tender. He placed me in the center of the four-poster bed and took his time worshipping my body from head to toe. So this was what it felt like to be made love to. It was as if his body was showing all of the emotions he couldn't form into words.

JOSH CAME in the next morning with a breakfast tray that included scrambled eggs, toast, and fresh fruit.

Now this was a way to start a day. I sat up and crossed my legs, tucking a sheet around me.

"Feel free to lose the sheet." He winked before going back downstairs for his own tray and then taking a seat beside me.

"This is really good as I was starving. I think I may have to keep you," I teased.

"Well, one of us has to cook. Otherwise we'd be eating nothing but cereal."

"You say that as if it would be a bad thing. I happen to love cereal."

"I know. I saw your stash of Frosted Flakes in your apartment."

"Tell me something?"

"This is the first time while on a vacation I haven't wanted to go back to work. Instead I'm thinking about the next opportunity we can manage some time down here. Do you like the house? I was thinking of buying it."

I'm pretty sure my smile was the goofy sort that you can't help when someone has made you gloriously happy. "I love it. Is it for sale?"

He looked at me with the expression of a man used to getting what he wanted. "Everything is."

With his money, I imagined most things were.

"Now tell me something, Haylee."

"I feel comfortable asking you almost anything. You have a way of never making me feel stupid for asking. I guess it's nice to feel this relaxed with someone."

"Hmm, sounds more like a compliment than a telling me something I don't know about you."

"Maybe. So what's on the agenda today?"

His face leaned in for a quick kiss. "I thought we could go snorkeling today. Maybe tomorrow we can take out a boat and go to one of the other islands."

"That sounds great except I don't have any clothes."

"Ah, that reminds me." He handed me a robe and then opened the master bedroom closet. "Take a look."

The first thought I had was that he had surprised me by packing my things. So when I glanced inside the closet to find at least twenty-five items of clothing I didn't recognize, I was momentarily confused.

"What is all this?" I took out one of the hangers. It held a white bikini that still had the tags and appeared to be my exact size. There were a couple pairs of shorts, some cover-ups, sandals on the bottom, and even a wetsuit.

"I called a shop on the island, gave them your sizes, and requested that they bring these things by for you."

"To borrow?"

"No, of course not. I bought them for you."

I kept my back toward him as I processed this. Finally, I turned around, trying to find the best way to say it without insulting him. "It's not that I don't appreciate it, but I could've brought my stuff from home. I thought maybe you meant that we would be naked the whole time or in robes like this. But I didn't think it meant you were going to buy me a new beach wardrobe." He'd just given me a first class ticket to Australia and then flew me down to the islands. For some reason the new wardrobe pushed it over an invisible threshold for me.

"Haylee, I'm a wealthy man who hasn't spent any money on you thus far. Can you please accept the gift?"

Great, he was offended.

I wished he would understand where I was coming from. "You bought me my iPad, a plane ticket to Australia, and this trip down here. Josh, I don't want anything from you but you."

That appeared to hit home as his features softened. He took my hand. "Come here. Let me tell you something about me."

I followed him over to the bed where he sat me on the edge and then kneeled so that he was eye level with me.

"I've never been overly generous when it comes to giving gifts or making frivolous purchases. I don't subscribe to trends. I've had the same suits for many years, the same furniture for many more, my father's watches. The same man has cut my hair for the last ten years who still charges me sixteen dollars. And clearly I have judgment issues regarding those I perceive who do make frivolous purchases."

"Oh, I'm well aware of that." I thought of London.

"Yes, and I was properly and justifiably put in my place, which leads me to you. Most women— Actually, you know what? I've learned my lesson with that. Let me clarify, my ex-wife and even other women I've dated tended to have an expectation about me. They assumed if we went out to dinner, it would always be a four-hundred-dollar meal with the most expensive wine. If we went on vacation, it would be lavish. If they hinted that they loved a friend's purse, then they expected I'd buy them one. Hell, my ex even went so far as to say I was cheap because I didn't want a million-dollar wedding."

"You're talking to the wrong person if you want to me confirm that spending less than a million dollars on a wedding is cheap."

"Exactly, and that brings me to you. From the very beginning, you didn't have that expectation. Hell, you took me to In-N-Out burger. And you don't hint or have an expectation for anything for Christmas, and then you get me an incredibly thoughtful gift."

"It was only a cereal bowl."

His eyes regarded me. "Haylee, it meant more to me than a lot of other gifts I've ever been given because you remembered something I told you and then thought about it. You didn't give it with any anticipation of receiving something in return. Giving you that plane ticket felt good because I know how much seeing your family means to you. And no offense, but your best pair of underwear shouldn't come from Catherine. And because I know you'd never splurge on yourself, it makes me incredibly happy to do it for you."

"Well, when you put it that way, how can I possibly say no?" I took his face between my hands and kissed him thoroughly.

"Thank you," he approved, obviously pleased that I was accepting the gifts.

"More like, thank you. Do you want a fashion show?" I wiggled my brows.

He laughed, helping me to my feet. "I would love one. But to warn you, it might mean that snorkeling gets postponed because I can't be responsible for my actions."

"Hmm, I like it even more, then."

I proceeded to put on a show with my two new bikinis, one in white and the other one a fun navy-and-white stripe. Then I modeled a couple cute sundresses, two cover-ups that went great with the bikinis, shorts, and T-shirts of the softest material. In addition, he'd purchased four sets of bra and panty combinations in various soft-hued colors. My favorites by far, though, were the camisole and short combinations for sleeping; two of them were silk and two of them were cashmere.

"I feel like all I want to do is pet myself in this." The feeling against my skin was luxurious.

"That gives me a whole lot of ideas," he marveled with his hands roaming over my back, giving me soft caresses.

"Ha, I guess this is your way of making sure I don't sleep in my oversized T-shirts and running shorts, huh?"

"You could wear a plastic bag and still look sexy."

I raised a brow. "I could pass for adorable, maybe pretty, but there's nothing sexy about this." I motioned to my short set.

"That's where you're so very wrong. You're sexy in the most understated way."

My face must've shown that I didn't think that was much of a compliment because he clarified.

"What I meant is that I didn't buy you red or black teddies or lingerie, because you're sexy as yourself. You were much sexier in that light blue corset from the photo shoot that covered the majority of you than you could've been in a thong and nothing else. It's almost like a hidden treasure trove of sexy underneath the cutest little package."

He took my hand and backed me onto the bed, taking his time unwrapping said package and making me feel sexy indeed.

It was late afternoon by the time we finally made it down to the beach to snorkel, but the best part about vacation was the luxury of time. I loved my new wetsuit and loved Josh's ass in his even more. I'd never snorkeled before, so he took a few minutes to show me my gear and, just like that, we were in the water.

The fish were amazing. I'd never seen so many colors, and the water was so crystal clear that it was easy to see them all. It was also warm, which was surprising as I'd grown up near the Pacific Ocean, which was anything but. After snorkeling for a couple hours and grabbing a quick lunch, we took a nice long walk on the beach. Hand in hand, we talked about everything and nothing. It was comfortable and peaceful to be completely free to show affection and to get to know one another even better.

After taking a shower in preparation for dinner and donning one of my new dresses, I went downstairs and saw a candlelit table set for two. Josh was in the gourmet kitchen with several dishes on top of the stove. I took a seat on the other side of the large counter and watched his graceful movement thinking there was something sexy about a strong man who could cook.

"I was upstairs only thirty minutes. Did you whip something up or call in some elves?"

He smiled across the stove and lifted a lid. "Elves, my lady."

"I won't say the R word, but this is lovely. Thank you."

"The R word. Ah, romantic. I guess that will be our secret, too."

He dished up our plates and crossed over to the bistro table on the other side of the kitchen. The window view was breathtaking, with the sun setting off in the distance. He pulled out my chair, and we both ate in silence.

It was nice to see him casual in his linen pants and shirt, barefoot, opening a bottle of wine. He looked relaxed with the slight stubble on his newly tanned face. It hit me once again how very handsome he was. The fact that he was mine, at least for now, gave me a great sense of pleasure.

"Tell me something on your mind right now causing that smile," he requested, narrowing his eyes across the table.

I was enjoying the poached salmon and risotto and getting full quickly. "I was thinking about how relaxed you look and how happy I am to get to see this side of you. The stubble and tan are very sexy, Mr. Singer."

He gave me a wicked grin that made my stomach do a flip-flop of anticipation.

"Tell me something," I returned.

"Hmm, I was thinking about something a little kinky I'd like to try later."

Lowering my fork slowly, I felt the liquid heat pool in my center.

"You keep looking at me like that, and we're not going to finish dinner."

"Promise?" I challenged, getting to my feet as he did the same.

Then we were on each other, hot like the very first time, mouths greedy, hands groping for skin contact. Suddenly I was being lifted and taken downstairs.

I'd been aware that there was a lower level, but hadn't yet explored that part of the house. Wondering what was in store, I watched as he turned on the lights. My eyes widened when I realized we were in a large bathroom that had a steam room on the far side and a huge mirror along one entire wall.

He put me on my feet gently. "Take off your clothes, baby." His voice had an edge to it that let me know how much he was fighting for control.

It turned me on to know I had that sort of effect on him.

He opened the door to the steam room and turned on the water. Then he watched as I peeled off the sundress down the length of my body, revealing that I had no panties on. "Ah, aren't you full of surprises? Thought you'd get lucky tonight?"

"I was hoping." I grinned.

I watched as he took off his clothes and marveled at how strong his body was while yearning to touch it. I didn't have long to wait as he crossed over to me, took my hand, and led me into the shower stall filled with steam.

His fingers found my warm, slick entrance, and I moaned into his mouth as he ravaged my lips with his kiss. My hand caressed his velvety flesh, finding him hard and ready.

"Turn around," he commanded. He'd opened the door of the

steam shower and led me back out to the bathroom in front of the glass.

Once I turned, I swallowed hard at the vision of us in the large mirror, naked with his arms around me from the back and his hands stroking my body.

"Why doesn't the mirror fog up?" I had to ask.

"It's no-fog, I guess. Maybe for this very purpose."

I was mesmerized, watching as his hand dipped lower and his fingers explored my sensitive flesh in the reflection. My knees felt weak with the heat of the steam and his hardness behind me. With his other hand, he reached for mine and led it down to where his fingers were settled over my clit.

"I want you to touch yourself, Haylee, and I want to watch. Like this."

We locked eyes in the mirror. The sheer intensity spiked my libido up another level.

"I'm not sure how…"

"Shh, I've got you. You're so beautiful, and I want to watch you as you come for me. Then I'm going to fuck you from behind and make you come again."

I was about to combust merely at the thought of it. He bent down, moving my legs wider and landing kisses over the backs of my thighs and up to my back and shoulders. I made small circles with my fingers and watched our images in the mirror as he straightened and splayed his hands over my breasts and down my stomach.

"Let me feel how you're doing." He dipped two fingers into me, and I gasped, wanting more. I ground my backside into his fingers, searching for the relief I couldn't seem to find.

"God, you're positively dripping. Easy now, unless you want me to play with your ass?"

I swallowed hard, and he gave me a slow smile, spreading my wetness up. I was quickly losing my ability to stand.

"Do you know how many times I thought of this since our

plane ride using instant messenger? Press harder, like this." He threaded his fingers through mine and rubbed smaller, more deliberate circles over my clit.

"Josh, I—"

His fingers left mine, and I watched as he positioned himself behind me. "Just my fingers, baby." He inserted a finger into my backside with his other digits slipping up inside my wet center.

A trembling groan left my body while my orgasm shredded me completely, ridding me of the capacity to stay upright. Luckily, his strong arms braced me from behind as I rode the last wave. He then brought me to the floor gently, folding his body behind me.

"Well, now, this position has possibilities, too." He stood briefly and came back with two plush folded towels. "Do you think you can sit up on your knees?"

I could only nod and do as he asked, not able to find my voice at the moment.

"Stay right there. I'll be back; don't move a muscle."

As if I could, I thought, watching him leave.

He came back a short time later with something in his hand. Pulling me to my feet, he revealed what was in his palm. "You're going to learn how to pleasure yourself."

It was a silver phallic dildo with what looked like two points on the top. I could only whimper when he turned toward me, taking my hand, and inserting my fingers with his into my wet, sensitive channel.

"Do you feel that? Now try it yourself while I watch. Then the next time we're apart and we play via iPad or phone, I'll know what you look like when you make yourself come."

Jesus, it was almost too much as he turned on the vibrator.

"This is the rabbit. I want to watch you insert it. Put it in all the way, as far as it goes. You're plenty ready for it, aren't you?"

I pushed it in and took a breath, moving it deeper. Closing my eyes, I gave myself over to the sensation.

"Open your eyes, baby. Look at me."

He moved behind me, and I met his gaze in the mirror's reflection. I couldn't help panting with desire. The new vibrating sensation inside of me and his burning gaze had me captivated. "I want you—" I started to say that I wanted him inside me, but he put a finger to my lips.

I took it into my mouth and heard his hiss. "Fuck."

His other hand ran up my backside. "Start with your fingers, rub that sensitive little nub for me. That's it. Do you know how much this turns me on? You're unbelievably sexy."

I felt feverish for him. Watching his heavy eyes through the mirror watch me, I knew he was having a hard time staying patient.

"That's it. Rub it harder, and I'm going to turn up the vibrator to high."

What the hell? I realized he had a small remote in his palm and felt the change in speed with a jolt.

"That's right. Feel it." His hands cupped my breasts and pinched my tender nipples, rolling and teasing them to sharpened peaks.

"You're almost there. Come for me, my Haylee."

That was all it took as my orgasm eviscerated me completely.

His hands reached down and took out the vibrator before nudging me onto all fours. He entered me from behind, and I reveled in the fullness of his hard cock fitting inside of me as if it was made for me. Looking up in the mirror at the visual of him behind me doggy style was erotic, especially with the heat and steam surrounding us.

"You feel incredible. Do you like this?"

"Yes. God, yes." My voice was gravelly, and my body felt like I wouldn't stay conscious if I had another orgasm. But Josh was unrelenting as he reached around and rained an assault on my over-sensitized center of nerves. I had no choice but to meet the silent demand of his eyes in the mirror as I tumbled over the cliff. His climax followed shortly after, sending hot wetness deep inside of me.

The intimacy and power of what just happened left me completely drained, and I collapsed onto the dewy, tiled floor with him lying down beside me caressing my back.

"I think I should have a steam room and mirror installed in my apartment. What do you think?"

I gave a little moan. "I think I might not survive it, but it would be a hell of a way to go."

"Ha, that makes two of us."

I lay there, unable to move a muscle.

He got up, scooping me into his arms from the floor and then carrying me upstairs to the bedroom. I was pretty sure I was unconscious before he even covered me with the comforter.

THE LIGHT WASN'T YET SHINING through the blinds, and Josh was in a peaceful slumber beside me when I woke the next morning. I didn't get very many opportunities to observe him sleep, so I propped up on an elbow and enjoyed soaking him in, from his long, soot-colored lashes to his full lips and impressively muscled chest and arms. This powerful, gorgeous, sexy man was in my bed, and he had made sure that the worst Christmas had turned into the best days after. Our relationship had reached a new intimacy where it was no longer purely sex but hand holding and soft kisses and tender moments.

I puttered into the bathroom, brushed my teeth, and then took a long look at myself. I would not start thinking of this as anything more than a nice progression to our romance.

"Are you thinking about experimenting on your own in the mirror?"

Josh filled the doorway. My pulse instantly spiked at the

sight of him in nothing but silk boxers, showing off solid chest, chiseled abs, and powerful thighs.

"Christ, Haylee, the way you look at me—it's the hottest fuck-me look in the history of them."

"You're kidding. Please tell me I don't have an actual *fuck-me* look."

His response was to quirk a brow. "You have a couple, but sliding your gaze from my head on down is perhaps my favorite and the least subtle of them."

I moved into his arms, hugging him close. "I can't be held accountable for looking at you that way with a body like yours on display. Any woman would do the same."

"Hmm, considering you're splendidly naked, I would say right back at you, and you're the only woman I want looking at me that way."

"Oh, good answer." My lips brushed over his.

"How about you go get the bed warm for us again? I'm going to brush my teeth, and we'll make out."

Giggling, I slapped his butt on my way back to bed and glanced at the clock, which indicated it was only four in the morning. I stretched in the bed, loving the feeling of having this time with him all to myself.

"Ready to make out?" he said, returning.

This wonderfully playful mood was contagious, but I made the mistake of trying to see if he was ticklish. Turns out he wasn't, and then the tables were turned.

"All right, all right. I surrender, I surrender."

He stopped, thank the good Lord, and grinned.

I had a moment where I contemplated revealing how I felt, but I couldn't yet. It was too soon. So instead I put all of my emotions into kissing him, loving the fact that we could go from such hot sex downstairs to making sweet love in the early morning light.

Later we took a boat out and spent the day cruising. Josh packed a picnic lunch, and we lazed around in the sun and water. I thoroughly enjoyed watching him sail the boat, looking tanned and in charge.

We arrived back at the house in the early evening, and after a nice long, hot, sexy shower, we went down to the kitchen where Josh took some time teaching me how to cook. We were slicing tomatoes and basil with his arms around me from the back as I wiggled against his arousal. I was enjoying the fact that we were essentially engaged in foreplay with every touch when his phone rang.

He glanced at the caller ID and set it down. Then, making the effort to be more communicative, his eyes darted over my face. "It's Catherine. I'll call her when we get back."

We got back to dinner prep, but my phone rang this time. I checked the ID. "Do you think it's urgent?"

He took the phone out of my hand and put it down. "This is our time."

I smiled, and then his phone rang again. "Josh, it's fine. You can answer it. It seems strange for her to be calling me unless she's trying to track you down."

He searched my eyes and then grabbed his phone. "Catherine, slow down. Take a deep breath. Now say that again." He gave me a look that conveyed she was upset, and I could hear her muffled voice on the other side.

While I rubbed his back in support, he gave me a helpless look. Considering I didn't normally see him at such a loss for words, I sympathized. Obviously, she was upset, and he didn't know what to say or do.

"Uh, I'm still out of town actually. No, I'll be back day after tomorrow." He gave me a pained look, and I picked up my phone to call Catherine back. Time to come to the rescue.

"Yes, I'll hold." He mouthed *thank you* to me.

"Catherine, hi—" That was all I got out before she started.

"He's engaged. He's engaged to that little actress. What is she, twenty-one or something? The divorce is barely final, and he's already engaged. She's probably pregnant. God, I almost forgot I have Josh on the other line. Let me release him and come back. Can you hold a second?"

"Sure." I watched as he hung up his phone. He then came over to kiss the top of my head in a gesture that told me he was very grateful.

"So tell me all of it from the beginning. Did he call you?"

This led to a long story of finding out from a friend of a friend and then a story about the twenty-one-year-old wannabe Broadway star, who evidently was dumber than a box of rocks.

I walked around the kitchen, watching Josh chop vegetables and enjoying the little touches while he kept reading my face to ensure I was all right with the conversation.

"Okay, I'm going to give it to you bluntly. You ready?" I tried to ignore Josh, who had turned around with his arms folded as if wondering what I'd say. "Do you want him back? I mean, is there any part of you that misses him and wishes you guys could be together right now?"

"No," she admitted in a small voice.

"That's what I thought. So now he's someone else's problem. You need to flip your way of thinking. You think of it as losing him, but in fact you tossed him back. The only woman who will have him now is one who's dumb enough to believe he's a catch. Honestly, if he had ended up with some foreign correspondent with a PhD and Nobel Prize, I'd be just as upset as you are, wondering why the world is so unfair. But it sounds to me like he got the only girl who would put up with him."

"I know, but it still hurts," she confessed.

I instantly felt sympathetic. "I know it does, and I'm sorry you're going through this. You don't deserve it."

"Turns out he's coming with her to the same New Year's Eve party that I go to every year, and I really don't want to see them there together."

"Then don't go. Why put yourself through that?"

Josh turned around to watch me again.

"Because I have my pride, and this has always been the party I go to. I shouldn't have to change my plans," she sniffed.

I sighed, wishing there was something more I could do. "I understand, but if it means you'll end up putting on a brave face and returning home to cry your eyes out, I say skip it. Go to a party where you'll actually have a good time."

"Maybe you're right. Hey, how's California? I've been blubbering, and here you are spending your first holiday without your family. I'm so sorry."

"Don't be, and thank you for asking. I'm doing fine. The day itself was rough, but I'm in a better place now."

"Good. I'll let you go, Haylee. Thank you for talking me down. Anyhow, I'll call you once you're back. I'd love to do dinner or something."

"Dinner sounds great."

We finished our call, and I walked over to where Josh was seasoning the steaks.

"She okay?" he inquired.

I put my arms around him. "Yeah, I think she will be."

WE WATCHED THE SUN SET, enjoying our dinner on the beach. Josh took my hand and stared into my eyes.

I could practically feel my heart in my throat.

"If I'm being honest, I didn't like that you and Catherine were becoming friends. Aside from the fashion, I wasn't sure that you two would have much in common. But now I appreciate you're good for her. You don't sugarcoat it, but you're still very kind with your words. Maybe your logical female mind can help counter her illogical one. Not that she's always like this. She hasn't been thinking clearly since the divorce, and I'm not equipped to be as sympathetic as you seem to be. Anyhow, I wanted you to know that I appreciate you coming to my rescue, and I understand now why you two are friends."

"It's always easier to be logical when you're not the one emotionally invested. I do feel somewhat guilty however."

"For what?"

"She'd give anything to be here with you, and here I am, happy, and there she is, miserable."

He shook his head. "She wouldn't be happy; she only thinks she would be. And more importantly, I wouldn't be happy, and you wouldn't be happy. I get that you feel somewhat guilty. Hell, even I did for a moment, but it is what it is."

Why he didn't get that he could avoid the whole guilt thing was beyond me. He could stop going out with Catherine on dates to start. It nagged at me, but the reminder that this was only temporary kept me from opening my mouth. "What do you want to do tomorrow on our last day?" I needed to change the subject.

He appeared relieved. "Lie around naked, enjoy the sun, take a walk on the beach, go for a naked swim, lay around some more naked."

"That's a lot of naked time," I laughed.

"Oh, I think it's just right. Matter of fact, I think we should start with naked dessert eating and naked dish washing tonight."

Pulling my sundress over my head, I revealed that was all it took to be naked.

"I'm loving this whole sundress no panties look." And just like that, he was chasing me into the kitchen and making good use of our naked time together.

CHAPTER SEVENTEEN

Going from the tropical climate back to the cold weather was quite the drastic change. On New Year's Eve the city of New York was magical with a buzz for the night's festivities, but it was also crazy town. For example, the way people stood freezing outside in Times Square for the entire day—I had no interest in that but woke early to go for a very cold and crisp run. Unfortunately, I found out the hard way that the sidewalks were icy by taking a spill.

With my knees and hands scraped from trying to catch my fall, I ran gingerly back to the building. When I hobbled out of the elevator, I met Josh's concerned look.

"Where were you?"

"I was running, but I fell as it's icy outside." I held up my hands to expose the evidence of my tumble.

He walked over and took my palms, inspecting them. "I don't want you running outside anymore. It's winter, and there can be ice on the ground or falling from the buildings. Not to mention on New Year's Eve all the whackos filter into the city."

"Well, as much as I think you being worried about me is

nice, try to be reasonable about such things. I need to run. I'll simply be more careful next time."

"You can use my treadmill."

"Where? In your apartment?"

"Yes, I have a gym that includes a treadmill, stair climber, and some free weights."

"Uh, okay. Thanks."

"Let's get these cleaned up."

I'd expected him to take me into my place, but instead he led me into his.

"So this is obviously the living room, kitchen to the left, down here's the master bedroom and bath." He led me through, giving me the abbreviated tour.

"What's this door?" I asked, looking at the closed door across from the master bedroom.

"My office, which is locked."

Uh, okay.

Back toward the kitchen, we went down a small hall. "Another bathroom and then this—" He opened the door. "—is the gym."

It was nice, with a large flat screen on one wall and on the other a view of the city through a floor-to-ceiling window.

"Oh, and here's the laundry room." He opened the door across from the gym to show me. "You can do your laundry here instead of going to the laundromat from now on."

"Thanks, but Josh—"

He shook his head. "No buts. There's no reason for you to be out in the freezing cold to run or do your laundry. Come over here instead. Matter of fact..." He led me back to the kitchen and fished out a key from one of the drawers. "Here's a key."

Whoa.

"Come on, let's get you cleaned up." He took my hand and led me into the master bath where he had me sit on the edge of the huge tub while he went into one of the drawers and brought back a small first aid kit.

"I appreciate the offer and the key, but I don't want to intrude on your space. It seems kind of sudden." Even last night upon our return from Tortola, we'd gone back to our respective places to sleep.

He met my eyes and frowned again. "It's not sudden; it's practical."

As if it wasn't enough that I was living in his guest apartment, now I was going to use his treadmill and washing machine, too? Sighing, I tamped down on the uncomfortable thought of becoming more reliant on him. By his own admission, his intentions were *practical*. Just a few weeks ago, I hadn't been allowed to see the inside of his space. This had to be a big step for him when it came to trust. "Okay, thank you."

He made quick work out of cleaning up my scrapes, even pulling down my pants to clean my knees.

"I feel like a little kid," I giggled while he blew on the antiseptic to keep it from burning too much.

"Well, I don't feel like a parent at the moment as I can smell your pussy, and all I want to do is shove my face in it."

Holy shit.

His hand cupped my sex through my panties. "Ah, you're soaking, baby." When he dragged them down, I protested.

"I was running and am sweaty—"

"I know, and I love it." He practically dove in, causing me to just about buck off the tub. "I feel like I know your scent now. That beautiful, sexy scent for me, and it makes me crazy for you."

That admission made me hotter. His mouth suckled my clit gently and then harder with his tongue circling it, ensuring I wouldn't last long. I climaxed quickly.

He stood up and stripped me swiftly, then turned on the

water, grinning. "It's not quite the same as in Tortola, but it does have possibilities."

Yes please.

After our sexy shower, Josh dried me off thoroughly and applied some ointment to my scrapes. "I always figured that shelf would be good for something other than holding shampoo," he quipped.

Kissing him deeply, I suckled on his bottom lip and caressed his face. "Are you telling me we christened your shower?"

"That we did, and the edge of the bathtub for that matter."

Well, now, that was a surprise. "I thought maybe you lived here when you were married or brought girls back here at some point."

"I bought the place after the divorce, and I like my privacy. You're the first woman I've had any physical relationship with here—and I can tell from your big old grin that pleases you."

"Matter of fact, it does."

"We can plan on christening the bed later this evening if that sounds good?"

"Or we could have a little preview now?"

"You know we're going to kill each other. Death by sex," he smirked.

"It's a little out of control, isn't it?"

He laughed. "I can think of worse things. At least we have tonight and tomorrow before we have to return to the real world."

"Sort of, but I won't be back until late tonight. New Year's Eve party, remember."

He looked disappointed but then finished up by applying a Band-Aid to my knee. "Right. You're going out with Will while I'm out with Catherine."

I had called Will yesterday when we arrived home as I refused to sit at home on New Year's waiting for Josh to get back from his evening with Catherine. We might have reached a new intimacy in our relationship, but that didn't mean I'd changed my resolve against sitting home pathetically.

JOSH WAS in a brooding mood while watching me get ready for my New Year's Eve date with Will. Standing there in his tux, he could hardly say much about it though considering he was taking Catherine out this evening.

"Whose party is it?" he asked for the second time today.

My answer didn't change. "I'm not sure. Will said it had something to do with a modeling gig he did. All I know is it's black tie and uptown."

He frowned. I knew his party was downtown and a much higher profile deal. "I think that Catherine could use the moral support if you were to come to the party we're attending."

It wasn't the first time he'd hinted. I was, in fact, tempted, if for no other reason than to be able to see him tonight, but the thought of watching him with her wasn't something I'd put myself through. Catherine might not want to follow my advice to avoid unnecessary drama, but I definitely would.

"I don't think so." I spritzed on my perfume.

"Give me one good reason. It'll be a better party than the one you're attending, and I'm sure Will could use the exposure in the fashion industry. It's practically a who's who."

Considering Will had just been signed by Calvin Klein, he didn't need any favors, but more importantly, Josh wasn't getting it. My glance conveyed my annoyance. "Okay, I'll give you two reasons. One, I don't want to watch you kiss Catherine at midnight, and two, I don't think you want to watch Will kiss me."

That instantly earned me an irritated look. "So you're planning to kiss him?"

And we were back to that again. "Everyone kisses everyone

at midnight. But with any luck, I'll just play his wingman to help find him someone else at the party."

"I quite like that idea. Yes, let's find Will a girlfriend."

So much for never wanting to play matchmaker.

WHILE JOSH WAS STILL sound asleep on New Year's morning, I eased out of bed and padded back to my room in order to don my workout gear.

The party had been a lot of fun the night before with Will and I enjoying dancing and then counting down to midnight. I'd arrived home shortly after one o'clock in the morning and was happy to see that Josh had beaten me there. I'd curled up into his arms and enjoyed slow, sleepy sex until we both fell into slumber.

What better timing than now to make use of his treadmill? I was sure Josh would be sleeping off a hangover this morning. Donning my headphones and turning on my music, I was five miles in before I noticed him watching me sleepily from the doorway. I slowed down to a walking speed and tossed him a smile.

"I hope I didn't wake you."

He shook his head. "No. I was simply enjoying the view. You know, I had this vision of you jogging all cute and burning a couple calories, but now I see what Brian was talking about. You truly run, don't you?"

I rolled my eyes. "Yeah, him making that comment in front of everyone in Charlotte annoyed me. It made it sound like I was slow-mo Baywatch running or something."

He chuckled. "Watching you run is much more real. I guess I get his initial infatuation now."

I pressed the stop button and wiped my face with my towel.

"Does that mean you're infatuated?" I moved in front of him, and he took my mouth in a searing kiss.

"Something like that."

"Happy New Year."

"Mm, Happy New Year. Did you have a nice time last night?"

"I did, actually. Will is a great dancer, and we spent a lot of time doing just that."

"Better him than me. I don't dance."

I smiled, remembering that tidbit written in all capital letters on his personal dislikes sheet. "How was your time with Catherine? Any drama with the ex?"

"No, luckily he was a no-show. All that workup, and he doesn't even come. It was fine, but I missed you."

"I missed you, too."

"Catherine said she called you about coming in the day after tomorrow for the photo reveal?" he inquired, taking my hand.

"She did, and I'm anxious to find out how they turned out."

"I'm sure they will be great. Now then, let's get to your post-workout routine."

His arms lifted me up, and I giggled, looking forward to it.

NERVES WERE GETTING to me about how the photos had turned out when I made my way, together with Sasha and Brian, to a conference room on Catherine's floor a couple days later. Will was there and gave me a kiss on the cheek. Sasha was humming with excitement, and I noticed that she and Brian appeared to be uncharacteristically quiet around one another. We all took our seats around the long rectangular table and faced the screen set up at the end of the room.

Catherine came in all smiles, looking like she was holding

back a secret. "Okay, please sit. Dim the lights, Erin," she directed her assistant. And there I was up on the big screen. "Here are the final shots we decided to go with for each look," she said, scrolling through them.

It was hard to believe that striking woman in the photographs was me. I was so engrossed in taking in all of the details that I barely noticed Josh come in. We went through each of the dresses and scenes, and I blushed when we got to the one with Will and me in my lingerie. It made us look like a couple. The photo was intimate and beautifully done with us lying on the bed looking at one another while he caressed my face. I silently applauded Bart for making the pictures look amazing and tasteful.

"And last, but not least, we have our cover shot." She flashed the screen to show me in my wedding dress draped across the chaise. Will stood behind me, reaching down.

"Wait, did you say cover?" Will asked.

She clapped her hands and squealed. "Yes, you guys have the February cover. I mean, I knew the shots were superb, but this one, it's just above. And then this last photo of Haylee alone in the dress will be the inside picture. Look at that ring, Sasha. The diamonds pop, and I think your client will be very pleased with the credits. I know I couldn't be happier with how they turned out, and I owe it all to you, Haylee. Well, you and your mother's beautiful dresses."

The lights came on, and I was still stunned. I was a cover model for Cosmo Life?

"So, as a big thank you, and because I can't imagine the dress without them, these are for you." She handed me a box with a bow.

I took off the lid and sighed with pleasure. The blush-colored Valentino lace shoes. "Catherine, these are amazing. I don't know what to say except you're beyond generous and thank you."

"I figured they can be your 'something new' for when you get married. Now you just have to find the man to buy you the rock and the pink diamond pendant," she laughed.

I didn't risk a look in Josh's direction.

CHAPTER EIGHTEEN

The next couple months flew by in a whirlwind. The cover shot garnered me several other modeling jobs, and I finally felt good about having plenty of money to get me through law school. Josh and I settled into something of a routine with a little less travel, and I was spending more time in his apartment. But what I loved the most was that he was becoming more open about his plans and not spending quite so many nights out. Part of me wondered if his lack of dates had something to do with ensuring I didn't go out with Will, but I didn't bother to read too much into it, opting instead to simply enjoy the time we had left.

It was the first weekend of March, and I'd been invited to a Cassius Rum party in Vegas for the weekend. I was getting ready to leave for the airport on a Friday morning when a knock sounded at my door and Josh came in.

"Hi," he murmured.

It didn't matter if it was one day or one hour since I'd last seen him, whenever I laid eyes on him, I still got butterflies. "Hi," I whispered back.

He leaned down to kiss me. "How's the packing?"

"Good. I'm all set, I think. The car should be downstairs in about ten minutes or so." It felt strange that while I was about to leave for the airport, he was heading into the office solo.

"I wish you could fly out with me tomorrow instead of leaving today." He was traveling to his brother's thirtieth birthday, also coincidently in Vegas. Meanwhile, it appeared he was feeling as anxious as I was at the thought of spending the night apart.

"Unfortunately, flying out tomorrow wouldn't do me any good as the Cassius Rum party is tonight. Plus, this is your weekend with your brother."

When he'd first found out about my Vegas commitment, he'd seemed wary about the timing coinciding with his trip, almost as if I could have known he'd be there over the same weekend. So the last thing I needed now was him thinking I would try to hone in on his plans with his brother.

"And if I want to see you tomorrow when we're both in Vegas?"

I kissed him on the cheek. "Then you'll either call me or text me. If I'm free, then we can get together."

"You should be staying in my hotel."

"The event is in my hotel. And since the client is paying, I couldn't exactly ask for them to lodge me somewhere else. I need to go, but safe travels. Maybe I'll see you there." I gave him one last kiss and wheeled my suitcase out the door.

"Haylee, please be careful there. I mean it. Watch what you're drinking and who is around you. Please text or call me tonight when you're back safe in your room."

I turned and smiled. I might not want to admit it, but it was nice to have someone worrying about me. "I will."

VEGAS. So far during the day, the city didn't look as spectacular as some of the photos, but it did look massive. Caesars alone was at least a block long. I checked in without a problem and went ten floors up to a beautiful tower room. The space was tasteful and comfortable with a view of the Strip that was amazing. Feeling somewhat lonely, I sent a text to Josh.

"Arrived safe at the hotel. On my way out to explore."

"Be safe, be good."

His response made me smile. Considering we mostly traveled together, I imagined this was new territory for both of us.

I spent the afternoon walking down the Strip and exploring various hotels, thrilled with the different themes, like the Venetian and the Paris. I was definitely getting my exercise, and the weather was a nice break from the New York temps in March.

For the party, I dressed in a Pucci print dress that was vibrant and fun in pink, green, and white. My white strappy sandals completed the look. I left my hair down and went with a smoky eye and some lip gloss.

The red carpet was intimidating, especially after some celebrities made their way in, but I was polite to the photographers and thankful to Lisa, the Cassius Rum representative, who let me know where to go.

An hour in, I was ready to leave. I didn't know anyone, and no one was overly friendly. But Lisa had asked that I stay for two hours, so I sucked it up and smiled at the bartender, who could barely hear me over the music.

Taking my gin and tonic outside onto the balcony, I smiled when my phone buzzed and I saw it was a text from Josh.

"I'm here early. A car is outside on the curb, gray sedan, license plate YY7 8954, driver is Henry. He'll take you back to my hotel and give you a keycard. I'm on floor 52 penthouse. See you when you're ready to leave."

I mingled for the last hour to ensure that Cassius Rum had a lot of photographs and that I was visible for my obligation to them. They'd paid for my trip; the least I could do was fulfill my end of the bargain. When the two hours were up, I said goodbye to Lisa and walked back to my room where I grabbed my laptop bag, filling it with my toothbrush and some things to wear back in the morning.

I found Henry curbside. As we started down the Strip, I got a fantastic gridlock view of the Bellagio water show. I sat in awe, taking in all of the people out late amid the lights and sounds of Vegas.

By the time I made it up to Josh's room, it had been two hours since his text. Opening the door to his suite, I found him sitting on his couch looking like he was waiting on me. I smiled at the sight.

"Hi," he whispered softly, rising and taking me in his arms.

"Hi, yourself." I sighed in contentment as he pulled me closer. "It took longer than I thought to get out of there, and then traffic was bad."

"I didn't mean for you to leave the party early." He took my hand and led me to the bed.

I quickly slipped off my shoes and stripped down to my undergarments. "I was ready to go."

He cuddled me close with my back to his chest and inhaled the scent of my hair.

"Do you want me to let you sleep?" I asked.

"Mm, you're stealing my line and no, I want to keep doing this." He peeled down my panties, and I felt his erection nudging up against my sex while his fingers found me wet and ready. "And this," he said, sliding into me to the hilt.

"Oh, yeah?" I managed.

"I had to come to Vegas early. You'd think it's been weeks, but it's only been since last night." His hips moved against me in measured rhythm while his hands reached around and kneaded my breasts. His fingers teased my nipples and then reached down, caressing my stomach.

"I was happy to get your text message. God, you feel good."

"So do you. Come for me," he groaned, rubbing my clit and increasing the tempo until I shattered all around him. He moaned, following me over the edge. Then he lay there inside of me, cocooning me fully while we both came back down off of our high.

"My Haylee," he murmured, kissing the back of my neck.

I turned over and caressed his face. "Hmm, I like that."

"Tell me something. Something you've wanted to tell me but haven't. A secret."

Did I dare? Maybe it was the alcohol or the amazing sex, but suddenly I had no filter. "Do you promise not to freak out?"

He smiled and looked a little wary, but nodded. "I won't freak out."

"I don't know if you're ready."

"Well, now that you have me intrigued, you have to tell me."

I felt the doubt creep up. "Maybe when I'm more sober so that I can decide if it's a good idea." I yawned and then found myself pinned down with him looming above me.

"Tell me," he demanded.

"Or what?" I challenged, and then I was being tickled.

"Oh, oh, no, no. Okay, okay. Please stop."

He relented and quirked a brow. "Spit it out."

"Okay, but lie back down and hold me first. No more tickling."

He cuddled me close and nuzzled my neck. "Haylee, tell me." He tormented me by running a finger along my rib cage, causing me to giggle.

"I love you." And there it was. I watched the words register, the surprise and intake of breath. "And before you do freak out or say something lame like 'gosh, Haylee, I didn't mean for this to happen,' just know that I feel it, I said it, and that's it. I don't expect anything in return. Our time is still up when I leave for school this summer, and I won't say the words again unless you ask me to."

He expelled a breath. "I'm not freaking out."

I wondered if he was trying to convince me or himself.

"And what do you mean you're leaving this summer? School doesn't start until fall."

I was grateful he'd changed the subject, but even more pleased that he didn't seem anxious for me to move away. "Most schools start in the middle or end of August, and I want to take some time to move there. Plus, I'll take a couple of weeks for Australia, so I'll probably leave New York in July."

"You don't even know where you're going yet." There was a hint of agitation in his voice. I guessed it was because, in his mind, he had thought September was the month, and I was speeding up the time table.

"I'm waiting to hear where I've been accepted. Matter of fact, I should receive the letters any day now."

He absorbed this information. "Are you sure you want to go?"

I felt a pull and a desire that was tempting to explore, but I didn't dare. In knowing that we had an expiration date, I had the control. I believed in short-term happiness and valuing relationships in the here and now. After my parents' deaths, I could definitively say that there was no such thing as a truly happy ending. If I started to believe there could be, I wasn't sure I'd survive the fallout when there wasn't.

"Yes, I'm sure about school. Now it's your turn. Spill it, Singer. Tell me a secret that I don't know."

"I think my secret would be lame."

"So you had one you were going to tell me, but now you aren't sure?"

He nodded and then relented when I gave him a pointed look. "Okay, my secret is that I didn't deal well with you traveling here without me. It put me in a weird place, and I couldn't get on the plane fast enough to join you again."

"Weird like how?" I wished he'd express some of his feelings.

"Just like I was being left out. I was worried about you being here by yourself, and I didn't like it."

I wanted to press him on that thought, but noticed he was already half asleep. "I'm glad you came out here," I whispered.

I AWOKE to hear Josh's voice in the other room talking to someone. Listening closer, I realized he was on the phone. I looked at the nightstand and saw a glass of water and Motrin, which made me smile. He was so thoughtful sometimes.

I quickly took the pills and slipped into the shower, happy that I'd brought a change of clothes since it would make it easier to go back to my own hotel room this morning.

"Good morning," he greeted, kissing me as I came into the living room where he was working.

"Good morning. Do you need any help?"

"If you don't mind. I know it's Saturday morning."

"Of course I don't mind. You're in luck that I have my laptop. I used its bag to bring some things." I took the computer out after putting away my dress and other things. "You know, I saw cinnamon rolls downstairs in a Starbucks. I think I'll skip down first and get a chai tea and a cinnamon roll. Do you want one?"

"Cinnamon roll yes, but make mine a large coffee, please." He kissed me again.

"I'll be back." I smiled all the way downstairs.

There was quite a line at Starbucks, but I didn't mind. I took myself upstairs, drinks and cinnamon rolls in hand. I had to knock on the door because I'd left my keycard and phone in the room. I was shocked to see a man other than Josh answer.

"Um, hello." I looked back at the room number to confirm I hadn't made a mistake, but he ushered me in with a large smile which looked familiar. This had to be Josh's younger brother, Colby.

"Hello to you." He took the tray of drinks and box of cinnamon rolls out of my hands, setting them on the table.

"Ah, Haylee, this is my brother, Colby. Colby, this is Haylee."

"Well, hello, Haylee." Before I knew it, Colby was on me, his lips descending to kiss me soundly while his hands gripped my ass.

I was in such shock that it took a full second to register what he was doing. Meanwhile, I heard Josh curse and then felt him pull his brother off of me. I could still taste the alcohol on Colby's breath.

"Dammit, Colby. Haylee is my assistant."

"Oh, shit. Wait. What?" Colby sputtered. He looked toward me as if he couldn't believe it. "Sorry about that. I thought you were the stripper for the evening. My birthday present. I had a few on the plane and just wasn't thinking."

I looked at Josh's face, which was a mixture of angry and apologetic. Then I glanced toward Colby, who shrugged it off. Before I could control it, my hand flew. Right. Across. His. Face. I don't know who was more stunned: Colby, Josh, or me.

"What in the hell was that for?" Colby asked, holding his cheek.

"For accosting me."

He looked contrite. "But I told you, I thought you were the stripper."

"I don't care who you thought I was, or if I was in fact the stripper. You don't just go up to any woman and shove your tongue down her throat and grab her ass. You don't know me, you've never met me, and my profession should have no bearing on how you treat me. Jesus." I held my hand as it began to throb.

"Holy shit, I think I'm in love." Colby looked at Josh, who was now shaking his head at his younger brother and eyeing me warily.

"Your brother needs therapy," I quipped.

"Not going to argue with you," Josh replied dryly.

Rolling my eyes, I walked over to where my laptop was sitting, thankful I'd put away my clothes and toiletries so Colby couldn't see that I'd spent the night.

He crossed over to the ice bucket, and I felt a sliver of sympathy as he pulled out some cubes and put them into a wash cloth. His face sported a bright red spot.

He walked toward me and handed over the washcloth. "Here, take this for your hand."

"I think you may need it for your face."

He gave me a grin, showing off dimples that I'm sure had all of the girls clamoring. "Oh, it hurts, but I deserved it. Your hand did not."

I took the ice pack gratefully.

"Well, aside from hitting horribly misbehaved younger brothers, what do you do for my older brother? I mean, he has Nigel."

I willed myself not to look at Josh and was glad when he didn't intervene. "Nigel is going through some personal things and isn't able to travel. I'm helping Mr. Singer in the short term."

He looked between the both of us. "So seriously, this is only professional?"

Josh held up his hands, evidently exasperated with his younger sibling. "Colby, I'm about to kick you out. Could you please act like a grown, mature man? Haylee is my assistant and was coincidently in town for the Cassius Rum party last night at Caesars. She and I were attending to the Gibson acquisition before you accosted her."

"Wait a second. You're the girl who did the modeling for Katrina Tross?"

"I am."

"And the cover for Cosmo Life?"

"Yes."

"So you'll be in town tonight?"

I nodded, wondering where he was going with this.

"Fantastic. You can come to my birthday party."

Before I could object, Josh was doing it for me. "Colby, your party isn't something Haylee would want to come to. She has other plans."

Colby focused his attention on me. "It's my birthday today, and I really, truly want you to stop by. I mean, come on, you and I could have a connection, and someday it will all come back to how you slapped me when I mistook you for a hooker, and then I invited you to my thirtieth birthday party in Vegas."

I shook my head and laughed.

"Come on, I like you, Haylee. Please come tonight, just for a short time. You don't have to stay, and I'm the one inviting you, not my brother."

That fact wasn't lost on me. Although I knew Josh might be irritated, I agreed anyhow. "Okay, I'll stop by for a few minutes. And I'm sorry for slapping you on your birthday, but you did deserve it. I brought extra cinnamon rolls if you'd like one."

He smiled and opened the box.

Josh gave me an annoyed look as I sat down to log into my laptop with my tea and breakfast on a small table to the side.

Colby took a seat on a nearby chair where he started on his cinnamon roll. "So, Haylee, tell me about my brother these days. Is he still a stick in the mud?"

I arched a brow. "Considering you thought he got you a hooker first thing on Saturday morning for your birthday, I'm hard pressed to believe you actually think that."

"Well, Vegas is a different story." He winked. "But back in New York, what's he like?"

"Professional, hardworking."

"See? Boring," he teased, looking bored himself.

"Haylee, can you email me the Gibson spreadsheet?" Josh interjected.

What the hell was that? Oh right, the Gibson acquisition. "Yes, of course." I emailed a fake document.

"Great, thanks. I'll make my notes and send them back to you if you don't mind making the changes later today?"

Was I being dismissed? "Uh, no, of course not."

"How long are you making her work on a Saturday in Vegas?" Colby inquired.

Josh looked a little uncomfortable but glared at his brother. "It won't take long."

"So, Haylee, what are you up to today after you finish your work? I could show you around Vegas."

"I appreciate it, but I already have some plans."

"Great. Maybe I could tag along. What's on the agenda?"

"Well, I'm doing M&M World and then Coke World. Then I want to see the inside of the Paris Hotel and ride the gondola at the Venetian. After that maybe I'll go up in the Stratosphere." I purposefully chose the touristiest things available.

"I feel like you may be trying to dissuade me from coming," he chuckled.

"Actually, those are the types of cheesy things I'd like to do. We'll see if I have time or not for all of it." I finished up the rest of my breakfast and looked toward Josh. "I'll talk to you later."

"I'll walk you out," he offered as I grabbed my computer bag.

We walked to the front door. "Sorry. He came in much earlier than expected. I tried texting you," he whispered.

I smiled tightly. "My phone was in my bag. It's all right. I'll see you tonight, I guess. Although I don't know where I'm going."

"I'll make sure you get an invitation."

"Does it make you uncomfortable if I go?" I already knew the honest answer to that question. After Josh hadn't invited me home for Christmas, I'd convinced myself it was for the best. I didn't want to get accepted into a family and become part of their lives only to have it torn away in a few months.

"No, it's fine." His voice was unconvincing at best.

"I won't stay long. See ya later."

I SPENT the day exploring the Strip and did end up in M&M World. There I requested Josh send me an embarrassing photo of Colby. A short time later, I left with my birthday gift in hand. Silly, but appropriate. I was about to go back to my room when I received a text from Josh.

"Moved you to a room in my hotel. See the front desk and they will give you your key. Henry is waiting outside your hotel when you're ready."

After gathering up my stuff, I checked out and then found Henry curbside. Once I arrived at the new hotel, I was treated like a VIP and given a lovely junior suite.

When I entered my room, I immediately noticed the large box on the bed with a bow. My interest piqued, I opened the gift and smiled at the glitzy silver, shimmery dress. Wow, he'd gone all out, I thought, when I noticed that underneath there were Jimmy Choo strappy shoes to match. At the bottom was an invitation to the party with the address of the hotel's rooftop dance club and bar. The dress was hot, and I couldn't wait for his reaction. Maybe he was looking forward to seeing me at the party after all.

I PURPOSEFULLY WENT LATE to the party as my intention was to drop in and then leave. Josh didn't need me honing in on his plans, and I didn't need Colby observing me with his brother. I took a deep breath and gave my invite to the large man at the door. The dress fit me beautifully, and with my outrageously overpriced, gorgeous shoes, I felt sexy.

When I entered, I was immediately offered a glass of champagne. The club was already filled with beautiful people. It was a good thing I had the dress as it was all glitz and glamour. My eyes scanned the crowd while I sipped. I smiled when Brian came up to me.

"Haylee, I didn't know you'd be here." He kissed both cheeks as I smiled awkwardly.

"I was in town last night for the Cassius Rum event and then met Colby this morning. He pretty much insisted I stop by."

"Ha, so you met the little brother. What did you think?"

"I think he makes you look like a wallflower. He's a lot to take in."

He threw his head back and laughed. "That's a very fair assessment, but I will tell you he's a pretty decent guy down deep."

As if on cue, Colby found us. "Haylee. Damn girl, you look hot."

"Way down deep," Brian quipped, completely amused.

I saw Josh approaching, his expression carefully masked.

"So, Haylee, how was your touring of Vegas and the kitschy places?" Colby inquired as his older brother came up to hear the conversation.

"Good. Here, this is for you. Happy Birthday." I handed him the small gift bag, and he looked intrigued.

"Hi, Haylee." Josh took in my dress as I gave my best *you're only my boss* smile.

"Hi, Josh."

We all three watched as Colby opened the box.

"M&Ms?" he asked as I hid a smile.

"Open them and take a look. I can't take all the credit; your brother helped."

He did so and then howled with laughter. "Holy shit. Personalized, embarrassing childhood photo M&Ms. These are classic. You really went to M&M World?" He ate a few, grinning like a teenager.

His face was adorable, and I found myself laughing. "I did, and it was pretty cool. So was Coca-Cola World, for the record."

"The dress looks even better on you than it did in the store," Colby declared.

I about spit out my drink. "This dress is from you?"

He looked amused, and I realized my mistake.

"Who else would it be from?"

Holy crap.

"Well, obviously the idea was from you as the invitation was from you, but I thought you waved your pinky and had some girl do the shopping for you."

Colby and Brian both raised a brow but thankfully stayed quiet. Josh didn't say a word at all.

AFTER THIRTY MINUTES, I figured I'd probably imposed enough on Josh's sensitivity since he kept stealing looks my way, so I walked over to Colby to say goodbye.

He was flanked by two beautiful women who looked as though they might have been a birthday gift from his big brother. I wasn't going to ask. Brian was also standing nearby talking with Josh.

"Colby, I have to go, but thank you for inviting me."

"Stay. You haven't been here that long."

"Thank you, but I've got other plans. Happy Birthday."

"I'm glad you could come and even happier I met you." He kissed me on the cheek.

"Good night," I murmured.

Josh kissed my cheek as well. I tried very hard not to let myself look weird when he did so. "Good night Haylee, be safe," he imparted as I swallowed hard.

"I'll walk you out," Brian offered, surprising me.

Josh looked surprised, too.

"Um, okay."

Brian took my arm and led me through the crowd until we were outside of the club.

"You still think your boss might not be into you? You should've seen him watching you all night," he confided once we could finally hear one another without having to yell.

"So why did you insist on escorting me out? Are you trying to make him jealous?"

He chuckled, and his eyes lit up with mischief. "Merely helping things along. Have a good night." He took off in the direction of the restrooms while I moved toward the elevator and went down to my room.

I was absolutely ravenous. But when I looked at myself in the mirror after making my way back to my room, I decided to change. This was a gorgeous dress for a Hollywood party, but not so much for the midnight buffet. I'd just slipped off my shoes when I heard the card slide in and the door open.

"I guess being the owner gives you all access to my room?" I smiled at Josh as he crossed the room in two strides while looking around. It dawned on me what, or rather whom, he was looking for. "You think Brian is here?"

"You left together."

"So obviously, you had to see for yourself."

"Obviously, I did. Seems you had an eventful day, with my

brother buying you clothes and then Brian needing to see you out."

My temper rose. "I'm not even sure how to respond to that. I thought the dress was from you, and Brian simply walked me out." I watched his jaw throb and knew he was angry, so I didn't think it would be a good time to mention that his friend had probably done it to get a reaction from him.

"And if Brian had asked to come up to your room, what would you have said?" Lifting me up onto the dresser, he pushed my dress up around my hips and stepped between my legs.

"I would've said I was hot for only one man, and he's not him," I whispered, stroking his face. Then his mouth was on mine, fierce, hot and demanding. I could feel a hum of anticipation between us as his hands moved up my thighs. Soon my panties were ripped in two.

"Those were my new ones," I muttered as his mouth left mine and then was on my very center. "Jesus, Josh…" I came within seconds and felt his lips skim the insides of my thighs. "Are you still annoyed with me?"

He pulled back and met my eyes. "No, and I should've never been. I'm sorry."

Holy shit, did he just apologize? My eyes must have conveyed my shock.

He sighed. "Yeah, an apology. I'm trying to get better at them."

"God, that's unbelievably hot," I admitted, kissing him with gusto.

He chuckled. "If only I'd known. Now I'll say I'm sorry all the time."

"Ooooh, say it again," I teased as he lifted me down.

"So very sorry. Now get on the bed on your knees," he commanded.

Aroused by his demand, I moved to do as he requested. I

heard his zipper and watched him over my shoulder as he shed his pants and knelt behind me.

"I'm going to have all of you next weekend, Haylee. We're heading down to my house in Charlotte early, and there we'll shut ourselves in for the two days and play. Do you understand?"

I whimpered as he stroked me with the tip of his cock.

"I didn't hear you," he coerced, putting in the tip as I moved back to urge him deeper.

"Yes, yes, this weekend."

Then he hit it home.

"Fucking Christ, Haylee, your pussy is so sweet." He pounded hard, causing me to almost lose my ability to stay on my knees. With his fingers rubbing my engorged clit he urged, "Come with me, honey."

I did spectacularly, feeling him do the same. I couldn't hold myself up any longer, so I lay flat on my stomach as he broke the contact slowly.

He went into my bathroom, and I heard him wash up. Then he was back with his face near mine. "Are you falling asleep?"

"Actually, I'm starving. I was planning to hit the buffet."

He kissed me softly on the lips. "I wish I could join you."

"I know. Me, too. But you should go and have fun with your brother." I slowly got out of the bed and righted my dress before unzipping it completely and stepping out of it.

He quirked a brow. "Are you trying to get me to stay?"

I smiled, enjoying a moment of female empowerment. "While that's tempting, I'm changing into jeans and now new underwear. I want to eat."

He watched as I crossed into the bathroom in order to wash up. He was still watching when I came out to don new clothes. "You all right?" He looked concerned, stopping me in my tracks.

"Of course. Why do you ask?"

"I want to make sure we're good, that you don't feel weird about, um—"

"A quickie?" I supplied and watched his wince. I crossed over, put my arms around him, and kissed him. "I know that you respect me for a lot more than my body. I only wish you could confide in me about where these trust issues come from."

"Haylee, we've gone over this. I'm not burdening you with my past."

"I don't think of it as a burden. I see it as helping me understand and maybe be a little more sensitive."

"I need to get back." He kissed me again and strode out, a man intent on returning to his brother's party and avoiding the subject at hand.

I WOKE up when I felt Josh climb into bed with me. Glancing at the clock, I saw it was three in the morning.

He nuzzled my shoulder, and I realized he was completely naked. "Haylee," he whispered.

I found his insistent lips. "Ugh, you taste like cigarette smoke and whiskey."

"Sorry, I just had to feel you tonight, but I can go."

"No, stay. But no kissing on the mouth," I giggled, turning back around and feeling his lips on my neck.

"Deal, and I'm sorry. I smoked a cigar, but no cigarettes."

"Mm, you don't have to answer to me. I merely want you to live longer because you're sooo much older than I am."

He chuckled. "Feisty. I like that."

I felt my panties being tugged down, and then his fingers were working me.

"You're ready for me, aren't you?"

"I am, always."

"Where are you going?" Josh questioned, his voice still rough from the night before. He sat up slightly and grimaced.

I sympathized. "I put some ibuprofen and a glass of water next to the bed for you."

"It's been awhile since I've had a hangover like this. Thank you."

"You do it for me, so it's the least I can do in return."

"My throat feels like crap, probably that damn cigar," he admitted. "Come here." He patted the bed, and I shook my head.

"I'm heading down to the gym before checkout. I need a good run."

He looked disappointed, and I was about to change my mind when a knock at the door surprised us both. "Did you order breakfast up?"

"No, I didn't."

The knock came again, and I waited to answer until Josh gathered his clothes and went into the bathroom. I looked through the peephole and sucked in a breath. Crap. Opening it slightly, I gave a tight smile to Colby.

"Hi, there," he greeted, entirely too chipper for someone who should be good and hungover this morning.

"Hi, yourself. What brings you by?"

"Well, I wanted to talk to you for a minute. Mind if I come in?"

"Uh, I'm on my way down to the gym, but we can talk on the way."

"Sure. Sounds good."

"Let me grab my iPod and I'll be right out."

Unfortunately, I underestimated him. As I turned and went toward the desk to grab my music, he put his foot in the door and let himself in. I spun around and flushed.

"Whatcha hiding, Haylee?" he asked, smirking.

I rolled my eyes, trying to play it off. "Nothing. I'm simply old-fashioned about having a man I barely know in my hotel room."

"Mm hmm. You know, it's funny. I went by my brother's room this morning, and he didn't answer the door."

"Maybe he's sleeping," I said dryly.

"Perhaps, but I was kind of hoping I'd find him here. That possibly you two were together."

"Why? So that you can make bang-the-secretary jokes and comment on my *qualifications*?" I did air quotes and moved again toward the door, ready to leave.

"I heard enough about your qualifications last night, actually, while talking with Brian and Josh."

"Please don't make me hit you again," I threatened and watched his smile.

"I like you, Haylee. You don't put up with crap. And for the record, I was being sincere. But all right, I'll walk you downstairs. If my brother isn't man enough to come out of the bathroom and tell me, his only brother who he should trust, that he's in fact with you, then I think I may have to do my best to convince you to give me a shot, after all."

The bathroom door slammed.

I didn't bother to turn around. Instead, I watched Colby's eyes light up with the satisfaction of being right.

"I'll be down at the gym," I muttered, feeling annoyed and embarrassed.

I felt Josh's hand on my shoulder. "Haylee, wait—"

"No, you two talk or whatever. I have stuff to do. See ya, Colby."

Colby moved in front of the door. "Haylee, I didn't call his bluff to shame you. I'm sorry."

His eyes reflected sincerity, but I still wasn't ready to talk about it.

"She has nothing to feel ashamed about." Josh's voice was angry.

I faced him, putting a hand on his chest where I felt the hum of fury.

"I'm not ashamed. This is just awkward. I'm heading downstairs and will be up later."

That seemed to calm him down some as I left the brothers to hash it out.

Josh was gone by the time I returned to my room, and there was no note. Sighing, I took a shower and started packing. My flight was leaving in a couple of hours, and I needed to check out. I was about to text him goodbye when I heard a knock at my door.

Opening it, I was surprised to see Colby again.

"He's not here this time." I didn't bother hiding my annoyance.

"I didn't come to talk to Josh. I came to apologize to you."

"What for? You weren't off base." And maybe that's what had bothered me the most. Colby had been able to read there was something between us, and yet Josh had denied it until he'd been caught.

He sighed and crossed the room. "No, but I didn't mean to disrespect you in the process. I wasn't trying to make it seem cheap or anything." He looked sincere, but it didn't matter.

"It's all right. It is what it is, and I know what it looks like. I'm his secretary, ten years younger, and we're sleeping together. I guess the only silver lining is that he's single, so I won't get the trifecta award for the cliché office romp."

"There's nothing cliché about the way my brother feels about you."

I sucked in my breath and must have shown my surprise.

"You don't know?"

I could only shake my head.

"Well, now you do. He's happier than I've ever seen him.

Although I think making it public with you instead of hiding it would go a long way to ensuring you're both happy."

"This is only temporary. Besides, you, of all people, know he has hang-ups regarding the general public knowing anything private about him."

He regarded me before speaking. "He does have good reason. Not that you should be penalized for that bitch of an ex-wife he was married to, but unfortunately, he's been burned. I guess the point I was trying to make in coming here this morning was one, to say it was really nice meeting you. Two, that I'm sorry for accosting you yesterday and embarrassing you this morning. And third, I think you're good for him."

"Thanks, Colby."

We both jumped at the sound of the knock at the door.

"Speak of the devil." Colby smirked.

I opened the door to see Josh. "Hi," he greeted softly and then stiffened upon noting his brother over my shoulder.

"I was just leaving." Colby moved toward the door. "See you in the lobby in an hour, Josh."

The door closed, leaving us alone.

"What did he want?" Josh appeared irritated to have found his brother in my room.

"He wanted to apologize," I said simply and watched Josh relax.

"Good. I'm glad he did. I was hoping to have you fly back with me today, but Colby and I have personal business for which we need to go to Florida. I should be back in New York later this week."

I waited for an explanation of his personal business, but that was all he was willing to share. Disguising my hurt that he wasn't confiding in me, I kept my voice light. "That's fine. I'm heading to the airport. Safe travels, all right?"

"You too," he responded, kissing me soundly and walking me out to the elevator.

CHAPTER NINETEEN

I didn't see or hear from Josh the rest of the week. Nigel mentioned that he'd gone to a funeral in Florida and then home to Virginia for personal reasons. It was a cruel reminder that I wasn't really a part of his world. I even wondered if we still had plans for the upcoming weekend in Charlotte. He'd mentioned it the last night in Vegas, but he'd been drinking and that had been before Colby had discovered us the next morning.

The bright spot, however, was that by Friday I'd found out I'd been accepted to all of my top schools, including Harvard, Stanford, Cornell, Yale, Columbia, and NYU. I was excited and wished Josh was with me to share the news. Meanwhile, I texted Sasha, Catherine, and Will, hoping at least one of them might be up for helping me celebrate tonight.

It was nearly six o'clock, the time I normally left work. According to Josh's itinerary, he'd just landed back in New York. Nigel had thought he would most likely head into the office, and I was torn whether or not to wait for him. Sighing, I looked up to see Brian coming off the elevator.

He must have had the bypass code in order to come straight

up. He looked amused. "It's Friday. Why the mopey face?" He surprised me by sitting down in Nigel's chair and scooting over towards my desk.

"Uh, Josh's plane just landed, so if he's coming into the office, it probably won't be for another hour or so. I'm packing up for the evening."

"I know. I just talked to him. He's meeting me here, and then we're going to dinner. Now why the mope?"

"I'm not. I was just trying to see if anyone was available to go out tonight. I wanted to share my news."

He seemed intrigued. "So share with me."

Why the hell not? At least he'd be happy for me. I handed over the letters.

He glanced down and read through them briefly. "Holy shit, Haylee, you got accepted to all of them?"

"I did." I smiled. It did feel good to tell someone.

"This is a cause for celebration. Did you tell Josh?"

And therein lay the root of the mopeyness, if there was such a word. "He's been out of town all week, so I haven't had a chance to talk to him."

He looked thoughtful and then went over to Nigel's phone to dial a number on speaker.

I felt my heartbeat in my ears when I heard Josh's voice answer.

"Josh, it's Brian. I'm at your office, but I need a raincheck on dinner tonight."

"All right, then why come to my office?" He sounded mildly annoyed, but that was nothing new.

"Well, I didn't find out that I had other plans until I came here, and now I'm taking Haylee out to celebrate, instead."

Silence. Brian glanced over at me and winked.

"Take me off speaker," Josh commanded.

Brian didn't seem the least bit concerned and picked up the phone mildly. "Okay. Done. Uh-huh. Yep. You got it. Talk to you later." He hung up and then smiled at me. "I suggest we go before he gets here because he's not in the best of moods."

"What did he say when you took him off speaker?"

"Not anything worth repeating and nothing to worry about," he said, smiling.

I doubted that highly, but I was anxious to get the hell out of the office. "Who are you calling now?" I asked as we got into a cab.

"Sasha. I figured maybe you would want her there, too. I know she'll be thrilled for you."

"I texted her earlier but haven't heard back."

"I think she's probably at the gym; she leaves early on Fridays."

"So where are we going?"

"Piano bar uptown. You'll like it. It's perfect for celebrating."

"Brian, you don't have to do this. I feel like I totally crashed your Friday night with my pity party."

"You're kidding, right? Come on, this is huge news. Did you let Mark know?"

"Uh, no, not yet."

"He told me how impressed he was with your essay. He can make the trip down, so we should call him."

"He told you he was impressed?"

Brian nodded and dialed his phone, putting it again on speaker. "Mark, I have Haylee here, and she has some news." He gestured for me to take the phone.

"I got into all of the schools."

"All of them?" He sounded astonished.

"Yep. Stanford, Harvard, Cornell, Yale, Columbia, and NYU."

"That's awesome. I've never known anyone to get into all of them. I told you your personal statement was incredible."

"Well, thank you for critiquing it and looking over my application. It meant a lot."

"Of course. Are you celebrating?"

"That's the plan," Brian replied, taking him off of speaker. "Meet us. I'm bagging on Josh for dinner, and I think you should come down. Yeah, so who cares?" Brian winked again.

I figured Josh would be plenty pissed off when he found out that all of his friends were aware of my news, but he wasn't—and that they were taking me out.

"Good. Prepare for a long night. Mark will meet us there in a couple of hours."

Once we arrived at the piano bar, he got us a great table within minutes.

"I can't thank you enough for this, but Josh is going to flip that both of his best friends are out celebrating with me, and he doesn't even know what for."

"Well, then, he should've asked," Brian quipped back but then relented a little. "All right, I'll text him the place. If he shows up, then good. But if not, you're going to have a great time anyhow, okay?"

Sounded good to me.

I WAS PRETTY MUCH DRUNK. It was after ten o'clock, which meant a firm four hours of drinking. Mark and Brian had been thrilled that I loved the beer that was on draft, and we'd done a chugging contest. I'd lost, big time.

Sasha sat beside me and handed me the glass of water that Will had been kind enough to order from the waitress. Catherine had unfortunately been out of town. Brian and Mark were recalling a story from college when I glanced up and saw Josh walking toward us.

"Hey, look who decided to join the party," Brian drawled.

Surprised, Josh looked toward Mark, "I didn't know you were coming, too."

"Well, Brian called me to come down for the celebration."

If Josh found this odd, he didn't say so.

Brian pulled out a chair. "Take a seat. Let's get you a drink."

"So what's the celebration exactly?" Josh queried, looking at me.

My face heated at the fact that he was the only one still in the dark. "I got into all of the law schools I applied to."

I couldn't read his expression, but at least his words were sincere. "That's terrific. When did you find out?"

"I started receiving letters Tuesday, and the last one from Harvard came today."

Josh held up his glass. "Cheers, then. Congratulations." His eyes flicked over mine, and then he turned toward Mark in conversation.

"You feeling okay?" Sasha asked me, and I faked a smile.

"Yes, a little bit tipsy. Excuse me. I'm going to make my way to the ladies' room and make sure my balance is still intact." Will helped me out, and I gave him a smile. I needed to get myself together. Seeing Josh again after a week of radio silence had me off balance. The drinks didn't help.

In the restroom, I took a deep breath and glanced in the mirror. At least I didn't look too bad for working a full day and then drinking for a few hours. And my stomach was cooperating thanks to the carb fest Brian had insisted on ordering before starting on the beer. As I came out of the restroom, I came face to face with Josh. I hadn't expected him to follow me, but he appeared to have been waiting for me in the hall.

"Why didn't you tell me?" He searched my eyes.

"I just did." I didn't mean to be flip, but I was a little drunk and a lot annoyed with the man.

"I meant before you told everyone else. Why didn't you tell me earlier this week?"

"It must have slipped my mind what with all of the phone

conversations we shared," I retorted sarcastically. He hadn't once contacted me.

"I didn't get a chance this week. I had the funeral and some things to take care of. How did Brian get involved?" His tone was light even if his question wasn't.

"He came by the office tonight, and I showed him the letters. It snowballed from there."

"He does have that effect," he noted wryly.

"I'd better get back. Thanks for coming."

"Haylee, look, I was busy, and I didn't want to burden you with stuff. And I knew it was that time of the month, so I figured spending the week away would be good."

My temper snapped. "You went from not being able to spend a night away to completely frigid. And if you're implying your silence was because I was on my period, well that makes me think that all you want me for is sex."

He balked. "You know that's not true, and I apologize if it came out that way."

"Why the distance this week? What happened after Vegas?"

"What? Nothing, I just—"

"Just what?"

"Look, I don't want to talk about it, but it has nothing to do with you, okay? It's been a bad week all the way around."

"Are you going to tell me why it was such a bad week?"

His eyes told me the answer before he did. "No. You'll have to accept that I'm a private man. I'm not going to tell you everything."

"Right. Because I'm just the temporary secret girlfriend with an expiration date. Why bother to confide in me?" There, I said it, and immediately I saw his anger.

"Is that what you really think?"

I gave a half shrug, turned around, and headed back to the table. It took all of my willpower not to cry. Instead, I pasted a smile on my face for the next thirty minutes.

I did my best to ignore Josh once he appeared back at the table. He also must have realized it would look awkward if he took off too soon, so we both went through the motions.

It was past my bedtime and I could feel myself fading. "You guys are the best, but I should get home. At this rate I think I'll be good and hungover, Brian." I gave him a pointed look.

He held up his hands, and we all laughed.

"I don't know what you're talking about. You accepted the beer chugging challenge and I have to say gave me and Mark a run for our money. Plus, you're in your early twenties and should have twice the stamina we do," he teased.

Hugging Sasha first, I promised to meet her for lunch soon. Will embraced me next and told me he'd call when he got back in town. He was flying out the next morning for a modeling gig. Next was Mark, which was kind of awkward. He'd seemed uncomfortable ever since Josh had showed up. Brian, of course, lifted me off my feet with exaggerated exuberance and kissed me on the cheek.

"Congratulations again," he said.

"Thank you." I faced Mark. "And thanks again, Mark, for looking over my application and statement."

Blushing slightly, he nodded and then gave me a thoughtful look. "Wait. You never said: which school are you choosing?"

Oh, that. "I honestly have no idea. I feel like I should play roulette with the letters and let fate decide. Although I talked to my father's former partner today, and he said that he could find me affordable housing near Stanford. But I guess I need to map it all out."

"Mark could probably find you affordable housing near Yale, too," Josh offered.

"Well, I vote Columbia or NYU, so you can stay in the city," Sasha remarked.

"Me, too. Stay in New York, Haylee girl," Will said.

I had to hold my tears back by biting my lip. I felt like the friends I'd made here would miss me when I left. That feeling hadn't been with me when I'd left high school, college, or LA. Looking at their faces, I tried not to get too emotional about the fact that each of them had taken time out of their busy schedules to be with me tonight. "Well, I'm going to try to figure it out by next week. I'll let you know."

Just as I was about to walk outside, Josh stood up. "I'll make sure you get a cab. Anyway, I need to get home myself."

We walked out in silence while I tried to get a handle on my emotions over having real friends for the very first time.

"My car is over here."

"It's okay. I don't want for people to see. I'll take a cab."

"I don't give a fuck if someone sees us. Get in my car, Haylee."

My feet thankfully decided to follow the direction of my brain which was screaming that he was being a complete jerk at the moment. I didn't budge.

We were in a standoff in the middle of the sidewalk. Finally, his eyes softened.

"Please get in the car," he relented.

That was better, and I knew we shouldn't do this publicly. After Josh opened the door, I scooted into the back seat and stared out the window.

We stayed silent during the entire ride and up until we arrived at our floor in the building.

"Get your bags packed, please. We're leaving for the airport," he finally said.

"Right now?"

"Remember, we have plans for a weekend in Charlotte. We're going now."

"I haven't heard from you all week long, and suddenly we have plans for the weekend?"

"It's not sudden; we discussed it in Vegas. Look, it's been a lousy week, and I thought I'd be worthless company." He paused and then closed the distance between us. "I didn't grasp that I was making you have a shitty week, too, when you should be nothing but smiles."

"You're making the wrong excuses. You shut me out completely; I want you to tell me why."

He sighed and hugged me closer. "I know I did. Can we talk about it tomorrow? We can fly down tonight, and we'll have the whole weekend, just the two of us, okay?"

I thought about insisting on hashing it out here, but between my drinking and the lateness of the hour, I agreed to wait. "All right. But we'll talk about it tonight, when we get there," I compromised.

He looked instantly relieved and kissed my forehead. "We'll leave in fifteen minutes. Do you need help packing?"

"No, I'm okay." I went inside my apartment and got ready for the trip.

THE CAR RIDE to the airport was quiet, but I was grateful when Josh handed me a large bottle of water. His hand curled around mine. For now, I let my mind let go of my anger. The flight gave me the opportunity for a couple hours of sleep. I barely registered when we left the plane for the drive to the house, but woke as the driver pulled up to Josh's beautiful mansion.

"Home sweet home. Come on, sleepyhead."

He led me into his spacious foyer and then straight up the spiral staircase to what must have been the master bedroom. "Let's get you in bed. It's really late, so I'll give you a tour in the morning." He undressed me slowly and then crawled in beside me.

I sighed, loving the feel of him naked beside me.

"You seemed emotional when we were leaving the bar. What were you thinking?"

"I was thinking about the fact that Brian went out of his way to ensure I had a good night. That Sasha, Will, and Mark all dropped their plans because of me. I've never had that before," I whispered, feeling his arms come around me.

"They all adore you, Haylee. I just wish I would've checked in this week. You should get some sleep, baby. We'll talk more in the morning."

"I'm not tired yet," I whispered.

"Hmm, I'm sure I can think of something to pass the time."

I felt his hips cradle my backside and the start of his erection.

"You promised we could discuss your week tonight."

"Not what I had in mind," he protested, kissing my neck.

"I can't keep sharing with you, Josh, and get nothing in return." I turned and faced him.

"I didn't want to pile my shit on top of yours. You have enough on your plate without dealing with my crap." He was unprepared for me to scramble out of the bed.

I stood just outside of his reach. "Try again. Was it when I told you how I felt about you that first night?" Had those three little words spooked him?

"It wasn't that." He ran a hand through his hair as he sat up in the bed. I tried not to let the fact that he had an erection distract me.

"Was it telling your brother about us? You wondered why I was awkward about that whole scene, and I'll tell you it's because I knew it would affect us going forward. That you'd get weird."

"Would you please get back into bed? Just let me hold you, and I'll figure out how to say this."

I reluctantly returned to bed and let him snuggle me into his arms, my back to his chest, where I waited him out.

Finally, he sighed. "I'll just start with my week since that's easier. I received the call on Sunday night while we were in Vegas that the driver I'd had when I was a kid had passed away.

He was with me up until three years ago when he retired. I left for the Keys on Monday night. The viewing was Tuesday and the funeral on Wednesday. My mom and Colby came, too. It was expected, but still rough. And then my ex showed up, which was completely unforeseen."

I had to bite my tongue and measure my response carefully. "When was the last time you'd seen her?"

"Three years ago."

I had a million questions I wanted to ask, starting with why she would've been there in the first place. I could only handle one issue at a time, however, so I chose to leave that alone for now. "Tell me about your friend."

He spent the next few minutes telling me about his longtime family driver and then was quiet. "I wish he'd had more time to enjoy his retirement."

"Sounds like an amazing guy. I'm really sorry." I paused and then pressed on. "So after the funeral you went back up to Virginia with your mom?"

"Yeah, where I met her new boyfriend."

"That must have been tough." I kept my comment simple, letting him choose what he wanted to tell me.

"He was all right. My brother had met him before. It's strange to see her with someone. But he's the first guy she's dated, and it's been ten years, so I don't know why I let it bother me."

"It would be hard at any point of time to see your parent with someone new. You're entitled to your feelings." I yawned and felt his kiss on my hairline.

"Thank you."

"For what?"

"Not asking questions about my ex."

"Mm, you know that I really want to ask why she was there."

He sighed. "She once told me that she spent more time with our driver than me during our marriage. I think she had a fondness for him, but I really couldn't say, and I didn't ask her."

I was grateful that he shared this fact with me. Flipping around to face him, I kissed his neck. "Sounds like a rough week," I commented lightly, waiting for more.

He reached out, stroking my face. "It was, and I feel terrible that I was the last to know that you got into all of the schools you applied to."

"I would've told you had you called."

"I thought about it multiple times," he said lamely.

"It hurt my feelings that you would go from not being able to spend a night away from me to going to a funeral for someone you cared about and not even telling me what happened. I know this is short term. I've accepted that, but the 180 degree turn was really abrupt. I'd like to know why."

"I'll admit that it was weird after Colby found out. Maybe I panicked a little. The rest really comes down to self-preservation. I know this is short term, too, which is why not being able to be away from you for a night isn't the direction we should be taking things. I'm not looking forward to ending this."

I let out a breath. "Okay, I can understand that." And I did. We both didn't want to change one another or our long-term goals. Yet the thought of breaking things off in just a few months hurt like hell. "So you needed some distance to put things back into perspective?"

"Yeah, and now that you've received your letters, it's sinking in that you're really leaving soon."

I hugged him tightly and realized that I might not be the only one who'd developed feelings I hadn't planned on.

THE NEXT MORNING when I woke up, it dawned on me that I was twenty-three years old today. Not that Josh or anyone else was aware of that fact. I'd told him it was in March but had never revealed the actual day. In his massive king-sized bed, I stretched out like a cat, enjoying the fact that we had nothing on the agenda for the day but each other. I couldn't think of a better way to spend my birthday than having sex and enjoying some downtime with my man, even if he didn't know what day it was.

We had slept in after our late talk last night, and Josh had been overly attentive with our lovemaking first thing this morning. He'd brought me breakfast in bed, and now I was contemplating a shower while he insisted on doing the dishes. I was pretty sure all this attention was his way of making up for the last week.

Padding into the adjoining master bathroom, I marveled at the size of it. Marble tile was everywhere, and the sunken Jacuzzi tub looked like something I would definitely need to try later on. For now, I had every intention of enjoying his oversized glass shower with jet sprays from all angles. It occurred to me that I'd only seen the bedroom and bathroom and I looked forward to a tour of the rest of his home later.

Turning around while rinsing my hair, I saw him walk into the bathroom. He put a silk robe on the door's hook and watched me.

"You could join me," I offered suggestively.

"I'm finishing up downstairs in the living room. Take your time, brush your hair out, blow dry, and do whatever. I have this robe for you. Make sure you have nothing on under it."

"You don't want me to come downstairs?" I was intrigued.

He only smiled and shook his head. "Nope, not until I come in and get you. Don't you like surprises, birthday girl?"

I yelped when he pinched my backside. "I can't believe you knew it was my birthday."

He gave me a look as if to say *is there anything I don't know*. "Mm, yes I knew, and I need you to stay in here, okay?"

Smiling, I was genuinely excited for my surprise.

I finished up my shower and saw that Josh had brought my suitcase in for me. He must really not have wanted me to come out to the living room. I took my time, blew out my hair, and carefully put on my makeup, ensuring that I was all done up for my birthday surprise. Donning my new silk robe in a beautiful lavender color, I smiled at the feel of it against my bare skin. I busied myself with making his bed and then sat in the middle of it, checking my phone while I waited.

"Hi." He peeked in and then walked toward me with wrapped boxes in his hands. "You look exquisite."

I blushed and looked toward the gifts that were wrapped beautifully with big bows.

"So, birthday girl, these are for you."

"Which one can I open first?" There were four wrapped boxes. I was eager to find out what was inside each of them.

"Doesn't matter. Pick one."

I could tell he was amused as I grabbed the smallest box, shaking it like a little kid and enjoying his smile. I ripped through the paper while he laughed.

"You're definitely not the sort to carefully open the tape and save the paper, are you?"

I shrugged and then laughed. "Nope, life is too short." I opened the lid and smiled. There sat ten pairs of the prettiest lace and silk thong underwear.

"That's probably more of a replacement *I'm sorry* gift for ripping some of your other pairs, but I do rather like the thought of you wearing lacy thongs that I picked out."

I did, too, and gave him a sexy little kiss before starting on another box. "Ha, yoga pants." I started giggling and loved the fact that he was making each gift so personal. I pulled out the pairs, one in black, one in navy, and the last in dark gray. When I glanced at the size, I was impressed. "I thought you said these torture you."

"Mm, such sweet torture, though. It seemed like you only had the one pair."

"You're right; I do just have the one. Very thoughtful of you since I love them. Running, long flights, torturing my boyfriend—they're very versatile."

I ripped into another package and squealed as it revealed new running shoes, the best rated ones on the market and far out of my price range.

"I love these, all of it." I went for the last package, which revealed three pairs of designer jeans. "Josh, this is too much. You went overboard, but thank you, truly." I held up the jeans and watched a funny expression cross his face.

"It wasn't too much and probably kind of practical gifts, but I thought you'd use all of them."

My lips kissed his softly. "The best gifts are the ones that will be actually used. Considering I've been living in the one pair of jeans Catherine got me and my one pair of yoga pants, I feel like I've just been given a whole new wardrobe of the things I love. So, thank you."

He smiled.

I was undone because Josh Singer smiling made me one very happy girl.

"Come on. I have another surprise."

He walked me downstairs and into the sunken living room, which looked like a romantic movie set. In front of the large gas fireplace aglow with flames was a makeshift mattress with satin sheets and beautiful cashmere blankets. There was champagne on ice and white roses on both the coffee and end tables.

"I've never seen your house before; does it always look like this?"

He laughed. "Uh, no, it had a bit of a makeover in honor of our weekend. I'll give you a tour of the rest of the house later. But for now…"

I turned, tipping my face up for a kiss. He didn't disappoint, tasting me leisurely, savoring my lips and mouth, and then making love to me slowly and thoroughly.

LATER THAT EVENING while Josh was toying with my breasts, he asked, "Have you thought about your school choices?"

I lay in post-coital bliss in front of the fireplace, still completely naked. It was difficult to concentrate on his question. "Hmm, not really. I've been otherwise occupied."

"Gloriously so, but you still have a big decision to make. Here, this should help." He laid the cashmere blanket over me, and I giggled.

"There's still a matter of you being naked, which is far more distracting," I teased.

Smiling, he reached over and grabbed his discarded flannel PJ bottoms and slipped them on.

"Do you have any guidance for a decision-making strategy?"

He seemed surprised. "You want my advice on this?"

"Not on my actual school choice. But considering you make big decisions every day, I would welcome a strategy."

He looked pleased that I was asking him. "All right, you have six choices, correct?"

"Yes."

"So first thing today is to eliminate two of them off the bat. The two that don't make sense based on rankings or the fact that the other four are better schools."

I thought about it for a moment. "Okay. I'd eliminate NYU and Cornell. They were safety schools."

"And now you have four. So you can put together pros and cons along with the costs."

I smiled and got up from where we had been the last few hours to cross over to my laptop. Booting it up, I put on the screen the Excel spreadsheet I'd already made regarding the various law schools. "So, since I eliminated those two, let me hide those columns."

He took the laptop from me and scrolled down. "Impressive. So Yale and Harvard are the two top-ranked schools?"

"Actually, Stanford is tied with Harvard for number two."

"And Columbia?"

"Is number four."

"You have here that Columbia is your most expensive."

"It is when you factor in housing in New York City." I didn't want to entertain the idea of staying in Josh's apartment.

"And Stanford is your cheapest?"

"Of those four, yes—especially with the break on housing my father's old partner can get me."

"Mark told me he thinks he'd have a line on housing in New Haven for Yale."

"That would be great."

"Okay, now that you're down to four, the next step will be going down to two."

"That seems less overwhelming. Thank you."

"And now you have many choices for dinner. You pick for your birthday."

I could hardly believe the day was almost over. After our first round of lovemaking, Josh had given me a tour of his house. Then we'd spent the rest of the day naked in front of the fireplace with more lovemaking and no agenda. It was the best birthday I could have imagined.

"Mm, I choose sushi," I decided.

"Good. I'll order and run out to pick it up, along with your birthday cake."

THE NEXT NIGHT Josh grilled shrimp and steaks and kept the red wine flowing. I was feeling buzzed and enjoyed our playful banter in the kitchen. After dinner, we relaxed in the living room and watched a movie, still on our makeshift bed of cashmere and pillows. I was having a hard time concentrating on the plot line because of his little touches throughout.

When the movie credits started rolling, we both stood up to clear our wineglasses and plates. He hugged me tightly and murmured seductively, "I want all of you, Haylee."

A whoosh of heat traveled through me. We had flirted with it and played around, and now I was shaking with anticipation.

"Do you know what that means?" he asked huskily.

"Yes," I whispered, feeling his fingers take mine and pull me into him.

His hands cupped my face, and a shiver went through me. "Talk to me. Does it turn you on?"

I nodded and felt his sigh of relief.

"Take off your clothes and lie in the middle of the pillows. I'll be right back."

My hands shook as I slipped out of my clothes and lay on the pillows, feeling a rush with this dominant side of him, but also nerves.

He returned without any clothes and with a couple of things in his hands. "I'll make this good for you, baby, I promise. And if you don't want to do it again, we don't have to, okay?"

My breath caught when he knelt down in front of me, putting the toys to the side. All I could do was nod.

"So beautiful," he murmured, pressing kisses over my breasts, slowly tantalizing and teasing each one, bringing my sensitive nipples up into a peak and then sucking them seductively as I moaned in delight.

My back arched, and my body responded to his hot mouth on my fevered skin. He made his way further down to my hot, drenched entrance. I don't know what I'd been expecting, but him taking his time like this wasn't it. Soon I found my nerves disappearing as the familiar sensations started to build. But his lips didn't stay long and instead were trailing down to the inside of my thighs and then to the curve of my knee and down further as he kissed the arch of my foot.

"There's no part of you that isn't perfection."

I shivered with his words.

He kissed a path back up my legs, and his mouth feasted on my pussy. My hands grasped his hair, pushing his face further into my center as I felt his groan of pleasure.

"God, I love it when you do that. It makes me feel like you can't get enough."

"I can't," I breathed.

His tongue swept my clit, his mouth sucking erotically. I gripped the pillows, feeling it build, only to have him pull away. He hovered over me, looking into my face.

I reared up, taking his mouth and enjoying his sounds of pleasure at the fact that I had no reservations about tasting myself on his lips. My hips moved of their own volition, trying to relieve the pressure and practically begging for his hand to find me again.

"You're so wet for me."

I moaned when his fingers finally found me and nearly cried out when they left again.

He nipped my bottom lip.

"Josh…" He'd never teased me this way, always going for multiple orgasms instead of delaying the one.

"Easy. We'll get there, but I want you ready."

"I am ready." I practically whined and wanted to pout when he just grinned. He was enjoying this torture way too much.

"Help me with the condom," he requested, and I was momentarily confused.

"This is so that I can have you the other way after."

"Oh," was the only thing I could respond with. I wasn't sure of the rules of anal etiquette, but that seemed sensible.

"Put the rabbit inside of you, but don't turn it on yet."

He reached over and handed the vibrator to me. It was all I could do not to start pushing it in and out as my body craved release.

"Patience. Now get up on your knees, put your elbows on the couch, and spread your legs."

I wasn't sure I could take much more as my body felt heavy and fevered. At the breaking point.

"Let me turn it on, but you're not going to come yet. Okay?"

"I, yeah—"

His one hand kneaded my breasts and I could feel him behind me. His fingers on his other hand found me pathetically drenched for him and then the hum of the rabbit was started with a flick of his remote control.

"Please…" I wouldn't be able to hold out any longer. His skilled fingers dipped down and spread my wetness up towards my back entrance and then his finger slid in.

"Come, Haylee, I want you to come and to move against my finger." I did. Whether he would have instructed me to or not, my hips were moving with a tempo I could no longer control. The rabbit deep inside of me and his finger were merely along for the ride. "That was so hot," he whispered in my ear.

I was coming down when I realized the intensity of the rabbit was now shooting back up. "Oh, God," I moaned. I was on stimulation overload when I felt his finger being replaced by something larger, and I knew it was the broad head of his penis. I heard the sounds of him coating his erection in lube and then felt his fingers working me, making the entrance wet and ready.

"Easy. Just feel it. We'll go slowly." I could hear his erratic breathing as he paced himself, pushing only a small measure forward and then holding still to allow me to accommodate his thickness.

But the problem was I was past the point of going slow. My body needed him. It craved him in that forbidden place so much that I couldn't wait any longer. I thrust back and heard his breath hitch. I'd caught him off guard and felt his hard cock push in past the muscle. It was such a mixture of pleasure and pain as he stretched me with his hard length.

"Fuck, slow down and relax. I don't want to hurt you—"

His thought was cut off. My body was moving without my brain in charge, and it wouldn't be denied. I pushed back again and felt him slide in further. His breaths were strained. I felt him trying to pull out a little to relieve the discomfort, but my orgasm was close, and I wouldn't be deprived. I wasn't sure if I'd survive, but I was almost there and, at this point, I wasn't sure I cared one way or another. On one final push back, he was completely filling me. Whatever control he'd thought he'd exercise was gone as both his hands grabbed my hips, and he started to drive in earnest.

"Christ, Haylee—"

The orgasm tore through me with such ferociousness that I felt like I might pass out from the magnitude of it. I was pretty sure I screamed his name and felt his primal groan on a final thrust into me.

I was trembling, and I could feel him shaking, too. If it hadn't been for the couch in front of me I would've been flat on my face. He withdrew slowly, and I managed to take out the rabbit. I couldn't take one more pulse from that little guy. All of my nerve endings were raw.

Meanwhile, he disposed of the condom.

I fell back into the pillows on my side as I wasn't sure I would be able to lie on my back for a while.

"Are you okay?"

I couldn't form words, but I felt him beside me.

He grasped my face, searching my eyes.

I nodded and curled into him.

"Jesus, I thought the teasing would work you into it slowly. I didn't know it would—"

"Unleash a wild animal?" I supplied and felt his chuckle.

"Kind of. I didn't hurt you, did I? Are you sure you're okay?"

"Mm hmm, but I think I'll probably be a little sore."

"Yeah, I'd say so. I didn't mean—I mean was it good for you?"

"I can barely talk, so yeah, the orgasm rendered me speechless."

"So you liked me in your—"

"Please—" I held up my hand, my entire face heating. "I can't talk about it like that, not yet."

He only grinned. "That's even more of a turn-on. A nice girl who likes the dirty things we've done but doesn't want to talk about them."

I groaned, putting my face into the curve of his shoulder and neck.

"Haylee, it's every man's fantasy, don't you know? I like that you blush, but I also want you to feel comfortable. Mostly I want to make sure you enjoyed it, and I didn't hurt you."

"I'm fine, I promise. I guess it just sort of shocked me how much I wanted to, uh, do that."

He smiled and kissed me fully, suckling my lower lip and tugging playfully. "I'm going to go run a bath. Meet me there in a couple minutes, okay?"

I nodded and then joined him a short time later. Wincing at the slight twinge in my backside, I sat down and saw his sympathetic expression.

"Bad?"

I bit my lip and blushed. "Not too bad."

His eyes shifted from concern to lust. "You do realize I'm going to have a difficult time this week watching you sit down in chairs without getting hard."

I giggled and loved straddling his lap, his lips kissing me intensely. He hardened almost instantly and I found his arousal with my fingers.

"Mm, are you sure you want to go again? We don't have to."

"I want to," I murmured, guiding his length into me and loving the feel as he slowly slid in and out, slopping water out of the tub and neither of us caring.

He stood up suddenly, and I wrapped my legs around his waist. He didn't break contact and took me out to the bed where he lay me down and, still attached, followed me, bracing his weight on his arms. "Sweet, beautiful, and all mine. You're my fantasy come true, you know that."

He was attentive and sweet and made love to me slowly and thoroughly. I appreciated that I needed it more than I'd thought in order to balance the mind-blowing kinky stuff from earlier.

IT FELT strange after our weekend together to dress up in business attire and make our way into the Charlotte office on Monday morning. Josh held my hand during the ride, but regrettably, we put space between us emotionally when we went in through the doors to start our day.

He had meetings for the majority of the morning, and I was glad to catch him in his office finally as he was finishing up a call. The blinds were shut. I wasn't sure if that was because of the sun pouring in or for privacy, but the fact that we had seclusion kind of did things to a girl when looking at her man in his suit and tie, sounding all powerful on a conference call. I took a seat in front of his desk to wait and winced, having forgotten about my tenderness there.

He hung up and looked at me in concern. "Still sore?"

"A little, but sometimes I kind of get hot with the reminder of why." I hadn't meant to say that last part out loud and paused at the carnal look he gave me.

His eyes closed, and he took a deep breath. "You do realize I have a raging hard-on right now and have another meeting in twelve minutes."

Before he could open his eyes and figure out what I was up to, I hurried to his side of the desk and dropped to my knees in front of him. Freeing his cock from his suit, I saw he hadn't exaggerated about being hard. This was one of my fantasies.

Muttering an oath, he hit some sort of switch that locked the doors. "Dammit, Haylee."

I glanced up and slid my tongue up his seam. "You want me to stop?"

His eyes were raging with emotion. Though apparently at war with himself, he shook his head.

This was all the coaxing I needed to continue. I swirled my tongue around the tip before grabbing his erection around its base with both hands and taking it deep into the back of my throat. I worked him hard and fast, increasing the tempo, aware that we only had a limited amount of time. I was pleased when he came after only a few minutes. Licking up every last drop, I saw that his eyes were still watching me.

"You didn't have to," he voiced softly.

"I never feel like I do. I wanted to, as this was kind of a fantasy for me, with you at your desk looking good in your suit, and me sucking you off behind it."

I watched a shudder run through him and let go so that he could get things, ah, put away. I smiled, satisfied with the fact that I had taken one Joshua Singer by surprise, and he wasn't yet recovered.

"So, you have two more schools to eliminate, and I have an email from Mark to show you," Josh said as we enjoyed a barbeque dinner back at his house later that evening.

He brought over his laptop, and I read the email out loud

about the possible housing for Yale. "Building is being refurbished, and I may need to move apartments at some point, but the one-bedroom looks more than reasonable regarding price," I remarked.

I went and got my laptop in order to update my spreadsheet. "All right, I'll eliminate Columbia: housing is way too pricey for me to remain in New York." I couldn't gauge what he was thinking, but I'd be damned if I made my decision regarding law school about him. "And as much as I loved Stanford for undergrad, I want something new, so now I'm down to Harvard and Yale."

"Well, there you have it. And then there were two."

"Actually, I already know my decision. I mean, there's no contest on the housing prices. Yale it is."

"Congratulations." He crossed and leaned down to kiss me softly.

I emailed Mark to confirm the housing situation and my lease start date of August first. This would allow me enough time to get things moved in before starting classes at the end of that month. I just had to send in my commitment letter, and in no time I'd be starting my new life. It wasn't lost on me that instead of the excitement over starting a new chapter, I felt sad I would have to leave the old one behind.

CHAPTER TWENTY

The next three months were a blur of trips all over the world. Josh and I spent nearly every night together, and it was getting harder to imagine not doing so. We didn't discuss me leaving, but I knew it weighed on both of our minds. When we arrived back home in New York on a Wednesday mid-June, I knew it was time for me to give notice at work.

I was at my desk and had just finished typing up my official letter of resignation. I wondered how Josh would react and kept telling myself it didn't matter.

Pulling back from these thoughts, I glanced at Nigel and saw he was looking pale. He'd been fighting an illness all week. "Nigel, why don't you go home? I can tell you're not feeling well."

"I may take you up on that. It's only a cold, but with David's last treatment three days ago and him being so weak, I want to be sure he doesn't catch anything."

"I completely understand. And I have this tomorrow, too, okay?"

"All right, my dear. I might have to take you up on that."

"Get some rest." I watched him go and hoped he felt better soon.

Josh was currently on a conference call and didn't look to have anything scheduled immediately after. I emailed a meeting request that was simply labeled 'discussion' and waited for his confirmation.

He accepted and then came out to my office area during our appointed time looking amused. "Everything okay?"

Fighting my nerves, I stood up and grabbed my letter of resignation. "Yes, fine. I just need a few minutes with you. Nigel left early as he was feeling sick."

"He sent me an email. I hope he can get some rest. Did you want to come into my office?"

"Uh, yes. Sure." I swallowed hard, following him in and closing his door.

He took a seat on the edge of his desk, looking casual as he studied me. "You look nervous."

"I probably shouldn't have made this so formal. I mean, we both knew it was coming. But I know for HR I need an actual date. Here." I handed him my typed letter of resignation detailing that my last day would be the twelfth of July, one month away.

He read it as he walked around to his chair and took a seat. "If you email a copy to HR and CC me, they can get the ball moving," he said thickly.

"Right, okay." I didn't know what I'd been expecting, but this wasn't it. I bit my lip, trying to fight my tears, not knowing why I wasn't relieved that he was processing this like any boss would.

"Was that all you wanted to discuss?"

I shuffled my feet. "Uh, well I'm planning on going to Australia after my last day and would vacate your apartment when I get back. I should be completely moved out by August first."

"That's fine. Take your time. Do you need help with the move? Are you shipping out some more things from California?"

We were being very civilized about this, but instead of feeling pleased, I felt sad. "I'm stopping off on my way to Australia to find out what I want to ship out. I'd like to bring some items to furnish my apartment. Not the antique stuff, but the couch, bed, et cetera." God, I was rambling on with details that he wouldn't care about.

"I'll pay for the move."

I waved him off. "No, I mean you've been generous enough and—"

"It wasn't a question." Agitation flashed in his eyes.

"Okay." I blew out a breath and opted not to fight about this. "Thank you."

"So that's it?"

That felt like a loaded question. One which I was going to avoid. "Yeah, unless you can think of anything else."

"Nope, I mean you seem to have everything all set. You know if you want to leave sooner, you can. You don't have to give a whole month's notice."

"I, um—did you want me to go sooner?" Now it was my turn with the loaded question.

"I was only suggesting doing so if it's easier for you. I know you're anxious to get onto your new life." His voice betrayed some emotion.

I softened. "This isn't easy for me."

He stood up and walked over to his window, refusing to meet my eyes. "Really? Because it sure seems like it is."

I wrestled with what to say. "We both knew this day was coming eventually." I fought the tears, not knowing how he was feeling. I didn't even have a finger on the pulse of my own emotions.

"You're right. Uh, if that's it, I'll let you email HR. I need to make a few phone calls before heading out to my next appointment."

He shifted back into work mode. I realized the best way to avoid breaking down was to do the same. "Of course. I'll leave you to it."

By the time I'd scanned my letter and made it to my desk, the tears were coming down. I knew I was doing the right thing. If it hurt like hell now, it would only devastate me in the future. Especially if I counted on him always to be part of that future.

"Haylee, I—"

I jumped at the sound of Josh's voice and saw that he'd opened his door and was staring at me.

I held up a hand as he moved toward me. "Don't make it harder," I whispered, meeting his eyes.

"I don't think that's possible," he replied quietly, pulling me up from my chair and enveloping me in a hug.

He stroked my hair, and we stood like that for a few minutes until I could get a handle on the tears.

"What if I take a look at the train schedule? I could take my plane up to see you, too, but Mark has always said the train is faster. We could do every other weekend. Maybe you could come to New York sometimes, too. I know you need to study, but you'd have breaks and—"

I pulled back, completely shocked. "What are you saying?" My heart was beating double-time and I felt the panic before he even said it.

"I'm saying I'm not ready to end things. I could give you a hundred reasons why you don't need law school, but I know you're set on it. The bottom line is New Haven isn't that far away."

"But we put it out there from the beginning that this was short term. We want different things." He'd been adamant he didn't want marriage or kids, so why would we continue with a relationship knowing this? As much as ending things hurt, prolonging the inevitable would be worse.

He looked frustrated. "Tell me, then. If you're so sad at the thought of it ending, why don't you want to continue?"

I swallowed hard, feeling like I was being put on the spot. "Josh, we've never even been out on an actual date. You don't want people to know about us, and you've never let me meet your family. Colby was the exception because he found out. Also, you don't always share what's happening in your life. Not to mention there's the dating other people thing. I've accepted all of that, even when it hasn't been easy, because our relationship was only temporary."

He sighed. "For the record, I haven't gone out with anyone since New Year's Eve. But I think I get what you're saying."

"You do?" I asked carefully.

"Yeah, I think so. You want more than just an extension of our time together."

I sighed in relief that maybe he did get it. "And I fully understand that you aren't in a place where you can do that. I've never tried to change you. I respect the fact that we both want different things long term."

He simply looked at me as I rushed on.

"And I really would like to enjoy our last month together. We have the hotel grand opening in Cancun to look forward to in a couple of weeks. Maybe we could get some personal time there as well?" A last few precious days with him would give me a chance to gather as many memories as possible.

"Yeah, I'd like that." He looked torn as the phone rang.

I picked up the call, gave a greeting, and then put it on hold. "It's Mark for you."

"Okay. I'll, um, see you later tonight, all right?"

I nodded, feeling relief that we were back to the original plan. Emotionally, I could prepare for the end if I knew when that would be.

ON A FRIDAY afternoon a week after giving notice, I received a beautiful bouquet of flowers in the office. Josh was in a meeting across town, and Nigel had the day off. Smiling, I read the card and felt my heart flutter.

"Please join me this evening for the opera. I will pick you up at your place at 7pm. –J"

He was asking me out on an actual date. I hugged the card to me and took a deep breath. The last week had been a little awkward, but he'd still climbed in bed with me each evening. We were enjoying the time we had left, and this was an indication he wanted to make the best of it. I might not believe in long term happiness, but I loved the moments in time where it was easy to forget that.

I dressed in my black Givenchy gown. It was made for a night at the opera. After touching up my makeup and hair, I was ready by seven o'clock. My pulse leaped with the sound of the knock.

I opened my door to see Josh standing there in a full tuxedo. The effect was panty-dropping for sure. "You look really good."

He closed his eyes, and when he opened them again, I could see the flash of desire. "That damn *fuck-me look* you have, Haylee, will be the death of me."

I couldn't help grinning. "It's really your fault for filling out a tux the way you do."

"Well, you are ravishing, and I'm really glad you wore that dress. I especially like the slit." He bent down and parted it to reveal my full leg and garters and then hissed through his teeth. "I knew doing that would be a mistake. Come on. Let's go before I blow this date before it gets started."

I grabbed my clutch and took his offered arm down to the waiting car. Instead of grabbing my pinky in the back seat, he moved me close and put his arm around me.

As far as dates went, I was already sure this was the best one I'd ever been on.

The opera was beautiful, and Josh's seats, of course, were the best in the house. Afterwards, the car took us a few blocks away to a restaurant, a swanky place that was humming on a Friday night. It was evident he was pulling out all of the stops when we were escorted to a private table in the back.

Once we were seated, he took my hand over the small intimate table for two. "I'm not hiding you. I just wanted privacy for us," he explained.

"I understand either way."

He frowned and appeared to want to say more, but we were interrupted by the waitress.

She took our orders and poured the bottle of wine.

He toasted and looked at me thoughtfully. "To new beginnings."

I smiled, clinking my glass with his. "New beginnings."

"I should've done this with you sooner."

Biting my lip, I searched for the right words. "I think it means more anyhow, that you would do this for me before I leave. Thank you."

His eyes flashed something, and then it was gone. We enjoyed a lovely meal and some more wine before making our way back to the apartment.

"I'd like to take that dress off of you myself, if you don't mind," he said quietly.

We'd just come off the elevator to our floor. I had thought I'd go change before going over to his place.

"Okay." I felt the heady combination from the romantic evening and the wine.

He took my hand and led me into his apartment, closing the door behind me. "You're so fucking beautiful," he whispered, raking his eyes over me from head to toe.

"You make me feel that way."

He peeled my dress off slowly with kisses along the way.

Finally, I stood naked in the middle of his living room, trembling with desire. "You're overdressed," I admonished.

He grinned. "We're going to play a game."

"Just so long as that game includes you touching me soon." I stepped into him, cupping his arousal through his pants and enjoying the look on his face as I did so.

"Oh, it does. Come on." He swept me up into his arms and carried me to his bed. After setting me on my feet next to the footboard, he walked into his closet. Reappearing with a silk robe tie, he smiled at me. "We'll play around-the-world and revisit our trips together. Let's start with Cancun, the first time, where I believe you were tied up. Considering we're heading back there in another week for the grand opening of my new hotel, I think it's only appropriate."

I nodded, licking my lips. "Do we have to go in order, or could we skip around?"

He crossed over to me as I held out my wrists. "What did you have in mind?" He secured my hands together and then loosened his bow tie.

I was filled with anticipation as he stood just to the side of the bed, kicking off his shoes. "I'd like to do Cancun and then maybe Hong Kong and perhaps finish with Charlotte."

His eyes flashed with recognition of our venture there, and a shudder ran through him. "Tell me what you said in Vegas that first night. I need to hear it again."

My breath left me in a whoosh, and I searched his eyes. He was finally ready to hear it again in our final weeks together. "I love you."

He closed his eyes as if soaking up my words. When he opened them, he crossed over and cupped my face with both hands. "I love you too, Haylee."

And then, suddenly, he was kneeling in front of me, his breath at my center.

"Jesus, Josh—" I'd hardly had a chance to absorb his words. My mind bounced between relieved that he felt the same way I did to sad that it would just make it harder to leave in a couple of weeks. Part of me wondered if my looming departure made it easier for him to be honest with his feelings. Almost like he had nothing to lose in telling me now. As I felt my orgasm build, all thoughts were replaced with a burning need to just feel him.

"Tell me again, baby," he implored, lifting me up to sit on the bed.

"I love you, Josh," I said, hearing him murmur his same response as he devoured me fully. We went on to explore our world travels. It was like playing the *Greatest Hits* one last time.

CHAPTER TWENTY-ONE

Just when I wanted time to slow down, it seemed suddenly in a hurry. I couldn't believe we were back in Cancun on a lazy Saturday afternoon, the place where it all started between us. We'd flown in last night, and today Josh had reserved a private cabana by the pool stocked with water, liquor, and snacks. The grand opening party would be later this evening.

It felt sublime to get these moments with just the two of us. I'd spent a couple of hours in the sun but now enjoyed reading a book while in my bikini and with him rubbing my feet. "This is heaven, but I kind of feel guilty monopolizing you." I looked up and smiled as he worked up my calf.

"This is heaven for me, too. Since tonight I'll be ridiculously busy playing host at the party and for the most part kind of ignoring you, I'm enjoying our personal time now."

"So how private is this cabana?" I raised a brow.

He looked at his watch, and I wondered what he had going on. But his fingertips then danced up my thigh before he rose quickly. "We have time. Let me put the sign on the outside, and it will be very private."

Swim trunks and bikinis sure made it easy to have a quickie in the cabana, I thought, giggling while he re-tied me from the back about twenty minutes later. But we both froze when we heard voices getting closer.

"Well, he's my son, and I'm going in," a woman's voice said.

"Oh, shit," Josh exclaimed.

It didn't register until Colby and an older, attractive woman came through the entrance that Josh had recognized his mother's voice.

My just-had-sex-hair had to give it away immediately, not to mention the cushions were scattered. Ten minutes sooner and she would have met me for the first time in the doggie style position. Not exactly the impression a girl wanted to go for when meeting her lover's mother.

"Mom, you're here early," Josh recovered, crossing over and giving her a kiss on the cheek.

Colby gave me a wink, and I blushed crimson, frantically looking for my cover-up.

"Mom, this is Haylee Holloway, my girlfriend. Haylee, this is my mom, Patricia Singer, and you know Colby."

Holy shit, did he just say girlfriend?

She glanced first at me, then back at Josh, and lastly toward Colby. "It's nice to finally meet you, my dear. I've heard a lot of great things."

I was in stunned disbelief. "Nice to meet you, too, Mrs. Singer."

"Josh, a word please," his mom requested.

Josh followed her outside but not before kissing my hand.

Colby turned toward me with a sympathetic look. "Sorry about that. I should've texted Josh to let him know we were ahead of schedule."

"Uh, it's fine. I guess I didn't know I'd be meeting your mom at all."

He chuckled. "Well, right after having sex probably wasn't the ideal time. I did try to tell her that sign was for a reason."

I could feel myself turn beet red as Josh came back in with his mother again.

"I'm heading to my room to get changed and unpacked. Then I intend to come back down if you two don't mind the company?" Patricia asked.

I realized she was addressing me. "No, not at all."

After she and Colby left, I expelled the breath I was holding.

"Sorry about that. She arrived earlier than expected," Josh apologized.

"You didn't mention I was meeting your mom and seeing Colby this weekend."

"I wanted it to be a surprise." He studied my face.

"I had thought you didn't want me to." I couldn't figure out my feelings. I was thrilled he would finally introduce me to his family but confused as to why he would do this when we were winding down our relationship.

"I love you, and I'm not ashamed of her knowing that." He hugged me close. "Are you?"

I leaned back. "Of course I'm not. It just took me off guard."

He kissed me softly and then straightened up the pillows. "Thank God she didn't come in any sooner."

We both giggled and put the cabana back the way that it had been before we'd gotten frisky.

JOSH'S MOM was polite and charming, but when she sent Josh and Colby to go get some food for us, I became nervous about being left alone with her.

"So, Josh says you're starting law school soon."

"Yes, at the end of August I'll be heading up to Yale."

Her face expressed appreciation. “Good school. Have you met Mark?”

“Yes, he’s been wonderful. He helped me get an apartment in New Haven and critiqued my essay.”

“How did you and Josh meet?”

Giving her the abbreviated version of the shoot in LA and then Nigel needing help, I hoped I wasn’t saying too much.

She was especially interested in the vintage spread in Cosmo Life. “I saw those pictures. I don’t know why I didn’t recognize you. Those dresses were amazing, especially the wedding dress.”

“Thank you. That’s my favorite, too.”

Josh and Colby came back in with a couple trays of food, and Josh handed me a cool beer.

“Thanks.” I smiled.

“So what are you two talking about?” Colby questioned, nosy as ever.

“Wedding dresses,” Mrs. Singer replied.

Josh inhaled his drink wrong with that comment. His brother patted his back, looking amused.

“Excuse me?” Josh finally made out.

Rolling my eyes, I responded, “Easy, there. We were specifically talking about the vintage dress shoot for Catherine’s magazine. Your mom said she liked the wedding dress the best.”

She nodded and winked at me.

“Nice. Thanks, Mom,” Josh quipped.

“Come on, dear. I want grandchildren, and I’m not getting any younger.”

I met Josh’s eyes and knew instantly his mom was not aware of his vasectomy.

“Well, considering how irresponsible my little brother is, I’d be willing to bet there’s a grandchild out there somewhere,” Josh contended sarcastically.

Colby shrugged and played into it. “Not a problem as long as I don’t know about them, right?”

"Not funny. Sometimes, Haylee, it isn't easy being a mother of two boys." Patricia shook her head.

Her expression made me laugh. I could picture the Singer boys growing up and many a time Patricia saying exactly this.

My eyes met Josh's, and I wondered what he was thinking. And why would he bother to introduce us now, I contemplated? Was he purposefully trying to make things harder to end? Or was he simply making the best of our time left? At the moment I didn't want to analyze it because it felt too good to be enveloped in this family atmosphere and get to see a side of Josh I hadn't seen before.

My last week in the office was bittersweet as I knew it would be. It was Thursday and both Nigel and David were taking me out for dinner. Tomorrow I was only coming in to turn over my laptop and finish up paperwork. After doing that, I planned to meet Will for lunch.

Since on Saturday I was leaving for Australia for two weeks, I wondered if Josh had anything planned for the Friday night before then. Our last night. Sure, I'd see him again before I moved out of the apartment, but by then I was convinced he'd have moved on. I tried not to think about the fact that he'd probably start dating again while I was in Australia. He'd never lack for company if he didn't want to; that was for sure.

Josh left early for a meeting, and Nigel suggested we do the same.

"Why don't we head out a little bit early? Josh won't mind as he knows we're taking you out tonight."

I smiled, grateful for the fact that they wanted to spend time with me before I left. "Sounds good to me. Is David meeting us there?"

"Yes, we'll see him there. You look lovely, by the way."

I looked down at my mother's black Tahari dress and realized it would be the last couple days I'd be wearing these clothes for quite a while. They definitely didn't have a place at school.

"Thank you. And it's so sweet of you two to do this for me." I would miss my New York friends more than I'd ever imagined. I'd never before felt like people were going to miss me. My father's business partner simply felt an obligation to look after me from afar. Although I loved my Aunt J, she'd never been around enough for me to miss her. No one I'd met here had an obligation toward me; they just seemed to genuinely want to be a part of my life.

Upon arriving at the restaurant, we were led upstairs and toward the back. As we entered the room, a resounding "SURPRISE" shouted out.

Holy shit. Everyone I knew from New York was there in that room, including Josh. He caught my eye and gave me a wink as both Sasha and Catherine rushed over.

"We wanted to give you a proper going-away party," Sasha said.

"This is—it's just wonderful. Thank you."

I couldn't believe everyone was there. Nigel and David, Mark, Brian, Will, and even Bart and Gina were giving me hugs.

"My dear, you are to have the seat of honor." Catherine led me to a chair in the middle of a long table.

Josh took the chair next to me.

Cocktails were delivered, and then Catherine spoke up again. "Right now we're going to go around the table and each say something about how we met Haylee and how much we'll miss her."

I felt my face heat at the attention. Josh's hand squeezed mine under the table.

Catherine continued, "I'll go first. I met Haylee in the ladies' room at a party in London."

I smiled in remembrance and hoped to God she didn't go into

detail about my needing a tampon. Thankfully, she skipped that part, focusing instead on our instant bond over vintage dresses.

"You have become a good friend, and I'm honored to have gotten to know you over the last few months. I'm going to miss you like crazy, but I hope I can talk you into coming to New York some weekends," Catherine finished up.

I nodded, fighting the tears as Brian went next. I couldn't help feeling embarrassed as he described meeting me running in the gym.

Then it was Sasha's turn. She described the opportunity for Delayne and getting to know me while we set up the proposal. "I wish you all the best. We will definitely need to plan on girls' weekends in the future," she concluded.

It was very emotional to hear about how everyone felt about me. Bart about had me in tears, and then Gina talked about the Bahamas shoot and seeing me in my mother's wedding dress. Will recounted our very first model shoot and how we'd become friends right away. By the time we got to Mark, I felt a little nervous. How the hell would he recount our first meeting, considering it had been in the middle of the night in order to sign a NDA so that I could have sex with his boss?

"Well, my story isn't quite so eventful as Haylee and I met over a contract deal via video."

I took a large gulp of my wine and felt Josh clasp my fingers.

Mark continued. "I was lucky enough to find out she was interested in Yale and even luckier that I'll soon be able to have her as a neighbor up in New Haven. I know you'll make a great lawyer."

I let out the breath I was holding and gave him a smile of gratitude.

Nigel and David were as sweet as they could be with their kind words about my being there with encouragement during David's treatments.

I shifted in my seat when they got to Josh.

"Everyone knows how we met, so anything you'd like to say, Haylee?" he said simply.

I wasn't sure if I was disappointed or relieved that he'd nothing to say. Swallowing hard, I finally found the words for everyone. "I can't tell you what it means to have you all together like this. This last year was shaping up to be the worst year of my life. Then I came here, and it's turned out to be the best. I have nothing but gratitude for each of you and your friendships. Catherine, Sasha: thank you for planning this. It really means so much."

Catherine interrupted. "We can't take all the credit. It was Josh's idea."

I hadn't been prepared to hear that and felt his hand stroke mine again. I turned toward him. "I would be remiss without thanking you, Josh. If it wasn't for you, I wouldn't have met anyone else in this room. You either directly introduced me, or I met them because of the opportunity you gave me with the modeling and moving me to New York. So, thank you for the chance you gave me and, more importantly, for the friends I've met because of you."

He looked a little taken aback. "I should be the one thanking you. You've made me a better man, a better friend, and even a better boss." He leaned over and whispered, "I'm going to tell them."

All eyes were still on us as I realized what he meant.

He brought my hand up to his mouth and kissed it.

I could feel the blood start to rush to my ears, and my heart felt like it would beat out of my chest. No, no, no, I screamed inside of my head.

"There was something special about Haylee when I met her. She was refreshing, candid, and I soon realized she had the biggest heart of anyone I'd ever met. She made me look forward to coming into work and even travel, which I haven't enjoyed for the last few years. When she gave notice, I recognized that I was in love with her."

I couldn't breathe, and I didn't dare look at the other people around the table.

"The timing is ironic to realize my feelings, considering she's now leaving. But hopefully it will mean that you'll see more of her in New York if I can convince her to try the not-so-long-distance route. And Mark, you'll definitely be seeing me more in New Haven, too."

"I don't know what to say," I whispered, finally recovering. I was saved from having to talk anymore when the food started to arrive.

"I'll be back, just need to go to the ladies' room," I said, turning to Josh.

He stood up and pulled out my chair like a perfect gentleman.

I forced myself to walk slowly to the restroom when all I wanted to do was run. Once I was alone in the stall, I felt myself start to panic. This wasn't what we had discussed. He was changing things after we had agreed. Doing it publicly just made it even harder to understand. It was tempting to sneak out the door, but all of these people had come for me. I couldn't possibly do that.

"Haylee, you still in here?" It was Catherine's voice.

"Yeah, just finishing up." I flushed the toilet and pasted a smile on my face.

"You all right?" She studied me as I came out of the stall.

"Yeah. Are we okay, Catherine? I didn't know that Josh would say that and—"

"We're fine, honey. He told me last week as he didn't want to take me off guard, and I'm happy for you both. Sincerely. It's a testament to how he must feel to make a speech like that, something so far out of his comfort zone."

I nodded, knowing she was right. Josh was an introvert who valued his privacy.

"I just wanted to check on you. Josh wanted to make sure he didn't scare you off. I assured him that you were probably just processing."

"Yeah, I was taken off guard." I washed my hands and returned with her a short time later.

The rest of the night was a blur as I engaged in conversation, smiled when appropriate, and finally said my goodbyes to everyone. Josh took my hand on the way home and thankfully left me to my thoughts until after we arrived.

"Are you all right?" he asked as I turned to go into my apartment off of the elevator.

"Yeah, fine. I just need to change."

He gave me a small smile and kissed my hand, letting me go into my space while he went into his.

As soon as my door shut, I leaned against it, fighting the anxiety that was threatening to crawl over me and take over. I changed quickly into my cashmere pajama set and then lay in the middle of my bed staring at the ceiling.

I heard Josh come in a short time later, not bothering to knock. His weight on the bed came before his voice. "Talk to me."

I sat up and saw the concern in his eyes. "Why did you make it sound like we were continuing things in your speech?" My voice was quiet even if my mind was screaming.

His eyes softened, and he took my hand. "Baby, wasn't it obvious? I took you on our first real date. I had you meet my mother. And tonight I made it public. You said you wanted more, and I'm showing you I can give you that."

I swallowed hard. "But we had agreed that once I left— I mean we want different things."

"I know we did, and I know it took a hell of a long time for me to figure out I want more. But I love you, Haylee."

I felt the tears. "Josh, I don't—I don't want this," I whispered.

Hurt flashed in his eyes. "Help me understand. I thought you loved me."

"God, I do, but you and I eventually won't work out."

"Why would you say that?"

I couldn't continue sitting so close to him knowing that he was hurting, so I got up and paced. "It's the truth. We want different things. You don't want marriage. You don't want children." I was firing off excuses and didn't understand why he couldn't grasp that he was only making things more difficult. I'd hit rock bottom before. I didn't need to do it again, eventually grieving yet another loss. I wouldn't survive trying to get over Josh Singer a year from now if I was already about to lose it now.

He shoved both hands through his hair. "I feel so strongly that the commitment between two people is much more than a piece of paper. As for kids, you know I can't give them to you naturally." He got up and crossed toward me. "Could we just agree to do the long-distance thing for a while and see where things go?"

"For every day that we prolong the inevitable, it just makes it more difficult to walk away."

"What are you so scared of?"

His rising temper made my stomach feel sick. "I'm just a realist. Breaking things off now is hard enough. Having to do it three, six, twelve months from now would just be too much."

"What can I do to prove that I'm in this for the long term?" His voice resonated with a touch of vulnerability.

"There isn't anything anyone can do. Sometimes it's out of our hands." My voice was resigned. I thought of my parents and the fact that they hadn't wanted to leave, but they had. No one could prove they were in it for the long haul, because no one really knew.

"So that's it, then?"

A roar of pain shot through me with the thought. I didn't trust myself to speak and only nodded.

He paused, and then I watched him walk out. Even if this wasn't the way I'd imagined it ending, I had to remind myself that I was getting what I'd asked for. The overwhelming pain hit me, and I took solace in the fact that it would only have been worse if we'd continued.

I MADE sure I got to the office before Nigel or Josh the next morning in order to turn in all of my things. I left a note for Nigel explaining that I had too much to do before leaving on Saturday to stay in the office the rest of the day. I hoped he understood.

It was difficult to see anyone from the party, considering that the impression they had from Josh's speech was so different from my stark reality of the moment. Therefore, I tried to cancel my scheduled lunch with Will, but he surprised me by coming up to my apartment with food in hand.

"How did you know where I lived?" I questioned after opening the door.

"I called Josh. I was worried about you, and this is the last day that I'll get to see you for a while."

I was shocked. "You called Josh? What did he say?" I could tell myself I didn't care, but the truth was I would always care. I loved him.

"He sounded torn up, but just told me where to find you."

I took the bag from him and looked inside to see burgers and fries. This unfortunately brought a fresh round of tears as it reminded me of Josh. If I was doing the right thing, why did it feel so bad?

"Oh, shit, Haylee. Don't cry."

"I'm sorry, Will. I'm just a mess."

"So, I take it you weren't thrilled with Josh's declaration last night?"

I shook my head. "I didn't even glance around the room. Was everyone shocked?"

He smiled. "I think most of us weren't. I know I wasn't." He dished up lunch and handed me my plate.

"You knew?"

He looked amused. "I suspected during the model shoot given the death stare I was getting. But I think it was confirmed the night we had your law school celebration. He got up shortly after you went to the ladies' room, and then you guys avoided eye contact after that."

He waited me out until I was ready to speak again.

"It's complicated."

"Try me."

"We just want different things. He doesn't want to get married again or have a family. Sometimes love isn't enough," I murmured.

"That's bullshit, and you know it. Why are you ending things if you're this miserable doing so? I can tell by your eyes that you cried yourself to sleep last night."

It was a fair question. "What happens when, two years down the road, he decides he's done, and I've invested three years in him? Or what happens when I want marriage after school, and he doesn't? We agreed this was short term, and we weren't going to try to change one another."

"Haylee girl, people change. We influence others all the time without even realizing it. He admitted to everyone last night that he's a better man from having met you. He loves you. Are you really telling me that two years from now he wouldn't hold on tight to you?"

"There are no guarantees." I had lost my appetite.

"No, there aren't, but you want my advice?"

I nodded.

"Take some time for yourself in Australia and figure out where this fear is coming from. Not everyone gets a shot at happiness. For what it's worth, I think you should hold on tight and buckle up for the ride no matter where it takes you."

CHAPTER TWENTY-TWO

I couldn't sleep. After a couple solid hours of weeping, I'd finally stopped crying. Now, six hours before my flight would depart, I stared at the ceiling and thought of Josh next door and how I'd hurt him. It was difficult to breathe past the ache in my heart.

I got up, flipped on my light, and took a shower. I sat back down on my bed. Three o'clock in the morning. Still three more hours until I needed to head to the airport.

The knock made me jump. When I opened up the door and saw Josh standing there, longing struck me hard and fast. I didn't bother to fight what my body craved. Instead, I launched myself at him, pulling his head down for my wild kiss.

His initial reaction of shock turned into unbridled desire for me. He weaved his fingers into my hair and walked me into my apartment, kicking the door shut behind him.

I was anxious to feel his skin upon mine and frantically undressed him. His mouth was hungry, feasting on mine with a need that matched my own. We were desperate, like we'd been starved for one another. As soon as I stepped out of my panties, he lifted me up, giving me only enough time to wrap my legs around his waist before pinning me against the nearest wall. His arms held my hips in line with his, and then he was thrusting into me, my back against the hard surface.

"Oh, God," I gasped, enjoying the carnal pleasure of being taken this way. My weight was completely supported by his strength as he pounded into me over and over. He angled himself, hitting just the right spot. My breathing stuttered, and my nails raked down his back as the orgasm took over. I clenched down, feeling his groan and the hot release deep inside of me moments later.

Instead of setting me back down on my feet, he carried me to the bed. I could feel him getting hard again as he lay me on my back and followed me down, all while staying inside of me. He lifted up to brush the hair from my face and then kissed me reverently.

Relentless in his lovemaking, he brought me to climax three more times during the next hour. As we lay there afterward, I could tell both our minds were on the ticking clock.

"I saw your light. I just wanted to tell you to have a safe trip." His voice was low and husky.

"I wasn't able to sleep," I replied lamely.

"Anxious for your flight?"

I shook my head. "Honestly, I was thinking about you."

Taking a deep breath, he stroked my back. "I put too much pressure on you with the announcement at the party. I was in the moment and went for it without conferring with you first about how you'd feel. I'm sorry."

"You don't have anything to apologize for. You were only doing what you thought I wanted," I said thickly.

"Sometimes I forget how young you are. You didn't get a chance to enjoy your undergrad years, and this opportunity in law school is one that's important. You need to figure out who you are and what you want. I was selfish in wanting you to change that."

"You weren't selfish, and you didn't ask me to give up anything. Besides, I'm the one who told you I wanted more. I just didn't pay attention when you started giving it to me."

"I should've done it sooner."

"I don't think it would have mattered. You're right about me being scared. But it's hard to articulate it."

"Give me something, Haylee. Anything. I'm trying to understand."

I fought the tears. He didn't deserve to think it was something he was doing or not doing. "I know you are." I paused and then said the first thing that came to mind. "Since the death of my parents, I haven't trusted happiness. I don't know how."

He hugged me tighter and took a few moments to process. "Tell me what I can do."

"I guess I just need time to figure out if I can change that."

"Time apart?"

I nodded sadly. "At least for the next couple of weeks." I desperately wished that I could simply open my mind and reveal all of my overwhelming thoughts and fears. I had shared such a small piece because I didn't understand it all myself. I could only hope my time in Australia would give me some clarity.

He held me for the next hour, and then we showered together, enjoying the last few minutes of cuddling before I needed to get ready.

He was silent while watching me dress and gather up my things.

When it came time to say goodbye, I felt the tears again.

He gave me a small smile and wiped under my eyes gently with his thumbs. "Enjoy your time with your family. I love you."

"I love you too, Josh," I whispered, leaning into him for one last kiss.

My two-week trip to Australia was good for me. I connected with the only family I had left and thoroughly enjoyed the vacation time. I came to the conclusion that I had a lot of unresolved feelings when it came to my parents' deaths. Feelings of anger, guilt, and resentment plagued me, and I wasn't sure how to deal with them, let alone admit those feelings to someone else. My confession to Josh had been a true statement: I didn't trust in happiness. Worse, I didn't know how to fix that belief. How did I shift my mindset? At this point, the answer completely eluded me.

While apart, I texted Josh daily to share what I was doing or send photos of the things I was seeing, such as Ayers Rock or the dolphins in the harbor. I didn't say I missed him because I'd been the one to force this separation. The truth was that I missed him terribly and relished every time I heard from him.

My flight back didn't get into JFK until after ten o'clock at night. By the time I made it through customs, it was closer to eleven. I came out of the international arrivals gate so intent on finding my luggage at the carousel that I almost overlooked Josh completely.

Seeing him standing with a small smile just beyond the security point jolted my system. It was all I could do not to run into his arms. I knew I had a goofy smile on my face.

"Hi, baby." He grinned as he walked up to me. He was finally close enough to reach out and touch if I wanted to.

I just stood there staring at him, tears in my eyes. Finally, I made my legs move and launched myself at him. "I can't believe you're here."

He put his arms around me and held me close. "I missed you, Haylee."

I leaned back and cupped his face until he put me down and my feet touched the ground again. "I missed you, too."

We collected my luggage and were sitting in the back of his

sedan before Josh spoke again. "How was your time in Australia?"

"It was really good. My family couldn't have been nicer. And the food— Oh, my goodness, can my Uncle Paul cook. His restaurant is fabulous."

"Good. I'm glad you had fun." He sighed.

I knew he wanted to know if I'd thought more about us. "The time went by really quickly," I offered lamely.

"It felt like it crawled here."

I snuggled into his arms while looking at our hands joined together. "I missed you a lot. I'd hoped to come back with all of the answers, but instead I seem to have more questions. I'm still working through them."

He was completely quiet.

I realized I was being vague and tried to clarify. "Do you think we could play it by ear and just not put pressure on things? I have three weeks before school orientation. Even though I want to get moved in and settled, it would be nice to spend time with you. We could just hang out with each other as our schedules allow and not commit to anything."

After an eternity, he finally spoke. "If that's what you need, I can do that."

As I walked back to my apartment from my last class on Friday morning, I couldn't believe I'd already completed week two of law school. The days after arriving back from Australia and before starting school had gone by in the blink of an eye, what with the move-in, orientation, and the time I'd spent with Josh. He hadn't pressured me into sharing any more insight into what I was feeling, and I hadn't offered up anything additional. He seemed to be content with living in the moment and leaving our relationship undefined for now.

Over the last two weeks, I'd fully embraced my academic routine and put in my time studying each night. It was tiring, but I was excited to be back in the groove of being a student.

My apartment was on the second floor of a four-story brick building. The unit was spacious, with a simple layout of living room and kitchen with two doors at the back that led to the one bedroom and bathroom. Most of the other floors appeared to be under construction, and I hadn't met any of my neighbors. Students kept weird schedules, so that wasn't surprising.

I'd had some of my things shipped out from storage and loved the fact that I got to sit on a familiar couch and look at my parents' art on the walls. Sometimes it was the little things.

The rest of my Friday consisted of studying until Josh arrived later this evening after work. He'd mentioned he needed to attend a golf thing with Mark here in New Haven tomorrow afternoon. I was pretty sure the golf event was only an excuse to come up so he wouldn't have to make the official reason be that he wanted to see me.

I'd just finished reading, completing most of what I needed to do this weekend, when the knock came that evening. I felt my heart flutter with anticipation despite my mind urging me to play it cool. After opening the door, I just smiled.

"That's quite the smile." Josh was still in his suit and tie from the office.

I moved into him and hugged him tightly. "I guess I couldn't wait to get my hands on you. I hope the train wasn't too bad."

He looked tired. "It was fine."

"Liar, but that's all right." I appreciated the fact that he didn't want to complain.

He smiled and kissed me deeply. "You okay?"

"It's been a hectic couple of weeks getting back into the routine of school, but I'm good. I can't believe it's already turning into fall." I led him into the apartment.

"It's beautiful up here in the fall. I think you'll really enjoy it. What do you feel like doing this evening?"

"I have Thai food and your favorite whiskey. I thought perhaps we'd lounge this evening and stay in."

"Sounds perfect to me. I should be done with the golf thing tomorrow by four o'clock. I was thinking if you don't have any plans, I'd like to take you out on a date. Dinner, maybe the movies."

He sounded so unsure that guilt crept up. Perhaps I had made him feel like this. "Dinner and a movie sounds amazing." I meant it because now that he was standing here I was the happiest I'd been in weeks.

He glanced at the books on the couch. "You've been studying."

"Yes, but it's been five hours, and I'm ready for a break."

"You've been studying for five hours?" He shook his head in disbelief.

I smiled. "Reading mostly and preparing early for Monday."

"Nerdy Haylee is kind of hot," he teased.

"Do you think coming up here like this is going to get old?" I blurted out, not sure what answer I was looking for after only his first trip. Maybe some sort of reassurance.

He searched my eyes and then responded carefully. "I'm not sure. All I know is that in this very moment I'm the happiest I've been in weeks."

My breath caught with his admission that echoed my own thoughts. I took his hand, leading him into the bedroom. "Dinner will have to wait because right now I've got other plans in mind."

An hour later we ate cold Thai food from the bed, enjoying each other's company.

"I KNOW it's only September, but my mother is chomping at the bit, asking if you'll come for Thanksgiving. I don't want to pressure you, but I figured I'd put it out there before she calls you directly."

We were on our Saturday night date at a quaint pizza place in town that Mark had recommended. It felt wonderful to hold hands across the table and act like a typical couple on a Saturday night out. But I wasn't ready for this question. Ironic, really, since last year I'd felt left out of Josh's family holiday plans.

"Wow, that's two months away." I said the first thing that came to mind and immediately regretted it when I saw the hurt look on his face.

"It's fine. I can tell her that we're playing our relationship by ear, and asking you too far in advance puts too much pressure on you."

Ouch. Here he'd offered up something new with regard to sharing the holidays with his family, and I'd sounded annoyed. "I didn't mean—"

He held up a hand. "No, I know. I shouldn't have brought it up." He sighed and then gave me a forced smile. "You ready for the movie?"

He was already changing the subject and signaled the waiter for the check.

We arrived at the movie theatre, and I could feel the tension rolling off of him as we took our seats. "Please tell your mother I'd be happy to come," I offered. The more I thought about it, the more I realized that looking forward to a holiday might be a good thing for a change. And if he was putting things out there for our future, obviously he was committed to it.

He didn't even look at me. "Why don't we wait until we get closer to the occasion? Who knows? By then you could be dating someone completely new."

I stared at his profile and fought the tears. He was starting to feel resentment toward me, and I couldn't blame him.

The lights dimmed, and I tried to focus on the movie. Finally, twenty minutes in, I couldn't bear it any longer. I couldn't sit miserable in a movie theatre while my maybe-boyfriend who was no longer a secret hated me for something I wasn't able to give him. I stood up, scooted out of the aisle, and made my way out of the theatre. Hopefully, he'd assume I'd gone to the restroom.

It was about a mile back to my apartment, but I didn't care. The problem was that I didn't know which direction to walk. I vaguely remembered the drive, but we'd gone to the restaurant first, and that had been further from my place than the theatre. I looked around, but there were no taxis. The difference between New Haven and New York was never more obvious than now.

"What are you doing?" Josh was suddenly beside me on the sidewalk.

"I just need to go home. This isn't working. You'll end up despising me, and I'll hate myself for letting that happen."

He looked at me for a moment before responding. "Let me drive you."

No arguments about how he wasn't going to hate me, no fight about how he still wanted to be with me. Just a cool resignation in his voice that broke my heart.

He pulled into the parking lot of my building.

I found myself unable to move. "Sometimes I resent my parents for leaving me," I whispered, staring straight ahead instead of meeting his gaze. "I get angry with them, with God, and then at myself for even feeling that way." This was the first time I'd ever admitted that out loud.

Josh sat there awhile silent and then cut the engine and got out of the rental car. He went around to my side, opened the door, and unbuckled me. He didn't say a word as he scooped me up and carried me into my apartment. He lay me down on my bed and undressed me like he would a child, shed his own clothes, and enveloped me under the comforter. We lay there awhile before he finally spoke.

"It means a lot that you would share that with me. The only thing I'll say to you is that I'm here to listen anytime without judgment. I could tell you until I'm blue in the face that you're entitled to feel that way, but it won't matter unless you believe it." He paused and leaned back so that he could kiss my forehead. "I'm sorry for what I said in the movie theatre."

"But?" I could hear the word in his voice.

"But you won't truly know if I'm what you want unless you have a chance to be without me. As much as I hate the thought, you need to figure out what you desire from your future and if you want me to be a part of it. The worst thing I could do is keep pressuring you into something you're not sure of. You'd resent me. And you're right; I am starting to begrudge playing it by ear."

I swallowed hard. "Are you breaking up with me?"

He shook his head and traced my face. "You did that the night of your party. I'm just ready to let you go now."

CHAPTER TWENTY-THREE

Josh had been right. Fall was beautiful in New Haven. The trees were brilliant colors, and the weather was crisp. I was six weeks post-Josh and moved through my daily routine in a fog. Instead of embracing the college social life, I threw myself into my studies. I wasn't trying to be a hermit, but I wasn't motivated to do anything except an occasional study group. Somewhere deep down, I knew I was fighting the depression that threatened to take over, but I couldn't seem to flip it off like I wanted to. I'd come to the conclusion that I'd blown it with Josh. It was ironic that in pushing him away, I'd brought on the very pain I'd hoped to avoid.

I spent Thursday night finishing up a paper for my Torts class when my phone rang. Will's number on the screen made me smile for the first time in weeks. I hadn't talked to him since I'd arrived back from Australia. I'd told him then that Josh and I were taking things day by day. It would be good to talk to a friend.

"Hey, Will."

"Hiya, Haylee. What are you doing this weekend?"

"No plans. Why, are you heading to New Haven?"

"No, but I was hoping you might be persuaded to come to New York. I have a shoot tomorrow and they need a female model. It's for Calvin Klein, and you'd be in men's underwear. They'd be thrilled if you were able to fill in last minute."

"Uh, what time?"

"Eleven o'clock, and it's only scheduled for ninety minutes. If I can steal you away from Josh for a couple of hours, we could go out for lunch after?"

It was on the tip of my tongue to tell him that we'd broken up, but I just couldn't seem to say the words out loud. "I'd like that. I've missed my friends." That part was true, but it was also true that I'd pushed them away. I'd opted to blow off Catherine and Sasha whenever they texted me by telling them I was busy with school. They'd stopped asking when I was coming into the city and I wondered if they were aware of the breakup by now.

"Cool. I'll text you the address and see you there."

THE NEXT DAY I was tempted to text Josh and tell him I was going to be in town. Or just show up on his doorstep tonight. The problem was that for all I knew he had a new girlfriend by now and I wasn't sure I'd survive seeing him with someone else.

I was a little ahead of schedule when the cab from the train station pulled up in front of the address in Chelsea that Will had texted me. The shoot was in a contemporary art gallery on the second floor of a repurposed warehouse. I headed in.

Will hadn't arrived yet, but the Calvin Klein rep greeted me by name and put me directly into hair and makeup. "We have men's sizes. You look to be about a size two-four in women's, is that right?" she asked.

I met her look in the mirror. "Uh, more like four-six."

She grabbed some briefs and brought them over.

I pulled them up and frowned. They were really baggy. I'd probably lost a couple of pounds in the last few weeks but definitely not a full size.

"Let's get you a smaller pair," she offered.

I slipped on the smaller size briefs and a white tank top and headed out to the main room. I was all smiles for Will, who was shirtless and in his own briefs.

"Hey, you." I gave him a hug and then cocked my head when he frowned at me.

"Jesus, Haylee, how much weight have you lost?"

"Maybe a couple of pounds," I answered in a small voice.

He didn't look like he bought it. "More like a full size, maybe more. I thought college was supposed to pack on the pounds," he teased as we took our places in front of the screen.

The scene was pretty straightforward. We were done in two changes and just over an hour later.

"Come on, let's go get something to eat before you fall over." Will took my arm and led me outside.

"Why do I feel like you're mad?"

"Because you're wasting away. What's going on with you?"

I rolled my eyes. "First I'm too fat to be a model at a size six. Now I'm down a size, and I'm suddenly too thin. I can't fucking win."

His eyes softened, and he studied my face. "Did something happen?"

I shrugged. "Josh gave me what I wanted. Space and the knowledge that the best way for me to keep from feeling abandoned by someone I love was to fuck it up before they have the opportunity."

"Shit. I'm sorry, Haylee girl. Let's get something to eat, and you can fill me in."

A half hour later we had a pizza in front of us, and I'd caught him up on most of the details.

"So you haven't reached out to him or told him that you're miserable without him?"

I looked at Will in surprise. "Why would I reach out? He said he was letting me go."

Will shook his head and sighed. "Yeah, until you were ready. He thinks he's giving you the space you need to figure things out. Why the hell haven't you told him you have?"

"So you think I should go there tonight?" I was suddenly hopeful.

"Uh, maybe you should call him first."

I knew instantly that he was thinking the same thing I had. There was a possibility Josh could be with someone else. The thought made me sick to my stomach. "I think I'll just take the train back to New Haven instead. I'm sorry to bag on the rest of our lunch, but I'm not feeling good."

He reached out and took my hand. "You're worrying me. You need to eat."

"I'm fine, Will, but thank you. I'm going to catch a cab and then a train home. Thanks for thinking of me for the shoot. We'll be in touch." I was suddenly too warm and too emotional to sit for one more moment. I threw down a twenty and got up too fast. The room spun, and I felt the blood leave my head.

"Fuck, Haylee. I've got you." His voice sounded like it was in a tunnel.

"I'm all right," I whispered and felt a cup lifted to my lips.

"Drink slow," he coaxed. "I'm going to sit you up. Easy, now."

I realized my upper body was being supported by Will while my butt and legs were on the floor.

He lifted me back up to the chair.

My face flushed with embarrassment at the fact that I had the waiter and half the restaurant staring at me. "I think I just stood up too quickly."

"I think you haven't been taking very good care of yourself," he chided, typing something into his phone.

I sighed. "I'll be fine. I just need to get home."

He glared at me, and I had to sit back in astonishment. I'd never seen Will mad before. "Don't test me, Haylee. Sit there and sip your soda a few minutes."

I felt like a petulant child but didn't trust myself to be able to get up without falling flat on my face.

He was totally engrossed in his phone, and I wasn't sure how long he intended to keep me here. My question was answered when I saw Josh step through the door fifteen minutes later. My eyes met Will's. I was a mixture of confused and hurt.

"Come on. We're heading to the hospital."

JOSH DIDN'T SAY A WORD, but the hard line to his mouth and the intense look in his eyes spoke volumes.

I knew better than to protest the fact that both men insisted on seeing me to the hospital. I was in the middle of the sedan's back seat with Will on one side and Josh on the other.

I wondered what kind of pull Josh had when I was shown to a private room upon arrival at the hospital. A nice nurse drew blood and took my vitals, and a doctor came in shortly after.

"Now then, Ms. Holloway, I'm Doctor Butler. I'm told you have lost some weight and had a dizzy spell today?"

I nodded and looked toward Josh, who was standing by the window. Will was seated in a chair.

"Have you felt a loss of appetite lately?"

"Yes, I've been nauseous."

"For how long?"

"About six weeks," I revealed reluctantly.

"What do you think you weighed back then?"

"I, uh—"

"She was one hundred-thirty pounds," Will offered. Why did he have to remember that from the Cosmo shoot?

"You're one hundred-eighteen pounds now," Dr. Butler provided.

I heard Josh curse.

"We ran some tests and should have some preliminary results in shortly. In the meantime, you're dehydrated. The nurse will start an IV and that should get you feeling better."

I winced at Josh's angry look and kept my eyes down. The nurse came back, started the IV, and then left us in quiet.

My heart broke at the sight of Josh. I tried out several conversation starters in my head but in the end chose to remain silent. At least Will scooted over and gave me a kind smile.

The doctor came back in fifteen minutes later with a sympathetic look. "Ms. Holloway, I have some things to discuss with you of a personal nature." His eyes flicked toward both men as if asking me to choose whether to let them stay or go.

"I'm staying," Josh declared, looking at me.

Will took my hand and leaned down to whisper, "Don't be mad that I contacted him. He loves you." He stood up and kissed me on the forehead. "I'll leave you two. You call me later tonight, yeah?"

I nodded and gave him a small smile. Once he left, I turned my attention back to the doctor.

Dr. Butler glanced toward Josh. "You sure you want to discuss this with him here?" Evidently the good doctor wasn't sold on his insistence without my approval.

I met Josh's eyes and knew that no matter what they had to tell me, I needed him to hear it, too. "Yes, doctor. Do I have cancer?"

He looked immediately confused. "No, you're pregnant, Haylee."

He'd knocked the breath out of me. "That's impossible," I whispered, glancing at Josh.

His face was pale and his eyes angry. "Obviously you chose the wrong man to stay. I'll let you call Will back in to give him the good news." He left abruptly without another look.

I blushed and could only stammer. "He, um, had a vasectomy years ago."

"Any other partners?" Dr. Butler asked kindly.

Clearly, Josh thought so. "No, none."

"Well, then I would conclude the vasectomy wasn't successful. Did he get tested afterwards?"

"I don't know. I mean, it was years ago, before we met."

"From the HCG count, I would put you about six or seven weeks, but you should make an appointment with an OBGYN. Do you need a recommendation?"

I couldn't think; I could hardly breathe. How in the hell could I be pregnant? I'd been barely hanging by a thread the last six weeks, and yet I had a tiny life growing inside of me. "I, um, live in New Haven, so I can find someone up there, I guess." I thought back over the last few weeks. "Doctor, I took some sleeping pills. They're prescribed, but I didn't know…"

He nodded. "How many? Did you take them nightly?"

I shook my head. "Um, four or five over the last few weeks." I'd only taken them the last few Saturday nights after crying jags left me sleepless.

"I think that's fine. If you were taking them nightly, I'd have been more concerned. You need to make an appointment soon, and they can get you on some prenatal vitamins. Now that you do know you're having a baby, you need to start taking better care of yourself. No more sleeping pills, and you need to gain back the weight you've lost. It's typical for women to lose some weight in their first trimester if they are throwing up, but I think in your case you're not eating enough. Do you, ah, want me to call anyone?"

I shook my head. "No, thank you, Dr. Butler. When can I go home?"

"Give it another thirty minutes to get some fluids in you, and you'll be on your way."

"All right, thanks."

IT WAS TEMPTING to just catch the train and go straight home, but instead I found myself in Josh's building. After waving at Rafael, I made my way upstairs, bracing myself for a scene that wouldn't go well.

After knocking, I waited patiently for him to answer. Just when I thought he'd keep ignoring me, the door opened.

He was still in his suit, but with his tie loosened and jacket tossed on the floor behind him. He already had a glass of amber liquor in his hand. "What do you want?"

I about lost my nerve. I loved this man more than anything, but right now the last thing I saw in his eyes was love for me. "I want to talk to you."

"I'm pretty sure everything I needed to hear was in the hospital room today."

"Can I please come in? I don't want to have this conversation in the hallway."

"By all means, come on in. At least this condo doesn't have stairs, so when you leave in tears after admitting it's not mine, I don't have to feel guilty if you fall down."

The pain of him comparing me to his ex-wife shot through me.

"I'm assuming it's Will's, but I guess the fact that he's not with you must mean that you either met someone else up in New Haven, or you wanted to see if you could trade up first."

"I haven't slept with Will or anyone else. I've been miserable without you the last six weeks."

"I had a vasectomy, Haylee." He shoved his hand through his hair and took a swig of his liquor.

"Did you ever get tested? I mean, given the other side effects, maybe that part was botched, too."

"You know, I didn't give my ex enough credit. At least when she was confronted, she came clean about cheating. But you're actually going with a botched vasectomy angle, huh?"

My temper flared. "I'm not going to stand here and have you treat me like shit because of what your ex-wife did to you. I don't deserve to pay for her transgressions."

"I trusted you," he tossed out, his voice thick with emotion.

"Did you?"

"My ex tried to trap—"

"Don't." I cut him off. "Please don't make me hate you by saying what you're going to say. I'm not her, and you need to get over yourself and what happened because you know what? It has nothing to do with this moment. And why on earth would I trap you? I'm in law school. Do you think this is convenient for me? I trusted you, and *you* got me pregnant after assuring me you couldn't."

"Well, that's a new spin, isn't it? Now you're the victim?"

"Why can't you believe I'm telling the truth?"

"Even if I were to buy into the whole botched vasectomy, we had sex for a year. A full year without getting pregnant. Then we break up, even though it shreds me to do so, and now you're pregnant. You were in New York with Will today without a word to me. I haven't heard from you in six weeks, but now you're telling me you've been miserable?"

"I thought maybe you'd moved on," I said lamely. How was I supposed to tell him that I'd waited for him to contact me since I'd been the one who had pushed him away?

"How far along are you?"

I knew instantly he'd start doing the math. "I won't know for sure until my OB appointment, but Dr. Butler estimated about six to seven weeks."

"Convenient," he said bitterly.

I had an epiphany. “All this time I’ve been beating myself up for not being able to get past my hang-up so I could be with you. But we’re not so different. We both have trust issues. I don’t trust that someone I love won’t let me down and abandon me. And you never really trusted that I wouldn’t do exactly what your ex did. The only difference is I was finally honest about my shortcomings. You were just moving forward, hoping that nothing ever triggered yours again.”

“I can have my car take you to Will’s place. It’s downstairs. It would be best if you left now.”

I swallowed hard. “Thanks for proving my fear was not unfounded, Josh.” I turned and walked away. There was nothing left to say.

CHAPTER TWENTY-FOUR

I didn't remember much about the train ride home. Numbly, I went through the motions, grateful when the cab dropped me off so I could go through my front door and finally curl up on my couch. The sobs started and led to getting sick in the bathroom. Somewhere in the back of my mind, I knew I had to get myself together for the sake of the baby. But in this moment, all I could manage was to sit on the bathroom floor in front of the toilet and lay my head on the cool side of the tub, closing my eyes.

I heard someone's voice calling my name. When I finally looked up, I saw Mark framing the bathroom door.

After taking one look at me, he cursed and knelt at my side. "Jesus, Haylee, do we need to go to the ER?" He pushed my hair out of my face and studied me.

I shook my head. "No, no. It's mostly hormones and the other part stress. I'm fine. Please don't take offense, Mark, but I just need to be by myself for now."

"Like hell I'm leaving you."

The sobs started again, and I felt his arms go around me. I

leaned into him and, finally, after a few minutes, calmed enough for him to talk.

"Come on out to the sofa. I brought you some soup and crackers."

He settled me out in the living room before heading into the kitchen to make a phone call. I took a few tentative sips of soup. My stomach growled, and I sighed, knowing I needed to force it down. If not for myself, then for the baby.

I looked over toward the kitchen and could hear Mark's quiet voice, but I wasn't able to make out the words. I wondered if he was talking to Josh.

He walked back and handed me a ginger ale, then took a seat next to me. "I have someone coming over I'd like you to talk to."

"Who?"

"His name is Dr. Mark MacNally, or Dr. Mac, as he prefers. He isn't too bad as far as shrinks go, and he specializes in grief counseling."

I shook my head. "I don't need anyone for that, Mark. My mom has been dead for over a year now, my father for five."

"I'll tell you from experience that it isn't always that simple. We need people, Haylee. As much as we want to deal with things by ourselves, we can't always. My fiancée died seven years ago, and I still have trouble sometimes. There's no such thing as an expiration date on grief."

The surprise of his admission must have shown on my face. I wasn't aware he'd ever had a fiancée, let alone that she had died.

"I'm guessing Josh didn't tell you. He's good that way," Mark said, sighing.

Shaking my head, I murmured, "I didn't know. I'm so sorry."

"I don't share it with a lot of people. The point is that when I saw you on that bathroom floor, I could see myself once upon a time. Normally I wouldn't push this, but considering what's going on right now, I think you need to talk to someone sooner rather than later. You have the baby to think about."

"You spoke with Josh, I take it?"

"I did. He's worried about you."

I couldn't help scoffing. "He told me to go see Will, who he thinks is the father of the baby. I don't think *worried* is a word I'd use."

"He reacted badly, I know. I got that impression just from what he told me. But Will called him to check on you, and I believe he had a few choice words for Josh."

"Great. It's like a Jerry Springer episode in the making," I muttered.

He gave me a sympathetic smile. "When Dr. Mac gets here, I'll head home to get some stuff, and then I'll be back. I'm going to sleep on the sofa tonight, all right?"

I shook my head. "Look, Mark, I get that Josh wants you to look after me, but—"

He interrupted. "He asked me to check on you. This I'm doing for you, one friend to another. Dr. Mac coming over isn't anything I'm letting him know about, either. This is about getting you to feel better. Okay?"

Feeling the tears, I hugged him and whispered, "I don't want to need help."

"No one ever does, but grief never really goes away. You just get better at coping."

DR. MAC MADE me feel instantly at ease, quelling my nerves. He appeared to be in his mid-forties, and it was apparent he had a friendship with Mark. He spent a lot of time, not surprisingly, focused on gathering information about the death of my parents and my previous episode of depression. He asked me a lot of questions about my relationships with others.

"Why do you think it is that you try to be such a good friend to everyone but want nothing in return?" Dr. Mac questioned.

"Because I'm scared," I replied in a whisper.

He looked enormously pleased with my answer. "Now tell me why."

Biting my lip, I sighed. "Because if I rely on anyone to be there for me, then I risk falling apart when they aren't. It's safer to be there for others instead. I've convinced myself that I don't need anyone because I don't want to be hurt again."

"I notice you said *again*. Haylee, it's natural for you to feel resentment regarding the death of your parents. Everyone has anger after they lose someone close to them."

"My parents wouldn't have wanted me to feel angry."

He looked at me thoughtfully. "But what do you feel? I think this is an important question and one you need to ask yourself more often. At some point real soon, you're going to have decisions facing you that weren't planned out with your parents. Decisions as a mother."

I nodded. "I know you're right."

"Tell me what you're thinking with regards to Josh at this point."

"I feel like he just verified what I'd always feared."

"I won't defend him since I don't know him. But I will say that if he still has residual trust issues of his own, most likely they took a priority in a moment of crisis. Just as you panicked, perhaps he did too. He did call Mark to check on your well-being. I'd like to think that's a sign of not completely abandoning you."

"I guess…" I was unconvinced.

He continued. "You have a lot of insight already into your feelings. I feel like we accomplished more in one session than some patients do in five. You should be proud of yourself for getting there on your own. We can't always contain grief or our emotions in a box or time limit, Haylee. That may have worked for you as a coping mechanism in the past, but you need to start giving yourself a break. This isn't easy stuff you're dealing with."

"I don't want to burden anyone with it."

He gave me a kind smile. "Do you see it as a burden when your friends want to talk to you about something they're going through? Or do you see it as an opportunity to be a good friend?"

If I had a light above my head, it would have been illuminating the room. "I'd see it as being a good friend."

"I think you've taken a step in the right direction by allowing Mark to be that for you this afternoon."

"I suppose I did." And Will had also been such an amazing friend to me earlier today. I needed to call him after my session and let him know I was doing okay.

"Let's set up an appointment for tomorrow as well as on Monday after your classes. I also do couples counseling if you'd like to suggest it to Josh."

"I don't see that happening, but I'd like to see you again."

In only one session, it appeared he understood me, and I was grateful. I wasn't sure about my future with Josh, but that would need to take a back seat for now.

SHORTLY AFTER DR. MAC LEFT, Mark returned with groceries and his overnight bag in hand. "I got you a couple kinds of soup, some crackers, and some Gatorade," he said, unpacking in the kitchen.

I gave him a watery smile. "Thank you."

He was true to his word and took the couch that night.

I was exhausted from the day, but still had trouble sleeping. I was worried that I'd already done damage to this innocent baby before it even had a chance. I stared at the clock until I heard voices. They sounded like they were coming from the living room, and they didn't sound happy.

I stood, trying to listen, and recognized one voice belonged to Josh.

"Why the fuck are you here?"

I opened the bedroom door before Mark could answer and just stood there looking at Josh.

His eyes moved over me, and I immediately saw the grim set of his mouth. Why the hell was he here if he was going to look at me with hostility?

"Before you go and accuse me of sleeping with Mark, I'd like to point out he was on the couch. Unless, of course, you think that's how I do things now. Shag and relegate to the sofa after." I couldn't help the sarcasm.

"I wasn't implying anything. Fuck, it just took me off guard when I came in," he said, sighing.

"I'll, um, head home," Mark offered.

I held up a hand. "Not so fast. It's the middle of the night, and I'm not certain Josh is staying at this point." Then a thought dawned on me. "Wait. How did you get in here? I locked the door. Matter of fact, now that I think about it, how did you get in yesterday, Mark?"

Both men looked at me, apparently without knowing what to say. I realized they'd only both have keys for one reason: Josh owned the building. "Unbelievable," I muttered, watching Mark's blush confirm my thought.

I turned around, shut my bedroom door, and collapsed back on my mattress. I didn't need this shit right now.

The voices continued for a little while, and then I heard my bedroom door open. I listened to the rustle of clothing on the other side of the room and then felt the weight of Josh climbing into the bed. "If this is Mark, I was only kidding about the shag and couch routine."

"Not funny," he muttered, putting his arms around me from the back. "Are you mad about the building?"

"Considering you thought I'd become the campus slut and

was trying to pin a pregnancy on you, I've got other things topping that list at the moment. Why are you here?"

He sighed. "Because I'm not going to let my trust issue prove a point with yours. I won't abandon you. And I love you too much to let you go again."

I flipped over so that I could face him. "So you got tested?"

He shook his head. "You know my history. Unfortunately, not much has changed in that department. I was unsuccessful in providing a sample."

"I suppose that's part of my devious plan, too," I remarked dryly.

"I deserved that."

I didn't know how to respond, so I just stayed quiet.

"You looked so thin when I saw you in the doorway. Why didn't you tell me you were so upset these last few weeks?"

"I just figured I'd blown it. If you were willing to let me go, then I reasoned you were ready to move on."

"You thought that I let you go because I didn't love you, but in fact I let you go because of how much I love you. I believed it was what you needed. I hoped every day to hear from you and thought maybe you'd moved on."

"I fucked that up, too, then." Tears stung my eyes.

He kissed me softly. "No, I did, for not understanding that I shouldn't have waited six weeks. I should've kept showing you that I wasn't going anywhere and known you'd feel like I was deserting you otherwise."

I shook my head. "If I didn't get that, how could you?"

"Because like you said, we're not so different. We both have trust issues. Different circumstances but the same result in that we expect others to let us down. You didn't trust that someone wouldn't leave you again. I should have known you'd view our separation as just that."

"You were so adamant when I left that this baby wasn't yours. So what changed?"

"I thought about how you looked in the restaurant after Will texted me. You looked like how I've felt over the last few weeks. More importantly, you've never given me a reason to doubt your honesty. I was lumping you into an old scene with my ex instead of looking at you as you."

Relief washed over me. "Thank you for that, but you still need to get tested. I could probably help you with the sample if you'd like?"

"You must really want me to get tested to offer that."

"I don't begrudge you getting confirmation. You had a vasectomy, and with what's happened in your past…"

"Are you planning to keep it?" His voice was a whisper.

I worked to stifle my temper. I well remembered him telling me he didn't want children. "Yes, I am, and if you intend on trying to convince me otherwise, you might as well leave."

"No, I just wondered with law school—" He took a deep breath. "I just needed to know. I don't get a lot of rights here, and all of the decisions are yours."

"So you would want this baby?" I whispered.

"Yes. I mean, if I get a vote, then, yes, I'd want you to keep it."

I breathed a sigh of relief. I'd barely had a chance to come to the realization that I was having a baby, and yet I was already fiercely protective. At the same time, the way he'd phrased things about getting a vote and not having a lot of rights made me think there was something he wasn't telling me. "Your words make it sound like you have been through this kind of discussion before."

He sighed heavily. "My ex got pregnant in the third year of our marriage. She didn't tell me. I thought she'd gone away with her sister for a spa weekend but found the discharge instructions from the abortion a month later. I had the vasectomy shortly afterward and never told her."

So this was the betrayal he'd spoken of. "How did she not notice the side effects?"

"Our sex life was basically nonexistent after I found out what she'd done. The handful of times we did, I just took the pill. She never noticed that I didn't finish. Then a month after I filed for divorce, she came to me and told me she was pregnant."

"And you told her about the vasectomy, I take it."

"Yeah, I threw it in her face along with the reason why. She admitted to cheating and told me that it was my fault for pushing her to do so since I'd emotionally cut her off. She was crying and went down the stairs. The rest you know."

"Do you believe she was pregnant?"

"I didn't at first, but the medical records became part of the divorce proceedings. She miscarried and blamed me. Anyhow, I don't want to talk about that anymore. What happened is old news, like you said, and now you know all of it."

"I imagine it wasn't easy to tell me that, but it helps me understand your reaction a little bit better."

"It doesn't excuse it, though. I'm so sorry."

"I'm sorry for not reaching out sooner."

"I'd like to set up an OB appointment for you Monday after class if you'd let me. I'm worried about you and the baby."

Yeah, I was too. "Okay. I have an appointment with Dr. Mac at two o'clock, but it should be done by three so we can make it for after."

"Dr. Mac, as in Mark's doctor?"

"Mark called him, and we spoke yesterday. Turns out you can't just flip a switch on depression." I smiled, recalling Josh's exact words last year in San Francisco when I'd first told him about my plan for dealing with it. "I'm working on my fears when it comes to long-term relationships. And I need to ensure I'm doing things the way I want to, instead of what I perceive my parents would have wanted. I need to get my shit straight before I have someone else relying on me."

"It takes a lot of strength to talk to someone."

"There's nothing strong about me, but I'll get there eventually."

"That's where you're wrong. It takes more courage to ask for help than to pretend like you don't need it. Trust me, I know." He stroked my face and took a shaky breath. "What do you think about me going with you for counseling? I mean, not tomorrow, but eventually. Work on things together."

I was stunned. "You'd agree to do couples counseling?"

"You're not the only one this baby will be relying on. It's time I get my shit together, too."

CHAPTER TWENTY-FIVE

We took the train Wednesday afternoon back into New York City to get the test done. Even though I was confident about the result, I was still anxious to get this over with.

During the last few days, I'd had three more sessions with Dr. Mac and also my OB appointment. The tests revealed that I was about six weeks along. We left with a sonogram picture and a pregnancy book. Josh had stayed the entire time and had become quite the food police, ensuring I was constantly eating or drinking something.

"How long do you think before we get the results of your test?" I whispered. We held hands and were just about to arrive at the station.

"I'm not sure. Today is the Wednesday before Thanksgiving weekend, so it may not be until Monday that we'd get the result, but I'll ask them to expedite it." Josh lifted my hand to his lips and kissed it.

"The sooner the better."

"We don't have to do this, Haylee."

"No, we absolutely have to. I don't want one little speck of a doubt."

"I trust you," he whispered, cupping my face.

I swallowed past the lump in my throat, knowing how hard it was for him to say that. "I believe you." I let out a breath. "But we're still getting the test. It's too important not to."

His fingers brushed my face, and he thankfully changed the subject. "Did you want to find out the sex with the blood test in a few weeks?"

"I'd rather let it be a surprise, but you want to know, don't you?"

He gave me a small smile. "I'm good with whatever you want."

"I THOUGHT we were going straight to your doctor's office." I turned toward Josh. After the two-hour train ride, the car had met us at the train station in New York City and now had pulled up in front of his building.

"I thought the condo might be more conducive for getting a sample. From here I can take it down to the doctor's office. They only require getting it within an hour."

That made sense and sounded better than a sterile room. Walking inside, I was filled with nostalgia. Last weekend I had barely made it past the hall. I missed the happier times here.

"Not much has changed," he voiced, watching me look around.

"I guess we should probably get on with it." I turned toward him, anxious to complete the task.

"Yeah. God, I never thought we'd ever be awkward about sex."

I smiled, feeling the same way. "Where's the cup?"

"Uh, it's on the nightstand. I guess you could help me. Fuck, this is horrible." He took a seat on the sofa and dropped his head in his hands.

Kneeling in front of him, I took his hands in mine. "Come on. It doesn't have to be. Despite everything that has happened, I did miss you. It's been too long." He hadn't made a move to do more than kiss me all week, and I hadn't pushed it. I'd simply needed his presence more than anything else over the last few days.

"Maybe we're putting too much pressure on this," he suggested. "We could do it on Monday or maybe over the Christmas break, when we'll have more time."

Yeah, right. There was no way I was waiting any longer. "I have an idea." Taking his hand, I led him into his bedroom.

"And what would that be?"

I grinned. "I'm going to tie you up."

He raised a brow, and his eyes looked wary.

"Come on, we've never done that, and it's not like I'm plotting to leave you here tied to the bed."

I could tell he was reluctant, but finally he undressed, never letting his eyes leave mine.

"Climb up on the bed," I suggested.

"You like the thought of tying me up?"

"It's kind of hot." I didn't reveal that last night I'd been searching on the Internet for ways to help him with this.

"There's nothing hot about doing this into a cup."

After quickly peeling off my clothes, I stood there in nothing but my bra and panties. "How do you know? You could get to the point where you insist on this."

He rolled his eyes but gave me a smile just the same.

I waited with a raised brow until he complied with lying on the bed. Then, taking his robe belt, I leaned over with my breasts in his face to tie his hands to the headboard.

"You smell really good," he groaned.

Smiling seductively, I went back to his closet and grabbed a silk tie.

"You aren't tying my feet," he warned, watching me sashay back toward him.

"You're right. I'm not, but I am blindfolding you." I could tell he was about to protest, so I sweetened the pot. "Please?"

He swallowed hard and then relented. "Okay."

It meant a lot that he trusted me this way. I placed his clothes neatly by the end of the bed, knowing he'd have to go to the doctor's office directly after. Then I grabbed the cup out of the nightstand drawer, along with a bottle of lube. I took both their tops off to make them readily available and set them down on the bed within my reach. I hoped I'd remember to use them in the heat of the moment.

"I wish I could see you right now," he voiced.

After shedding my bra and panties, I crawled up on top of his body. "How about you feel me instead?" My chest hovered over his face and he leaned up to take one of my nipples fully in his mouth, teasing it mercilessly. Moving down, I stroked his chest with my fingertips, letting little kisses follow.

"I missed you so fucking much."

"I missed you, too." I slowly moved my body down the length of his, ensuring my wet sex rubbed against his skin, making him all too aware of my need.

"Oh, God, you're so wet. I wish I could touch you. Put yourself on my face, Haylee," he pleaded.

"Mm, maybe next time."

He growled in protest, and I grinned.

I lined my wet sex up with his hardened length and gripped his shaft with my fist. Rubbing his tip between my swollen lips, I rocked my hips, coating him with my desire.

He swelled even further in response. "Jesus," he hissed, thrusting his hips up, searching for penetration.

Straddling his powerful thigh so that he could feel my wet

center, I lowered my head and licked his shaft from tip to base. My tongue curled around his crown, and I loved hearing him groan in pleasure. Enclosing my lips around him, I coated his cock with saliva, stroking him with my mouth, and finally put him in the back of my throat. Increasing the pressure, I sucked in a rhythm and felt his hips arch in response.

I reached for the lube with one hand, coating my pinky finger with it. I wasn't sure if he'd like this or not, but when in Rome, I thought. I sucked harder and then slid my finger into his backside.

"Jesus Christ. Fuck, I'm coming," he groaned, his entire body taut with his orgasm.

Thankful the cup was within reach, I grabbed it quickly and released him from my mouth, capturing as much as I could. Putting the cap on the sample, I set it to the side and then gave his tip a little kiss, regretful I'd been denied the enjoyment of tasting him. Lastly, I reached up and untied the blindfold.

"Well, aren't you full of surprises?" he smirked.

I smiled in response, untied his hands, and then squealed when he immediately put me on my back, arms pinned above my head.

"I wish we had more time," he whispered regretfully. His fingertips caressed the length of me while his lips fluttered kisses down my breasts and stomach.

"Don't you have to go?" I sucked in my breath as he nibbled at my waist.

"Oh, this won't take long. I can tell you're already halfway there, aren't you?"

"Yes," I rasped, arching off the bed.

His mouth suddenly crashed down on my throbbing sex while his fingers invaded me completely. When he brought his index finger out and sucked on it, savoring the taste, I almost convulsed.

"Do you know how much I missed the taste of you?"

I could only quiver in response, watching him bury his face back into my center. He brought me to a climax, and then, unrelenting, he went for another.

"Josh—" My whole body tensed again, and then the wave hit me from top to bottom.

Raining gentle kisses on the inside of my thighs and grazing his mouth up to my breasts, he laid his head gently on my stomach and rubbed it with his hand.

"I guess I'd better go, but I'll be back as soon as I can." Kissing me with tenderness, he reluctantly got off the bed, dressed quickly, grabbed the cup, and left.

"Hi, beautiful." His voice felt like a soft caress in my ear. Opening my eyes, I saw Josh kneeling in front of me. I looked at my watch and realized two hours had passed since he'd left. I had taken a shower and then must've fallen asleep on his couch.

Stretching, I moved over, allowing him to wedge between me and the back of the sofa. His arms came tightly around me and squeezed.

"I'll find a way to make it up to you," he sighed into my hair.

I turned around to search his face. "How did you get the results so quickly?"

"My doctor was able to see some sperm in the sample under the microscope. He'll send it out for more specific results, like the count, but he said it was pretty obvious that there were some."

I breathed a sigh of relief. "Well, thank God that's over."

Stroking my face, he commented, "We have a lot of things to talk about."

"First I need to get out of the initial trimester. Until thirteen weeks, the miscarriage rate is, like, fifty percent with first-time pregnancies."

"What?" He looked immediately concerned.

"It's nothing that can be prevented in most cases. That's why most people don't tell others they're expecting until after the first trimester."

"Jesus, that's depressing. I had thought we'd tell my mom this weekend over Thanksgiving. That is, if you'll still come. Or we could stay here for the weekend or go to the islands. Whatever sounds best for you."

The fact that he was anxious to share the baby news with his mom made me happy. But he sounded so nervous that I wouldn't want to visit his family. "As long as you're there, I don't care where we go."

Pleasure filled his eyes, and he gave me a sweet kiss. "Right back at you."

"I'll be at thirteen weeks closer to Christmas. We could tell her then."

"Okay, yeah. So you'll be able to finish out the year at Yale?"

"Yes. I suppose I'm lucky with the timing. I'm due the first week of June, and classes will be over the last week of May. I'll have the summer for maternity leave."

"I'm assuming you want to stay at Yale next year?"

"I guess that's up for discussion. I could transfer to Columbia as I don't want to keep you from seeing the baby every day. That is, assuming you'd want to. We should talk about how much you want to be involved."

"Of course I want to be involved, Haylee. I'm fully invested. I mean, we'll get married, and the more I think about it, maybe New Haven would be a better place to have a baby. We can walk to parks and drive places. I don't like the idea of raising a baby here in a penthouse in Manhattan. I know people do it all the time, but New Haven feels more like family, at least until you're out of school."

I had stopped listening after the word *married.* "Josh, wait a second. Back up. We're not getting married."

Looking at me funny, he sounded incredulous, "Of course we're getting married. We're expecting a baby."

"A lot of people have babies without being married. Plus, you always said that you would never get married again."

"I said a lot of things that I'd like to take back. I want us to be a family."

The thought of living happily ever after as a family paralyzed me with a fear that was greater than any I'd felt before. The stakes had never been higher as I'd never wanted something so much. But I was so nervous about the health of the baby. In an effort to share my fears, I decided to come clean with Josh.

I took a deep breath. "I have to be honest and tell you that I'm really worried about the baby. I lost twelve pounds and took some sleeping pills during the first six weeks because I didn't know I was pregnant. I fainted and was dehydrated. I didn't take care of myself, and I feel just sick about it."

He caressed my face and kissed me softly. "Haylee, you had no clue. And I share in that responsibility by thinking I couldn't get you pregnant and not being there for you."

"So you see, talking marriage is a moot point until we get past the first trimester. After that, we can talk about the future."

He stared at me for what seemed an eternity. "All right."

CHAPTER TWENTY-SIX

"You have to marry me," Josh whispered in the quiet. It was Thursday night, and we'd just enjoyed Thanksgiving Day with his mother and brother in his childhood home in Virginia.

"I'm not out of my first trimester yet," I reminded him.

"Are you having second thoughts about us? About me? I know I'm not easy to be with, but I love you so much it hurts."

I rose up and looked into his eyes. My strong, powerful man still had his own insecurities he was working through. And I was responsible for some of them. "Do you know why I love you?"

Shaking his head, he looked apprehensive.

"I admired your fairness when you made sure I got paid for my first modeling shoot. You made me feel beautiful when I kept catching your eyes on me that day. It still gives me a rush when your eyes watch me across a room or walk toward you."

Caressing my back, he kissed me sweetly.

"I loved that you wanted to get In-N-Out burger with me on our first date."

"Jesus, if you think that was our first date, I think I'm the worst boyfriend ever."

Giggling, I continued, "Well, I thought it was wonderful, but I digress. I love when you called Mark in the middle of the night because you couldn't wait another minute to touch me. I love that you gave up smoking for me. I love that you agreed to do couples counseling and that you trust me." I took his hand and kissed his palm. "You make me feel important and that I matter."

He let out a breath. "You are so fucking important that I don't even have the words to express it. The best feeling in the world is knowing that you mean something to someone. You need to know how much you mean to me. And for all the reasons you love me, I love you for so many more. In my whole life, I've never met anyone like you. I think I knew it from the moment I met you. I couldn't figure out why I was drawn to you. Why every time our eyes met, I felt a jolt, almost like I was destined to be with you. God knows you deserve better, but I'm a selfish man when it comes to you, baby."

"You're not selfish, Josh. We've come so far in the last couple of weeks. Just let me get through this first trimester before we start talking about the future. And before you think I'm putting you off, just know that I feel like I can breathe again. I can finally say I *need* you without it feeling like a character flaw."

He ran his hand down my hips and over my stomach. "I need you too, Haylee."

THE WEEKS LEADING up to Christmas went by quickly. Feeling less nauseous by the day and more energetic, I was already gaining back some of the weight I'd lost and feeling a lot healthier.

Josh hadn't brought up marriage again, which I assumed was because he was waiting on the second trimester and agreed we needed some assurance of the baby's health before taking that next step.

Dr. Mac had told me that it was natural to have the first trimester be a milestone at which many expectant parents felt relief, but with my additional concerns, it was especially pivotal for me. He'd challenged me to think about how I'd feel once I was past the thirteen weeks, though. Would I find another reason or obstacle to keep me from believing in our future as a family? Or could I do away with my tendency to put limitations on things as a habit of protecting myself?

Ten days before Christmas while walking back from class on a Friday afternoon, I sent Josh a text to find out which train he was on. I expected him to visit that evening. However, when I stepped into my apartment, I was at a loss for words. The entire living room was covered in roses and candles. There were rose petals on the floor, with dozens of them in pink, white, and red on every surface. Small tea lights gave a glow and soft music played in the background. I put my backpack down at the door and simply stared.

"Josh?" I called out.

He came out of my bedroom dressed in a tuxedo.

My heart pounded at the sight of him. "What's going on?"

Smiling, he took my hand, and led me to the center of the room. Then, to my absolute amazement, he dropped to one knee. "Haylee Lynn Holloway, I'm an ass for not realizing sooner that I didn't do this properly. I was so caught up in what we needed to get done before the baby came that I neglected to actually propose to you. This shouldn't be an item on a to-do list. You are the most important thing in my life, and I don't want to spend one day without you in it. I love you, I trust you, and although I know I'll continue to need to ask for your forgiveness down the road when I screw things up, you make it easy to admit when I'm sorry. Will you please do me the honor of becoming my wife?"

"But the first tri—" I started to protest, only to have him cut me off.

"I don't give a damn about the first trimester." He stopped and winced. "God, I didn't mean that the way it sounded. I'd be devastated if you miscarried, but I still want to marry you. Our future happiness isn't only dependent on the first thirteen weeks because no matter what happens, we're in this together. And it's okay for you to be frightened about what's to come. I'm scared, too. We'll still go see Dr. Mac, and we'll work through things as they come, but I want to do it together."

Where he held my hand, I could feel his shaking. With his other hand, he reached inside his jacket pocket and brought out a box.

When he opened it, I gasped. It was the same stunning vintage diamond engagement ring from the Cosmo shoot.

"I want to see you in your mother's dress standing across from me saying your vows, and I want this ring on your finger."

I was speechless.

In a moment of clarity, I realized the lengths Josh had gone to in order to show his love and commitment to me. Whether it was for one day, one year, or a lifetime, I knew I needed to grab onto happiness with both hands. There would never be guarantees in life, but for the first time, my hope for the future outweighed my fear of losing it. "Yes," I whispered.

"Yes?" he confirmed in a choked-up voice. If I'd ever questioned his love for me, watching my powerful man with moisture in his eyes when I accepted his marriage proposal sealed the deal.

"Absolutely, yes." The tears of happiness streamed down my face.

"Thank God." And just like that, he stood up, raining kisses over my face and then on my mouth. He slipped the ring on my finger and gave me a beaming smile.

I could only look at it with awe. "It's gorgeous."

"It needs to be because so are you, my love."

"This is amazing." I gazed around the room and breathed in the scent of the roses.

"I wanted it all to be perfect."

"You are perfection, especially in that tux."

"You're getting that look on your face." He had a knowing smile.

Ah, the infamous fuck-me-look. "Mm, the apartment won't burn down if we leave the candles lit for a while longer, will it?"

"No, they're small tea lights. Mark actually helped me."

The picture of the two of them setting up this romantic scene made me laugh. Maybe there were advantages to having Josh own the building.

I made short work of ridding him of clothes and found he was equally as frantic to shed me of mine. Pure happiness overwhelmed me when he lowered me to the rose-petal-covered couch. "This is wildly romantic," I remarked, savoring the feel of his hands on my sensitive breasts.

"I'm glad you think so because I can't even wait the time it would take to get you into the bedroom. Your breasts are getting heavier. Are they more responsive, I wonder?"

Jesus, I about came as his mouth feasted on one.

"I'd say so," he observed, switching to the other one.

Moaning, I arched toward him and felt his hand make its way to my tender folds.

"Ah, you're more sensitive everywhere, aren't you?"

"God, I think so. I've been really hot thinking about you all week. I think the second trimester is coming on."

"I think I feel more than that coming," he murmured, sucking hard on my nipple and bringing me quickly to climax with his magic fingers on my clit.

"Holy crap, I think the orgasms are even better." Feeling his lips trail kisses up my neck, I gasped again in pleasure.

He ravaged my mouth, plundering it with his tongue and

tugging on my bottom lip with his teeth. "I love kissing your sweet mouth," he mused, parting my legs and easing inside of me slowly as we both savored the feeling. "You'll tell me if I hurt you?"

"You won't." I was frustrated when he moved slowly and carefully. I didn't want slow and gentle like he'd been doing over the last couple of weeks while my stomach hadn't been feeling up to par. Right now I was beyond turned on and needed him to recognize it. Wrapping my legs tightly around him, I rocked my hips, thrusting up and forcing him deeper inside of me. "Fuck me, Josh."

His shocked expression made me smile as did the lust that shaded his features.

"You never cease to surprise me, soon-to-be Mrs. Singer," he chuckled.

Giggling, I clenched around his hard erection, enjoying his grunt of pleasure. I knew flexing made him lose control.

"Haylee…" he moaned. Gripping my ass, he lifted my hips up to meet his thrusts, taking me over the edge and following shortly after.

OUR BREATHING finally returned to normal as we lay there in the romantic glow of the room with my head on his sculpted chest and our legs wrapped around each other. "Tell me your answer again," he asked, kissing my temple.

"Yes, I will marry you, Joshua Robert Singer."

He leaned back and quirked a brow.

"Did you really think I'd marry a man whose middle name I didn't know?"

"Baby, I wouldn't have cared so long as the answer was yes," he laughed.

"It's a yes."

Breathing a sigh of relief, he nuzzled my neck. "We need to talk wedding plans. I know you have a whole binder and things planned out, but in the interest of time—"

Kissing his face, I made up my mind. I was ready to make my own decisions about my future instead of thinking about what my parents would have wanted. "All I care about is that I get to wear my mother's dress with my amazing shoes and stand across from you."

Smiling, he hugged me tight. "Really? You don't mind if I take over and we get married, say, New Year's Eve?"

"That's only a little over two weeks away."

"Yes, it is, which means we need to get moving on the logistics. First things first, where do you want to have the ceremony?"

"What do you think about that beach house in Tortola, if it's available? We could maybe do tents outside? Or if the house isn't vacant, just anywhere on a beach."

His face lit up, and I could tell he was pleased with the idea. Kissing me deeply, he glided his fingertips down the side of my face. Pulling back, he stood up and looked around for his pants, grinning. "I love that idea. I'll see if it's open, and we can start on the guest list. I know it's short notice, but considering it'll be one hell of a New Year's Eve party, hopefully most people can come last minute. It'll only be a small group, anyhow. I'll have Maria start on travel logistics, and I should have a list of questions for you by morning. For now, let me start calling people so that they have a chance to change their plans."

I couldn't help smiling. "You truly don't mind planning the wedding?"

He helped me up and hugged me tightly. "As long as you don't feel like you're settling. As much as I want you to be my wife as soon as possible, I don't want you to be disappointed. If you desire the grand wedding that you and your mom intended, we could do it after the baby comes. It would give us a year to plan."

I thought a moment before replying. “We can talk to Dr. Mac about it tonight during our session, but I planned my wedding before I was in love and before I knew what mattered most. My mom would understand that a wedding of my dreams is the one with the man of my dreams. I need to do what feels right to me.”

His eyes closed, and he clearly savored my words. “God, I love you. Now, come on. Get dressed before I take you to Vegas because I’m too distracted to plan anything.”

I giggled. “Tell me something, Josh.”

He put his hands on either side of my face, looking serious. “You’re my second chance at happiness. One I never thought I’d deserve but that I will never take for granted.” He kissed me sweetly. “Your turn.”

My smile was just one indication of how happy he made me. “I’m still scared. But now I realize what terrifies me the most is imagining a future without you. Everything else we can face together.”

EPILOGUE

As I watched my gorgeous bride come down the aisle, I fought the overwhelming emotion that clogged my vision. Haylee looked exquisite in her mother's wedding dress, absolutely the epitome of beautiful, inside and out. I was the luckiest man on the planet. I couldn't take my eyes off her and shared her small smile as her father's former business partner gave her away. She'd insisted on keeping it simple, without a bridal party, for which I was relieved.

We were surrounded by our friends and family in Tortola. All the family. Yes, the best had been Haylee's reaction to her relatives making the trek from Australia.

We had told everyone about the baby individually over the last week since we were officially out of the first trimester. All of the tests had revealed a normal pregnancy. Although there was still some anxiety over this little life for which I'd be responsible, I was ecstatic about becoming a father.

Haylee loved me in a way that I'd never felt before. She wanted me for who I was instead of for anything I could give her. She'd taught me what it was to love unconditionally, and although we were still working on our trust issues with Dr. Mac, I felt confident that we'd conquered the biggest hurdles.

After the ceremony and during dinner, I pressed a kiss to her cheek and stood with the microphone so that everyone could see me. I felt a sense of déjà vu. Most of the faces were the same we'd seen at her going-away party last July, although now they included family. The big difference with this party, though, was that I'd put a ring on my love's finger, and she wasn't going anywhere. We were in this life together.

"I'd like to say a few words to my lovely bride." I waited as the chatter died down. "To know you, Haylee, is to love you, and I'll spend the rest of my days showing you how very much I do. You are my rock, and I have every intention of being yours, forever and always. I will adore you until my last breath."

She gave me a watery smile and stood, hugging me tightly.

Taking a moment, I kissed her sweet lips. "Now then, I would like to share a first dance with my bride." I smiled at her shocked expression. My friends had much the same look on their faces. I was not a man who danced. Not at a prom, not at a club, and not with my first wife. Not ever. But for Haylee, well, I'd do a naked jig on the table if it meant she'd look at me the way she was in this moment.

The music started, and I watched the recognition on her face as the song, "Thinking Out Loud," by Ed Sheeran started.

"How did you know?" she whispered.

Taking her out on the dance floor, I answered, "I took a peek at the wedding binder you made with your mom. Matter of fact, if you look at the wedding centerpieces and the cake, they're also from that binder." Every detail was important for making this special for my wife.

She tipped her face toward mine and kissed me sweetly. "You've made this the very best day for us, from the song to this necklace." She fingered the beautiful diamond piece around her neck.

I'd had it delivered to her as her wedding gift while she'd been getting ready earlier. It wasn't the same one from the model shoot, but Catherine had helped me pick it out as something unique for today.

"I plan on seeing you in nothing but that later tonight." I could picture it already and needed to stop before I became hard on the dance floor.

"I like that idea. And maybe after everyone leaves the day after tomorrow, we can enjoy the steam shower."

God, the way she looked at me, like she could never get enough—It was a powerful thing.

"I love you." Even though we were on the dance floor, I felt like it was only the two of us.

"I love you, too. So tell me something, Mr. Singer."

Smiling, I knew this game would never get old with her. "Hmm, something you don't know. Let's see. Do you think we'll ever run out of things we don't know about each other?"

"I certainly hope not. I like this game."

"All right, I'll tell you something. How about the fact that I bought this house?"

She about stumbled over my feet. "What?"

"It holds special memories of our first trip here, not to mention now our wedding day. And of course, there's the steam shower."

Tears were swimming in her eyes. Her smile that was purely for me gave me a punch in the gut.

"I think you've given me the world."

"Tell me something, Mrs. Singer." God, I loved the sound of that and the fact she had wanted to change her name to mine. It was possessive as hell, but having her take my name made me feel good about soon becoming the Singer family of three.

"Oh, I'll tell you something. Come here."

I bent down so that she could whisper in my ear.

"We're having a girl."

I was stunned. "Wait. What?"

"Did you not hear me?" she asked, clearly amused.

Whispering, I repeated, "We're having a girl? You found out with the blood test?"

"I knew you wanted to know, and I figured I would surprise you with it. I mean, what do you get as a wedding gift for a man who has everything?"

Emotion pulled at my throat. Putting my arms around her, I lifted her up and twirled her around in celebration. Everyone must have liked that since they clapped. It dawned on me that, in fact, everyone was still watching us. To hell with them, I thought, kissing her soundly. The room erupted, and I loved the sound of her giggle.

"You already gave me you, which was the best gift. But this is pretty amazing, too. God, a girl. My mom is going to flip." When the song ended, it was tempting to pick up my bride and carry her upstairs where we could be alone, just the two of us.

"I know what you're thinking, and we're only a couple hours away. Then you have me for a lifetime. And maybe you should tell your mom about her granddaughter when you ask her for a dance." Haylee knew how much my dancing with her would mean to my mother.

"I'll go ask her because for you I'm always hard pressed to say no."

She laughed. "You're going to have a daddy's little girl soon enough, so you'd best get used to that."

I grinned. "I look forward to spoiling you both."

Read the next book in the Something Series! Sasha and Brian's story is up next in Ask Me Something.

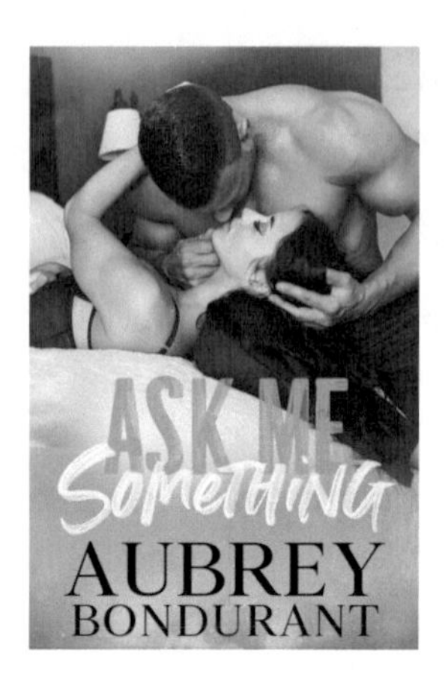
ASK ME
Something
AUBREY
BONDURANT

ACKNOWLEDGMENTS

The first step is always the hardest to be able to share your writing with someone and to leave yourself vulnerable. A big thank you to my friend Katie for listening to me talk about my books for years and always being so supportive. Your excitement over my characters gave me the confidence I needed to get them out there.

To my husband and children who respected "mommy's laptop time" and enabled me to fulfill a life-long dream of publishing my first book. I love you and appreciate your patience with this endeavor!

A huge thanks to Alyssa Kress who taught me things like character arc, verb-ing and guided me to write a better story. This journey would not have been possible without your invaluable support and knowledge. www.alyssakressbookediting.com

And finally, to all of the would-be authors out there who have characters and stories that run through your head. Go for it! Finish that book and share those characters with the world. Life is too short not to!

ABOUT AUBREY BONDURANT

Aubrey Bondurant is a working mom who loves to write, read, and travel. She describes her writing style as: "Adult Contemporary Erotic Romantic Comedy," which is just another way of saying she likes her characters funny, her bedroom scenes hot, and her romances with a happy ending.

When Aubrey isn't working her day job or spending time with her family, she's on her laptop typing away on her next story. She only wishes there were more hours of the day!
She's a former member of the US Marine Corps and passionate about veteran charities and giving back to the community. She loves a big drooly dog, a fantastic margarita, and football
Sign up for Aubrey's newsletter to find out about new releases here
Stalk her here:
Website
Facebook
Twitter
Email her at aubreybondurant@gmail.com

Made in the USA
Thornton, CO
11/04/24 16:13:59

169c4925-729e-41b2-a9a7-e4c65307e200R01